She's the one.
She's the goddamn strings
attached to my heart.

love with STRINGS

USA TODAY BESTSELLING AUTHOR

NIKKI ASH

She's the one.
She's the goddamn strings
attached to my heart.

No Strings

PROLOGUE

BENJAMIN

"Brody's been kicked out of school and refuses to listen to me. I can't do this anymore."

"Can't do what? Parent?"

The mother of my son glares my way, but I'm unfazed. I've been on the receiving end of her wrath for the past fifteen years.

"You've been traveling since he was born. It's easy to play dad from afar, but you haven't actually *been here*. He's been getting into fights and failing his classes. Now he's been expelled." Her tear-filled eyes lock with mine, pleading. "He needs his father."

Her words hit me like a punch to the gut. I didn't ask to become a father and never wanted to become one. I watched what having kids did to our parents. Listened to their constant arguing over finances and parenting until our mom, someone who was supposed to love and protect us, had finally had enough and did the unthinkable, leaving us all to drown in our guilt and grief.

I never wanted that for myself or my kids. I didn't want the responsibility that came with parenting, and I didn't want my kids to ever be put in the position my sister and I were in, which is why I made it clear to Paola I didn't want to have any. She promised she understood and swore she was on birth control. But she lied. She went behind my back and got pregnant, thinking that I'd magically change my tune. The only thing that changed when she told me she was pregnant was our relationship status. I walked away that day, losing any trust and respect I had for her.

It took some time for me to come around, but I went to the hospital when Paola called me the day Brody was born, planning to give up my rights. This wasn't an accident. She did this on purpose. But the second I looked at my son, my heart swelled with a kind of love I had never felt, and despite my disdain for his mother, I became a father that day and promised Brody I would do whatever it took to be there for him.

"You're not around," she adds. "And I can't do this on my own anymore."

Her accusation knocks me out of my thoughts.

"Yeah, I've been busy working. You know, to pay your child support and the private school our son *was* attending. I had no idea he was getting into trouble because you never said anything."

She could've called, texted, emailed. I spent part of Christmas break with Brody, and neither of them said anything. Yeah, he seemed moodier than usual, but I figured it was just a part of him being a teenager.

"It's only gotten worse as of lately. It's like one minute, he was a sweet little boy, and the next, he's skipping school and getting into fights. Please, Benjamin. I need you to take him. I...I can't do this." Tears leak from her eyelids, sliding down her cheeks, and I'm reminded of my mother. Of the last time I saw her alive...

"I want to watch the TV!" my sister, Amalia, yells.

"It's my turn!" I shout back, snatching the controller from her.

"Both of you shut up!" Mom screams, tears streaming down her cheeks. "I can't handle all the fighting. Get in your rooms now!"

We both groan but do as she says, not wanting to upset her more.

A few hours later, I'm playing my PlayStation when Amalia comes running into my room. "Hey! Get out!"

*"Benjamin," she sobs. "Mom…" She drops in front of me, covered in…*is that blood?

"What's wrong?" I jump up and run over to her. "What happened?"

"Mom's bleeding everywhere. I think she's…I think she's dead."

"Benjamin," Paola says, bringing me back to the present. Her eyes are rimmed red, and her nose is running from crying. Her cheeks are splotchy and tearstained. A part of the reason I stayed away from Paola was so that what happened between my parents would never happen to us. If I wasn't around, we couldn't fight. Yet somehow, here we are.

"Okay." I walk over to her and wrap her in my arms. "I'll take him."

I might've been too young to save my mom from ending her life, too young to understand she needed help, despite my dad thinking he could fix her himself, but I'm older now, and I can make sure Paola is never in the same position as my mom.

"Thank you."

As she sobs into my chest, I catch a bit of movement out of the corner of my eye. Brody. He's home. He must've come in through the garage. He's listening and watching from around the corner. Our gazes clash, and the sad as fuck look in his eyes tells me he's been listening.

"Brody, come out here, please," I tell him, stepping away from Paola.

He stumbles from around the corner. "Hey, Dad," he mumbles, completely ignoring his mom.

"What do you say to your mom?" I'll be damned if he's going to disrespect her anymore.

"Hi, Mom," he mutters without looking at her.

"How would you feel about moving in with me?" I ask.

His hazel eyes, identical to mine, remain devoid of all emotion as he shrugs.

"Hey." I step toward him and tip his chin up, locking eyes with him. "I asked you a question."

It's then I notice his eyes are bloodshot. I inhale and smell it—weed. He's high. Jesus Christ, when did he get old enough to smoke?

"Does it really matter what I want?" he retorts.

"Of course it matters," Paola cries, fresh tears sliding down her cheeks. "But you fight with Ted every day, and I don't know what else to do."

Brody glances up at his mom with a sadness in his eyes that breaks my heart. "Does Ted make you happy?"

His question comes out of left field, shocking me. I'm not sure what her happiness has to do with anything.

"O-Of course he does," she stammers, sounding as confused as I am at the turn of this conversation.

Brody nods once, looking almost resigned, then he looks at me. "Yeah, I'll go live with you. I hate this city anyway."

"Oh, well, then you better start liking it because I'm moving home."

Paola gasps, and Brody's eyes widen at my words. Since Paola told me she was pregnant, and I walked out the door, I've never lived in a place longer than a few years. Only long enough to open another nightclub and then move on.

It's not until at this moment, as I stand in front of my son—who's almost as tall as me and is as high as a kite and sad as fuck—and his mother—who's in tears, looking exhausted and confused—that I realize I've messed up.

"Home?" she breathes.

"Yeah, I'm back for good." I look at Brody. "Go pack whatever you need, and don't even think about bringing any drugs with you."

After he walks out of the room, I turn my attention back to Paola. "I'm sorry. I should've paid more attention and come home sooner."

I was so caught up in running from my own demons, pissed at Paola for her betrayal while trying to make a name for myself—when she told me I'd never amount to anything after I dropped out of college—that I lost track of the important shit, like my son. I told myself quality was more important than quantity, but I was wrong. My son needs us both. But right now, it's clear he needs *me*. He's hurting and lashing out, and opening a new club sure as hell isn't more important than taking care of him.

Paola sniffles. "For how long?"

"I meant what I said. I'm back for good."

SAVANNAH

"I'm sorry. We didn't mean for it to happen," Lois says, attempting and failing to sound sincere.

Too bad I know her well enough to know that the way the corner of her lip is quirking up just slightly, along with the brightness in her shitty brown eyes, means she's anything but sorry, and she most definitely meant for it to happen.

Like me, Lois spent most of her childhood in foster care. It's where we met. We would talk for hours at night from our beds in our crappy, loveless foster home about how we would find love when we got older. We might not have had a loving home growing up, but we would create our own once we were old enough.

The men of our dreams would sweep us off our feet and love us and take care of us. They would buy us the biggest houses with the whitest picket fences, and then we would have the most beautiful babies. And we would love them and cherish them. We wouldn't take what we have for granted because we know what it's like to be on the other side of that fence.

When we graduated from high school, Lois stayed behind, working at the local gas station because she didn't have the grades or ambition to go to college, while I went off to the University of Tennessee on a full academic scholarship.

While there, I met Neil when I interned at his father's company, Everton Construction. He wasn't the white knight I imagined, and he didn't sweep me off my feet, but he offered me everything I dreamed of on a silver platter, so I went all in. Beggars can't be choosers after all.

He proposed after I graduated, and three months later, we were married and living in his home. It didn't actually have a white picket fence because he said they were ugly and preferred wrought iron. Maybe that should've been my first clue he wasn't really the one.

Lois came to visit for the wedding and fell in love with the city. Since she had no money or means to move and live on her own, I offered to let her stay with us. Until Neil, she was the closest thing to a family I've ever had.

"How long has this been going on?" I ask, glancing at the two of them while keeping my tone under control so I don't show just how much my heart hurts.

It's not over the fact that my husband cheated on me with another woman—our relationship has been over for a while since I came home from work and smelled the woman's perfume on him—but because it was with my best friend. The irony that she was my maid of honor isn't lost on me. Or that she told me dozens of times how lucky I was and how she hoped to find a man like Neil one day.

"For a little while," Lois says softly.

I nod and stand, ready to leave and get as far away from my ex-husband and ex-best friend as possible. *Too bad I have nowhere to go.* "Him, I understand. He has zero respect for women, including his wife. But you...you were supposed to be my best friend."

"I really am sorry," Lois cries, crocodile tears skating down her cheeks. "We didn't mean to fall in love. It just happened."

Yes, she did. Like me, she has been so desperate for love and attention for years. I have no doubt the second Neil paid the slightest bit of attention to her, she soaked it up—just like I did.

Looking over at Neil, whose features are devoid of any emotion, I wonder what I ever saw in him. How I could be so desperate to find love that I would allow myself to fall for a man like him.

I pluck my keys from my back pocket and hand them to Lois. "I guess these are yours now."

"Where are you going to go?" she asks. "If you need to stay here…"

I bark out a humorless laugh at my ex-best friend's offer to stay in my ex-home with her and my ex-husband. The same home I opened up to her, where she and my husband proceeded to have an affair behind my back.

At first, when I called him out on his cheating and told him I wanted out, he begged for forgiveness. Promised he was just stressed. I didn't accept that as an excuse and made it clear I wanted a divorce. For several days afterward, he pleaded with me to change my mind, offered to go to counseling, and came home with gifts galore, thinking I would forgive him.

Then, one day, something in him changed. I came home from work and was served divorce papers. And because he's rich and I'm not, I lost everything. Because everything of mine was because of him. I gave him all of me, and now I'm left with nothing. I'll never make that mistake again.

I spend the next hour packing up my clothes and putting them into boxes in the back of my SUV while Neil and Lois make themselves scarce. Technically, Neil didn't kick me out, but there's no way I'm staying under the same roof as them. I still have an iota of my dignity intact.

Once I've gotten everything that's mine from the house—which isn't much—I get in my vehicle, refusing to let the tears fall. But the second I turn on the ignition, it hits me. Aside from a little bit of money I've saved and the car Neil gave me as a wedding gift that's in my name, I literally have nothing. No home, no place to go. I have my clothes in my trunk and nowhere to take them.

Because Neil's father holds a lot of weight in this town, our divorce was expedited. I couldn't afford a lawyer, and I didn't want to fight, so I let him handle it. It only took seven weeks to finalize the divorce and leave me homeless.

I knew Neil was having an affair, but I didn't know it was with Lois. I knew I would need to move out, but I thought I would have some time. It all just happened so quickly. In the blink of an eye, I lost everything. Then again, maybe I never really had anything to begin with.

My phone rings over the Bluetooth, startling me out of my thoughts. I glance at the caller ID and see it's Brianne. It's like she knew I needed her. "Hey."

"Oh my fucking God! That trifling, no-good, husband-stealing skank! Did you see her post? Did you know?"

I bark out a watery laugh, loving that my friend has my back. "I'm assuming you're referring to Lois and Neil."

"Yes! That bitch. I knew I never liked her."

It's the truth. I met Brianne in college, and we immediately clicked. She was my dorm-mate for two years, and then we shared an apartment off campus for another two. Every time Lois would come to visit, Brianne would tell me something about her felt off. *Guess I should've listened…*

"You can't steal someone's husband. He obviously wanted to be with her. Besides, we're no longer married. Our divorce was finalized today, and I moved my stuff out."

"And you really let him get away scot-free?"

When I told her I would agree to whatever Neil wanted, she offered to hire a lawyer to fight him. Since he cheated, she thought I'd have a shot at walking away with some money and maybe even the house.

"I don't want anything from him. None of it was ever really mine."

It might've been my dream—the doting husband, the loving home, the kids, the dream job—but it wasn't my reality, and fighting with him over stupid, materialistic possessions wasn't going to change anything. Our relationship was over several months ago when he turned to another woman instead of his wife.

"You're a better person than I am. What are you going to do now?"

My stomach sinks at her question. "I don't know. Start over...For tonight, I plan to check into a motel."

"A motel? No way! Move here."

"What?"

She can't be serious. She lives in New York, almost a thousand miles away.

"Our CFO retired unexpectedly, and Lucas and my dad have been interviewing people to replace him. It's perfect timing! You've spent the past four years working for a construction company. You're more qualified than anyone they're interviewing."

"Brianne, you're crazy! A CFO? Me?"

"Yes, you! You're a freaking math genius! You could move here and start fresh. Plus, you know how much I miss you. And you would love living in New York."

She's lost her mind. That has to be it. I can't possibly pick up and move my entire life to the East Coast. At the same time, is it really such a crazy idea? Not to work for her family's architecture and construction company because there's no way they would actually hire me, but to move to New York. I've only been there twice, but she's right. I did love it.

"I'm a licensed CPA in Tennessee," I point out.

"So, you'll transfer it to New York." She's quiet for a moment before she says, "I texted Lucas, and he said he can interview you tomorrow."

"I can't fly out there tomorrow!"

Brianne laughs. "Through video chat, silly. Although I hate the idea of you staying at a motel and am tempted to get you on a flight out tonight. I'm not sure if the company jet is in use..."

"One, I'm fine staying at a motel." I've lived in worse. "Two, are you serious? He's willing to interview me? This isn't a pity offer, is it?"

"Savy, you're practically the smartest person I know, and when it comes to math, you might as well be an alien. You can do math in your head quicker than I can with a calculator. You got your degree *and* MBA in the time it took me to get my single design degree. Sharp Architecture and Construction would be lucky to have you. This is not a pity offer. This is a smart business decision with the bonus of having one of my best friends living in the same zip code as me."

I can't be considering this. It's insane. Absurd. Senseless. Yet…

"I would have to find a place to live."

New York isn't cheap, and it'll take time to save—

"Shut up! You'd live with me, of course! I have the extra room, and my father owns the building, so if you want to live on your own once a place opens up, you can.

"He would rent to you for cheap since you work for the company. And before you argue, he does it for all of our employees. There's also a garage where you can park your vehicle. Though I would recommend you sell it since having a car here is kind of pointless. It would give you some extra cash in the bank."

"Bri…"

She has this all figured out, and I can't think of a single reason to say no. I might not have the marriage, or the family, or the love, but at least I could have a career, which would allow me to create my own future without depending on anyone but myself.

Maybe I set my expectations too high. Instead of looking for love, I should've been working for security. Love got me a broken heart, but a career will give me stability, which is more important.

"Eeek!" she shrieks when I don't come up with a new argument. "It's totally happening. You're moving here!"

"You don't even know if your brother and father will hire me."

She might be a part of the company, but her brother and father own the other two-thirds. Brianne focuses on what she loves—design—and leaves them to make the business decisions.

"Oh, I know they will. The interview is just a formality. What do you say?"

"I don't know. Let me think about it. I'll interview with your brother tomorrow and let you know."

"Fine." She sighs. "I want to beg, but I know this has to be your decision. If you need anything, call me. I'll just be over here pricking my Lois and Neil voodoo dolls with needles."

I laugh as we hang up, totally imagining her doing just that, and then once it's quiet, I stare at my phone for a moment. Could I really do it? Move to New York? Tennessee is all I've ever known. It's where I've lived my entire life...but at the same time, what life have I actually lived?

My screen flashes with a notification I missed while I was on the phone. I click on it, and it takes me to a post. It must be the one Brianne was talking about. It's a picture of Lois's ring finger with a big rock on it, and in the caption, it reads: **It's official! Neil and I are engaged! #longtimecoming**

I exit out of the post and shoot a text to Brianne.

SAVANNAH

If your brother thinks I'll be a good fit, I'm in.

Then I pull my ring off my finger. *Wonder how much I can pawn this for?*

CHAPTER ONE

BENJAMIN

ON MOST MORNINGS, MY EYES OPEN BEFORE THE ALARM goes off. I look over at my phone and see it's 5:59 a.m. Before it changes to six o'clock, I quickly switch off my alarm, preventing me from being forced to listen to the ridiculous loud buzzing sound. I'm not even sure why I set it since my brain and body know I wake up every morning at six.

Getting out of bed, I head to the bathroom to begin my daily routine. After I take a quick piss and brush my teeth, I wake Brody to get ready for his first day of school.

Once I know he's half-awake, I throw on my workout clothes and head down to the gym located on the basement level of the building where I live.

I enter the gym and grab a towel from the rack to wipe down the treadmill. Then I click on the television to watch the morning news on the big screen in front of me as I start my warm-up.

Before I step it up to a run, I check my emails. How is it possible I already have forty-six new emails? I checked them before I went to bed not even three hours ago.

Exhaustion sets in when I think about my lack of sleep. I always say I'm going to go to bed earlier, but then insomnia keeps me awake. Before I know it, it's after three in the morning, and I'm prying my eyes from my laptop and forcing myself to get a few hours of shut-eye.

Scrolling through the emails, I see one from my sister with Valentine's Day on the subject line. I click it open and quickly skim through it, noting it's about the upcoming event happening at Lush —the restaurants/nightclubs I own.

Next month is Valentine's Day, and since Amalia oversees all the events for my clubs, she's planning a big event to celebrate the holiday.

I notice my on-site managers are copied in the email, so I ignore it, clicking on the next one. It's from Moti, the assistant manager at the Las Vegas location, asking about the food and beverage report. Some numbers aren't adding up, and he'd like to seek clarification.

He's emailed my dad, who is the accounting manager, but hasn't heard back...*Weird.* My dad's always on top of his shit. I forward the email to my dad, then put my phone back into my pocket. I'll deal with the rest later.

The biggest hurdle I've had to overcome in the past fifteen years since I bought my first club is delegating and trusting that they'll do their job right. I'm a firm believer that if you want something done right, you do it your damn self, so letting go of the reins has been challenging.

While I'm justified in my need to manage everything myself—the mother of my son *handling* the birth control herself, only to lie and get pregnant, as just one example—I also understand the other side of it. When you own a half dozen nightclubs and restaurants, it's impossible to control every detail. I can't be everywhere at once, especially not now.

Increasing the speed on the treadmill, I bring myself to a steady pace of nine miles per hour while I get lost in the news, trying to block out the shit running through my mind.

I have a meeting with Lucas, my best friend and architect, this morning before he takes off on a business trip to discuss the property I recently acquired as a gift to my sister and her new husband, Gerald.

Gerald is a fabulous chef and hopes to open a French restaurant. Only it'll have a twist. Since my sister loves art, she wants to attach a gallery to it and call it Artfully Delicious.

I think the concept is brilliant and will do well here, so I'm meeting with everyone to go over the plans.

I also have a conference this afternoon with Brody's guidance counselor to go over the expectations for the remainder of the year.

Since he was expelled from his private school, I enrolled him in the local public school, and he's behind on credits since he failed so many classes.

Paola damn near lost her shit when she found out our son is attending a public school, but I don't care—and I told her as much. My sister and I both went to a public school, and we turned out just fine.

I'm about ten minutes into my run when the door opens, and a woman I've never seen before walks in. Instinctually, my eyes roam over her, taking her in.

Caramel hair with various shades of blond highlights are pulled up into a loose ponytail. Tanned, toned legs are barely covered with yellow cotton shorts—if you can even call them that. I'd bet all my money, if she turned around, I'd see a hint of her ass cheeks peeking out.

I chuckle at the shoes on her feet. Instead of wearing tennis shoes, she's sporting light pink fluffy boots. Her face is free of makeup, and her tits look real—perky but not in the so-perky-they-hit-her-chin sort of way.

It's not often I see a naturally beautiful woman free of plastic surgery and makeup. Especially living in the places where I've lived. You want a fake woman? They're a dime a dozen.

I've learned the hard way women are good for one thing, to sink into and find release with. It doesn't matter if their tits are real or fake. As long as they can handle their own in the bedroom and understand what the term *no strings* means, we're good to go.

Realizing I'm still staring at her, I drag my eyes back to the television, but when she comes over and steps onto the treadmill next to me, I can't help but check out her backside.

I was right. Her ass is firm, just like the rest of her body, and her shorts are so tiny, the bottom swells of her cheeks are popping out. She has this thickness to her that I can imagine grabbing ahold of in bed.

This woman is either new to this building or has changed her workout time because I damn sure would've remembered seeing her here before. Then again, I haven't been around much for the past several years, so it's possible we just haven't crossed paths.

When I force my gaze to move from her ass back up to her face, I notice she's staring at the treadmill screen with the most adorable look. Her nose is scrunched up in confusion…or maybe frustration. Either way, she's staring at the gym equipment like it's from another planet. Based on her furry boots, I'm going to assume she's new to working out.

"Need some help?"

She turns her attention to me and hits me with the bluest eyes I've ever seen. It's like getting lost in an ocean of warmth. I'm in such shock by how beautiful she is, I almost trip over my feet. In fear of face-planting, I grab the emergency stopper and yank it out, bringing the machine to a sudden halt. Not realizing how quickly it would stop, my feet keep running, and my stomach hits the front of the machine, causing me to release a loud grunt.

She smiles wide at the scene in front of her and giggles. *Fucking giggles.* I almost ended up facedown on a potentially deadly machine, and she's laughing at me.

"I think I should be asking you that question."

Her words are wrapped in a cute Southern twang. It's not strong, but enough to tell me she's not from here. When I look at her pink shirt, I notice it reads *Southern girls do it better* across her chest. I would *definitely* like to find out what it is exactly they do better.

I clear my throat and force my attention back up to her face, *again*. Her eyes dance with mirth, telling me she caught me checking out her assets.

"I was reading your shirt," I say dumbly as a way of explanation.

"Uh-huh," she says with humor in her voice.

She goes back to looking at the treadmill, except now with what looks like determination in her eyes. *Is she willing it to turn on?*

"You just pick a program, enter the info, and hit start," I explain, pointing at the program button.

She lets out a sigh and presses the button, then begins to enter all the necessary info:

Sex: female—damn right she is.

Age: 24—ten years my junior. A bit young for me, but I'm an equal opportunist. Age is just a number, after all.

Weight…

She looks at me and gives me a mock glare. "You already know my age. At least let my weight remain a mystery."

I bark out a laugh and press the start button on my treadmill. She hits start on hers as well and begins to walk. Her machine makes a faint screeching sound my machine doesn't make, like it's scratching against the bottom. *Screech, screech, screech, screech, screech, screech.* Holy shit, it's annoying.

She picks up the pace a little, and the sound gets louder. Thank God I never use that machine. How is it not bothering her? Then I notice at some point while I was once again ogling her, she put earbuds in. I can faintly hear the sound of country music playing from them.

After several minutes of this annoying noise, I look to see how long she set her workout for. She catches me staring and takes one earbud out. "Whew! This machine is gonna work me hard."

Is she serious? She's walking at an unhurried pace. The people on the streets of New York walk quicker on their way to work.

"How long are you planning to walk for?" I ask while I slow my run down to a brisk jog.

"I'm not really sure. I guess until I get tired."

Great. At that speed, she'll be here all day, which means I'm stuck listening to that screeching noise for the rest of my run so this woman can go for a leisurely stroll.

"Have you worked out before?"

"Nope. A part of the new me is to become healthier, and because there's no way I'm giving up my fried chicken or ice cream, I figured my best bet is to work out. It just so happens my new living situation means I have this gym at my disposal, so I thought, what the heck."

Would it be piggish of me to tell her that her body looks just fine and there's no reason to waste her time on that treadmill—driving me nuts with that screeching noise while I'm trying to listen to the news and enjoy my workout in peace?

If she wants a workout, I can *gladly* accommodate her, and I guarantee she'll work up more of a sweat than she's doing right now. The thin material of my shorts stretches against my growing erection. It's been a while since I've gotten laid. Between finishing up the club in LA and moving back here with my teenage son, who hates his parents and the world, I've been a little preoccupied.

A few minutes go by and then she presses stop on the machine.

"You're done?" She's only burned thirty calories.

"Yeah. Don't want to overdo it on the first day. Figure I'll work my way up slowly."

I stifle my laugh at how ridiculous this woman is, but I'm also pleased that horrid machine is now quiet.

"Have a good day," she says, waving as she walks out of the gym. "Maybe I'll see you around."

You bet your fine ass you will.

CHAPTER TWO

SAVANNAH

"Is that what you wore to the gym?" Brianne laughs, handing me a steaming mug of coffee. "Your UGGs and pajama shorts?"

"I don't own any workout clothes. And anyway, I only lasted like ten minutes before I got winded."

We both crack up laughing.

"Are you going tomorrow?"

"Sure. Why not? New city, new me, right?"

Plus, aside from my appointment on Friday to fill out paperwork and get a tour of the office, I have the remainder of the week with nothing to do but get acquainted with my new living arrangements. Monday will be my first official day of work.

Brianne smiles sadly. "There's nothing wrong with the *old* you. You're perfect."

I want to believe her, I do. But it's hard to believe you're perfect when nobody in your life has ever wanted you enough to keep you… to put you first. To show you that you're their everything. Not my parents, not my foster parents, not my best friend, not even my husband.

Cue pity party for one.

"I guess I just want to figure out who I am."

"You will. And when I get back, I'll help you." She winks playfully. "This city is filled with wealthy, yummy men. Trust me."

"You aren't lying," I agree, remembering that sexy man jogging on the treadmill.

When Brianne quirks a brow, silently asking me to elaborate, I do. "I ran into some hot guy at the gym. I didn't plan to get a workout *and* a show, but hey, I'm not complaining. If I have to suffer through a grueling workout, a bit of eye candy makes it worth it."

She shakes her head and giggles. "There you go! Did you ask him for his number?"

"No! My divorce was finalized like five seconds ago."

Brianne's answer to getting over Neil is to get back out there, but I don't agree. I put myself out there once, gave Neil my all, and ended up husbandless, best-friendless, and homeless. This time around, I'm going to do things differently, starting with focusing on myself.

Brianne takes her cup to the sink, rinses it out, and then comes back with her luggage.

"I hate that I'm leaving you when you just arrived. You sure you don't want to come? The resort we're staying at has a ski lodge. You can sit by the fire and drink hot cocoa."

She and her brother, Lucas, scheduled a trip to Wintergreen to meet with a huge investor to discuss remodeling a ski resort. Since it was planned before I knew I would be moving here, they couldn't reschedule—and there's no reason for them to. I'm a big girl and can handle being in the city by myself. Besides, their dad is meeting me Monday morning to walk me through my responsibilities.

"No, I appreciate it, but I'm going to spend this time getting settled...working out." Maybe, if I'm lucky, that guy will be down there working out again tomorrow.

Brianne laughs. "Yeah, okay. Just don't overdo it. Wouldn't want you laid up in bed before you start working." She rolls her luggage to the front door. "There's food in the fridge, or you can order from any of the takeout places listed on the board. Those are the good ones. On Friday, take a cab, not the subway. It's quicker from where we're located." Her green eyes scan the area, trying to think of anything else, but before she can convince herself to cancel her trip, I walk over and hug her.

"I'll be fine. I promise."

"If you need anything, I'm only a phone call away. I have a meeting this morning, but my flight isn't scheduled until after lunch."

"Got it, but I'll be okay."

I spend the morning putting my clothes away and organizing everything in my new room and en suite bathroom. Since Brianne used it as a guest room, it was already furnished with beautiful white wood furniture that easily holds my clothes. And what doesn't fit in the drawers, I hang up in the walk-in closet. I set out the few picture frames I have left that don't include Neil or Lois and then line up my paperbacks on the bookshelf. I don't have a whole lot, but they're all my favorites.

By lunch, I'm going stir-crazy, so instead of making something to eat, I grab a jacket and venture out. The elevator dings, bringing me to the lobby, and I step out, taking in my surroundings.

When I arrived yesterday, I was so overwhelmed that I didn't pay attention to the area, so I have no clue where I am, but I do know this building is high-class. Between the gorgeous fountain, the marble floors, and the sleek front desk with someone behind it twenty-four hours a day, the lobby alone looks like it belongs in an architectural magazine. It's no wonder Sharp is one of the most sought-after architectural and construction firms.

"Good morning, Miss Cartwright. Can I assist you with anything this morning?" My eyes go wide at the elderly, gray-haired gentleman who apparently knows my name. "I'm Fred, the concierge," he says with a light chuckle. "I work Monday through

Friday, seven a.m. to three thirty p.m. If you need anything during that time, I'm your man."

I smile, remembering Brianne telling me about Fred, who is like an uncle to her. He came from the previous building they lived in and has worked here for several years.

"Nice to meet you. You can call me Savy. I'm just going to go for a walk to find some food."

"Very well. Enjoy your hunt." He winks, making me laugh.

As I'm exiting the building, tightening my hold on my jacket since it's chilly outside, I run smack into another person. "Oh, I'm so sorry."

When our eyes connect, he glares before a sly smirk graces his lips as his eyes descend over my body. He has a cigarette between his fingers, yet he's clearly too young to be smoking.

"Damn, you're hot," he says with crass only a teenager could pull off.

"One, you don't tell a woman she's *hot*. You tell her she's beautiful. Two, smoking kills, and women don't think it's sexy. It makes you smell and taste like an ashtray, and *nobody* thinks that's sexy." I pluck the cancer stick from his fingers and toss it into the ashtray part of the garbage can. "Now, if you'll excuse me…" I let out a huff and head down the street in search of somewhere to eat.

A few seconds later, I hear him yell out for me to wait. "Sorry," he says, looking at me sheepishly, "for saying you're hot. It worked on a show I was watching."

"Apology accepted." I stop in my place to give him my attention. "How old are you?"

"Uh…" He clears his throat. "Eighteen."

"Try again," I say with a laugh.

He sighs and runs his fingers through his shortish yet floppy brown hair. "Fourteen."

"Shouldn't you be in school?"

"Yeah, so?" He smirks, and the way his hazel eyes catch with mine, I have no doubt that one day, when he's older, *much older*, he'll be a heartbreaker, but right now, he's just a teenage wannabe bad boy. I grew up with dozens of them in foster care.

"Like smoking, dropping out of school isn't a turn-on either. Women like men who are educated, so you might want to get your butt back in school and get an education. That's if you ever want to meet a woman."

He scoffs. "Doubtful. My dad has women falling all over him, and he dropped out of college."

Little shit…

Before I can think of a comeback, he points behind him at the building. "Do you live there?"

"Yeah, I just moved in. I'm new to New York."

"I live there too. Just moved in, but I've lived in New York my entire life." Like a gentleman, he extends his hand. "I'm Brody."

"Savy." I shake his hand. "Do you still have time to get to school?"

"Nah, school gets out soon. It's a half-day. My dad's totally going to kill me for skipping." He says it like it's a fact—one he's not at all worried about, reminding me of the foster kids I'd lived with growing up, who'd do things like skip school to get a rise out of the people taking care of them. I don't know this kid, but based on his comments, the smoking, and the truancy, I'd bet he's seeking attention.

"Well, I need to find somewhere to eat. How about you show me somewhere good, and I'll buy you your last meal?" I wink playfully, making him chuckle.

"I know just the place."

We end up a few blocks down at a little hole-in-the-wall deli that, according to Brody, serves the best sandwiches. He tells me how he's recently moved in with his dad and was supposed to start school today.

"So, what happened?"

Brody shrugs, averting his gaze.

"You get scared?"

"Pfft," he huffs. "I'm a man. We don't get scared."

I raise a brow. "Even *men* get scared."

He sighs and takes a bite of his sandwich. When he's done chewing, he swallows it down with a gulp of his lemonade and is about to speak when his cell phone rings.

"Shit, it's my dad."

"Shoot," I correct, feeling a bit of sympathy for his dad. "And you better answer it. He's probably worried sick."

I know I would be if my son were wandering around the streets of this vast city on his own.

Brody rolls his eyes as he hits answer. "Hello?"

I can't hear what his dad is saying, but I can hear him yelling.

Brody huffs, then says, "Whatever...I'm sorry." His tone doesn't match the last two words. He's not sorry. His eyes meet mine as he tells his dad where he's at. "Fine...I'll be back soon." He hangs up and groans. "I forgot he was meeting with my guidance counselor today to go over my credit-retrieval schedule. He's at my school now."

"And you're not."

He nods.

"What's credit retrieval?" I ask curiously before taking another bite of my delicious sandwich.

"I failed a few classes last semester, so I have to take them online to get credit."

"What are you, a freshman?"

"Yeah." He shoves the final bite of his food into his mouth, chews, then swallows, sucking down his drink to wash it down.

"That's a bad way to start high school. You planning to go to college?"

"Nah, I'm going to work for my dad. He has the best job there is." His eyes light up, making it clear, despite his act of rebellion, that he loves his dad very much.

"What does he do?"

"He owns a bunch of nightclubs. His job is literally to party."

I cough out a laugh. "I think there's more than that to owning nightclubs. I doubt he makes money by partying."

Brody shrugs. "I don't know." His phone rings, and he curses under his breath. "It's my dad again."

"You should probably get going."

"Or we could have cake for dessert. This place makes the best éclair cake. It is my last meal after all."

"Nice try." I reach over and tousle his hair. "You made your choice, and now you have to face the consequences."

CHAPTER THREE

BENJAMIN

MY ALARM GOES OFF, AND I GROAN, EXHAUSTED. Yesterday felt like the never-ending day from hell.

After a shitty meeting, where I learned we've hit some red tape on acquiring the permits to get started with Artfully Delicious, I headed to Brody's school to meet with the counselor.

When I got there and learned he wasn't there, I nearly lost my shit. Apparently, my damn kid thought school was optional.

After a long talk about our roles and responsibilities—where I did all the talking, and he grunted and rolled his eyes—I took his phone away.

He stormed out pissed and stayed in his room for the remainder of the day, refusing to come out for dinner. Hopefully, today goes a bit smoother.

After getting dressed in my workout clothes, I wake Brody up so he can start getting ready. To ensure he makes it through the doors of his school today, I'm going to have to deviate from my routine and drop his ass off myself.

When I enter the gym, I'm taken aback by the woman already on the treadmill. Caramel hair up in a ponytail, tiny cotton shorts that show off her thick thighs and plump ass, fluffy boots—beige today—and instead of a T-shirt, she's sporting a tank top. She's walking, once again, at a leisurely pace. Only, unlike yesterday, today her treadmill isn't squeaking…because she's on mine.

I stalk over to her and cut around the front so I can look her in the eyes, and when I do, I'm stunned silent. The woman is eating a goddamned bag of Doritos while walking on the treadmill. Is she fucking for real?

My gaze slides from her mouth to her ample cleavage peeking out of the confines of her top. The saying on the front reads *Mind your own biscuits & life will be gravy.*

"Oh, hey," she says with a bright smile, pulling one earbud out of her ear. "Fancy seeing you here again."

"You're on my treadmill," I deadpan, ignoring the way her smile and accent fuck with my head.

She glances around, confused. "Really? Do we sign up somewhere to reserve certain equipment?"

"No, but I use that treadmill every day at this time." I've been using it for years at this time—since I bought a place in this building to use as my home base—and not once has anyone else ever joined me to work out…until now.

"Oh." She pops an orange chip into her mouth. "Well, good thing there're two."

She plucks another chip from the bag and drops it into her mouth, then wraps her lips around the tip of her finger, sucking the orange residue off. My thoughts go to her using those same lips and tongue to suck my dick. Fuck, I need to get laid.

She puts her earbud back in and hits something on her treadmill. Frustrated in more ways than one, I walk around to get on the screechy machine next to hers and see she has a tablet resting on the front of her treadmill. What. The. Hell. She's reading a book. This woman is barely walking while eating a bag of Doritos and listening to a goddamned audiobook.

I jump on the treadmill and hit the quick start, pushing the speed up to my usual nine miles per hour. The screeching begins immediately, and the faster the speed, the louder it gets. This can't be happening. I'm never going to make it for an hour.

I pound my feet onto the belt of the machine, trying to rid myself of the anxiety and frustration I'm feeling. One minute, I was building nightclubs, partying it up and getting laid in LA, and the next, I'm trying to raise a teenager—one who's failing out of school, almost burned my apartment down a few days ago when he was trying to smoke in his bathroom, and refuses to speak to me unless I force him to.

My schedule is fucked, and my routine is shot. I don't even know which way is up, and this goddamn woman is messing with my morning workout.

After several minutes of the obnoxious noise, I give up. Getting off the machine, I instead focus on my upper body. When I glance over, I find her stepping off the machine. I still have a good thirty minutes, so after she smiles and waves, dumping her empty chip bag in the garbage on her way out, I jump on the machine to get a few miles in.

Tomorrow, I'm getting here early, getting my damn treadmill, and unplugging that screechy-ass other one. If she wants to go for a stroll, she can take a walk through Central Park.

After I shower and get dressed, I take Brody to school, stopping at a deli for breakfast along the way. I need to order food so we can start eating at home. I just haven't found the time.

"Have a good day at school," I tell him once we reach the front of the school.

He nods, looking bored. "Yeah, okay."

"Come home right after school, and I'll pick up dinner."

"'Kay," he says, walking through the gates.

I wait until he's all the way in and then start to walk away, only I get a weird feeling, so I turn around and go back. And sure enough, there he is, walking out of the damn school.

"Are you kidding me?" I bark, making him jump.

"Shit, I mean shoot." He blanches.

"Get your ass in school!"

"All right, all right." He raises his hands in a placating manner, then turns around and goes in.

This time, I wait until I hear the bell ring before I walk away. This kid is going to be the death of me.

"BENJAMIN, HOW ARE YOU?" MY DAD ASKS WHEN I WALK into the deli to meet him and my sister for lunch. "How's Brody?"

"He skipped school yesterday, so I'm hoping he actually stays put today."

"He'll be okay," Dad says. "At his age, you were doing the same thing."

"Yeah, because my mom killed herself, we were living in our car, and I was lashing out," I point out. "What does he have to act out about? He has a damn good life."

Dad flinches. "Sometimes people are going through things we don't know about. Maybe cut him some slack."

I'm about to ask what he means by that when the waitress walks over, interrupting our conversation to ask what we'd like to drink.

"Water, please." I don't drink during the business day.

"Same for me," Dad says.

"Make it three," I tell her. "We have someone on their way."

"Sorry I'm late," Amalia says, rushing over. "With Valentine's Day coming up, we're slammed with the upcoming events." She leans over and kisses our dad's cheek, then mine before she sits down. "I can't believe Valentine's Day is—"

Her words are cut off by the sound of my phone ringing. "Give me a second. It's the office." I raise a single finger, halting our conversation. "Benjamin Fields."

"Mr. Fields, it's Owen Ross...from accounting."

"Yes, I know who you are. Is everything okay?" While all my employees have my cell phone number, very rarely does anyone use it since, up until recently, I'm usually out of town, and they have a person of contact in the office. For Owen, it's my dad.

"I've been trying to get ahold of your dad, but I can't seem to track him down. There's an issue with—"

"Benjamin," Dad cuts in. "Everything okay?"

"Owen's been trying to get ahold of you."

His brow furrows, and he extends his hand, silently asking for the phone. "Owen, I'm going to put my dad on." I hand him the phone.

"Owen, I'll be in this afternoon." He pauses to listen to whatever Owen is saying. "Okay, I'll handle it when I get back." He hangs up and hands me back my phone. "Sorry about that. I was out of town for a few days."

"Where'd you go?" I didn't even realize he was gone. But then again, I've been so busy with Brody I don't even know what day it is.

"It was just a quick business trip. I'll get everything sorted this afternoon."

"Thanks, Dad." I pat him on his shoulder, thankful to have him on my team. For a long time, I was worried about him, afraid he would regress and go back down the dark path he spent too much time on after Mom's death, but he's stayed on the straight and narrow, and I'm damn proud of him.

The waitress sets our drinks down and then takes our orders.

"How'd the meeting go with the city this morning?" Amalia asks once the waitress leaves.

"Good. We got the green light to move forward."

She squeals. "I can't believe it's really happening. Gerald and I owe you so much."

"You don't owe me anything. It's a damn good investment. Between your love and knowledge of art and his culinary skills, it's going to be a huge success. Besides, everything else is running smoothly, and with me here for the foreseeable future, it's the perfect time."

It's taken close to fifteen years, but I'm finally at a point where it feels like all my business ventures are running like well-oiled machines.

I'll have to travel occasionally to check on them, but I'll be able to handle everything from here for the most part. Which is good since my son needs me to be as hands-on as possible. Paola texted me last night that Ted is going out of town for business, and since Brody is with me, she's decided to go.

"Maybe it's time to finally settle down," Amalia says for the millionth time.

"I already told you—" My phone rings again, and when I glance at the screen, I groan, recognizing the number. "Hello."

"Good afternoon, I'm looking for the parent or guardian of Brody Fields."

"This is his father, Benjamin Fields."

"Hello, this is Dean Thomas. Your son was in a fight and has been suspended. We're going to need you to come down so we can discuss this in person, and you can pick him up."

"I'm on my way." I stand, and Dad and Amalia both look at me curiously.

"Brody was in a fight and got suspended. So much for him staying at school."

"RISE AND SHINE." I SNAG BRODY'S BLANKET AND PULL IT off his body.

"What the hell?" he rasps. "What time is it?"

"Quit cursing. You're fourteen, not thirty. And it's five thirty. Time to get up."

"What? Why?" he whines.

"Because you're suspended, and I don't trust you to stay home alone."

His eyes pop open.

"You're coming to work with me. I'm going downstairs to work out. Be dressed and ready to go by seven thirty."

He groans, grabbing a pillow and placing it over his face. I snag it and toss it onto the floor.

"I'm not kidding. Get up."

I enter the gym with a bounce in my step, knowing that I'm early and will get my treadmill. But when I turn the corner and find *her* walking on my treadmill, I growl under my breath.

"Hey!" She waves with a cheerful smile. "You're here early."

"So are you."

"Yeah." She nods, taking a sip of her Starbucks coffee before setting it back down. "I couldn't sleep, so I figured I would start my day early. Got coffee and then came here."

My gaze slides down to her shirt of the day: *If you love Southern women, raise your glass. If not, raise your standards.*

"How many of those shirts do you own?"

She looks down and laughs. "A lot. There was a gift shop in the quad of the college I attended, and every time my friend would see a new shirt, she would buy it for me as a joke because, as you can tell from my accent, I'm a little Southern."

When she winks, I can't help but smile, despite my workout being ruined yet again. Something about her is sexy, and it's not just her looks. Maybe it's her carefree attitude.

"Where did you go to school?" I find myself asking.

"Tennessee."

Wait a second…

"What's your name?"

"Savy."

"Short for Savannah?"

"Yep."

Well, shit, either it's a small world or a coincidence. Lucas told me about her before he left. Said she was a friend of Brianne's from college, and he hired her as his new CFO. Apparently, she's some sort of math genius. I skim over her once more, a bit confused. It's got to be a coincidence.

"What's your name?" she asks.

"Benjamin."

She grins, showing off her perfectly straight white teeth. "Benjamin, huh? Mind if I call you Benji?"

"It's Benjamin," I repeat. No respectable businessman would agree to being called *Benji*.

She snorts. "How about Ben?"

"Benjamin."

This time, it's a giggle that shouldn't shoot straight to my dick but does. "Benjamin is so long and formal. How about…"

"Benjamin," I repeat.

At the same time, she says, "Benny?"

"Benjamin," I deadpan. "Ben-ja-min."

"We'll see," she says, stopping her treadmill. "You can have it. I'm done for today."

She takes one last sip of her coffee, then chucks it into the bin on her way out, leaving me standing here speechless.

"BRODY, LET'S GO!" I YELL, CHECKING THE TIME. IT'S seven thirty, and we need to get going. I scheduled an early meeting, and it looks bad when the boss is late.

"I'm coming," he groans, stepping around the corner.

He's wearing a beanie on his head, a hoodie with a skateboard across the front, also covering the top of his head, and jeans with more holes than material. He looks more grunge than professional, and if I had time, I'd make him change. How did I not notice the way he dresses until now? Maybe because his private school required a uniform.

"What?" He glances down when he catches me staring.

"You look like the homeless guys under the bridge. Your mom lets you dress like that?"

He rolls his eyes. "It's a vibe, Dad. You don't get it."

"I make enough money for your *vibe* to be a bit more polished than that. Appearances speak volumes, and yours says you don't care."

"Because I don't," he says as he walks past me and out the door.

I grab my briefcase and lock up behind me. Once we're downstairs, I nod toward Fred, so he can hail us a car.

As I'm opening the door and sliding in after Brody, I hear a woman yell, "Hold, please!"

I glance out from inside and see Savannah running out the door and straight for our car. Oh no…This won't do. I have a schedule to keep and can't be sharing a car. There are a million cabs in the city. She can't grab one of those?

But before I can tell her this, she stumbles in, knocking me into Brody, and slams the door shut. "Whew, thank you! I'm running late."

"Must've been that *long* workout," I mutter sarcastically, annoyed that now I'm going to have to be a gentleman and allow for her to be dropped off first. This is going to set my entire morning back.

Savannah laughs, the sound melodic and carefree. "Probably. I might need to get up even earlier if I'm going to make working out part of my routine once I start working."

Well, at least if she does that, she'll be out of the gym before I arrive since she doesn't seem to walk more than ten minutes.

"Hey, Savy," Brody says, sounding more chipper than I've heard him the past several days.

Savannah looks around me. "Hey, you. I didn't see you there."

"You two know each other?" I dart my eyes from her to him.

"Brody showed me a delicious restaurant to have lunch at the other day."

When the hell would he...and then it clicks. "You were eating with her when you were skipping school?"

"Where to?" the driver asks impatiently before Brody can answer.

I glance at Savannah.

"Oh! Umm..." She pulls her phone out and taps away at it. "Fields Tower? I can't find the address."

Well shit, I guess she *is* the friend Lucas hired. At least I don't have to worry about being late since we're going to the same place.

"Yep! Fields Tower," she repeats. "Have you heard of it?"

"Yeah...my office is there as well."

Brody snorts, and I elbow him, making him chuckle.

"Really?" Savannah asks. "Do you work for Sharp Architecture and Construction?"

"No, but Uncle Lucas is Dad's best friend and my godfather," Brody announces.

Savannah's bright blue eyes go wide. "Oh, wow, what a small world."

She smiles at my son, who smiles back. The kid hasn't done anything more than grimace and occasionally grunt since he's moved in, and now, he's over there grinning like a damn fool.

Brody spends the car ride telling Savannah about other restaurants he likes, and she makes note of them in her phone so she can check them out.

Once the driver stops in front of the building, I quickly swipe my card as Savannah opens the door and scoots out, and I follow while Brody gets out on the other side.

As she steps onto the sidewalk, sliding her coat on since it's a bit chilly outside this morning, I take in her attire from behind.

She's dressed differently than what she's been wearing to the gym, more professional, which makes sense since she's going to work.

Her black pencil skirt is tight in all the right places, hugging her ass. It's just long enough to be deemed professional and short enough to show off those toned legs of hers, which are unfortunately covered in black pantyhose.

She's sporting come-fuck-me heels that have me imagining what they would feel like digging into my back as I fuck her on my office desk.

"Benny," Savannah says, knocking me out of my thoughts.

"Benny?" Brody laughs, knowing I hate nicknames. "Can I call you Benny too?"

"You can call me Dad." I glare at him. "The building is right there." I point at the twelve-story building in front of us that reads Fields Tower in mirrored letters across the front.

"Thanks." She tips her head upward. "It's big."

When she doesn't make any move to walk in, Brody and I stay standing by her. He gives me an odd look, and I shrug.

"You okay?" I ask.

Her eyes dart over to me. "Yeah, just nervous, I guess." Her Southern accent comes out heavy. "It's intimidating. New city, new job. I guess it's all just hitting me." She glances around. "I was hoping to get breakfast, maybe coffee, before my meeting." She looks at her watch. "I have some time. I wasn't sure how long it would take to get here. Do you know of anywhere? Maybe a bit of food and caffeine will help."

Her azure eyes meet mine, and it feels as though my breath has been knocked out of me. With her hair down in waves and a bit of makeup on her face, she's gorgeous.

But it's the way she looks at me, with vulnerability in her eyes, that has my attention. It feels as though she's cracked open the vault to her soul and is giving me a glimpse. She's so open, like what you see is what you get, and I'm not used to that. I

n my world, people put up a wall and hide behind it, only showing what they want others to see. But with one look, it's as if Savannah's bared herself to the world.

"You can come with us," Brody says first. "Dad's house has no food, so he has to feed me anyway."

Savannah looks at him and laughs. It's carefree and melodic, and I know I'm fucked.

"I know of a place," I tell her, extending my hand.

She takes it, and I lead her and Brody to a deli that serves breakfast and coffee.

After we order our drinks and food, we find a small table near the window to sit at while we wait. When our number is called, Brody surprisingly offers to grab it all. He passes out everyone's food and drinks when he gets back.

"Thank you," Savannah says to him, handing him a napkin. "This smells delicious."

"So, how did you two meet?" I ask them, taking a sip of my coffee.

Brody averts his gaze while Savannah shrugs. "He told me I'm hot."

"What?" I glance at my son, who has the decency to look sheepishly at me.

"And I explained women are beautiful, not hot." She laughs softly. "I also told him women prefer men who are educated, so he should stop skipping school."

Brody smirks and looks at me. "And I told her my dad dropped out of college and still gets plenty of women."

I internally groan. "I graduated high school, and I did attend college. It's where I met your mom."

"Yeah, but then you dropped out and bought a strip club," he argues, making me choke on my coffee. Shit, I never realized how much kids pay attention.

"Brody," I warn, ready to strangle him.

It's not that I'm embarrassed. I don't own them anymore, but at the time, it was a damn good investment. After I renovated and sold them, my return on investment was fifty percent. I used that money to open Lush after paying Lucas back in full with interest.

"What?" he asks, oblivious to the problem with his word vomit. "I don't see why it's a big deal. My friends think it's awesome."

"You don't go around telling people your dad owns strip clubs. Besides, I don't even own them anymore." I look at Savannah, who's hiding her grin behind her cup of coffee, obviously amused at the direction the conversation has taken. "I own several nightclubs called Lush."

"Oh! I've heard of that place. Bri mentioned it when we would talk. I've never been to a nightclub before, but the pictures she showed me were gorgeous."

Before I can think about what I'm doing, I say, "We should go some time."

Savannah's eyes lock with mine. "That would be fun. Bri and Lucas will be back next week. We can all go."

My phone rings, reminding me of my morning meeting that I'm late for. "We need to get going. I'll walk you to where you need to go."

"Is your school over here?" she asks Brody.

"Um, no." He shakes his head, actually looking ashamed. "I got into a fight and got suspended."

She frowns at him in concern. "You're on quite a roll, huh?"

"I guess," he mutters with a shrug.

"Hopefully, he's not going to make this a habit," I add in, glaring at my son, who makes it a point to avoid my gaze.

After we leave Savannah in the reception area of Sharp, Brody and I take the elevator upstairs to where my company's offices are housed. I set him up at my desk to do the schoolwork he needs to have finished before returning next week and then head into my meeting.

CHAPTER FOUR

SAVANNAH

"THIS WILL BE YOUR OFFICE," DAVID SAYS, STEPPING INTO the spacious room.

To the left is a large window that overlooks the city, and in the center is a beautiful mahogany desk. There's a comfy yet elegant-looking couch in the corner with a coffee table and several rows of bookshelves lining the walls. Near the window is a small round table with four chairs, and behind it is a little nook with a Keurig machine and a mini fridge.

"This is mine?" I splutter in shock, taking it all in.

When I finished filling out my paperwork, I ran into David Sharp, Brianne's dad. He said since I was here and he wasn't busy, he would show me around himself.

After only two minutes into the tour, I quickly realized how different Sharp is from the company Neil and his dad run.

For starters, Sharp is warm and inviting. The people actually seem happy to be here, and instead of shitty cubicles, everyone has their own little—or in my case, big—space.

"Of course," David says with a genuine smile. The entire time he's been giving me a tour, I keep looking for a hint of calculation or fakeness, but I've yet to see any. "You're a vital part of this company and will be treated as such. This floor houses the finance and accounting department. We'll hold a meeting on Monday so you can meet everyone and get brought up to speed."

"Thank you. I can't wait."

I step farther inside and run my fingers along the smooth top of the desk, excited to make the space my own. While I was in college, I dreamed of having my own office one day, but when I went to work for Neil, he stuck me in a small cubicle. Not only did he claim he didn't want to play favorites, but it was also pointless because I wouldn't be there long.

Once I got pregnant, I was expected to quit and stay home with the baby. It turns out, he was right. I wasn't there long...but it wasn't to stay home with a baby.

After letting me know he'll be around if I need anything, David excuses himself. I walk around the desk and slide into the comfy plush leather chair. This is mine, all mine. All those years of my parents, and then later my foster parents, telling me I'd never amount to anything only made me want to succeed and work that much harder, and it paid off. I did it. I really freaking did it. I'm a CFO.

I can't help the squeal that escapes my lips as I spin in my chair, fist-pumping the air.

When the chair swivels back to the front, I find Brody standing in the doorway with a grin splayed across his face.

"I could hear you screaming from the lobby." He steps into my office and plops into a guest chair on the other side of my desk.

"Oops." I cover my mouth. "I guess I couldn't contain my excitement."

"Over getting a job?" He laughs.

"Yeah." I nod. "I worked hard in school, and it feels good to see it finally paying off. I graduated at the top of my class and passed the CPA certification on the first try. I'm excited to work."

Brody's face sobers. "My dad loves working too." He doesn't say it, but I can hear it in his tone—his dad works a lot.

"Speaking of which, what are you doing here?"

The last I heard, he was supposed to spend the day in his dad's office doing schoolwork since he's suspended.

"Dad got caught up in his meetings and forgot about lunch." He shrugs, acting like it's no big deal. "I ordered a shitload of food, so I came to see if you wanted to join me."

My heart aches for the sadness in Brody's words. He's lonely, craving attention, and his dad doesn't see it. I only do because I can relate.

Before my mom took off and my dad lost custody of me, all I ever craved was their attention, but the only thing *they* craved was the drugs they were addicted to. Ben isn't addicted to drugs, but it's clear, based on what Brody's just said, he might be addicted to his work.

"I'd love to." I don't have any plans for the rest of the day anyway.

Brody grants me a small smile. "Cool."

I say goodbye to Doris, who works in HR, on my way out and follow Brody to the elevator. When we get off on the top floor, the large sign in the expansive, opulent lobby reads: Fields Enterprises.

"Your dad works here?" The company owns the entire building, and from what Doris said, it's worth millions, possibly billions.

"My dad is Benjamin Fields. He owns the company and this building."

Well, Christ on a cracker. Who knew Mr. Uptight was some big shot business owner? He mentioned owning some clubs...Guess this explains why he's a workaholic.

When my features display my shock, Brody chuckles. "One day, I'm going to work here too." The pride in his voice makes me wonder if Ben knows how much his son looks up to him.

Brody shows me back to Ben's office, which makes mine look like a cubicle. The entire eastern wall is glass, showing off the beauty of Central Park, and in the far corner is a table and chairs that seat eight people. A couch and loveseat are set up in another area with a massive oak desk. I swear this office is bigger than most people's apartments.

"The food should be here soon," Brody says. "I'll go grab us some drinks. What do you drink?"

"Any chance you have sweet tea?"

"We should."

"Can you point me in the direction of the bathroom?" It's been a long morning, and I need to use the bathroom and freshen up.

"Yeah, umm...it's straight down the hall. Make a right, and then it's on the left, I think. My dad has a bathroom in here..." He points at the closed door. "But he forgot to unlock it."

"Thanks."

I find the bathroom quickly, and after relieving myself and washing my hands, I head back.

Somewhere along the way, though, I must make a wrong turn because the next thing I know, I'm walking into a conference room where a meeting is being held by none other than Benjamin Fields.

Everyone is quiet as he speaks, his tone brooking no argument. It's clear he's not reprimanding anyone, but he means business. He isn't rude in any way, but he's authoritative. Every word demands respect. His employees are all typing away on their laptops, I'm sure taking notes.

My thoughts go back to the past few mornings at the gym. How serious he was about his precious treadmill and workout. When the other one made a horrible screeching noise that sounded like a poor cat on his death bed, he almost lost it. It was so much fun to see him all riled up. I planned to return anyway, but seeing the look on his face when he arrived early, and I was already there...Priceless.

Oh! And when I asked if I could call him Benji or Benny...The way he corrected me all deadpan and broody like the idea of his name being shortened was going to give him an anxiety attack.

Before I can stop myself, I let out an extremely unladylike snort, capturing everyone in the room's attention, including Ben—yeah, I refuse to call him Benjamin. Our eyes meet, and the wolfish look in his gaze has the V between my legs tightening.

"Can I help you?" His question comes out more like a demand. His voice is deep and throaty, dripping with sexy confidence. I briefly wonder if he's this way in *all* aspects of his life. I bet he fucks the way he runs his company—with complete and utter control.

Images of him tying me up and having his way with me flicker through my brain, heading straight to my lady parts. Would he let me ride him or demand to be on top? I bet his dick is big, too. Neil was extremely insecure, and he had a small dick. Ben, on the other hand, seems very, very sure of himself.

"Ms. Cartwright, can I help you?" he asks again, popping my fantasy bubble.

I clear my throat. "No…umm…Yes?" I squeak out.

He tilts his head to the side slightly. "Which is it? No or yes? In case you haven't noticed, I'm in the middle of conducting a meeting right now."

I don't know what comes over me, but when he raises a single brow in what looks like half-curiosity, half-impatience, the words just fly out. "Sorry to interrupt, *Benji*"—his team of employees gasp at the nickname—"Brody ordered lunch, and I was wondering when you'll be joining us." It's a simple question, but my tone conveys how I feel about him forgetting about his son.

Ben's jaw ticks, no doubt in anger and probably annoyance, but I can also spot a hint of regret. He glances down at his watch, then looks back at me. "It would seem I lost track of time." He turns his attention to his employees. "Everyone, go ahead and break for lunch. We'll reconvene in thirty minutes."

"Make it sixty," I say. "Thirty minutes is hardly enough time to eat lunch."

His eyes go wide, and a devilish smirk plays in the corner of his mouth as his employees' gazes volley between the two of us, waiting for their boss to confirm one way or the other.

"Sixty minutes." He shakes his head slightly as if he can't believe he's agreeing to something so ludicrous.

Once everyone is gone, and it's only the two of us, Ben closes his laptop and stalks over to me, only stopping once he's cornered me against the wall with our faces mere inches apart.

Up close, his hazel eyes are like nothing I've ever seen—different shades of greens and blues and browns all mixed in a beautiful, chaotic way.

His chocolate brown hair is cut short on the sides and slightly longer on the top. My fingers itch to run through the strands to see if his hair is as soft as it looks. He's sporting several days of stubble, yet it's trimmed neatly.

When his eyes sear into mine and his tongue darts out to wet his lips, I wonder what it would feel like to kiss him, like *really* kiss him. So deep his stubble would burn my face. And then my thoughts shift, as I imagine that same stubble burning between my legs as he licks his way—

"Nobody interrupts my meetings, ever," he says, knocking me out of my erotic fantasy. "They don't argue with me or question me, and they sure as hell don't call me *Benji*. Who the hell are you, and what are you doing to me?"

His questions come out less accusatory and more in wonderment. They're clearly rhetorical, more or less aimed at himself.

I open my mouth to answer him—something sarcastic at the tip of my tongue—when Brody crashes into the room.

"I thought you left," he says to me, hurt and relief woven in his features.

Ben backs up slightly, taking his eyes off me to look at his son.

"I was just telling your dad we were about to eat. He lost track of time, but once I snapped him out of it, he ended his meeting so he could have lunch with us."

Brody's lip quirks up enough to hint at a tiny smile. "Really? You ended your meeting?"

"I did," Ben tells him. "Is the food here?"

"Yeah. I ordered Italian. Your favorite."

Ben smiles. "That sounds good. I just need to have a quick word with Savannah, and then we'll meet you in my office."

Brody looks confused but shrugs. "All right, but hurry. It's going to get cold."

He leaves through the same door he came in, and once we're alone, I turn to Ben, trying to appear nonchalant when I'm anything but. Being this close to him has me feeling things I have no business feeling.

"What's up?"

"I can't remember the last time I felt this way," Ben murmurs, scarily voicing my same thoughts. "First you take over my gym, messing with my morning workout, then somehow you win over my son...a kid who seems to hate everyone these days." He steps forward, encroaching on my personal space. "Then, you crash my meeting, undermining my authority with my employees..." He drags his eyes over my face. "Calling me a name you know I hate..."

I swallow thickly as he drags his tongue across the seam of his lips, looking at me like I'm a puzzle he can't figure out.

"I can't decide if I want to hate you or fuck you." There's a predatory gleam in his eye, one that says the desire to fuck me is winning over the want to hate me. And I get it because as much as he's pissing me off, I can't help but feel this attraction toward him... this pull...

A neon red sign flashes, as if saying, *"Not good, Savy. Not good. Back away and run. Men like him will chew you up and spit you out,"* snapping me back to reality.

I can't afford to be under this man's spell. I've already lost everything: the idea of a loving home and a devoted husband, the possibility of creating a family. Ben is the type of man who'll take and take and take. And I have nothing left to give. And with that thought, I erect a wall ten feet high to protect myself.

"I don't particularly want you to hate me," I say, internally cringing at how breathy my words come out. "I think your kid is pretty damn cool, we live and work in the same building, and our best friends are related, which means we'll probably be seeing a lot of each other, but if it's between fucking me and hating me, you can consider me a foe because I just divorced a man like you: an uptight, control-driven, selfish asshole, and I have no desire to ever go back to anyone like that again. So, hate me or like me, I don't care. But you will *never* fuck me."

I turn on my heel and saunter out without looking back. He's hot on my heels, but he doesn't say a word until we're back in his office and seated with Brody, who's dishing out the food.

"How's your schoolwork coming along?" Ben asks Brody once our plates are full.

"Fine," Brody mumbles.

"Do you need help with anything?"

"Nope."

Ben nods, then tries again. "Did you ask about the football team at your school? Are they any good?"

This time, Brody just glares.

Ben sighs, clearly frustrated Brody isn't participating in the conversation. Poor guy is at least trying, and Brody isn't giving him an inch.

Feeling like maybe I should do something to thaw the ice a bit, I do what my grandpa used to do when I was little and things got awkward.

"What happened to the Indian who drank too much sweet tea?"

Both guys look at me like I've lost my mind.

"He slept in his teepee. Get it?" I cackle. "Tea...Pee?"

Brody is the first to crack a smile, then Ben follows.

"Tough crowd." I take a sip of my sweet tea—which is nothing like the sweet tea from where I'm from—and try again. "How do you organize a space party?" The guys' smiles grow. "You planet...Get it? You *plan* it."

This time, they both grant me a full-megawatt grin, but neither actually laughs.

"Really? That's it? That one was one of my best." I pout playfully.

"If you want us to laugh, you have to actually be funny," Brody smarts. "I've got a good one. What do you call it when Batman skips church?"

Ben snorts out a laugh. "Christian Bale."

They high five, both apparently thinking the joke was clever, while I'm left stumped.

"Get it?" Brody asks. "Christian Bale?"

When I shake my head, he looks at me like I have two heads. "Haven't you seen *Batman?*"

"No."

"What?" they both say in unison.

"How is that possible?" Ben asks. "Everyone's seen *Batman.*"

"Not me." I shrug. "What's it about?"

For the rest of our meal, Brody and Ben explain to me all about *Batman.* Apparently, there are several movies, but the one with Christian Bale—who's an actor, in case you didn't know—is the best one. They're so animated as they talk, so I simply listen while they finish each other's sentences, recounting the entire movie.

When they've finally replayed the entire movie for me, Brody says, "So, Savy, what's your favorite movie?"

"*Sweet Home Alabama.*"

They both raise their brows, obviously not having heard of it, and now it's my turn to tell them all about the best movie ever.

Lunch flies by, and before I know it, my plate is empty, and my belly is full.

"That was some good food," I say, setting my fork and knife into my container and closing the lid. "Thank you for the invite."

I stand, ready to clean up, when Ben's hand lands on top of mine, making my heart skip a beat. A simple touch from him shouldn't affect me like that, but it does.

"Leave it," Ben says. "My assistant will clean up."

"Okay, well, then I better get going." I remove my hand out from under his, breaking the connection. "Your lunch is about over." I shoot him a knowing wink, and he shakes his head.

"Can I go with you?" Brody asks. "It's boring as sh—" When I give him a pointed look, he stops in his tracks and changes his wording. "It's boring here."

"Brody—" Ben begins.

At the same time, I say, "I don't care if your dad doesn't mind."

Ben's eyes meet mine. "I'm sure you have better things to do than have a teenager tagging along."

"Not really. Plus, I enjoy Brody's company, and he knows the city. He can show me where the store is and carry my bags for me."

"Can I go?" Brody asks.

Ben groans. "Fine." He pulls something out from his desk and hands it to Brody—his phone. "You're still grounded. This is only to be used if I call you or you have an emergency." He looks at me. "I should be off around six. I'll come by and get him on my way up."

"Sounds good. Try not to work too hard, *Benji*."

With a smirk that I know is sure to drive him nuts, I gather my purse and walk out of his office with Brody laughing as he follows.

I GRAB A CAN OF TOMATO SAUCE AND HAND IT TO BRODY. "Wanna invite your dad for dinner?"

"No."

"Why not?"

"Because I'm not speaking to him," he says, sounding very much like the surly teenager he is.

"You spoke to him during lunch."

He rolls his eyes. "That was about Batman. Besides, he'd say no anyway. He works twenty-four seven. He won't really be by to get me at six. More like nine or ten. I have a key, though, so I can go home any time. I don't need a babysitter."

"You sound like you hate his job, yet you told me you want to work there."

He glances at me and shrugs. "I figure if I'm there to help, he won't have to work so much. There'll be two people doing the work instead of one."

Oh boy, I'd bet Ben has no idea how his son feels.

Brody's phone rings from his pocket, but he ignores it, continuing to push the buggy down the aisle.

"I think your phone has rang a dozen times since we left your dad's office. It's not your dad calling, is it?" I grab some dough for the pizza we're going to make and drop it into the buggy.

"No. It's my mom."

"Ahh. So, I take it, you're not speaking to her either?" Until now, I haven't heard a single word about his mom.

Brody fidgets, suddenly looking uncomfortable. "We got into it." His eyes drop to his feet. "I got in trouble at school, and I..." He clears his throat, still refusing to look at me. "I don't get along with Ted. He's a dick." He lifts his head, and something about the way he looks at me makes my chest tighten. "She had enough of my shit, so my dad moved home and moved me in with him."

I ignore his foul language. "Okay, that explains why you're not talking to her." We'll get back to that later. There's obviously more to that situation. "But that doesn't explain why you're giving your dad a hard time." I toss a container of cherry tomatoes at him, and he sets it in the buggy.

"He only asked me to move in with him because my mom made him. Can we get mushrooms? I love mushrooms on pizza."

"Sure." I snag a container and hand it to him. "I don't think anyone can make your dad do anything he doesn't want to do." I've only known him for barely a minute, and I can already tell that about him.

"Maybe." He shrugs. "He doesn't even want to live here."

"Yet, he *is* living here. So why are you trying to push him away?"

"I'm not." He scoffs.

"Yes, you are." I stop in the middle of the produce section and look at Brody. "I was raised in a foster home, so I've seen it a million times. The smoking, the skipping, the attitude. You're pushing your dad to see if he'll stick or run."

"He never stays!" Brody barks. "He always leaves. Might as well get it over with now."

Ding. Ding. Ding.

"And then where will you go? Back to your mom's?"

He blanches, as if he hadn't thought of that.

"I'm not going back there. I'd rather live on the streets."

Whoa, okay then.

"You'd rather live on the streets than live with your mom?"

"Than live with Ted," he spits.

"Who's Ted? Your stepdad?"

"My mom's fiancé. I hate him."

"Okay, so you hate him, and you don't want to live with your mom. That leaves your dad. Do you *want* to live with your dad?"

"Yeah, but he's going to leave. I'm telling you…he always does."

"One thing I've learned from being in foster care is that we can't control others. We can only control ourselves. Maybe your dad's here for good…" He opens his mouth to argue, so I raise my hand to stop him. "Maybe he's not. But while he's here, maybe you should try to give him the benefit of the doubt…get to know him, let him see the good in you instead of trying to push him away. Maybe he'll prove you wrong and stick around."

"And what if he doesn't?"

"Then it's his loss. Because I've only just met you and I already know you're worth sticking around for." I grab a container of pineapple and toss it to him.

"Eww, pineapple?"

"Best pizza topping ever."

CHAPTER FIVE

BENJAMIN

I can't think.

Can't focus.

I'm trying like hell to get some work done, and my only thought is Savannah fucking Cartwright. She and her Southern accent and her goddamn sass are going to be the death of me.

Between her messing with my workout routine, undermining me in my own office, and giving me attitude when I confronted her, she has my head spinning every which way.

Most women would've jumped at the chance to fuck me. But not her. She gave that shit right back and then walked away, shaking those delectable hips of hers.

And of course my son likes her. If I'm honest, I'm a little jealous of the way they get along. As if they've known each other for years when they only met a few days ago. The kid is mad at the world, but not at her.

While we were eating lunch, she even got him to talk to me for a few minutes, something he hasn't done in a long time. When we were done discussing our favorite movies, the remainder of lunch was spent with the two of them talking about random shit, laughing and joking. Without him even realizing he was doing it, he opened up to her.

Through their conversation, I learned more about my son than he's given me since he moved in. He hates going to a new school because he misses his friends and knows nobody there, which is hard for a freshman who's been going to school with the same kids his entire life. Their football team sucks, so he doesn't want to play. There's a girl he has a crush on, but he's not sure if she feels the same way. Of course, Savannah told him to go for it and gave him advice on how to go about it—in person and with her favorite flowers. The woman is obviously a romantic.

I put a call into his private school, and with a donation that could probably buy them a new damn wing, they've agreed to let Brody back in on academic probation. I'm planning to tell him tonight—and hopefully win some points.

When I eye the clock and see it's just after four, and I'm clearly not going to get anything else accomplished today, I shut everything down and head out early—something I don't think I've ever done before.

I stop by my dad's office to see him, but when I ask his secretary if he's available, she tells me he's in a meeting.

I shoot him a text, letting him know I stopped by and that we should do lunch soon to discuss our upcoming projects. It seems like since I've been home, aside from the one lunch Amalia insisted on, I haven't seen much of him lately.

When I arrive at Savannah's place, I knock, but the sound of music coming through the walls must drown it out because nobody answers.

I knock again, and when it goes unanswered, I turn the knob to see if it's unlocked. My kid is in there after all.

The door opens easily, and I walk in—I'll have to mention to her later that even though our building is safe, she's still in New York and needs to keep her door locked.

When I step over the threshold, I'm shocked by what I see—

although, at this point, nothing Savannah does should surprise me. With the music at a deafening volume and their backs to me, Savannah and Brody are standing in the kitchen, flipping what looks like pizza dough into the air.

Brody's head is thrown back in laughter while Savannah shakes her ass to the beat of the music, singing the lyrics at the top of her lungs. The entire area looks like a flour bomb exploded. The white powder covers the counters, the floor, their faces and hands.

Flashbacks of my mom flipping out over messes in the house sneak up on me. Of her trying to bake cookies with us but getting upset when we got icing everywhere. Of Amalia begging for Play-doh and then getting spanked when it got stuck in the carpeting. Every memory, every holiday, every family moment was tainted. Eventually, we stopped trying to create new memories and did our best to avoid making Mom mad. But we were young and still did things to upset her until the day she had enough and ended her life.

Brody glances at Savannah, raising the pizza dough roller to his lips to join in the musical duet like they're on stage. His smile is spread across his entire face, and his laughter is so loud, I can hear it over the music.

As I watch them sing and dance and laugh, something in me cracks. I don't know what it is. I can't explain it, but the sight of my son looking so fucking happy damn near brings me to my knees.

Maybe it's because in the fourteen years he's been alive, I've never once heard him laugh so carefree. We've hung out, gone to dinner, spent holidays together. I've heard him laugh, seen him smile, but right now, at this moment, I realize I've never seen him like *this*.

And I know it's my fault. I was scared to be a parent, to fuck my kid up the way my mom fucked up my sister and me, and because of that, I've kept my son at arm's length over the years. I've been going through the motions, but I've never allowed myself to really be a part of his life. I told myself I was doing what was best for him, but I was lying to myself.

As if sensing my presence, they both turn around at the same time. Savannah grins, but Brody's face falls slightly, and my heart shatters. I've done this to him. I've pushed him away, and now I need to fix it. He deserves better, and I'm going to give him that. I have a second chance, and I'm going to make the most of it.

Savannah grabs the remote and turns the volume down. "You're home early."

*Home…*The four-letter word lands in my gut like lead. I don't think I've been *home* in years—if ever.

"You guys making pizza?"

"Yeah," Brody says. "Can I stay for dinner? Mine is going to blow Savy's away."

Savannah hip checks him playfully. "Mine is going to be delicious."

"Pineapple doesn't belong on pizza ever," he volleys, making Savannah roll her eyes.

"We're about to put the toppings on and throw them into the oven. We have plenty if you want to stay."

"Dad can't. He makes calls until—"

"I'd love to," I say, cutting him off. "I'm done with work for the weekend."

Brody's brows fly up in shock. "Oh…okay. Well, you can have some of my pizza. Trust me, you don't want hers."

Savannah laughs. "Pineapple is good, and you promised you would try it."

Brody just shakes his head and rolls his eyes.

"I have beer and wine in the fridge," she offers. "We're almost ready to put the toppings on, and then it'll take about thirty minutes to bake."

"No rush." I open the fridge and grab a beer, then walk over to where they're rolling out their dough on blocks of wood. "Can I help?"

"You can slice the veggies if you want," Savannah says with a soft smile.

We work in comfortable silence with the music playing in the background for a few minutes before I remember I need to tell Brody about his school situation. I'm hoping it'll be the first step in defrosting the ice between us. "I spoke to your principal today."

Brody groans.

"The one at Trinity."

This gets his attention.

"He's agreed to let you back in."

"Seriously?"

"Seriously. But you're on academic probation and will have to prove yourself. One slip up and it's over, and you know they'll be watching."

"Hell, yeah! Thanks, Dad!" He stops chopping and looks at me. "I swear I'll behave. No more fights, and I'll get my grades up."

My eyes lock with Savannah, and she nods once. I'm not sure why, but her nonverbal approval gives me hope that I can make things right between Brody and me.

"I can't believe you got me back in! I need to call Ishmael and Sam."

"You're still grounded," I remind him. "Through the weekend. Monday, we start fresh, and you can use your phone again."

"Alright," Brody agrees easily. "Thanks."

Once we've piled the toppings on the pizzas, Savannah puts them in the oven. Brody goes out to the living room to mess with the TV and add some more songs to the queue while Savannah and I clean up the kitchen.

I'm washing the dishes when my phone rings. I dry off my hands and pull it out of my pocket, silently groaning when I see who it is.

"Paola."

"I received an email from Trinity. Brody's back in?"

"He is."

"Wow, that must've cost a fortune." When I stay silent, she says, "Thank you."

"I did it for him."

"Still, I appreciate it. How's he doing?"

I glance over at him and Savannah debating country versus R&B. Brody must win because a few seconds later, a song that's clearly not country starts to play.

"He's doing good," I tell her truthfully.

Paola sighs. "He hasn't always been like this. It's why I haven't said anything to you. I don't know when it happened or why, but suddenly everything was just spinning out of control."

"It's okay. That's why he has two parents. I'm sorry I haven't been here more, but that's changing now."

It sounds like she's sniffling on the other end, but I don't ask her.

"I'm going to be back in town next week," she says. "I have an appointment I can't reschedule. I was thinking he could come spend the night. I hate how we left things."

"I'm sure we can figure something out. Do you want to talk to him?"

"I've called and texted him several times, but he hasn't responded."

"He's been grounded from his phone," I explain, even though I know he has it on him. "But he's here with me now."

"At your office?"

"No, we're at a friend of ours having dinner. Hold on, and I'll get him." I walk into the living room. "Brody, your mom wants to talk to you."

That easy smile he's been sporting disappears. "I'm grounded from the phone."

"Not from speaking to your mom." I extend my hand, but he doesn't take it.

"I don't want to talk to her."

Unsure of how to handle the situation, I look at Savannah since she seems to get through to him, but she just frowns, keeping her mouth shut.

"He's busy right now. Can I have him call you later?"

"You mean he doesn't want to talk to me. I could hear everything."

"Yeah, I'll speak to him."

We hang up, and I pocket my phone, letting it go for now. Dinner at Savannah's isn't the place to discuss our family shit—even though he'd probably open up to her before he would me.

While we wait for the pizzas to bake, we discuss everything Savannah wants to see in the city. She's planning to spend the weekend playing tourist before she starts work on Monday. She has her phone out and is taking notes on everything we mention.

"Dad, you know the city better than anyone," Brody says. "We should just show her around."

"Oh, I couldn't ask you guys to give up your weekend."

"We'd love to," I say, shocking the shit out of myself.

I hate the city. Sure, it's where I live and grew up, but when you live here, you rarely go anywhere. The city is overpopulated and ridiculously busy.

Her face lights up. "Really?"

"Sure," I insist. "We're not doing anything this weekend. It'll be fun."

"Cool. What time should we go? After the gym?" She shoots me a playful wink.

"Actually, I go jogging in Bryant Park on Saturdays. You're more than welcome to join."

Savannah cracks up laughing. "Jogging? I'd croak over and die. I think I'll pass. Saturdays are for sleeping in anyway."

"I DON'T KNOW ABOUT THIS." SAVANNAH EYES THE ICE AS Brody takes off on his skates like a pro.

We've spent the weekend doing all the cliché touristy shit everyone does here in the city. We went for a walk through Central

Park, visiting popular attractions like the Delacorte Theater and the Belvedere Castle.

We ate dinner in Times Square and did a little shopping, and then, at Brody's request, we went back to our place to watch a movie—*Batman*, with Christian Bale, of course. Savannah fell asleep halfway through it, and once it was over, and Brody went to bed, I walked her back to her place.

Today has been just as busy. After we had breakfast, we explored several of the museums, shared our favorite bakeries with her, and went up to the observatory deck of the Empire State Building. Now we're in Bryant Park at the ice-skating rink.

If I'm honest, I was dreading playing tourist. When you live in New York, you avoid all the places we've visited. But from the moment we stepped out of the building and began our weekend of showing Savannah around, my tune changed.

Savannah was so excited about every damn thing we showed her, I couldn't help but enjoy myself. Her upbeat personality is contagious. She's taken picture after picture everywhere we've stopped, insisting on taking pictures of Brody and me, of Brody and her, and of the three of us.

Of course when she posted a few on social media, tagging me, Lucas made it a point to message me, asking what the hell I was doing and warning me away from Savannah. *"I can't have you fucking my new CFO. My luck, you'll break her heart, and she'll hightail it back to Tennessee."* I messaged him back that it's not like that, but I don't think he believed me.

"I'm going to fall and break my body, and then I won't be able to start work on Monday, and I'll be fired," she whines, making me chuckle.

"I've got you." I step into the rink and turn around. "Take my hands."

She eyes me skeptically for a second before she reaches out and intertwines her glove-covered fingers with mine.

Brody skates by with a couple of his friends he ran into when we got here, yelling for Savannah to get out here and skate.

She forces a smile and nods, then looks back at me. "I'm going to die…or break something and then die."

"You're not going to die." I tug her toward me. "C'mon."

She flies forward, her legs shaking like a baby deer. "How do you know how to skate?" she asks as I glide backward, pulling her along with me slowly.

"I played hockey growing up. Both Lucas and I did. It's how we became friends. We went to the same school but didn't really know each other until we were put on the same hockey team."

Her gloved hands tremble, and I close the space between us, sliding my hands down to her waist to hold her easier. She moves her hands up to my shoulders, latching on tightly in fear of falling.

"I have you," I murmur.

She nods, focusing on moving her feet while I focus on her—something I've caught myself doing several times this weekend.

She's dressed for the cold weather in a fuzzy ivory sweater and tight dark blue jeans that show off her curves. Her hair, which is down and straight, is lighter today, the blond overpowering the brown.

Her eyes have a bit of makeup around them, making her blue eyes pop bright like the sky.

And her lips…fuck, her lips. Because of the cold weather, she keeps reapplying some lip-gloss shit that makes her mouth look all wet and kissable—and no less than a dozen times today, I've had to stop myself from doing just that.

We do a lap around the rink, and since Savannah has caught on, I turn around so I can skate forward.

"Don't let go," she breathes, grabbing my hand.

"I won't. I promise."

Our eyes meet, and I look away, uncomfortable as hell at the way she's got me feeling. I can't remember the last time I spent an entire day with a woman, let alone a weekend—and completely enjoyed myself.

"It's so cold." She shivers dramatically.

"After we're done skating, we can get some hot chocolate."

Her blue orbs light up at the idea.

As we're turning the bend, Brody decides to be funny and sneak up on us. "Boo!" he yells, doing a skate-by with his friends, who all laugh at his antics.

Savannah jumps in shock, losing her balance, but before she can go down, I slip in behind her, wrapping my arms around her torso to steady her.

"Oh my God! You saved my life," she says, sighing into me in relief. Her backside rubs against the front of me, and I stifle a groan, needing to get off this ice and away from her before I make a move on her—proving Lucas right. And as tempting as it is—and trust me, it is—she's the best thing to happen to my son in a while, and I can't risk it getting awkward if I fuck her.

"I think I'm ready for the hot chocolate now," she says, glancing back at me.

"Sounds good."

We skate to the side, and I help her out of the rink so we can take our skates off. Once we both have our shoes back on, she offers to return the skates while I grab us some drinks. On my way to the café, I spot the igloos, giving me an idea.

"What are you doing?" Savannah asks when she catches up to me. "It's sooo cold!"

"I'm ordering us an igloo."

Her adorable nose scrunches up in confusion. "A what?"

"C'mon. You'll see."

CHAPTER SIX

SAVANNAH

THIS WEEKEND HAS BEEN AMAZING. I CAN'T REMEMBER the last time I simply let loose and had this much fun.

With Neil, everything was about show. If we went out, it was done with a purpose—to meet with a client, to discuss business.

Looking back, I can now see where Neil and I went wrong. I wanted a family, a partner, a home. He wanted a trophy wife on his arm to have his babies and make him look good.

And as much as I would love to one day have a family, I want it with a man who actually desires that—and not because it will make him look good.

"All right, this way," Ben says, leading us toward an area filled with…What are those?

"Oh my God, they're igloos!"

"I told you," he says with a chuckle.

He did, but I didn't understand what he meant.

We step into the see-through dome, and I glance around in shock. The area isn't huge, but it's big enough to house four comfy-looking chairs, a table, and a couple of ottomans. It's the coolest thing I've ever seen, and then I realize…"It's heated!" I turn around and look at Ben, who nods.

"It is. And our hot chocolate, apple cider, and dinner have been ordered." He sits in the two-person chair, patting the seat next to him for me to join, so I do.

"Thank you for this weekend. I've had such a good time. The perfect weekend leading up to starting my new job."

I never would've thought, after the first day I met him in the gym —all uptight and asshole-y—we'd be sitting here a few days later, in an igloo in Bryant Park, hanging out.

But after spending the past few days with him, it's clear there's more to Benjamin Fields than meets the eye—more than he wants people on the outside to see. He's not just a stuffy, cold businessman in an expensive suit. He's a caring, thoughtful man, and despite the rocky start he and Brody had, he's a really good father. And surprisingly, I really enjoy his company.

"You're welcome. It's the least I could do after everything you've done for Brody and me."

"What have I done?" I ask, confused.

Ben laughs under his breath. "Of course you don't realize it." He shakes his head. "These past few days are the happiest I've seen my son in a while. And the most pleasant. I even found his cigarettes in the garbage this morning. His cursing has decreased, and it's almost as if he doesn't hate the entire world."

"And you think I did that?"

"Yeah, I do," he says, his tone serious. "I don't know what's going on with him and his mom, but he's clearly taken to you during a time when he can use a friend, and I appreciate that."

"You don't have to thank me. He's a great kid. Just a little lost. I saw it many times over the years in foster care."

A gentleman steps inside and sets a carafe of hot chocolate on the table, along with a bowl of marshmallows and some peppermint sticks. Then he brings in a pitcher of apple cider and a plate of chicken tenders with fries and several dipping sauces.

"Thank you," Ben says, pulling out a bill to tip him. Once the gentleman exits, he returns his attention to me. "You grew up in foster care?"

"Yeah." I grab a mug and fill it with hot chocolate, then top it with some marshmallows and drop a peppermint stick inside. "Since my parents couldn't get their act together, choosing drugs over me, I was in and out, starting at seven years old."

"You didn't have any other family?"

"My grandpa on my mom's side tried to help, but he passed away when I was little, and my dad's parents refused to acknowledge us. I have one aunt, but she hated my mom so much, she wouldn't help, so that left me stuck in the system until I aged out at eighteen."

"I thought most get adopted."

"Some do, but many don't. Kids like me, whose parents refuse to give up custody even though they shouldn't have had kids, nor do they want them, get stuck in foster care. It's like having one foot in and one out. And by the time their rights were revoked, I was no longer a cute kid people wanted to adopt."

Ben nods slowly as if contemplating what he wants to say. I hand him a steaming mug of hot chocolate, and he thanks me.

After taking a sip, his eyes lock with mine. "I never wanted to be a dad. My mom always wanted to have kids. She and my dad were high school sweethearts and dated all through high school and college. They were together for almost twelve years before they decided to start a family.

"They had me and, shortly after, my sister. But after Mom had my sister, something in her changed. She would fight with my dad every day and yell at Amalia and me over everything. As the years went on, it got worse, but my dad refused to get her help. He was in love with her and kept saying things would get better."

I can see it in his face as he looks past me, stuck in his own head, that things didn't get better.

"When I was twelve, she committed suicide." His eyes meet

mine. "My sister is the one who found her bleeding out on the floor in her bedroom, knowing we were home.

"My dad lost his shit and his grip on reality. He lost his job, our house. At one point, we were sleeping in the car. He finally somewhat got it together, got another job, and rented a shoebox-sized apartment. Watching my mom and dad…" He sighs. "I never wanted to have kids. Before she had us, she was perfect. Their relationship, their marriage, their life was perfect."

"You can't possibly blame yourself." It sounds like she might've had postpartum depression or some kind of chemical imbalance.

I'm not a doctor, but in foster care, you see so many kids coming and going, all sharing their stories, that you learn about the various diseases that affect people, especially parents.

"I heard my dad say dozens of times she wasn't like that before she had kids." His elbows land on his knees, and he rubs his palms up and down his scruffy face. "I've never told anyone this before."

"You don't have to tell me."

"I need you to understand why my relationship with my son is so strained. Why I'm such a shitty dad."

"You're not a shitty dad."

"You compared his issues to those of kids in foster care." He chuckles self-deprecatingly. "I don't think I'll be winning any parent of the year awards."

"I didn't mean…I just meant I've seen kids lost like him." I try to backtrack, feeling bad for making it sound like Brody comes from the same type of home the other foster kids and I came from. "I wasn't implying that—"

"Stop." He smiles sadly. "I know you weren't trying to put me down or compare me to those other parents. But the fact you can even make the comparison is why I know I need to work on my relationship with my son." He sighs and shakes his head. "I just hope it's not too late."

"It's not. It's never too late." For years, I wished my parents would get their act together and come for me. Even when I was old enough to know better.

He nods and takes a sip of his drink. When he sets it down, he releases a harsh breath. "Paola and I started dating our freshman year of college. I told her from the get-go that I didn't want to have kids. I made it clear I had no intention of ever starting a family. I was up front because I knew, for most women, a man not wanting to have kids is a deal breaker. She told me she was okay with that, but apparently, she thought it was a phase I would grow out of. She swore she was on birth control, but she lied."

Holy shit.

"When Paola told me she was pregnant, I was scared shitless and pissed as fuck that she would deceive me. She showed me the ultrasound picture, and all I could see was our relationship turning into my parents'. The fighting, the name-calling, it turning physical. Her being driven to commit suicide. I couldn't do it. I couldn't put us in that position. I knew if I stayed, it wouldn't be good. I was filled with hate and resentment toward her, so I walked away. And I've been running ever since."

"But you're back now."

"Yeah, and I barely know my son. Fourteen years wasted."

"That's not true," I tell him, remembering some of the stories Brody shared with me when we were talking the other night before his dad arrived. "He loves you and looks up to you. He wants to work with you, run your business together."

"He doesn't like me."

"He's scared you're going to leave."

Ben's gaze connects with mine. "I'm not going anywhere."

"Then tell him that." I take his hands in mine. "And show him."

"Hey!" Brody steps into the tent. "This is so cool. I never knew these existed." His eyes drop down to our hands, and he smirks. "Am I interrupting something?"

"No." I pull my hands away. "Your dad and I were just talking."

"While holding hands?" He laughs. "I would ask if you're dating, but I know my dad doesn't date."

"Ha-ha, very funny, you little punk." Ben grabs Brody by the neck and ruffles his hair, which provokes Brody into reciprocating.

As I watch the guys roughhouse, glad to see them laughing and joking, I'm thankful for the reminder that Ben is off-limits.

Not that I was planning to pursue him or anything because I'm off-limits as well. Taking a break. Focusing on me. But hearing it is a good reminder that even if I were interested in Ben like that—which I'm not—he's not emotionally available.

Good thing I'm not interested in him that way.

"LET'S WATCH A MOVIE," BRODY SAYS WHEN WE STEP ONTO the elevator.

"Not tonight. Savannah starts her first day at work tomorrow. I'm sure she wants a little time to decompress. Plus, you have school tomorrow."

"Fine." Brody pouts.

"We should have dinner tomorrow night," I suggest. "You can tell me how your first day back at school and seeing Sariah went." Sariah is his crush, who he's planning to ask out.

Brody perks up. "All right, cool."

The elevator dings on my floor, but before I get off, I look at Brody and Ben. "Thank you for this weekend."

Matching grins spread across their faces.

"You're welcome," Ben says. "Good luck tomorrow."

CHAPTER SEVEN

SAVANNAH

asks, filled with humor.

I twist around and find Ben walking into the gym, dressed in a pair of gray sweatpants slung low on his hips and a white T-shirt stretched taut across his chest. The sleeves are short enough that I'm able to get a peek at the ink on his biceps. It's weird seeing him like this, dressed down and looking all normal. Even when we were hanging out this weekend, he was dressed nice.

"I wish," I tell him as he walks around to the front of the treadmills until he's facing me. "That would imply I actually slept."

He chuckles. "Nervous about your first day?"

"I spent the entire night tossing and turning. When I'd finally fall back asleep, I would get trapped in this horrible nightmare where I was calculating numbers, but every time I got so far, I would lose track and have to start all over again. It was exhausting."

"Sounds like it."

"I finally gave up on sleep and settled on going for a walk."

"I can see that." His gaze descends, and a sexy smirk quirks up in the corner of his mouth. "You're on my treadmill."

"Should've gotten here earlier." I lift my bag of peppermint-and-chocolate-covered pretzels. "Want some?"

"No." Ben snorts out a laugh.

"Whatever. Your loss." I pop a delicious pretzel into my mouth.

"Nice shirt." He raises his brows to his forehead. "Is that a warning I should heed?"

My shirt reads, *Here in the South, we don't hide crazy. We parade it on the front porch & give it a lemonade.*

"I don't know. You planning to do something that brings out my crazy?" I sass, stepping off the machine. Since I couldn't sleep, I've been walking for a good thirty minutes while drinking my coffee and eating my snack.

I stop at the trash can to throw my garbage away, and Ben joins me. "If you're not too full from your morning snack, want to go to breakfast before work? We can share a cab."

"Wow, you're offering to share a cab *and* buy me breakfast?" I make my eyes go dramatically wide. "Things are getting serious rather quickly. I'm not sure I'm comfortable with this. Will Brody be joining us as a chaperone?"

Ben's mouth stretches into a wide smile that turns my insides to mush. "Brody gets a ride to school since his private school is closer to where his mom lives, so you'll have to settle for just me. But don't worry," he murmurs, his hazel eyes shining with mirth. "I don't do serious, *ever*, so you're safe."

"Hmm…" I tap my lips with my pointer finger in mock contemplation. "I guess I could share a cab with you, and I'm sure in a couple of hours, I'll be hungry again."

Ben chuckles. "I'll pick you up on my way down."

"Sounds good."

When I'm back home, I take an extra-long hot shower, then focus on doing my hair and makeup until they're both perfect.

Afterward, I go through several outfits, finally deciding on a flowy white blouse and black dress pants paired with my favorite

Louboutin heels. I'm not a name-brand snob, but Neil was, and he insisted his fiancée—and later wife—be dressed to impress.

At the time, I felt bad for letting him purchase such expensive clothes for me, appalled at the ridiculous amounts people spent to clothe themselves, but now...well, at least I have nice clothes at his expense, which means I'll fit in at Sharp.

How one looks shouldn't represent how they'll do their job, but maybe looking the part will give me the confidence to get through my first day. Because the truth is, I'm nervous. While I spent years interning at Neil's company and then working for him, this is my first real job, and I want to succeed.

I'm checking myself out in the mirror one last time when there's a knock on the door. Since Ben told me he'd pick me up on the way down, I grab my purse so he doesn't have to wait, but when I swing the door open, I find not one but two guys standing at my door.

On the left is Ben, dressed in his crisp expensive gray suit that looks like it was tailored for him, and to the right of him is Brody, dressed in a pair of navy-blue dress slacks and a white button-up shirt with a blue, white, and maroon vest, complete with a matching tie. And in his hands is a..."Why do you have a plant?"

Both guys laugh.

"It's for your office," Brody says, handing it to me. "For good luck."

I take the plant from him and hold it close to my chest as Ben takes over. "It's a money plant. The guy at the store said it's supposed to enhance the energy of wealth. And since you deal with money..."

"You bought me a plant?" I choke out, suddenly filled with raw emotion. "For good luck?"

They both nod in unison, looking at me like I'm borderline crazy.

"Nobody's ever bought me flowers or a plant before," I explain. "Thank you." I pull Brody into a hug and then Ben. "This means a lot to me."

My eyes sting with unshed tears, but I keep them at bay, not wanting to scare the guys away. I've learned over the years that men hate women who cry.

"I hope you have a wonderful first day back at school," I tell Brody a few minutes later as he steps into the hired car.

"Thanks. See you tonight." He looks at his dad. "Thank you again for getting me back in."

Ben nods once. "Have a good day."

Once he's gone, Ben snags us a cab. We stop in at the deli to have breakfast and coffee and then head into the building.

"You look nervous," Ben says, handing me my plant. Being the gentleman he is, he held it for me while we were walking so I could finish my coffee.

"I am. I want to be great, and this is all I have left. If I'm not great at this, then…" My words trail off, and Ben lifts my chin with his thumb and forefinger.

"You're going to be great. But remember it's your first day, so you'll probably be a little overwhelmed, and if you're not great today, it's okay."

His words relax me slightly. "Thank you."

The moment I step off the elevator, I'm met by David, who greets me with a smile.

We spend the first part of the morning going over my job in detail as well as the expectations, and the second half is spent in what he calls the Monday morning meeting.

Apparently, once I get the hang of things, I'll be running it for the accounting department. Everyone is warm and welcoming, and the morning flies by.

Before I know it, it's after noon, I'm in my office running numbers, and my stomach is rumbling.

I'm about to ask Florence, the accounting department's secretary, if she knows of anywhere good to eat when there's a knock on my open door.

I glance up and find Ben standing in the doorway with a brown bag dangling from his fingers. My stomach tightens, but I push the feeling away.

"Figured you might be hungry," he says with a small smile. "I brought Greek."

"I was just about to attempt to find somewhere to eat," I tell him, standing to greet him.

"Whenever I get busy with work, I forget to eat." He walks over to the table and sets the food down. "How's it going?"

"Really good." I sit while he dishes out the food. It all smells delicious and has my belly growling in want. "I was a little worried because the company I used to work at was owned by my ex-father-in-law and ex-husband, and both of them were horrible, and then the other day when I ran into your meeting…"

He chuckles. "So, you were scared every company comes with an egotistical, cold-hearted asshole?"

I shrug. "If it's worth anything, you're different outside of your boardroom."

He nods. "I'm not always like that. I was having a bad moment. I bought my team breakfast this morning to apologize." He pops open a can of sweet tea and hands it to me. "So, you were married?"

"Yeah. Stupid decision on my part. We're divorced now. It's the reason I moved here. For a fresh start."

"Savannah, I'm going to grab—" David pokes his head in, and when he sees Ben, he stops his train of thought and grins. "Oh, I'm sorry. I didn't realize you had a lunch date." He steps in, and Ben stands to shake David's hand, but he's pulled into a hug instead. "I heard you were back."

"I am. It's good to see you."

"You, too. How's your dad? I haven't seen him at the club lately, and he's missed the past few men's nights."

Benjamin frowns. "Really? He wasn't with you this weekend?"

David's brow furrows. "No. Did he say he was?"

"I must've misunderstood him," Ben mutters, but his tone conveys something is wrong.

"I'm leaving on a business trip tomorrow, but when I get back, we'll have to do dinner."

"Sounds good," Ben says. "I'm sure Brody will love to see you."

David laughs. "That's right. I heard from Lucas he's living with you. How's he doing?"

"He is." Ben's face lights up. "He's doing better. Was going through a rough patch, but I think we're getting through it." His eyes land on mine, and the corners of his lips spread into a sexy smile, making my heart beat faster.

"Good, good. I'm sure he's no worse than you and Lucas were at his age." David chuckles and glances at me. "It was a full-time job just to keep those boys out of trouble and in school." He clasps his hand on Ben's shoulder. "I'll let you two eat your lunch. I wanted to make sure Savannah was settling in okay and taking a break for lunch. But I can see she's in good hands." He turns his attention to me. "In case I don't see you before you leave today, Lucas and Brianne will be back in tomorrow, as I'm sure you know, so if you need anything while I'm gone, let them know."

"Thank you," I tell him. "Have a good trip."

Once he's gone, Benjamin and I continue our lunch, but he feels off, sort of distant. He's not rude, but his mind is clearly elsewhere. When his phone goes off with a text, he doesn't even notice until I point it out to him.

"It's Brody," he says. "The football coach invited him to join the team for practice after school, so he wants to know if he can stay."

"That's good. He said he wanted to play, and if I recall, participation requires good grades."

He nods absently, typing on his phone. "Yeah. I told him he could." He collects the trash and shoves it into the bag.

"Thank you again for lunch," I tell him as I walk him to the door.

"You're welcome. Enjoy the rest of your day."

He saunters out of the office with a confident swagger most couldn't pull off, and I can't help but notice all the women—and even some of the men—stare.

I spend the rest of the afternoon learning the ropes, and when five o'clock comes, I shoot Ben a message asking if he wants to share a cab home. We exchanged numbers the day I took Brody with me in case of an emergency, but I haven't used it until now.

A few seconds later, a text comes through.

> **BEN**
> It'll be late before Brody gets home, so I'll probably stay and get some work in. Rain check?

> **SAVANNAH**
> Sure. Have a good night.

When I get home, I rinse off and change into some comfy pajamas. I'm about to find a menu and order in when there's a knock on the door. Peeking through the peephole, I see Brody and Ben on the other side, and I can't help the butterflies that flutter in the pit of my belly as I swing open the door.

"What are you guys doing here?"

Brody steps in with Ben following. "Dad didn't realize practice only goes until five."

"We brought dinner," Ben adds. "Hope you're in the mood for tacos."

"Um, always."

"Perfect." Brody grins. "I can't wait to tell you about my day!"

We sit at the table, and Ben doles out tacos to each of us while Brody grabs us drinks.

"Did you see Sariah?" I ask, taking a bite of my delicious taco.

"I did." He beams, chomping on his food. "I asked her out, and she said yes."

Ben pats him on the shoulder. "That's awesome."

"Thanks." Brody glances at Ben and then me. "How was your guys' day?"

Ben goes first, telling us about his day, and my heart swells in my chest as it hits me that this is the first time I've experienced this—

everyone coming together after a day of school and work to eat and talk and laugh.

Neil and I never did this. He worked late, and I usually ate alone. My foster families had too many people, so we ate in shifts. My parents were too drugged up to even remember to feed me. But here with Ben and Brody, I imagine this is what a family does—

"Savannah, you okay?" Ben asks, shaking me from my thoughts. He and Brody are both looking at me with worry etched in their features, and it's then I realize, without meaning to, I've teared up.

"Yeah, sorry." I laugh softly, grabbing a napkin to dab at my eyes. "I'm just…" *I'm thankful to have met you, I enjoy spending time with you, your company makes me feel warm inside, and for the first time in my life, I don't feel alone.* "I just had a really good day."

CHAPTER EIGHT

BENJAMIN

DAD

Sorry. Headed out of town for a few days.
Last-minute appointment.

I'm staring at the messenger app on my computer, confused about what emergency Dad has that would justify canceling our bi-weekly meeting for the third time.

When I got a notification the meeting was canceled, I checked with his secretary. She told me it's not on his calendar, which means it's not related to Fields Enterprises.

Something feels off, and it's starting to grate on my nerves. My dad knows I don't do secrets and have zero tolerance for lying. He lied about how bad off Mom was for years, and she ended up taking her own life.

I won't allow lies and secrets to worm their way into my business and destroy it from the inside out.

"Holy shit, I thought for sure when I returned, you'd be gone."

I glance up from my dad's cryptic message and lazily raise a hand to flip off Lucas. "I told you I'm back for good." I click out of the messenger app. *I'll deal with my dad when he returns.*

Lucas undoes the buttons of his suit jacket and drops into the seat on the other side of my desk, lacing his fingers together behind his head. "Yeah, but after almost fifteen years of you being gone, you can't blame me for being skeptical."

He smirks, showing off his annoying two-dimpled grin that he swears is half the reason the ladies can't deny him. The other reason, according to him, is his big dick. I can't confirm whether it's true, nor do I have any desire to.

"I fucked up, but I'm fixing it."

"Good." Lucas nods, sitting up. "It's Tuesday…Poker night at my place, if you want to join."

"Hell yeah, I'm in."

I always join whenever I'm in town. The weekly tradition started in high school. Our dads are good poker players and taught us how to play when we were younger.

We were looking to make some extra cash—for me—and saw on a movie where some guys hosted a poker night and charged an entry fee. We took everyone for what they were worth, and so the tradition began.

Every week, we would all play in Lucas's pool house with a hundred-dollar minimum buy-in. During the years my dad was checked out, it was how I got the money to buy us food—that and Lucas would raid his pantry and fridge for anything his dad wouldn't notice was missing.

We continued to play during college until I dropped out, Paola got pregnant, and then I ran. But Lucas continued the tradition over the years.

Only now, the stakes are higher since we're all rich as fuck and have nothing better to blow our money on.

"I saw the city gave you the green light."

"Yeah, about damn time." I lean back in my chair. "I also looked at the revised plans you sent over. I have a few minor changes I want to discuss, but aside from that, it all looks good."

"Sounds good." I expect him to excuse himself to go back to his own office since it's his first day back and he's as much of a workaholic as I am, so when a small grin spreads across his face, I know he came here for another reason that has nothing to do with poker or architecture.

"What?"

"Nothing." He shrugs.

"Sharp, get to whatever point you came here for. I have shit to do."

Lucas chuckles. "How was your weekend playing tourist with a certain blonde?"

"Fine."

"Despite my warning, you guys seemed pretty damn close."

"Are we gossiping like teenage girls now?"

Lucas laughs. "Does that mean there's something to gossip about?"

"No. We're friends. No need for a second warning," I say dryly.

Another laugh. "Friends? Since when do *you* have friends who are girls?"

I don't bother to argue because I wouldn't have a case. I don't have friends who are girls because I don't trust women. More often than not, they tend to have ulterior motives. They expect you to read their minds and then get pissed when you can't.

They play games, aren't up front and honest about what they want, and I don't have time or the inclination for that nonsense, which is why I have no desire to settle down. I have a business to run and now a son who needs me.

But Savannah…She's different. I don't know why. I can't quite put my finger on it. Maybe it's the way she is with Brody. The way she's connected with him.

We spent the entire weekend together, and I should've been

ready to walk away from her. She should've done something, said something to piss me off.

Instead, yesterday morning, I was dragging my son out to buy her a goddamn plant, then making plans for dinner.

Hell, this morning when I ran into her at the gym, I asked her to come over for dinner again, offering to feed her since she's been feeding us.

"She's different." When Lucas's brow hits the top of his forehead, I immediately wish I could take my words back. "She's been really good to Brody," I explain, trying to backpedal.

I ramble on for several minutes about the shit Brody gave his mom and me, how he's taken to Savannah, and how, in such a short time, he's done a complete one-eighty, all while hoping Lucas will buy what I'm saying and not ask questions. Because if I'm honest, I don't have the answers.

I don't do serious, but I can't get Savannah off my mind. And it's not just her gorgeous body or beautiful smile, or her sexy Southern accent, or the way she always seems to say what's on her mind, calling me out on my shit. It's more…Fuck, I'm screwed.

"So, you're really just friends," he says once I'm done speaking.

"Yep, just friends."

I can see the wheels turning in my best friend's head, but thankfully, before he can argue or ask questions, there's a knock on my door.

"Come in!" I call out, assuming it's my assistant.

The door opens, and *not my assistant* saunters in wearing a long-sleeved dress—the top half black and white polka-dotted, and the bottom half straight black with a belt that sits just below her tits—that covers the majority of her upper body, yet shows off every delicious curve.

My gaze drags down her tanned thighs and lands on her tall heels that make her legs look long and toned. When I rode to work with her this morning, she was wrapped up in a black overcoat, hiding what was underneath.

She's carrying a bag in one hand, drinks in another, and wears a bright smile. But when she realizes I'm not alone, she stops in her place, her lips curving into a soft frown. "I'm sorry. I didn't realize you were in a meeting. Your assistant said you were free."

At her words, Lucas swivels around. "Savy?"

"Lucas," she says with a sincere smile.

Lucas stands and approaches her. "It's nice to finally meet you." *They've never met?*

"You too," she says, setting the drinks on the table so she can properly shake his hand while I get up and head over to them, taking the bag from her and setting it on the table.

"What are you doing here?" Lucas's tone is casual even though he's digging.

As if suddenly remembering he's her boss, her blue eyes widen slightly. "Oh, umm…" She darts her gaze back and forth between us before settling on him. "I'm on my lunch break. I wrote down the time like we're supposed to, and I'll be back in—"

"Whoa, whoa, it's okay," he says, cutting her off. "I wasn't questioning you. I was just asking what you were doing *here*."

"Oh." She sighs in relief. "I'm having lunch with Ben."

"*Ben*," he repeats, humor in his tone.

"Savannah doesn't know anyone," I explain, "so I stopped by yesterday with lunch, and she insisted on returning the favor today."

"That's very *friendly* of him." Lucas stretches out the word friendly like the asshole he is.

"There's plenty if you want to join us," she offers, her voice cracking a bit.

"Thank you, but I have to head into the office and play catch-up, and then I'm meeting Laura for a late lunch. I was just stopping by to welcome *Ben* home." Laura is his girlfriend of two years.

Savannah nods. "Is Bri back too? I haven't heard from her today."

"She is, but she's in a meeting. We wrapped up sooner than planned and took an earlier flight, so she rescheduled an appointment. I'm sure she'll be by to see you later. She's excited to have you here. Wouldn't stop talking about it all week."

Savannah laughs softly. "I'm very happy to be here. It hasn't even been two days, but I love it at Sharp. Everyone is extremely helpful and friendly."

"Good," he says. "Enjoy your lunch. We'll talk later."

He turns on his heel and walks over to me. *"Friend, my ass,"* he mouths as his hand lands on my shoulder. "See you tonight," he says out loud.

Once he's gone, Savannah releases a loud sigh.

"That was…" She trails off, trying to figure out what to say.

"Lucas," I finish.

"Huh?" She raises a single brow.

"That was typical Lucas." I open the bag and take out the cartons of food. "He thinks because we hung out and you posted some pics on social media, something is going on between us."

I keep my eyes trained on her face to gauge her reaction, but she doesn't give shit away as she says, "I'm sorry. I should've asked you if it was okay to post pictures. I didn't even—"

"Stop." I wave her off. "It's all good. Lucas has recently gotten serious with his on-again, off-again girlfriend, so now he thinks he has the right to play matchmaker. He wants everyone to be as happy as he is." I roll my eyes. "Between him and my sister, they're determined to make me join the Hitched Club. He saw those pictures of us and tried to make something out of nothing."

I wait to see what her response is—if she'll hint that she wouldn't mind making something out of nothing—not that I would…But at least if she tries to wrangle me in somehow, I can cut the strings before she attempts to tie a knot.

Savannah opens the boxes and pushes one toward me, the smell of chicken lo mein filling my senses. "Oh, I know all about *that* club. I terminated my membership and have zero desire to reinstate it."

Either she's a damn good liar, or she really doesn't see me like that because she genuinely sounds like she means it.

She twists the top of her sweet tea and gulps down a large sip before she continues. "Besides, I've only been around you for like a week, and even I know you're not the *getting hitched* type."

Her statement should make me happy. It's exactly what I wanted to hear. She knows the score and accepts it. We're friends and nothing more.

Then why the hell do her words make me want to defend myself?

"You know my reasons," I say instead. "But what are yours? What has you running from commitment when most women are running full speed toward it?"

"Been there, done that." She takes a bite of her food and swallows it down with a sip of her sweet tea. "Met my now ex-husband while I was in college. I was interning at the company his father owns. We dated for a short time, and then he proposed. We were married right after I graduated."

She exhales a deep breath, mentally preparing herself for whatever she's about to say next. "I was blinded by my desire to have that whole happily ever after and didn't see how selfish he was. That he didn't love *me* but loved the *idea* of having a trophy wife on his arm. He thought a woman's place was barefoot and pregnant, supporting her husband."

She smiles sadly. "When I couldn't be what he needed, he found someone who could. And the worst part? It was my best friend."

What an asshole. I've only known Savannah for a short time, but even I can see the amazing person she is. She's someone you dote on and cherish. If she were mine, I'd—

Fuck, nope, not going there. She's not mine, nor will she ever be.

"Just because he was a piece of shit doesn't mean every other guy is."

"True, but growing up, I had the worst home life. I would dream of that elusive family. The husband and kids and career and home. I think I need a break from those dreams. I have a fresh start, a career that most would dream of. I live in a beautiful apartment and have friends like Bri…"

"And Brody and me," I add.

"Yes." She smiles her first sincere smile since she started telling me about her ex-husband. "I have a lot to be thankful for, and maybe it's not the way I dreamed it, but it's mine. So I just want to focus on those things for a while. Maybe one day…"

She clears her throat, and it seems like there's more she wants to say but doesn't. "Enough about me." She changes the subject. "Tell me, what are you cooking for me tonight?"

"Do you ever stop eating?" I joke. "You're eating and asking what I'm going to feed you next."

She shrugs. "It's all those workouts. They burn a lot of calories."

I chuckle. "Must be. Who said I'm cooking? Maybe I'm planning to order in."

"Oh, no. You said, and I quote, 'It's our turn to make you dinner.'" She points her finger at me. "There better be homemade food there."

CHAPTER NINE

SAVANNAH

"Ahhh!" Brianne runs toward me as I stand, just in time for her to wrap her slender arms around me. "You're still here!"

"Of course I'm still here."

"I was so scared you would be here alone and second-guess your decision, and then I'd come home, and you'd be gone."

"You're crazy," I say through a laugh. "I'm not going anywhere." Besides, where the hell else would I go?

Brianne releases me, taking my hand and guiding me over to the couch. "Okay, spill. I let you get away with your vagueness while I was gone because I couldn't corner you over the phone, but now I'm back, and I want all the deets."

"About what?" I ask dumbly, knowing she's referring to my time spent with Brody and Ben.

When Brianne gives me a look that says, *you know what,* I sigh. "We're just friends, so please don't make this more than it is. I enjoy their company, and if everyone tries to push us together, I'm afraid Ben'll push me away."

"Fine." She rolls her eyes. "Any plans tonight? The guys are playing poker, and Marcus will be there. Will you be my wing-woman, pleeaasssse?"

Marcus is Lucas's friend and Brianne's secret crush, but he doesn't even so much as look at her, let alone return her feelings.

"I'm having dinner with Ben and Brody."

She smirks saucily. "After…Lucas said Ben will be there."

"Oh." He never mentioned it. "Well, I guess."

"Great!" She claps her hands together. "How's it going?" She glances around the office. "Need anything?"

"Nope. It's going great. Sharp uses the same program as Everton, so the transition so far has been smooth. Your dad is so sweet, and I met your brother in person today while I was having lunch with Ben. He told me he'd be by to check on me."

The two times I visited New York, Lucas was out of town, and when Brianne and I graduated, we walked at separate times because our majors were different.

She invited me to dinner with her family to celebrate, but Neil insisted we go to dinner with his family instead. So, while I've met Lucas plenty of times through video chat while he and Brianne were chatting, and once during the interview, I hadn't met him in person.

"Good." She nods. "But if you need anything, I'm here." She leans over and hugs me tight. "I'm so glad you're here."

"WOW, THIS IS DELICIOUS!" I TAKE A BITE OF THE spaghetti and meatballs Ben and Brody made.

Ben texted me that he had to leave early for an appointment and to come over at six o'clock for dinner, so when I showed up after work, I thought for sure they would have ordered in.

So I was delightfully shocked when I found the table set with salad and garlic bread to start, along with a bottle of wine.

Both guys nod as they shovel food into their mouths and refuse to meet my eyes…weird. We eat for a few minutes in silence until Ben's phone rings. He glances at it and groans. It stops and then starts again.

"She won't stop until I answer." He sets his fork down and picks it up. "Paola…" He's quiet for a moment before he looks at Brody, who doesn't look back at him. "Okay, we're having dinner right now…Yes, dinner…Let me ask, and I'll call you after."

He hangs up and goes back to eating, not saying another word.

"How was your day?" I ask Brody to make conversation.

"Good. Football practice about killed me, but Coach says I'm a natural, and if I keep playing the way I am, I'll be starting."

I don't know much about football, but starting sounds promising. "What position do you play?" Not that I would know what he did if he told me.

"QB." He shovels a forkful of food into his mouth.

"Quarterback," Ben clarifies. "He throws the ball, and another guy catches it."

"Thank you," I say with a laugh. "I was trying to pretend I had a clue, but I don't think I've ever even seen a game."

"What?" Brody asks. "Didn't you go to UT? Their college team is the shit!"

"Language," Ben chides.

"I was, um…" Warmth creeps up my cheeks. "I was kind of a math nerd." I shrug. "I was on the math team and spent more hours than not tutoring others."

"So, no sports?" Brody asks.

"Nope."

"Parties?"

"Not really."

"How did you become friends with Brianne?" Ben chuckles. "I'm almost positive Lucas joked she majored in partying."

I nod and laugh, taking a sip of my crisp wine. "That's not far from the truth. She was my dorm-mate, and we hit it off. I guess it's true when they say opposites attract.

"Speaking of which...She's dragging me to poker tonight. She mentioned you're going."

"I am. It's been a while." He glances at Brody. "You okay with me going to Lucas's for a few hours?"

"I don't care," Brody says. "I'm not a baby. I've been left alone plenty, and he only lives one floor down."

"I know...Just checking." Ben takes a large gulp of his wine. "Your mom will be back in town tomorrow."

"Yeah, she texted me."

"Which you ignored. She wants to know if you can come by and spend some time with her, maybe spend the night."

Brody's fork stills. "I have school during the week and football and homework."

My heart cracks, seeing the sadness in his eyes. At some point, they're going to have to all talk. From the comments he's made, I don't think the issue is with his mom but her fiancé.

Since it's not my business, I keep my mouth shut, enjoying the dinner they made.

Ben looks like he wants to push Brody, but then he sighs. "All right, maybe this weekend. Ted's out of town, so it's just her at the house until Sunday. Then she's flying back out to meet him."

Brody nods his okay, then goes back to eating his food.

"What if instead of Brody going over there, you guys go out to dinner?" I suggest, going against my previous thought to keep my mouth shut.

Ben glares, but Brody's face brightens. "Will you go too?" Brody asks. "Please?"

"Oh, umm..." I glance at Ben to save me, but he just smirks, as if saying I walked into that one all on my own.

When I look at Brody, he's eyeing me as if waiting for me to say no and let him down. "Sure. If she's okay with it."

"Cool," Brody says, snatching up his now empty plate.

"Dishes," Ben calls out as he walks away.

"I'll do them," I offer. "You guys cooked. It's the least I can do."

Ben clears his throat. "No, you're the guest. We got it."

Taking my plate up to the sink, I stop at the trash can to dump the little bit of remaining scraps into it.

As I'm pressing my foot on the pedal to pop the top to the garbage, both guys yell, "Wait!" But it's too late. The open lid has exposed their lie.

"Seriously?" I accuse through a laugh, lifting the disposable aluminum dish. "You ordered food and pretended you cooked it?" Ben looks at me sheepishly while Brody cracks up laughing. "You both owe me a home-cooked meal!"

"THAT'S WHAT YOU'RE WEARING?" BRIANNE SCRUNCHES up her nose at my jeans and hoodie combo paired with my favorite comfy gray UGGs.

"What? It's cold out, and I was in heels all day."

She sighs. "There are going to be good-looking guys there, Savy."

"So?"

"So, you need to move forward."

"Bri," I warn. "I'm going as *your* wingwoman. That's it. And I'm only staying for a little while, so whatever you need me to *wing* better happen quickly."

She rolls her eyes, returning back to her mirror so she can finish putting her makeup on. Once she's done, we head upstairs to Lucas's apartment, where the poker night is happening. When we arrive, a group of guys is sitting around a large circular table, drinking and laughing, with cards in their hands. I look around and count five guys total, all good-looking, just as Brianne mentioned.

"Geez," I mutter under my breath, making Brianne laugh.

"Told you. Hot guys flock together."

"Does that include your brother?" I joke.

She crinkles her nose. "I don't see him like that, but you can't deny he isn't ugly."

"What are you doing here?" Lucas asks, glancing over at us, repeating the same question he asked me earlier today.

Great...not off to the best start with my new boss. First, I'm hanging out with his best friend, and now I'm crashing his poker night.

"Hello to you too," Brianne snarks, walking over and hugging the one other woman who's here. "Savy, this is Laura, the saint who puts up with my brother. This is Savy, my best friend from college and—"

"And the new CFO of Sharp," Laura finishes. "It's nice to meet you. I've heard wonderful things about you from Lucas."

"Thanks," I mumble, glaring at Brianne.

How did I not think about the fact that coming here meant hanging out with my boss?

"Oh my God, stop!" Brianne scolds. "Lucas, your annoying attitude is scaring Savy. Tell her it's okay to be here."

Lucas's face softens. "It's okay to be here."

"Damn right it is," Ben says. "Drinks are in the kitchen." He shoots me a playful wink before going back to his card game.

"Which one is Marcus?" I ask Brianne once we're in the kitchen, and she's mixing us each a Jack and Coke.

"The one on the right of Ben. The other two are Ian and Scott. Ian owns an investment firm, and Scott's a divorce attorney. Both single." She waggles her brows.

When I glance behind us to check them out, my eyes land on Ben instead. He's laughing as he slams his cards on the table and claims the chips while the other guys give him shit.

As if he can sense me staring, his gaze ascends, and he locks eyes with mine. His lips quirk into a soft smile, and butterflies that have no business residing in my belly spread their wings and fly.

"Oh my fucking God!" Brianne shrieks, making me jump.

"What?" I wait with bated breath for her to call me out on the way I'm reacting to Ben, but instead, she turns her phone around so I can read what's on the screen.

It's a picture of Lois and Neil with their hands on her stomach. The caption reads: **Baby on board! #16weeks**

Lois is pregnant…with Neil's baby. And based on how far along she is, he knocked her up while we were still married. I stare at the picture of the two of them. Lois is smiling at the camera, looking as if she's just won the lottery. But Neil doesn't look like a man in love at all. No, he looks like a man who cheated on his wife and mistakenly got his mistress pregnant and has to make it right.

And now the rushed divorce makes sense. He's from a Catholic family. It was one reason he pushed for us to get married—said his mother would be disappointed if we were living together out of wedlock.

I'd bet his parents found out about Lois being pregnant and threatened his life and job if he didn't make it right. His parents are all about appearances. Although, anyone with a brain will be able to do the math and know she got pregnant while he was married to me.

I click on the next photo, and it's of the ultrasound. My hand instinctively goes to my stomach, and my heart clenches in my chest. When Neil insisted that we try for a baby right away, and month after month, I found myself unable to conceive, Lois was there. I cried to her, worried something was wrong with me. And when I had a feeling my husband was cheating on me, she's the person I whispered my fears to.

After over a year of not getting pregnant, the doctor didn't have any answers as to why I couldn't conceive and referred us to a fertility specialist.

The next day, I found out Neil was cheating on me, so I didn't bother following up. I guess between me refusing to stay home and not giving him the family he so desperately wanted, he replaced me with someone he thought would be better suited to meet his needs.

In hindsight, it was a good thing I couldn't get pregnant because had I succeeded, I would be stuck in a loveless, controlling marriage with a cheating husband and a baby.

But it still hurts to know she could get pregnant so easily while I'm broken.

"Hey," Brianne says, knocking me from my thoughts. "You're not seriously upset about them, are you?" And then, as if the light bulb in her head clicks, her face falls, remembering every time I cried to her over the phone. "Shit." She pulls me into a hug. "Your time will come."

"Maybe." I shrug. But based on Lois being pregnant, it obviously wasn't Neil who was the problem—it was...*is* me.

"No, not maybe. It'll happen. You dodged a bullet, Savy. That guy is a grade A douche. That kid is so fucked with the two of them as parents."

I laugh under my breath at her attempt to lighten the mood.

"You know what you need, right?" She backs up and raises a single brow. "To get laid." Her face lights up as if her answer is the cure to world hunger.

Typically, this is when I would argue with her and tell her that's not who I am, but as I stare at my lying and cheating ex-husband and ex-best friend on the screen, I can't help but think maybe she's right.

Growing up, my world revolved around my parents—trying to be the perfect daughter so they would want me. And when nothing I did made them want to keep me, I focused on trying to make a foster family want to adopt me—which of course never happened.

Next came school. I worked my entire way through college to create a future for myself. I was the model student, afraid if I slipped, I would end up failing and be on the streets.

And then there was Neil. My entire sham of a marriage was all about him—his wants, his needs, his desires.

I've been so focused on everyone else, I never focused on *me*. I made it through the years with my parents and in foster care, I grad-uated college and have the job of my dreams, I'm living in a beautiful home with my best friend in the city that doesn't sleep, and I'm single.

"You know I'm right," Brianne says with a knowing grin. "What you need is to find some hot guy to have some no-strings, no-emotions sex with. A few mind-blowing orgasms, and you'll be saying, 'Neil who?'"

Before I can respond and tell her I'm already over him, a deep throat clears behind me.

When I spin around, Ben's standing there with his cup in his hand, his gaze searing into me. "Needed a refill." He holds up his glass while his eyes remain on me as if Brianne isn't right next to me.

"Friday night," Brianne continues, refusing to be deterred. "We can hit up a club."

"Bri!" Laura shouts. "Where's my drink?"

"Coming!" Brianne yells back, snagging her phone from me and pocketing it before grabbing two of the drinks she made and heading out of the kitchen. "Friday night, Sav, it's on!"

"What was that all about?" Ben asks once Brianne is gone.

"Like you didn't hear." I roll my eyes playfully.

"I was just wondering if I heard her *correctly*." The corner of his lips quirks into a sexy smirk. "You looking for some no-strings sex, Savannah?" The way my name rolls off his tongue sends a shiver down my spine.

"What if I am?" I volley, trying like hell to come across as nonchalant while knowing full well I'm playing with fire. Ben is the type of man who picks up the gauntlet when it's dropped.

And his next statement proves me right. "Then I'll tell you if stringless orgasms are what you want, you don't need to leave this building to have them."

I pop a brow, silently asking him to clarify while I swallow thickly at the thought of Ben pleasing me over and over again.

He sets his cup down and backs me against the counter, one of his hands landing on the countertop next to me and the other on the curve of my hip.

His breath is warm against my face as he murmurs, "You already know I have no desire to commit, and I have no doubt that the number of orgasms I could give you would have you forgetting about that asshole ex of yours."

His tongue runs across the seam of his lips, and my brain turns hazy, imagining his tongue on my body…until his phone rings. He pulls it out and frowns, taking a step back.

"Brody, you okay?" His son's name on his lips clears the fog from my sex-filled head.

Ben is Brody's dad. My friend. My neighbor. He's best friends with my boss. Brianne was right. I do need to get laid, but not by him. He might not do commitment, but with everyone we're linked to, he's the definition of strings.

"I'm actually with her. Let me ask." Ben looks at me. "Can you do dinner Friday night?" It takes me a second to understand what he's asking, and then it clicks. I agreed to go to dinner with Brody, Ben, and Paola.

"Umm, yeah, sure, I can do dinner."

"Did you hear her?" he says to Brody. With him momentarily distracted, I skirt past him, grabbing my drink and heading for the exit. "Okay, I'll be home in a couple of hours."

Before I can make it out of the kitchen, strong hands grip my hips and spin me around, backing me up against the fridge.

"No," I blurt out before Ben can say a word.

"No?" He says the word as if he's never heard it before, and I'm sure he hasn't. He's a beyond good-looking, wealthy man. I'd bet women throw themselves at him all the time.

"No," I repeat, my tone firm. "We're friends and neighbors. I care about your son. There are already strings. So, no. No stringless sex."

He opens his mouth to argue, but before he can, I duck under his arm and run out of the room to safety.

CHAPTER TEN

BENJAMIN

I offered her stringless, unemotional, endless orgasms—just like she wants—and Savannah Cartwright flat out said no.

It's been three days since she looked me in the eyes and told me no, and I can't stop thinking about it.

Of course, she lightened the blow by mentioning all the reasons the sex wouldn't be stringless, and her reasons make sense. I'd already thought about those same reasons when I considered making a move on her.

We do live in the same building, we have become friends—good friends actually—and she has gotten close with my son. But when I heard them discussing their plan to find Savannah a guy to get her laid, all those reasons went out the window because even though I know I shouldn't, I want her. In my bed, screaming my name.

But her turning me down is for the best. At least that's what I keep telling myself.

I thought after our conversation, Savannah would pull back, but every morning she's been at the gym working out—*if you can call it that*. We haven't ridden to work together since Brianne got back to town because they've been going in together.

But we've had dinner both nights with Brody at our place, and the entire time, she acted like I didn't proposition her with sex, and she didn't tell me no. Hell, she even stayed after dinner and watched a movie with us last night.

Now, we're at Three Amigos, Brody's favorite Mexican restaurant, waiting for his mom to arrive for dinner, and I can't take my eyes off her as she talks to Brody about his day.

I can tell he's nervous about meeting with his mom, but Savannah keeps him talking and laughing. She's good at making people feel comfortable around her.

We're going out after dinner tonight to Lush. I insisted we go there since the women want to go out, and I offered to show Savannah my club. She'll have no problem picking up a stranger to fuck. She's beautiful, sweet, genuine…She'll have guys lining up a mile away, and unless I can come up with a good reason to stop it from happening, there's not a damn thing I can do.

"What do you think?" Brody asks.

"Huh?" It's then I realize I've spaced out, staring at and thinking about Savannah.

"Can we take Savy skiing? She's never been." His face lights up in excitement.

Fuck, how the hell did I go all these years without this kid in my life full-time? I might've been running from Paola, but really the only one who was affected and hurt was Brody and me. I can't take back the past fourteen years, but I'll make damn sure all the years coming up count.

"Yeah, for sure," I tell him. "That'll be fun."

We're discussing the different places we can go when Paola arrives. To be cordial, I stand and give her a hug before introducing Savannah as Brody's and my friend.

Paola looks like she wants to ask questions but wisely doesn't. Instead, she shakes Savannah's hand and then gives Brody a hug.

"How are you?" she asks, sitting next to him.

"I'm good," he says softly—very unlike him.

Aside from the day I picked him up from his mom's, this is the first time in years we've all been together.

When Brody was younger, they were close, and it seemed they remained close as he got older, so I was shocked when she told me how bad things have gotten.

He's started to see a therapist, and although he's only gone to one appointment so far, it seems like it went well. I don't know what they talked about since it's about Brody, but he seems to like the guy, so that's good.

"How's school?" she prompts, wanting to catch up.

"Good." The kid was talking up a storm before she got here, but now it's like he's shut down.

As if sensing the same thing as me, Savannah jumps in. "Tell her about football."

Brody's gaze goes to Savannah, and he grins, his face full of pride. "Coach says I have a good chance at starting QB."

"What's that?" Paola asks.

As Brody explains the ins and outs of football, his mom gives him her complete attention. Savannah and I stay quiet, only adding to the conversation when Brody includes us.

We order dinner, and the conversation switches from sports, to school, to the girl Brody's dating—which in teen speak means they meet by her locker in the morning, and he walks her to class.

By the time dinner is over, Brody's a lot more comfortable with his mom, so much so that when she asks if he'll spend the weekend with her, he agrees.

"She seems nice," Savannah says when we get into the Uber I called for.

"Yeah. Thank you for coming."

"Of course. Brody is awesome. It was my pleasure."

"What time did you want to head to Lush?" I ask once we arrive and are in the elevator.

"I'll text you once we're ready," she says as the elevator doors open, and she steps out.

I consider grabbing her by her hand and pulling her back in, begging her not to do this, to go back to my place with me and let me take care of her, but I don't do any of that.

Instead, as the doors close, I watch as she walks down the hall, praying for the strength to get through tonight.

It's for the best, I tell myself. But even I don't believe a word I'm saying.

"HOLY SHIT," MARCUS CURSES, MAKING ME LOOK AROUND to see what has his attention. We're standing in the lobby of the building, waiting for the women to come down. Since a bunch of us are going out tonight, I ordered a Navigator to take us and pick us up so we wouldn't have to deal with snagging several cars.

My eyes follow Marcus's line of vision, landing on the three women walking our way. Brianne and Laura look beautiful, but Savannah has my attention.

With her honey-blond hair down in waves, her face full of makeup that makes her blue eyes pop, and her lips looking fucking edible, she's a far cry from the woman—in her southern shirts and work attire—I've come to know.

Her dress is a glittery silver number with chains for straps and a plunging neckline that exposes her ample cleavage. The dress stops short, with slits on both sides, showing off her toned thighs, with her tall black heels that have me imagining what it would be like to fuck her while she's wearing only those.

As she takes her coat from over her arm and puts it on, hiding her sexy as hell body, her eyes momentarily lock with mine. She smiles sweetly before looking at Brianne and throwing her head back in laughter at whatever she's just said to her.

"Fucking hell," Marcus mutters under his breath.

I know he isn't looking at Laura since she's with Lucas, so that only leaves Savannah and Brianne.

"Savannah is off-limits," I tell him point-blank, not giving a shit that it makes me sound like a caveman.

"Oh yeah? You calling dibs?" He laughs, knowing damn well I wouldn't do that. For one, I'm not in high school, and two, I haven't *claimed* a woman since Paola.

"She's off-limits," I repeat, refusing to give him anything more.

"Got it, but she isn't who I'm looking at. Although, I kind of wish I was. You're a scary bastard, but if I'm honest, I'm more scared of Lucas."

Hold up. "You like Brianne?"

"What's not to like? Look at her." He nods toward the women who are almost over to us. "I've tried to push her away, but I don't know if I have it in me to resist anymore."

"You're both grown adults. Just tell Lucas." Marcus isn't the type to fuck over a woman, so if he's saying he likes her, I'm sure he has good intentions.

"Tell Lucas what?" Lucas asks, stepping over to us.

"Uh..." Marcus stammers like a fucking teenager. "That your girlfriend is walking over."

Lucas glances at Marcus, ready to call him out on his bullshit, but then Laura wraps her arms around him, and he forgets the conversation as he tells her she looks beautiful.

When Savannah makes her way over, I grab her hand and pull her toward me, not giving a shit at the look of shock on her face. "

You look gorgeous," I tell her, kissing her cheek.

We pile into the SUV, and twenty minutes later, we arrive at Lush and are seen to the VIP section I had Val book for me.

The club's two levels are sectioned off into different areas. On the first floor is an upscale restaurant and bar as well as a lounge. On the second floor is a nightclub, but unlike most clubs, Lush is chiller and more laid-back.

The music isn't as loud, isn't thumping as hard, and it doesn't play the garbage most clubs play. Big names such as The Chainsmokers, Calvin Harris, and JB have performed at several of my clubs.

The cost for VIP is over a hundred dollars a person, and bottles start at four figures, going up as high as six. People know that when they come to Lush, they're getting a high-class experience only a few other places can provide.

When the bottle-service girl—Nadine—who's been assigned to us, comes over to take our order, I ask Savannah what she drinks.

"I don't know!" She laughs. "This place is too fancy for this Southern girl. I doubt you'd even have what I drink."

"Nonsense," I tell her, pulling her into my side. "We have anything you want."

"Umm…" She averts her gaze to think, then looks up at me. "I like Grey Goose."

Out of the corner of my eye, I notice Nadine scrunches up her nose at the mention of the cheap vodka, but when I raise a single brow, she smooths her features.

"Grey Goose for the ladies," I tell Nadine, not giving a shit about anything other than giving Savannah what she wants.

Most women would rattle off a bottle way more expensive just because she knows she can but not Savannah. She's as real as it gets.

"And a bottle of Macallan 25 as well," I add because there's no way I'm drinking that shit.

Nadine smirks at the difference in prices between the two bottles before she quickly schools her features *again* and scurries away to put in our order.

"What's Macallan?" Savannah asks as I guide us over to one of the couches in our section to have a seat.

"Damn good whiskey."

While we wait for the drinks to arrive, some of Brianne's friends show up, along with a couple of Lucas's and my friends.

Introductions are made, and then a few minutes later, Nadine returns with the bottles and glasses, asking everyone which bottle they'd like so she can pour the drinks.

"To great friends and even greater women," Lucas says, raising his glass and locking eyes with his girlfriend.

Everyone agrees and clinks glasses before downing their drinks. It's been a while since I've drunk, but the whiskey flows smoothly down my throat.

A few more friends of Brianne's join our table while everyone talks and drinks. Eventually, the women make their way to the dance floor while the guys stay put.

I sit back and watch as Savannah dances with Brianne to the beat of the music.

At some point, she lifts her hair on top of her head and turns her back to me, and I damn near choke on my drink.

From the front, she's gorgeous, but from the back...*fuck*. The chains holding her dress up wrap around her slim neck, leaving her entire back on display, and the material picks up again at the top of her ass. She's stunning, and I'm positive, before long, some asshole will be hitting on her.

The guys bullshit about various topics, catching up on sports and business. I keep half my attention on their conversation while keeping an eye on Savannah, watching as she lets loose.

The women eventually come back for another drink and then head back out to continue their dancing.

My restraint is about gone, and I'm considering joining Savannah on the dance floor when it happens...a guy approaches her.

I wait with bated breath for her to tell him no, but instead, she extends her hand and allows him to guide her away from her friends and over to the VIP bar.

Fuck, he's buying her a drink.

She doesn't need a drink, but of course she doesn't tell him that. I can't see what she orders, but a minute later, the bartender hands her a glass. She turns toward him, her body way too fucking close to his, and smiles, no doubt thanking him.

"You going to let him slide in on your woman?" Marcus says.

"She's not my woman." I grab my drink and drain it in one fell swoop.

But fuck if I don't want her to be.

CHAPTER ELEVEN

SAVANNAH

I can feel Ben's searing hot gaze on me, but I ignore it, focusing on the gentleman in front of me.

His name is Dexter, and he's a CEO of some big company that he's spent the past twenty minutes bragging about while I nurse the disgusting drink he bought me. He insisted on buying it for me after I told him I was drinking Grey Goose, telling me we could do better than that.

He hasn't once asked me anything about myself, and if his self-involved personality is any indication as to how he'd be in bed, I'd be better off using a toy than counting on him to give me a single orgasm, let alone countless ones.

"I think I see my friend calling me over," I say to him when his mouth stops moving long enough for me to get a word in. "But, um, thanks for the drink."

He opens his mouth back up to say something, but before he can get a word out, my back is to him—and I've left my drink on the bar top.

I'm searching for my party when another gentleman stops me.

"Are you here alone?" he asks, his Spanish accent on the strong side.

"I'm here with some friends."

"Can I buy you a drink?"

I'm about to tell him no thanks—been there, done that—when my eyes land on Ben. He's sitting in the same spot with his glass of whiskey in his hand and his gaze locked on me, drinking me in and waiting for me to fail so he can swoop in and seduce me.

Not going to happen…

"Sure," I tell the guy, plastering a fake smile on my face.

He grins and places his palm on my back, guiding me back over to the bar where I just left Dexter. Thankfully, there's no sign of him. The bartender—the same one who took Dexter's order—comes over and raises a single brow as if silently judging me.

"Two glasses of your finest champagne," the gentleman requests, not even bothering to ask me what I want.

Seriously, what is up with these men thinking the key to a woman's pants is through expensive alcohol?

Once she disappears, he turns his attention on me. "I'm Javier."

"I'm Savannah."

"A beautiful name for a beautiful woman," he says, laying it on thick.

We stand in silence while we wait for our drinks, and I use that time to assess Javier. He's a good-looking man with inky black hair and tanned skin, but the way he carries himself is kind of…stuffy. His face is freshly shaven, and he's dressed in a pin-striped suit complete with a tie and a watch that all scream, "I'm loaded."

My gaze flicks over to Ben, who's still watching. Tonight, he's dressed in a suit as well, but unlike Javier's stuffy one, his gives off an *I don't give a fuck* vibe. His gray pants are sexy casual, and as soon as we got here, he shed his jacket, leaving him in only a white dress shirt, sans tie, with the top few buttons undone, exposing a small spattering of chest hair.

As Ben sits back in his seat with his ankle crossed over his knee, his sleeves are now rolled up, showing off his ink. He scrubs his few-days-old scruff with his palm, his eyes never leaving me.

It's not that I don't want him. I do. But I'm also happy for the first time, and he and his son are a part of the reason for that.

When I first met him, I thought he was some stuffy asshole, but he quickly shed those tough layers and showed me the real Ben he keeps hidden underneath. And that man is someone I enjoy having in my life. I look forward to our lunch dates and dinner plans with Brody. He's become someone I can talk to and have a good time with. Crossing that line with him will only complicate things, and is it really worth it for a few minutes of sex?

"Here you are." Javier hands me a glass. "To meeting new people," he toasts.

We spend the next several minutes at the bar while he tells me about himself. By the time I finish my glass of champagne—which I must admit is delicious—I'm bored out of my mind. If I'm going to meet someone, I think I'm going to need to be a bit tipsier because doing this sober sucks.

"Would you like to dance?" Javier asks, gesturing toward the dance floor. I run my eyes over him again, trying to imagine this going anywhere, but I can't. Because he isn't who I want...not by a long shot.

"No, I'm sorry, I don't," I tell him, not wanting to lead him on further. "It was nice talking to you, though. And thank you for the drink."

His brows furrow, but he doesn't argue as I give him a small smile and then walk back toward my friends. Brianne spots me walking over, and I catch the pitying look on her face.

"Another dud?" she asks, obviously having seen me talking to the guy before him.

"Why are men so egotistical?" I grab the bottle of Grey Goose and pour myself a shot, quickly throwing it back, then pour another one and down that one just as fast. "They both couldn't stop bragging about themselves long enough to even ask me about myself." I roll my eyes. "I was already married to one selfish asshole. There's no way I'm wasting my time on another. I'd rather get drunk and Savy myself."

Brianne cracks up laughing, understanding the *One Tree Hill* reference—we spent countless hours watching reruns of it in our dorm—but Ben gives me a confused look, so I explain.

"It means to pleasure myself."

His eyes fill with mirth. "Now that's something I'd like to see."

"Of course you would because it would mean not having to do anything!" I huff, taking my annoyance out on him. "Typical man. Would rather watch a woman pleassure herself than do it himself."

Ben's gaze burns a hole into me, but I ignore him because I'm on a roll.

"I'm over it," I announce, pouring myself another shot, ready to drink it down. "I'm oh for two in the men department tonight, and I'm not sure my liver can take much more."

I raise my glass, toasting the air—because I'm obviously tipsier than I thought I was—but before I can down it, Ben stands and grabs my drink, dropping it onto the table. I stare at him in shock for a quick beat before he takes my hand in his and drags me away from the table, up a hidden set of stairs, and through a door marked PRIVATE.

When we enter what looks like an office, he swipes the papers off the desk and sets me on it.

"Ben," I breathe, meeting his lust-filled eyes. "We can't go there…"

"We definitely can," he argues. "You want no-strings sex, and I want to have sex with you. It's that easy."

I shake my head, trying to remember my argument, but one of his hands is now gliding up my thigh, making it hard to think clearly. He grips my legs and spreads them wide, stepping between them.

"Ben," I groan when he pushes my hair to the side and places soft kisses along my neck. "Nothing about us would be stringless."

"Savy," he murmurs into my ear. He's never used my nickname before, and the way he says it is such a turn-on. "I promise you, no strings." He sucks on my earlobe, causing my entire body to shiver in anticipation.

"I'm serious. I…I can't do commitment. I already did that with Neil and—"

He pulls back slightly to meet my eyes and presses his finger over my lips to silence me. "I'm a man of my word, and the only thing I'm committed to is making you come…several times if you'll let me."

His last words are my breaking point, and before I can second-guess myself, I'm fisting the front of his shirt and pulling him toward me for a desperate, needy kiss. He tastes like expensive whiskey, and I find myself sucking on his tongue, wanting to get drunk off him.

He moans into my mouth before he pulls back, gripping my nape and exposing my neck.

He slowly trails open-mouthed kisses along my overheated flesh, stopping with each one to suckle on my skin.

When he draws a full-body shiver out of me, he chuckles lightly.

"Stand," he demands, stepping back.

I find myself pouting when his touch leaves me, but I do as he says, completely under his spell.

"Turn around."

Again, without question, I follow his command, turning on my heel to face his desk.

He steps behind me and dusts my hair to the side. Then he unclasps the chain straps holding my dress up and unwinds it from around my neck.

When he unzips the bottom half—since nothing is holding it up anymore—it drops to the floor, making a clanking sound.

Because the dress is revealing, I'm left in only my heels and a tiny black thong.

Ben groans under his breath as he runs his palms across my

shoulders and sides, over the swells of my ass, and then down the backs of my thighs.

When he reaches my ankles, he has me lift each foot, so he can pick up my scrap of a dress off the floor. "Now, put your hands on the desk."

My palms hit the top of the sleek wood, forcing me to bend slightly due to the height of my heels. I'm completely on display for Ben, but I don't care because when I glance back through my lashes, the look on his face is pure unadulterated lust, and at this moment, I've never felt sexier. He could have any woman he wants, but he wants me.

"Fuck, Savy. Do you have any idea what the sight of you like this does to me?"

He doesn't wait for a response—and it's a good thing because I have no idea how to respond to that—before he closes the space between us.

He plants a kiss on my shoulder as he spreads my legs with his thigh. His hand glides up my back, pushing my shoulders down until I'm flush with the desk. My ass is in the air, my breasts are smooshed against the cold, hard wood, and my legs are open for him.

Since he's put me in the perfect position to fuck me, I'm expecting him to do just that—get right to it—so I'm confused when his touch disappears momentarily and then reappears between the apex of my legs. *He must want to make sure I'm wet first.*

But I dart my eyes behind me and find him on his knees. I can't see what he's doing, but his lips kiss my left butt cheek and then my right. His fingers slide under the thin material and enter me with ease, causing me to release a groan I attempt to muffle.

"No way. Nobody can hear you. I want to hear every noise, every scream, when I make you fucking come."

My thighs clench at his words, and he chuckles softly, going back to what he was doing.

He pumps his fingers in and out of me, and this time, when I moan, I don't hold back, enjoying the feel of him.

He peppers kisses across the globes of my ass, then pulls his fingers out and tugs my panties down my legs, helping me step out of them.

A second later, my legs are widened, and his hot, wet tongue slides across the seam of my center.

My forehead hits the hard wood, and I moan in pleasure.

With languorous strokes, he licks me from back to front. I can feel my arousal dripping down the insides of my thighs, but I just don't have it in me to care. His tongue feels too damn good.

He adds his fingers back to the mix, hitting something deep inside me, building up the most delicious orgasm, and within seconds, I detonate around his fingers and tongue.

My pussy clenches, my body trembles, but Ben doesn't stop until I'm begging him to, telling him it's too much and that it feels too good.

"Fuck, yes," he growls, turning me around and crashing his mouth to mine.

Our tongues mingle, and I taste myself on him. I just came, but the scent of me on him has me wanting more.

My fingers find the buttons of his shirt, and with shaky hands, I undo each one until they're all separated, and I can remove his shirt.

Without breaking our kiss, I find the button to his pants next and pop it open, unzipping his fly.

As if the sound snaps him out of whatever trance he's in, he breaks our kiss and shakes his head. "No, this is about you."

"But—"

"Multiple orgasms," he murmurs against my lips. "Now, how about while I work on making you come for a second time, you play with those pretty tits since I won't be able to?"

Before I can argue, he lifts me onto the desk, spreads my legs, and then drops back onto his knees. He spreads my lips apart, and his tongue lands directly on my clit.

"Oh, God," I breathe as my eyes roll to the ceiling.

The vibration of Ben chuckling while he sucks on my clit sends sparks through my body, and I find myself doing as he asked—grabbing my breasts and rolling my nipples between my thumbs and forefingers.

My climax is already on the precipice, and when he glances up and sees what I'm doing, his tongue still licking my clit, the heat in his gaze sends me over the edge.

My elbows hit the desk, my eyes closing—black specks of pleasure blurring my vision—and if the music wasn't thumping through the place, I'm positive everyone would hear me coming undone.

When I reopen my eyes, I find Ben standing over me with a satisfied smirk on his face.

With his shirt off, I take a second to appreciate his body. I knew he worked out daily, but holy shit, he's a sight. With a chiseled chest and rock-hard abs, I mentally pout that I won't get the chance to explore every inch of him more closely.

"I say we go for one more," he deadpans, his eyes trailing my body as if trying to decide how to accomplish the task.

"Only if it's with your dick inside me."

"Not tonight. You've had too much to drink."

"Yes, tonight," I argue, refusing to accept what he's saying. I'm a grown-ass woman and capable of making my own decisions.

I grab his pants and pull him toward me. "I need you to fuck me right now," I demand, yanking his hard as steel cock out of its confines. There's no way I'm ending this night, this one time with Ben, without him fucking me.

I stroke his shaft a few times before he groans and gives in, grabbing my ankles and yanking me to the edge of the desk. In one hard thrust, he enters me and bottoms out, making us both groan.

"Wrap those gorgeous legs around me," he growls, his palms smacking against the wood on either side of me.

I do what he says just in time because, in the next second, he's fucking me fast and deep, and had my legs not been linked together, holding me to him, the force of his thrust would've damn near sent me flying.

My arms snake around his neck, my nails digging into his back as our mouths connect once again. Ben kisses the way he fucks—passionately and thoroughly, giving me every ounce of himself.

All too soon, a climax I'm not sure I'm capable of experiencing pushes to the surface, and with one final drive into me, I'm soaring high with Ben following.

As I come down from my orgasm, I know I'll never be able to be with Ben again. Three mind-blowing orgasms and I'm already addicted. There's no way we're ever doing this again.

No strings, my ass.

He might be able to keep things stringless, but I have no doubt if I have another night like tonight, I'll be asking him to marry me and make me come every damn day for the rest of my life.

CHAPTER TWELVE

BENJAMIN

For the third day in a row, I step into the empty gym.

No Savannah on the treadmill, wearing her cheesy-ass shirts, drinking her coffee while eating her crap food.

On Saturday, before I went for my run, I stopped in during her usual workout time to see her, only to find the place empty. I chalked it up to her wanting to sleep in. We were out late, and she did have a good amount to drink.

Later that day, after Brody got back from his mom's, he texted her asking if she wanted to go bowling with us, but she said she wasn't feeling well.

I thought for sure I would see her yesterday. She might not actually work out while she's at the gym, but she's been down there every day...until now apparently, because once again, the gym was empty.

When Brody asked her to join us for dinner and a movie, and she said she still wasn't feeling well and needed to catch up on work, I knew something didn't sound right, but I let it go.

But now it's Monday, and she's once again not here.

Something tells me she's avoiding me—though, I'm not sure why. When we parted ways Friday night, she didn't seem like anything was wrong—quite the opposite actually. She was sated from the multiple orgasms I gave her and had a blissed-out smile on her face the rest of the night.

After we cleaned up and met our friends back at the table, we drank and danced until the early morning.

Brianne shocked the hell out of her brother by leaving with Marcus and, after saying bye to everyone, Lucas, Laura, Savannah, and I took the SUV back to our place. I walked her to her door and, after a kiss good night, told her I would see her tomorrow.

Everything in me wanted to ask her back to my place or worm my way into hers, but since she looked exhausted and mentioned passing out as soon as she rinsed off, I didn't push it.

Now I'm wondering what the hell happened, or if I did something to upset her. I know damn well she enjoyed herself, and she definitely got off several times. Those screams of pleasure couldn't be faked, and neither could the way her cunt squeezed my cock as she came for the third time.

I attempt to work out, but I can't stop thinking about Savannah the entire time. The woman drives me nuts, stealing my treadmill every damn day, yet when she isn't here, I miss her.

Fuck. No, I don't miss her. I'm worried. Yeah, I'm worried something could be wrong. Because that's what friends do. They worry and care. She mentioned not feeling well on more than one occasion. Maybe she really is sick but didn't want to make a big deal about it.

Did Brianne even come home this weekend? For all I know, Savannah could've been home all weekend alone, sick in bed with no one there for her.

When I can't stand another minute of not knowing what's going on with her, I turn off the treadmill and head back upstairs to take a shower and get dressed so I can catch her before she leaves for work —if she's even going. If she's sick, she might still be in bed, in need of medical attention.

Brody is dressed and ready for school, sitting at the table eating his breakfast when I come out dressed for work.

"I'll be right back," I tell him as I head out the door and straight to the elevator.

When I get to Savannah's place, I knock several times, but there's no answer. Dammit. I knock again, but when there's still no answer, I go back up to my place, finding Brody still eating and staring at his phone.

"Have you talked to Savy?" I ask nonchalantly as I grab a muffin and join him at the table.

He looks up from his phone and raises a brow. "Since when do you call her Savy?"

"I didn't—" Shit, he's right. I called her Savy. I shake my head. "Have you talked to Savannah?"

"Not since yesterday." He goes back to watching whatever stupid videos he's watching on his phone—that are undoubtedly killing his brain cells by the dozen.

"Do you have practice after school?"

"Yep," he answers, not bothering to look up.

"Want to order in dinner and watch a movie afterward?"

"Sure." He still doesn't look up.

"You should invite Savannah."

"All right."

"Text her now," I urge. "Before she makes other plans."

I eat my muffin in silence, waiting to see if she responds. His phone vibrates a few minutes later, and then he looks up at me, wearing a scowl on his face. "Something going on with you two?"

"No," I scoff.

"Really?" He turns his phone around for me to see. "First, she bails on bowling, then on dinner. Now, when I ask her to join us for dinner tonight, she tells me she'll be stuck at the office late. Dammit, Dad, what did you do?"

"Don't speak to me like that. And I didn't do anything." But even to my own ears, I can hear the guilt in my words.

"Yeah, right," he mutters. "I gotta go. Whatever you did, fix it."

He hits me with a pointed glare before slinging his backpack over his shoulder and stalking out of the house.

Damn, why does it feel like I've just been reprimanded by my teenage son? Oh, right, because I was.

I consider texting Savannah but figure it's probably best to just show up unannounced. That way, if she's avoiding me, she won't have a chance to run.

I have my Monday morning meeting, and I'm meeting my dad for lunch since he's back in town, but afterward, I'll head over to her office.

"SON, HOW ARE YOU?" MY DAD ASKS, SITTING ACROSS from me at the table in my office.

I give him a once-over and note that he looks tired. He's getting up there in age, and I wonder if maybe life is catching up with him. He's close to retirement age.

I don't want to throw that out there and risk offending him, so I store it away for later when I can broach the subject without it coming across like I want to push him out. I would never do that to my dad. He's the only parent I have left, and he's been through hell.

After Amalia and I lost our mom, I thought for sure we'd also lose our dad. We watched him hit rock bottom, and it was a hard, long journey to help him get back on his feet.

He's told me on numerous occasions his family and work are all he has left, so I wouldn't want to take that from him, but if it means taking the stress off his shoulders, I'll do what I have to do to keep my dad around as long as possible.

"I'm good." I hand him his sub and drink from Rosario's, our favorite sub shop that's been around since my father was a kid. "Brody seems to be back on track. He's back at his school and is playing football. He spent the night at his mom's Friday night, and it seemed to go well. We went bowling Saturday, and he kicked my ass." I chuckle, remembering the way he rubbed it in my face every time he rolled a strike.

My dad smiles, but it seems forced, and that has me worried. "I'm glad to see you home and in his life. He needs you."

"Yeah, he does. And I need him." I never realized how much so until recently. Now I can't imagine him not being in my life. "I fucked up, and I'm lucky he's making it easy for me to make shit right."

Dad nods. "I'm happy for you."

"How did your trip go?" I ask, still having no clue where he went and why.

"Good," is all he gives me.

"Was it for Fields?"

"Uh, no. Just a personal trip."

When he doesn't say anything more, I consider pressing him on the subject, but then his phone rings, and he tells me he needs to get it.

I expect him to take the call, but instead, he gathers up his food and drink and stands. "I'm going to take this in my office. Let's do dinner soon, all of us."

Confused, I stand as well. "Dad, is everything okay?"

Without answering my question, he pulls me into a hug. "I love you, Benjamin. I know I don't tell you enough, but I'm so proud of you. I fucked up when you were growing up. I didn't get your mom the help she needed, but instead of you and your sister letting it keep you down, you both soared."

"Dad," I choke out. "If something's going on…"

"It's nothing I can't handle," he assures me. "You focus on that boy of yours, you hear me? I got this." And without giving me a chance to argue, he walks out the door.

Since my meetings are done for the day, I finish eating, then let my assistant know I'm heading out and not to call unless it's important.

I take the elevator down to Sharp and go straight to accounting. Savannah's secretary is at her desk, and when she sees me, she lets me know that Savannah is alone, and I can go right in.

If she knew Savannah was avoiding me, she probably would've had a different answer.

I walk in without knocking and find Savannah at her desk, eating a sandwich while typing on her computer.

She glances up, then does a double take, her eyes going wide when she realizes it's me.

I close and lock the door behind me so we're not disturbed, then walk over to her desk and drop into the guest chair.

"Glad to see you've recovered." When her brows pinch together, I shake my head. "You know…because you were sick."

She swallows thickly. "I—"

"Save the lie. We both know you weren't sick, so you want to explain the real reason you blew Brody off all weekend?" Yeah, I'm hitting her with a guilt trip. You gotta use what you got. And she may be avoiding me, but she has a soft spot for my son.

Her face falls. "It's not that. You know I care about Brody."

"Then what is it?" I lean forward and shoot her a hard look that hopefully conveys I won't tolerate being lied to.

She closes her eyes for a moment, inhaling a deep breath before she releases a harsh exhale, reopening her eyes. "I needed some time alone to get my head on straight."

"Because of what happened between us Friday night?"

"Because while I was under the influence, I made reckless decisions."

"You're a grown adult, Savannah. I'd hardly call what we did reckless. People do it all the time."

"Do they also have unprotected sex while not on any type of birth control?" she asks, raising a brow.

It takes several seconds for her words to sink in, but once they do, I damn near lose my shit because holy fuck, we had sex without a condom.

I never have sex without a condom. Ever. Not since Paola tricked me into impregnating her.

This can't be right. She has to be confused. She'd been drinking and...

I stand, my heart thrumming in my chest, and pace the room, trying to recall the details from Friday night.

Unlike Savannah, I had barely drunk anything. A couple of glasses at most. My mind goes back to us in the office.

The clothes coming off.

The orgasms.

Her begging me to fuck her.

Me telling her no.

Me giving in.

I not only had sex with her without a condom, but I also came inside her.

My eyes land on her midsection that's hidden behind her desk. I fucked up, and I only have myself to blame. She didn't force me or trick me. I willingly fucked her bare.

"I'm clean," she says, mistaking the reason for my look of panic. "My husband was the last man I slept with without a condom, and after I found out he was cheating on me, I was thoroughly tested."

"I was ... I've never..." I stammer, unable to finish a damn thought. Fuck! I had sex without a condom.

I stop in place and look at her. "*I always* use protection."

"I'm sure you do," she says dryly.

"I'm serious." I step over to her. "I'm always careful. I can't believe..."

"It was both our responsibility," she says. "Like I said, I made reckless choices Friday night, and I needed time to sort through my head. I wasn't avoiding you. I just…" She shrugs. "I've scheduled an appointment with my gynecologist."

"Are you pregnant?" I blurt out, my eyes dropping back down to her stomach, which is stupid since it's only been a few days. Even if she is pregnant, she wouldn't be showing yet. Hell, I don't even think they can tell this early.

"Probably not," she says, and if I'm not mistaken, she almost sounds sad. "But I'll find out for sure in a couple of weeks. Either I'll get my period or the doctor will run a test."

My skin goes clammy, my insides turning ice-cold. There's a chance she could be pregnant. We only had unprotected sex once, so she's probably not, but there's still a possibility. It only takes one time.

"Look," she says softly. "I know you're freaking out, but the chances of me being pregnant are slim." She averts her gaze over my shoulder, and I notice her eyes are now glassy. "Neil and I tried to conceive for well over a year and couldn't. Then he got my ex-best friend pregnant, so I'm almost positive I was the problem."

She blinks several times before she releases a harsh breath. "So, don't worry. You couldn't have fucked up with a better person than me," she chokes out, forcing a watery smile. "I'm broken."

Oh shit. I'm over here freaking out that she might be pregnant, and she's sad that it's most likely not a possibility because she can't get pregnant.

"No." I close the gap between us. "Come here." I pull her up into my arms for a hug, and she lets me. Her face lands against my chest, and I can feel her body shaking with silent sobs. "Shh, it's okay," I murmur. "You're not broken."

She sniffles then backs up, wiping her tears away. "I am, but it is what it is." She shrugs. "We're quite the pair, aren't we?" she says with a humorless laugh. "I'd give anything to be pregnant because it would mean I'm able to be, and you're praying to God that I'm not."

She releases a shaky sigh. "If by some chance I am pregnant, I won't ask you for anything, I promise. I knew from the get-go how you felt—"

"Stop," I say, cutting her off. "Do I want to have any more kids? No, I don't. But I was there in that office on Friday night, and I know how it all went down. If you are pregnant, I'll one-hundred-percent be there for you and this baby." And I mean that with every ounce of my being. "I'm not the same boy I was fifteen years ago. I'm not going to run. I am just as responsible, if not more so, for what happened, and I'll be there every step of the way."

Savannah sighs in relief. "I was scared you'd think I tricked you."

"I don't think that at all." Had it been any other woman, I might've jumped to that conclusion, but from the beginning, something about Savannah made me feel at ease. She's not the kind of woman who would trap me into impregnating her.

"Thank you." She laughs softly. "This just got real deep for a Monday afternoon."

She's telling me…I came over here to call her out on avoiding me, only to find out I could be a dad *again*.

"I better get back to work. Please tell Brody I'm not avoiding him, and I'll see him soon."

"You can tell him yourself when you come over for dinner tonight," I find myself saying.

Her eyes widen, clearly shocked by my suggestion.

"Savy." Reaching out, I brush a wayward strand of hair from out of her eyes. "We're friends, and I don't want what happened Friday night to change that. I meant what I said about it being stringless. If we find out you're pregnant, we'll go from there, but nothing needs to change between us until then. Besides," I say with a laugh, remembering my conversation from this morning with my son. "Brody knew you were blowing us off, and he's blaming me. Practically threatened me to fix it."

Savannah's face lights up. "He's a good kid."

"He is. And it would mean a lot to him if you'd come over for dinner tonight so he can see everything is okay."

"All right. I'll see you guys tonight."

When she forces a too bright smile, telling me she's still worried, I lean over and kiss her forehead.

"It will all be okay," I promise her.

And for some crazy reason, even though I should be freaking the hell out, I actually believe that.

CHAPTER THIRTEEN

SAVANNAH

"WHERE ARE YOU GOING?" BRIANNE ASKS FROM THE doorway, eyeing me as I put the finishing touches on my face.

I considered going straight to Ben's after work but instead made a detour home first so I could change into something more comfortable, which turned into me rinsing the day off, fixing my hair, and then reapplying my makeup.

I glance in the mirror and note she's dressed in a gorgeous slinky dress, and her hair is done in beach waves. I saw her earlier today, and she wasn't wearing that at work.

"I could ask you the same."

A huge grin spreads across her face. "Marcus asked me to dinner."

"So does that mean I can expect you out all night again?" I ask with a laugh.

Since Friday night, when Marcus gave in and admitted to Brianne that he wants her—and told her brother as much—she's been gone more than she's been home.

"If it goes well, I hope so," she replies with a saucy wink. "And where are you going?" she asks again.

"Just over to Ben and Brody's for dinner." I turn around in time to see her brows kiss her forehead.

"What happened to no strings?"

Sunday morning when she got home after her weekend sexcapade with Marcus, I told her what happened between Ben and me in the back office—leaving out the part about not using protection. Not everybody needs to know about my lack of brain cells.

"I'm going over as a friend. Brody invited me."

Brianne side-eyes me but doesn't comment. "All right, well, one night with Ben was good, but we need to get you back out—"

"Nope," I say, cutting her off. "That one night was good enough to last me a while." Total lie. That night only has me wanting more —specifically more of Ben—but I'm not going there. "I'm not a one-night stand kind of girl," I admit, not lying. "For right now, I just need to focus on work and me, and if or when the right guy comes around, then he does."

"So, you're *not* opposed to dating?" she asks, confused, and I can see why she would be. The entire reason for my no-strings sex was because I said I didn't want anything serious, but being with Ben made me realize I don't want to have sex with some stranger. At the very least, I want to know and like the person I'm engaging in sexual relations with.

"I think it's safe to say one-night stands aren't my thing."

"Was Ben that bad?" she jokes, making me laugh. "Or that good?" she adds at the last second.

I'm saved by a knock on the door, which has Brianne squealing in excitement. "Have fun at dinner," she says, kissing my cheek. "And don't wait up."

"YOU LOOK BEAUTIFUL," BEN SAYS, OPENING THE DOOR for me. Like me, he's changed out of his work attire and is sporting a pair of navy-blue lounge pants and a white Henley, his feet bare.

"Thank you." I step inside, the smell of something delicious hitting my senses. "Did you guys cook again?" I joke when I see the Japanese food spread out on the table.

"No." Ben chuckles. "I ordered in, and since Brody ended up going to his mom's house to spend the night, there's way too much food."

Wait…"He's not here?"

"I might've forgotten to tell him you agreed to come over," he admits, at least having the decency to look apologetic. "Paola is heading back to Seattle tomorrow, so when he asked if he could spend the night and go to school from her house in the morning, I told him okay, realizing I forgot to tell him you were coming over. I didn't want to make him feel bad or cancel on his mom, so I just left it alone."

"Oh, well, we can just"—I wave my hand in the air—"do this another night."

"No way. We have tons of food. Please, stay."

There *is* a lot of food on that table, and it would be a shame for it to go to waste.

"Okay, sure," I agree, walking over and having a seat at the table. "You got all the good stuff."

I grab a pair of chopsticks and load my plate up with some sushi, pad Thai, rice, and shrimp tempura while Ben pours us each a glass of white wine.

"How was your day?" I ask, making conversation as I dip my sushi into the soy sauce.

"It was good," he says with a lazy smile. "Although, I'm not sure my assistant knows what to do with me being at the office all the time. I've been working remotely for so long…"

He laughs out loud, and I try and fail to ignore the way his throaty laugh shoots through my veins like the best kind of drug, giving me an instant high.

"Since my team has everything under control, I've been focusing my attention on Artfully Delicious," he adds.

"I bet your sister and her husband are excited."

"Yeah. She loves handling the PR and event planning for Lush, but her passion has always been art." He takes a bite of his food, and I'm so distracted by the way his throat bobs as he swallows, I don't hear what he says next. It must've been a question, though, because he's looking at me as if he's waiting for me to answer.

I nod and shove a mouthful of food into my mouth, hoping that was the correct answer, but when he throws his head back in a laugh, I know it wasn't.

"I zoned out," I mutter, embarrassed. "What did you ask?"

"I *said* you're staring at me like you want to eat me instead of that sushi."

"You did not!" I fling a piece of rice at him.

"No, I didn't." He leans over and runs the back of his knuckles down my cheek, sending a shiver up my spine. "If you want a repeat of Friday night, all you have to do is say so," he murmurs, taking a sip of his wine.

"Not happening," I say with more force than I feel.

Ben nods in understanding, but the way his gaze heats up feels like a direct contradiction.

As we talk about our day, he keeps his eyes locked on mine, only glancing down briefly to see what he's eating. The action feels intimate as if he's so enraptured in our conversation he can't stand to look away for longer than a second.

When my glass of wine is empty, he pours me some more, moving closer.

"What is that?" I point at the white strips on his plate.

"Calamari." He picks a piece up with his chopsticks. "Have you ever had any?"

When I shake my head, he brings the piece of food up to my

mouth, feeding me a bite. I chew slowly, tasting the meat. It's chewy yet also tender and has a mild flavor to it.

"Good?"

"It's…different."

He chuckles. "It's an acquired taste."

We finish our plates, and then Ben pulls out a box of colored circles. "What is that?"

"You've never had Mochi?"

"Never even heard of it."

Tonight is clearly a night for trying new foods.

Ben picks up the pink circle and brings it up to my mouth. "Take a small bite," he instructs when I open my mouth.

The circle is cold as my teeth bite down, breaking it apart. Inside is…ice cream, I think. It's strawberry and refreshing. The outside is kind of chewy, but the inside is soft and so good.

"What do you think?" Ben asks, popping the other half into his mouth.

"It's delicious."

I finish chewing and swallowing, already glancing into the box to see what other ones he has.

When I reach my hand out to grab a white one, he pulls the box back and shakes his head, making me pout.

"Uh-uh." He grabs the white one I was eyeing. "This is vanilla." He brings it up to my lips. "Take a *small* bite."

This time, when I open my mouth, I make it a point to chomp down on his fingers, taking the entire piece of Mochi into my mouth just to mess with him. It's super cold, and the inside of my mouth damn near freezes, but it's worth it when Ben's eyes go wide in shock, making me laugh.

"Now you're gonna get it," he warns just before he flies out of his chair and scoops me into his arms. He takes us over to the couch and drops onto it with me in his lap. "That was my favorite." He tickles my sides as I chew the delicious dessert, laughing so hard my belly hurts.

"Sorry!" I say through a laugh, but because my mouth is full of cold vanilla ice cream, it comes out muffled.

He stops suddenly, his gaze landing on me, and then his mouth collides with mine, his tongue demanding entrance. I part my lips, allowing him access, and he swipes his tongue across mine, moaning into my mouth.

"Mmm," he murmurs against my lips, "my favorite."

I open my eyes and find his already open, staring at me with his intention clear.

"Ben," I breathe. "We can't do this."

"Why not? We want each other...We both know the score. Wouldn't you rather be with someone you know than with some strange guy you have no idea about?"

I nod in agreement. That's exactly what I was talking to Brianne about earlier, but...

"I'm scared of getting attached," I admit. "Of mixing sex with emotions."

"I'll remind you every day that you can't get attached to me. That I'm not the guy for you. I promise you, Savy. You're safe to have your no-strings sex with me. And then, when you're ready to give that whole family plan a go again, I'll let you go so you can find the man you're meant to spend your life with."

He makes it sound so simple, so easy. And maybe for him it is, but for me...I don't know if I'm capable of this. Of not getting attached.

But then he drags his tongue across the seam of his lips, and I let my hormones, instead of my head, do the talking. Because my lady parts, they're begging for Ben, begging me to throw caution to the wind and, for the first time, live a little. No analyzing, no planning, just having some fun.

His hazel eyes bore into mine, begging me to say yes, and before my head can talk my hormones out of it, I pull Ben to me for a hard kiss, silently communicating my decision.

He pulls back slightly, raising a brow. "You sure?"

"Yes, I want you. Just...please, don't let me get attached."

"Not a problem," he growls, lifting me so I'm now straddling his lap. Because I'm in a jersey dress, when my legs land on either side of him, my center rubs against his hard length. I moan into his mouth, the friction of his sweatpants and dick turning me on.

In one fell swoop, Ben removes my dress, leaving me in only my bra and panties. He reaches behind me and unclasps my bra, sliding the straps over my arms and then tossing it to the side.

He cups one of my breasts in his large hand, and his lips latch onto my nipple, bringing the hardened peak into his mouth and between his teeth. When he bites down, scraping my sensitive flesh, the mixture of pleasure and pain damn near send me over the edge. I've never come like this, but based on the way my body is humming, I almost think it's possible. When he does it again, this time rougher, I grind my pelvis against his, making him groan.

"I need you inside me," I beg, not caring how desperate and needy I sound.

"Nuh-uh," he murmurs, releasing my breast and taking the other into his hand. "We have the place to ourselves and nowhere else to be. I'm going to enjoy every single inch of you."

He picks me up and walks us to his room, laying me out on the middle of his bed.

With one hand, he reaches behind and pulls his shirt off, and I take a second to appreciate the sight in front of me.

He pulls his pants down, leaving himself in only a pair of black Calvin's, and joins me on the bed.

Spreading my thighs, he drags himself between them and wastes no time exploring my body.

He nips and sucks and kisses along my breasts, across my torso, and down the apex of my legs until he gets to my center, where he eats me like *I'm* his dessert.

I come loud and hard, tugging on his hair and begging for him to fuck me.

Thankfully, Ben is thinking straight because Lord knows my

brain is hazy from my orgasm. He grabs a condom from his bedside drawer, rolling it over his shaft before he climbs on top of me and enters me in one fluid motion.

His lips brush mine, and his fingers tangle in my hair as he fucks me. It's different from the other night, though. It's not hard or fast. It's slow and methodical. He takes his time, hitting all the right places deep within me until we're both flying off the edge together.

After we're done cleaning up, Ben pulls me back into his bed, wrapping his arms around me from behind.

"Should I go?" I murmur, unsure of the protocol when you have stringless sex with someone who isn't a stranger.

"No." He tugs me closer so my back is flush with his front. "You should stay right here."

With two mind-blowing orgasms at the end of a long Monday, I sigh into his embrace without arguing.

But as my eyes flutter closed, I can't help but wonder if maybe I'm making a huge mistake because as Ben holds me in his arms, it feels an awful lot like strings are holding us together.

CHAPTER FOURTEEN

BENJAMIN

My alarm goes off promptly at six, and I quickly shut it off. Half-asleep, I reach over to pull Savannah to me and consider skipping the gym in place of a better way to get some cardio in, only to find she's gone and the sheets where she was sleeping have gone cold.

Hoping she's still here, I search my entire condo without luck, then shoot her a text, asking if she's okay since she apparently skipped out sometime last night after we fell asleep.

When she doesn't respond, I throw on my workout clothes and head down to the gym. She hasn't been down in a few days, but now that we're talking again, maybe she'll be here.

I walk in, and sure enough, she's on the quiet treadmill with a coffee in her hand and earbuds in her ears, no doubt jamming out to some country song.

Either she doesn't notice me walk in or she's ignoring me, so I walk around the back, checking out her peach of an ass in the tiny purple cotton shorts she's wearing. She's in her usual UGGs—today's color gray—and walking at a snail's pace.

I step onto the treadmill, wrapping my arms around her from

behind in a sneak attack, and she squeals in shock, quickly shutting the machine down and removing her earbuds.

"What in the—"

"I don't appreciate you running this morning," I murmur into her ear. Her hair is up in a messy bun, giving me access to her slim neck, so I take advantage, bringing my lips to her warm flesh and suckling on the area just under her ear.

"Ben," she groans, her body doing that full-body shiver thing it always does when I touch her.

"I rolled over, hoping to wake you up with my tongue"—I run my hand up the side of her smooth thigh and then, spreading her legs, glide it over to the inside and straight up—"only to find you were gone."

A whimper escapes her lips as my fingers slide under her shorts and underwear, finding her cunt ready for me. "I'm…I'm just trying to make sure no strings—"

Her words are cut off when two of my fingers plunge into her heat. "Fuck, Savy, you're so fucking wet." I grab her mane with my other hand and twist her head to the side so I can kiss her. "Stop running." I crash my mouth against hers, tasting her sweet as hell coffee.

I fuck her mouth with my tongue while I fingerfuck her tight pussy until her body begins to tremble under my touch.

"That's it, baby," I coax against her lips as she rides my fingers, seeking out her pleasure. "Come for me."

My words seem to be her undoing because several seconds later, she's doing just that—moaning into my mouth while she comes all over my fingers.

I'm just pulling my fingers out of her when she pushes against me, wiggling her ass.

I'm about to tell her we can't do that here—hell, I shouldn't have even fingered her here—the gym might be empty, but anyone can walk in at any time—when she twirls around and drops to her knees, pulling my shorts down and grabbing my dick. Of course it's hard as hell since I was just knuckles-deep in her pussy, and she wastes no time wrapping her plump lips around the head and taking me all the way into her mouth.

When my cock hits the back of her throat and she gags slightly, glancing up at me with glassy eyes, I damn near shoot my load. But there's no way I'm coming without feeling her tight cunt wrapped around my dick.

So when her mouth slides off my shaft and her tongue swirls around the tip, teasing the shit out of me, I pull her up, yank her shorts and underwear off, and lift her onto the edge of the treadmill so I can get a grip on her.

"Wrap your legs around me," I growl.

Using the treadmill as a backboard, I lift her on to my dick. With her body clinging to me, I palm the bottom of her thighs and enter her in one fluid motion.

"Oh my God," she breathes when I bottom out in her. "Fuck me," she moans, throwing her head back. "Fuck me hard."

Needing something sturdier, I turn us around and step off the treadmill. Her back hits the wall, giving me a grip to fuck her how we both want—hard and fast and deep.

Her fingers tug on my hair, and our mouths collide as I fuck her like I'm possessed. I can't remember ever wanting a woman as much as I want Savannah. The thought scares the shit out of me, so I push it to the side, refusing to focus on anything but the here and now.

Her orgasm hits her quick, and when her walls choke me like a fucking vise grip, I have no choice but to follow. Once she's milked me dry, she releases a harsh breath, then opens her eyes.

"Well, that's one way to start the day," she murmurs, a small, sated smile gracing her lips.

"That's the *best* way to start the day," I correct, ignoring the deep truth mixed in my words.

I lift her off me and set her on her feet, then grab her shorts and underwear so she can put them back on. I'm tucking my dick back into my pants when she gasps, her eyes going wide.

At first, I assume someone's come in and she's freaking out, but then my gaze hits her still bare thighs, the ones that are dripping with my…

"Fuck!" I look at Savannah, who seems to be in shock. "I'm so sorry."

I grab a bunch of paper towels from the holder and hand them to her.

"It's like I can't think when it comes to you," I grumble, scrubbing my hand down my face. "I didn't mean to…*fuck*." I don't even know what to say.

"It's okay." She quickly cleans up and puts her clothes back on. "I'm sure it's okay. I wasn't kidding when I said I had issues getting pregnant. We even charted and did temperature checks, but nothing worked." She grabs her crap off the treadmill and then stops at the door. "Maybe this wasn't a good idea. Lines feel like they're being crossed."

She's probably right. I can't seem to keep my head on straight when I'm around her, but for the first time in a while, I'm happy and in a good place, and I know it's because of her.

She brought Brody back to life, and she's easy to talk to and be around. And maybe it's selfish as hell, but I'm not ready to give her up yet.

The smart thing to do would be to cut the sex out of it and go back to being friends, but the thought of going days without being inside her has me thinking like an idiot.

"Things got a little carried away, and for that, I'm sorry." I close the distance between us. "But I'll make sure that from now on, I'm more careful. I'll use protection, and we'll stick to sex only at night and in my condo. That way, the lines are firmly in place."

She looks like she wants to argue, but thankfully, she just nods, forcing a smile. "Okay." She juts her chin toward the door. "We should probably get going, or we're going to be late for work."

I don't point out that I usually work out longer than this because it's clear she's just trying to make her escape.

"All right. Let's go."

"DID YOU FIX SHIT WITH SAVY?" BRODY ASKS WHEN HE walks through the door, throwing his backpack and gym bag on to the couch.

"Watch your mouth," I say over my shoulder from the kitchen where I'm putting together a salad to go with dinner.

I have a few pieces of salmon and potatoes baking in the oven. It's weird getting home early enough to make dinner, but it's nice getting to spend my evening catching up with Brody, especially since he's been busy all week between football practice, going to his mom's, and hanging out with his friends.

He texted asking if he could have dinner at his friend's after practice, but I told him I was already making dinner and to come home. I've barely seen him all week, and I miss him.

It's crazy to think I ever went weeks, sometimes months, without seeing him, and now I'm whining like a little kid about him being busy all week.

"Well, did you?" he asks, walking into the kitchen and bringing his foul body odor with him. "I want to invite her to my birthday party."

"Damn, kid, you stink."

You'd think with it being cold as fuck outside, he wouldn't sweat as much, but clearly, he does.

"Go jump in the shower. Dinner will be ready soon," I tell him, ignoring what he's said about wanting to invite Savannah to join us for his birthday festivities.

The fact is, I haven't spoken to her all week. At first, my goal was to give her some space so she wouldn't question our arrangement and end things. I even skipped the gym, opting to use the treadmill in my office instead, so I wouldn't crowd her.

But with every day that has passed, I'm wondering if I'm being stupid, and by not texting her, creating more of a rift between us. I promised her nothing would change between us, yet here I am making shit awkward by not texting her.

"I will," he says. "But first answer me."

I should've known he wouldn't drop it.

"Yes, I fixed things. It's all good." I mean, technically, nothing's wrong, so it's not exactly a lie.

He eyes me speculatively, not buying what I'm saying. "You sure?"

"Yes."

"Prove it. Invite her over for dinner tonight."

I bark out a laugh. This fucking kid is too much like me it's scary.

"There's not enough food," I lie.

Brody opens the oven, then slams it closed.

"Fix it," he barks, stalking out of the kitchen.

"In case you forgot, I'm the parent!" I yell after him.

"Oh yeah? Then act like it!" he shouts back, slamming the bathroom door behind him.

I finish cutting the veggies and set the salad on the table, then text Savannah.

BENJAMIN

Brody thinks you're not speaking to us.

SAVANNAH

Why would he think that?

BENJAMIN

He hasn't seen you since last Friday.

SAVANNAH

I'll text him.

BENJAMIN

Or you could come over for dinner…

SAVANNAH

Can't.

BENJAMIN

Why not?

SAVANNAH

I'm busy.

BENJAMIN

Doing what?

SAVANNAH

I'm on a date.

I drop my phone into the sink, and it clangs against the dirty dishes, cracking a plate. This can't be right...She can't be...I grab my phone and wipe it down, chuck the plate into the trash, and then type out a response.

BENJAMIN

What do you mean you're on a date?

SAVANNAH

Bri asked me to double with her and Marcus.

BENJAMIN

Who are you on a date with?

Before I hit send, I stop myself, realizing my text sounds a lot like a jealous boyfriend. Although, if Savannah were my girlfriend, you can bet your ass she wouldn't be on a date with another guy.

I delete the text, then pull up Marcus in my contacts.

BENJAMIN

Hey, how's it going?

MARCUS

Good, you?

BENJAMIN

Chilling. What are you up to?

MARCUS

Out to dinner at The Cove with Bri, Savy, and
Scott.

What in the actual fuck? They set her up with Scott? The guy is a womanizer. He's a divorce attorney who doesn't believe in marriage. Of all people, him?

As I'm about to text back, another one comes in from Savannah.

SAVANNAH

I have to go. I'll text Brody later and let him
know everything is okay.

I stare at my phone, wondering what the fuck just happened and how we went from fucking in the gym to her agreeing to go on a date with another guy.

I'm still staring at my phone when Brody comes out and informs me that the oven has smoke coming out of it.

"Food's ruined." I switch the oven off and grab the pan from inside, throwing it onto the stove.

"Great, what are we going to eat? I'm starved."

"I'll make—" But then an idea hits me. "Let's go out to eat."

"All right." Brody shrugs. "Where?"

"The Cove."

"Can we invite Savy?"

"No, she's out with some friends tonight. But you never know... maybe we'll run into her."

CHAPTER FIFTEEN
SAVANNAH

"It's a shame I didn't know you during your divorce," Scott drones on, refusing to drop the topic since I made the mistake of telling him about it.

In my defense, he asked me what prompted my move to New York, and I gave him the abridged version.

Only I didn't think about the fact he's a lawyer, and my vagueness would turn into him questioning me like I'm on trial.

Next time Brianne suggests we double, I'm going to laugh at her and then politely decline.

"I could've gotten you a nice settlement, even if you were only married for a short time."

As he rambles on about how much money he could've gotten me and how my situation is a perfect example of why couples should never enter a marriage without a prenup, I zone out, thinking about Ben's texts to me.

I might be overthinking it, but it seemed like he was almost jealous. Which doesn't make any sense since he hasn't contacted me all week.

I figured, after our slip up—times two—he was second-guessing our arrangement and had moved on—and I wouldn't blame him.

He made it clear he doesn't do commitment, and possibly knocking up your stringless hookup is kind of the definition of commitment.

Yet when we were texting, he seemed way more invested in what I'm doing and who I'm with than he should've been.

"Savy? I thought that was you."

My name being called shakes me from my thoughts, and when I look around to see who the owner of the voice is, I find Brody and Ben standing at our table.

"Hey," I say to Brody, getting out of my seat to give him a hug. "How've you been?"

"Good. Haven't seen you in a while."

I don't miss the way he side-eyes his dad, who rolls his own like a teenager.

"We'll have to change that soon," I promise, needing him to know I wasn't purposely avoiding him.

"What are you guys doing here?" Brianne asks.

"Dad burned dinner," Brody answers, "so he suggested we come here."

"Quite the coincidence," Marcus says with a chuckle.

When I look over at Ben, he's glaring at Marcus.

There's no way…He wouldn't have…

"I asked Dad to invite you over for dinner tonight, but he said you were out," Brody says. "My birthday is this weekend, and my friends and I are going to the arcade. It has laser tag and shit—I mean stuff…You should come."

"That sounds like fun," I tell him noncommittally since I'm not sure where Ben and I stand, and I'm not about to make things awkward.

"We're doing a family dinner for him Sunday," Ben adds. "Lucas and Laura will be there." His gaze flits from Brianne, to Marcus, then to me—skipping over Scott like he's ignoring him. "You guys are welcome to join. We'll be eating at Dragon Fusion."

"Hibachi's my favorite." Brody grins. "Savy, you'll come, right?" His features morph into a frown. "My mom can't make it because Ted needed her back in Seattle." He shrugs, trying to play it off, but it's obvious his mom choosing her fiancé over her son has hurt his feelings.

I've never been in her situation, and I hate to judge people, but I can't imagine missing my child's birthday. Maybe it's because I spent too many birthdays alone, wishing my parents would simply remember, let alone actually care enough to celebrate.

"I'll definitely be there," I tell him, no longer giving a shit how things are between Ben and me. "I wouldn't miss it for the world."

When his face lights back up, I know I made the right decision.

Everyone's silent for a few seconds, and then the hostess walks over and tells Ben their table is ready.

Of course it's in the same area as ours, not just nearby, but close enough that we're in direct line of each other and able to lock eyes.

Thankfully, our meal arrives, and I'm able to focus on eating my dinner.

Several times, though, my eyes find their way over to Ben's table and catch him looking at me.

BEN

I'm making pancakes for Brody's birthday.
Join us?

I STARE AT MY SCREEN, CONFUSED AS ALL HELL, BUT know I'm going to say yes. For one, it's Brody's birthday, and I got him the best gifts ever. I've been chomping at the bit to give them to him, and I won't be able to wait much longer.

And two, I'm curious to see how Ben acts around me. Aside from the brief conversation when they just *happened* to run into us at dinner, he didn't say another word to me all night. Not even after we finished eating and stopped by their table on the way out to say good night.

When Brianne and I got home, she confirmed my suspicions. Ben had texted Marcus, asking him what he was up to, and Marcus replied that we were out to dinner at The Cove.

Brianne proceeded to tell me that it was obvious Ben was jealous and making his claim on me, and while I totally got that vibe, I waved her off, saying that Ben isn't the claiming type.

SAVANNAH

Sure. What time?

BEN

10:00 after I get back from my jog. He should
be awake by then.

I climb out of bed and jump in the shower, then get dressed and do my hair.

Once I'm ready to go, I wrap Brody's present, then head up to their place. I knock once, then again when no one answers.

He did say 10:00, right?

I'm about to text Ben to let him know I'm here, thinking maybe he's still out for his jog when the door swings open.

My jaw drops, and I'm almost positive drool drips from the corner of my mouth as I take in an almost naked Ben.

His hair is shaggy and wet, and his shoulders and torso are dripping with fresh droplets of water.

Around his waist is a plush towel slung low, revealing his happy trail that leads down, down, down to what's become one of my favorite spots.

"Sorry," he says with a knowing smirk, not sounding sorry at all. "I was in the shower. Have you been knocking for long?"

"No, I just got here. I take it the birthday boy isn't up yet?" I step inside and try with everything in me not to let my gaze descend.

"No, not yet. I'm going to wake him up soon, though." He eyes the present in my hand. "You didn't have to get him anything."

"I know, but the gift kind of fell into my lap. I mean, I had planned to buy him something. But then this happened." I shake the box, giddy inside. "So, yeah."

"All right. Well, I hope you didn't spend too much. The kid's already spoiled."

"I actually didn't spend anything."

Ben eyes me curiously but doesn't ask about it. "I have fresh coffee in the kitchen if you want some. I'm going to get dressed."

I expect Ben to retreat to his room, so I'm momentarily stunned when instead he closes the distance between us—his body so close to mine I can smell the fresh masculine scent of his body wash.

"You look beautiful this morning." He leans in and kisses my cheek. "I'm glad you came."

And with those parting words—which leave my head spinning—he retreats to his room, shutting the door behind him.

I'm making myself a cup of coffee when Brody enters the kitchen.

"Hey," he says, his voice still gruff with sleep. "What are you doing here?"

"Your dad invited me over for breakfast." I finish stirring my coffee and drop the spoon into the sink. "Happy Birthday."

"Thanks." He leans against the counter and grins. "Dad said once I turn fifteen, even though I can't get my permit until I'm sixteen, he'll take me to practice driving in one of his badass cars outside of the city."

"That sounds like fun."

It also reminds me that I need to put my SUV up for sale. Brianne was right. There's no need for a vehicle while living here in the city. I might as well bank the money instead of dishing out hundreds every month for insurance.

"You're up," Ben says, walking out, dressed in a pair of dark wash jeans and a hunter green collared shirt that makes his hazel eyes pop. "Happy Birthday." He pulls Brody into a hug.

"Thanks. Savy mentioned breakfast?"

"Yep, I'm making chocolate chip pancakes. Your favorite."

Brody beams, like *literally* beams. "Cool."

"I brought over your gift," I tell him, handing him the wrapped box.

"You're not coming to the arcade later?" Brody asks with a small pout.

"I'm not really much of a video game person," I admit. "But I'll be at dinner tomorrow night."

"I'm not either," Ben says. "You can keep me company while Brody and his friends spend all my money playing."

Brody laughs, playfully punching his dad in the arm. "It's *gaming*, Dad, not playing."

He takes the box from me and unwraps it, pulling a football jersey out. "Thanks, Savy." He grins. "Jennings is my favorite." He's referring to Toby Jennings, the quarterback for New York.

"I know," I tell him. "You mentioned that at dinner with your mom. Flip it over."

He does as I say, and when he spots the signature, he gasps. "Holy shit. How'd you get this signed?"

"He offered. He's using Sharp to remodel his home, and when I was in a meeting with Lucas, he stopped by to pick something up.

"He introduced himself, and when I asked if he was the same guy you mentioned, he said he was.

"I told him how much you loved him and wanted to play like him one day, and when he came back to drop something off, he brought that for you."

"Wow." Brody sighs. "I can't believe you met him, and he signed this. This is awesome. Thank you."

"You're welcome." If he loves the jersey, he's going to freak out over the next part of the gift. "There's something else in there."

Brody pulls the envelope out and tears it open. After a few seconds, he glances up at me, his eyes bugging out of their sockets. "Are you freaking serious? Four tickets to the first home game of next season? Thank you!"

"You're welcome."

"I gotta go tell Sam and Ishmael! Thank you!" He hugs me quickly before he sprints out of the kitchen.

Once Brody is gone, and the sound of his door being slammed closed echoes, Ben cuts across the kitchen, cornering me against the countertop. "You must've made quite the impression on this guy."

"Or he's all about his fans."

"Maybe…" He tucks a strand of hair behind my ear. "Or he saw a beautiful woman and wanted a way in."

His eyes land on my mouth, and he wets his lips. The action has my lady parts clenching in memory of what his tongue is capable of. "Can't blame him if that's the case. If I would've seen you strutting around at Sharp in your sexy work attire, I damn well wouldn't be able to resist."

With his finger and thumb, he pinches the tip of my chin and raises my face, placing a lingering kiss to the corner of my mouth. "…ask you…number…?"

I'm trying to focus on what he's saying or whatever it is he's asking, but my head is fuzzy.

He kisses the other corner of my mouth, and I swear my brain literally turns to mush.

"Is that what happened?"

"Huh?" I can't focus on what he's saying with him this close to me, with his hands and mouth on me.

"Did he ask you out? Ask for your number?"

"Yes," I breathe, unable to lie to him.

"And what did you say?" He kisses my cheek this time, then trails his lips downward, along my jaw.

"I…I said no to dinner."

He hums his approval, then works his way up my neck. "But you gave him your number, didn't you?"

His teeth close around my earlobe, sending shocks of pleasure through my body.

"Yes," I whimper, shifting my head to the side to give him better access.

He peppers kisses along my neck and back over my jaw, stopping at my lips. "You seem to have quite a few men courting you."

"No, only two." I'd hardly call that quite a few.

He takes a step back, and his eyes meet mine.

I'm waiting to see what he's going to say, but instead, he simply swallows thickly and nods. "I better get started on the pancakes."

He walks away, taking his warmth with him, and I'm left standing here wondering what the hell just happened.

CHAPTER SIXTEEN
BENJAMIN

Two. Not three. Two. Because I'm not courting her. And I need to remember that. Because she obviously has. And that's the way it should be. I'm not the settling down, commitment type.

Commitment leads to expectations, like babies and families, and with those expectations come the inevitable disappointment—I witnessed it firsthand with my parents. The fact that Savannah gets it and accepts it and knows I'm not trying to court her should make me happy.

So then why the hell am I so goddamned jealous of the fact that when I mentioned she has several men vying for her attention, she didn't include me in that scenario?

I whisk the pancake batter a bit too hard, trying to get myself under control. Out of the corner of my eye, I can see Savannah standing there, watching and assessing, wondering why I went from being all over her to giving her the cold shoulder. She wants to ask but doesn't want to cross over that stupid invisible line that we have to stay behind.

No, it's not stupid.

It's smart.

It keeps us in our place.

Reminds us what we're doing…and not doing.

"Do you want any help?" she finally asks softly, making me feel like an asshole for the way I reacted.

"If you want to make the eggs, I won't stop you."

I make sure my voice is playful so she understands I'm not being cold to her. She did nothing wrong and doesn't deserve my shit just because I'm stuck in my own head.

When she visibly sighs and smiles, I know it's worked.

We work side by side getting breakfast ready, neither of us saying a word, and when I can't take the silence anymore, I turn on some music—a country playlist since it's Savannah's favorite.

A song comes on that Savannah must really like because she starts to sing along, knowing all the words, shaking her ass and using the spatula as a mic.

"I wouldn't quit your day job," I joke, bumping her hip with mine.

"Hey!" She pouts. "I'm a good singer."

"Maybe to the tone-deaf…"

She glares my way, then grabs a pancake from the pile on the plate without a second's hesitation and throws it at me. It smacks the side of my face, then falls to the floor with a plop.

I glance at her, shocked as hell that she just hit me with a hot pancake. She tries to hide her smile by grabbing another one and taking a bite of it.

"Mmm." She moans dramatically. "These are yummy."

"I wouldn't know," I say dryly.

Her attempt at tamping down her smile fails when an adorable giggle bubbles out of her.

"You think that's funny, huh?" She's so busy laughing that she doesn't see me grab the bottle on the counter and quickly shake it before I aim it at her. "How about some whipped cream to go with your pancake?"

Her eyes go wide, her head already shaking back and forth, but it's too late. I press down on the top, and white shit shoots out all over her face.

"Oh my God!" She shrieks, coming after me to steal the can. I turn away from her, and she jumps on my back. "You're so dead!" she yells through her laughter.

I carry her on my back over to the living room, then shake her off so she falls onto the couch. She hits the cushion, her face dripping with white cream, and before I can back away, she grabs me by my neck, pulling me to her.

I'm not sure what she's going to do, but when she rubs her face all over mine, transferring the cream onto me, I crack up laughing.

When she finally stops, our eyes meet, and I drink her in. She should look ridiculous with white stuff dripping all over her nose and mouth, yet she looks gorgeous. Her eyes are filled with mirth, and her cheeks are stained pink from laughing.

I plant my hands on either side of her head and press my lips to hers. The kiss is meant to be chaste, but it quickly turns heated. Our tongues tangle with each other, tasting, coaxing...until I hear the sound of Brody's voice getting closer.

"Mmm," I murmur against her lips, repeating the same sound she made a few minutes ago. "Delicious."

I push off the couch and step back just in time because a second later, Brody enters the living room, his phone still pressed up against his ear.

He stops in his place, looking at us like we've lost our minds. "What's all over your faces?" he asks, his nose scrunched up in disgust.

"Whipped cream," I tell him with a shrug. "We were hungry."

He quirks a brow. "Did you at least save me some food?"

Savannah snorts out a laugh. "In the kitchen, just don't eat the pancake that's on the floor."

Brody gives us both another look before he shakes his head and walks away.

"ARE YOU FREAKING SERIOUS?" SAVANNAH SHOUTS. "I swear you're cheating."

"How?" I laugh, throwing my arms up in victory.

"You just are!" She drops the striker onto the air hockey table and glares. "I want a rematch."

"Again?" I round the table and pull her into my arms. "I already beat you four times." I kiss the tip of her nose. "You gave it your best shot, Sav, but I think you need to know when to cut your losses."

"I hate you," she mutters as I kiss her chin.

"No, you don't." I kiss her lips, tasting the sugary sweetness from the cotton candy she was munching on a little bit ago.

"Hey, Dad!" Brody yells, causing Savannah to jump back like I'm on fire. "There you are!"

We've spent the afternoon hanging out in the arcade, eating, drinking, playing games like air hockey and Whac-A-Mole while Brody and his friends run rampant through the place.

Shortly after we arrived, I loaded them up with credits and told them to let me know when they're hungry. They disappeared and haven't returned once…until now.

I clear my throat. "You hungry?"

He gives me an odd look, telling me he saw how close Savannah and I just were, but he doesn't call me out on it. "Yeah. Can we get some pizzas?"

"Of course. I'll order them and call you once they bring them out."

"Cool, thanks."

He and his friends take back off, leaving Savannah and me alone again. "What kind of pizza do you like?"

"Pineapple." She smirks. "But I doubt they have that, so anything is fine."

I take her hand in mine and guide her over to the counter to order, then head back to our table and have a seat while we wait for the food.

Since the table is in a private room and the boys won't be back until I call them, I pull Savannah into my lap so she's straddling my thighs.

"What are you doing?" she squeals, wrapping her arms around me. "We can't have sex here!"

"Who said anything about sex? I just want to kiss you." I fist the back of her hair and pull her face toward mine. We stay like this, kissing like horny teenagers until the server drops the pizza and drinks off.

When we separate, Savannah looks at me curiously.

"What?"

"I'm just…confused."

"About what?"

"This…" She gestures back and forth between our bodies. "Us… What we're doing."

"I'm pretty sure we were just kissing."

I'm only half-joking since I know she means something more than that, but I'm not sure what she's talking about.

She rolls her pretty blue eyes to the ceiling. "I'm not an expert on stringless sex, but I don't think people who have it go around making out and holding hands."

She isn't wrong. I've had plenty of stringless sex, and never once did we hang out and act like we're dating. But I'm not about to tell her that—and I'm not about to think about why I'm not about to tell her that.

"There are no rules," I tell her instead. "We're grown adults, and we can do whatever the hell we want. And what I want to do is kiss you." I press a hard kiss to her lips.

When we break apart, her eyes flutter open, and she hits me with a hazy smile. Her lips are slightly puffy, and her cheeks are tinged pink. Fuck, she's so goddamn beautiful.

As I stare at her, wanting her back in my arms, in my lap, kissing me, a truth I haven't been wanting to admit hits me like a freight train doing a hundred with no working brakes.

This no-strings shit isn't going to fly much longer…because I want Savannah Cartwright. Every goddamn part of her.

"YOU LIKE HER, DON'T YOU?" BRODY GLANCES AT ME FROM the other side of the couch where we're watching *Breaking Bad*, a show that has become part of our nightly routine after he got me into it one night.

"Who?" I ask dumbly.

There's only one woman he would ask about. The same woman who's been on my mind since we dropped her off at her place a few hours ago, agreeing to meet back up tomorrow afternoon to ride to dinner together.

I wanted to ask her to come back here to watch a movie or something, but at the same time, I needed some space to think about shit.

My head is all over the damn place since I've come to the realization that just sex with Savannah isn't enough for me.

"You know who." He throws a pillow at me. "Savy. I saw you kissing her." His tone isn't just a statement of fact. It's an accusation.

"Is that a problem?" I don't technically need his permission to kiss someone, but I find myself wanting his approval for some reason.

"Depends on what your intentions are," he says, sounding older than his newly fifteen-year-old self. "If it's just to fuck her, then yeah, it's a problem. Because she deserves better than that."

I blink once, twice, taking in what my son just said, because holy shit, when the hell did he grow up? I mean, I know how old he is, but I guess I didn't think about what that means. He's fifteen and in high school. The same age I was the first time I stuck my dick into a woman.

"Have you had sex?" I ask, ignoring his foul language.

This time, it's his turn to blink several times while I wait for him to answer. "No," he finally says, making me sigh in relief.

"You planning on it?"

"Sure not planning to stay a virgin for life," he deadpans, making me chuckle. Fucking asshole.

"Soon?"

A shrug. Shit, he's planning to have sex soon.

I think for a moment about how to respond. I have two options: tell him not to, or use this moment to be real with him.

I'm not sure what the right way to go is, but I'm learning there are no instructions when it comes to being a parent. You just have to go with your gut, and my gut is telling me that he's going to have sex—just like I did—whether I give him permission to or not, so it's probably best to make sure he's safe about it when he does do it.

"Sex isn't something you should take lightly," I begin.

When his brows rise to his forehead, I internally cringe at my choice of words—it's clear my son knows how I've been living my life.

"What I mean is, while sex can be good, damn good, there's a lot more to it than just getting your dick wet..." Jesus, I'm fucking this up. "What I'm trying to say is you need to think about STDs, pregnancy..."

Brody groans. "Dad..."

"Don't 'Dad' me. If you're old enough to have sex, then you're old enough to discuss it." *Damn, I sound like a dad.* "When you have sex, you need to use protection. If you don't have any, I'll buy you some. I don't give a shit if she says she's on birth control. Things happen, and the last thing you need is to get her pregnant while you're in high school. Also, STDs are no joke. Some have no cure and can be life-threatening."

He swallows thickly but nods.

"When you have sex, remember to be good to her. Women, by nature, are romantic. Make sure she gets off first. No woman likes a selfish lover."

Another audible swallow and nod.

"Do you have any questions?"

He shakes his head.

"All right, well, if you do, I'm here."

We go back to watching *Breaking Bad* for a few minutes before Brody clicks pause and looks at me. "You never answered my question."

I quirk a brow in confusion.

"What are your intentions with Savy?"

"I like her," I admit out loud for the first time.

"So why don't you ask her out?"

I laugh at that. "Because I'm not fifteen."

He rolls his eyes. "Well, maybe you should be ... because I'm fifteen, and I have a girlfriend."

Point well made, kid ... Point. Well. Made.

"Dad, this is Savannah Cartwright. Savannah, this is my dad, Olivier Fields."

"It's nice to meet you," Savannah says, shaking my dad's hand.

"You too," he says back.

I assess him for a moment, noticing the black circles under his eyes. He looks tired ... more than the last time I saw him. I make a mental note to talk to him soon—demand to know what the hell is going on with him. Not today, though, since this is about Brody's birthday.

"There he is!" Amalia saunters in with her husband, Gerald, on her heels, carrying a stack of gifts. She grabs Brody and hugs him. "Happy Birthday, my favorite nephew!"

"I'm your only nephew," Brody points out, making everyone laugh.

More introductions are made, and then we're shown to a private room with a long rectangular grill situated in the center. Several chairs are surrounding the outer perimeter with a wooden bar-like table attached. This restaurant is one where the chef cooks your food in front of you.

Brody sits in the middle, and I sit to the right of him at the same time my dad sits to the left of him, leaving a seat empty for Brody's girlfriend. He asked me last night if she could join us, and I didn't see why not. Her parents had to first confirm with me that I would be there and they wouldn't be left alone, and once I agreed, they allowed her to come. Next to my dad is Amalia and her husband.

"Sav, sit next to me," I insist, pulling her into a seat. Lucas and Laura sit next to Gerald, leaving two seats open next to Savannah for Brianne and Marcus.

"Sariah's here," Brody says. "I'm going to go meet her in the front."

"Who's Sariah?" Amalia asks once he's gone.

"His girlfriend," I tell her.

"What?" She shrieks.

"Don't embarrass him," I warn. "I've never met her either. They only started dating a couple of weeks ago."

A few minutes later, Brody walks in, holding hands with a cute little blonde. She's dressed nicely in an appropriate dress and flats, and her makeup isn't done up too much. When he introduces her to everyone, she smiles shyly and waves, then follows him to the table to sit down.

"She seems sweet," Savannah murmurs into my ear.

I turn my head, and our faces are close ... so fucking close. I want to kiss her right here, but it would raise questions. "Yeah, she does."

Dinner is loud but fun, with everyone talking and laughing over each other. I didn't realize how much I've missed doing shit like this. It reminds me how long I've been away and that we need to do this more often.

At some point, my hand finds Savannah's knee, and I spend the entire meal massaging circles into her flesh. I've never been like this with a woman before, needing to touch her in some way at all times, and it only helps to cement my newfound truth: I want more with Savannah.

CHAPTER SEVENTEEN

SAVANNAH

I WAKE UP TO CRAMPS STRONG ENOUGH TO MAKE ME double over in pain. I tuck my legs up to my chest and stare at the wall, not wanting to get up, because I know that when I do, I'll sit on the toilet to go pee and wipe crimson.

My period has arrived.

I'm not pregnant.

I should be ecstatic.

Ben and I played a game of Russian roulette and dodged the bullet.

Yet my heart hurts.

Because as a woman who has wished and hoped and prayed to one day start my own family, I was hoping by some miracle I was pregnant.

I knew the chances were slim, and really, it's for the best since Ben isn't the man I'll be spending my life with—but a part of me still wanted to be pregnant. To carry a baby in my womb, to feel him or her kick, to see the creepy yet beautiful skeletal face and body on the ultrasound screen, and at the end of the nine months, give birth to the most precious baby in the world.

The pain in my lower belly worsens—like a subtle reminder that I'm not pregnant—and I squeeze my eyes closed, wanting to go back to sleep and wake up in five days when my period is over.

For most women, a period is a necessary annoyance, but for those like me who can't conceive, it's like a flashing neon sign that points out month after month that I'm broken.

And with that thought, I find myself lying here, wondering where the hell I'm going and what I'm doing with my life. What kind of person am I to wish for a man, who has no desire to have any more kids, to impregnate me? And of course this is the same man I'm falling for—hard and fast.

No strings, my ass.

My thoughts go back to the past few days, to the way Ben held my hand and kissed me. We haven't had sex in over a week, not since our gym session, yet somehow after this weekend, it feels like we're closer than ever. I'm not sure how kissing and holding hands can feel more intimate than the act of sex itself, but with Ben, it does.

I should break things off, tell him I'm done, but every time I think about doing so, sadness blankets me. Because with every kiss, every touch, every look he gives me, I'm falling deeper and deeper. I know it's going to end with my heart broken, but I just can't find it in me to walk away. God, I'm such a masochist.

The alarm goes off on my phone, and I shut it off, not wanting to get up but knowing I need to. Until I take some pain reliever, the cramps won't lessen, and I don't want my clothes and sheets to be stained red. I roll out of bed and head straight to the bathroom.

Sure enough, my period has started, and my underwear is coated red. I peel them off and throw them into the sink so I can try to keep them from staining. Then I jump in the shower to rinse off.

Once I'm out, I pop a couple of pain pills. I can already tell this month's cycle will be bad, and mixed with my feeling sorry for myself, I'm in no mood to go to work.

After pulling up Sharp's employee website and putting in for a sick day, I crawl back into bed, tucking myself under the blankets, and go back to sleep.

I wake to Ben staring down at me, his features marred by a deep V in the middle of his brows.

"I was worried about you. What are you doing in bed?"

I glance around, taking in my surroundings. "How did you get in here?"

"Brianne. She let me in on her way out."

She was still asleep when I decided to stay home, so I didn't tell her, not wanting to wake her up.

"You didn't show up at the gym this morning. You okay?"

I think about his question for a moment…Am I okay? Physically, yes…Emotionally, not so much. But how do I explain that to him?

No, Ben, I'm not okay. Remember when we had unprotected sex? Well, I didn't get pregnant, and now I'm heartbroken. That's one way to push him away. Hell, if I told him that, he'd probably run the other way.

When I don't answer right away, lost in my head and heart, he sits on the edge of the bed and tips my chin up so I'm forced to look at him. "What's wrong, Sav?"

"I'm not feeling well. I'm…" I take a deep breath. "My period started, and I have bad cramps."

He nods once, then dips down to kiss my forehead. "I'm sorry, baby."

"It's okay," I mutter. "Only the first day is bad. I took pain pills and—"

His eyes lock with mine. "Not about that."

I was already on the verge of crying all morning, so his words—the fact he's apologizing I'm not pregnant when he should be throwing a party—push me over the ledge.

Hot, fat tears well up, blurring my vision, and then spill over, sliding down my cheeks.

"Hey," he coos, sliding his thumb across my cheek to swipe a tear away before he stands, kicks his shoes off, and then climbs onto the bed next to me—still dressed to the nines in his business suit.

He pulls the blanket off me, envelops me in his arms, and then throws it back over us. I nuzzle my face into him, and in his warmth and comfort, allow myself to cry.

He doesn't say a word the entire time, just rubs circles on my back and holds me tight while I cry for the baby I want and may never get. For the family I never had and crave. For the love I desire and wonder if I'll ever truly experience.

When I've cried all the tears and have calmed down enough to think rationally, I tense up, embarrassed I've just spent who knows how long crying on Ben's shoulder—literally.

"I'm sorry," I mumble into his chest. "This isn't what you signed up for."

His thumb and forefinger pinch my chin, lifting my face so I'm looking at him. "Maybe not, but there's nowhere else I'd rather be."

His words confuse me, but I'm too exhausted—mentally and physically—to ask him what he means, so instead, I nod once and slide out of his arms. "I need to use the restroom."

I spend several minutes in there, using the bathroom, taking some pain pills, and washing my face, and once I feel like I'm halfway decent, I go back out. My bed is empty, and I find Ben in the living room talking on his phone.

"I won't be in today. Grab the permits on my desk and have a courier drop them off." He pauses to listen to whatever is being said on the other line, and then he says, "Yes." Another pause. "Perfect, thanks. Only call if it's an emergency."

Without so much as a goodbye, he hangs up and glances over at me. "You okay?"

I shrug. "I will be. Who was that?" I nod toward his phone as he's putting it back into his pocket.

"Lenora." His assistant. Bless her heart, I don't know how she's worked for him as long as she has. "She sounded a bit too happy when I told her I won't be in today," he says dryly.

I snort a laugh. "She probably needs a break from seeing your grumpy ass every day."

Ben glares. "I'm not grumpy. It's called running a business."

I roll my eyes. "You are *totally* grumpy. That day I ran into you during your meeting, you were all growly. If I were working for you, I would've quit after the first day."

Ben stalks forward, and shocking the hell out of me, he scoops me into his arms bridal style, walking us back to my bed. "I bet I could convince you to stay." He sets me down and crawls over me, his muscular arms framing my head.

"And how would you do that?" I breathe.

"I can be very persuasive." He drops a kiss to the side of my neck.

"Oh, really?" I turn my face to the side, giving him access. "And what would you do to persuade me?"

He runs his tongue across my pulse point, then nibbles playfully on the skin above my collarbone. "For starters, I would buy you coffee. The vanilla latte mocha frappe shit you love."

I bark out a laugh. "Oh, baby. Coffee *is* the key to my heart." I flutter my lashes dramatically. "What else?"

"That lemon pound cake crap you always get. The one with the frosting on the top...I'd buy you an entire loaf."

"Mmm...n ow we're talking. Tell me more," I say as butterflies flutter in my chest over the fact that while he's joking around, he knows exactly what I eat and drink—because he pays attention.

Ben kisses his way along my jaw, stopping at the tip of my chin and nipping at it. "I would bring you lunch every day, alternating between Italian, Thai, and the sub shop since those are your favorites." He sucks on my bottom lip. "And for dessert, I'd give you...me."

His lips brush against mine in a soft, sensual way…and then my stomach growls, making both of us laugh.

He pulls back, holding himself up so none of his weight is on me. "You stay here, and I'll go get us coffee and breakfast."

"You don't have to do that," I tell him, not wanting him to miss an entire day of work because of me.

"I want to." He kisses me again before he climbs off the bed. "Besides, I already told Lenora I was taking the day off. Don't want to disappoint her."

A half an hour later, he returns with a carrier filled with coffees, orange juice, and water.

"I know you love coffee, but you also need water to stay hydrated, and orange juice is good for you."

He sets it on the nightstand, then starts pulling stuff out of the bag he's carrying. He produces an entire loaf of lemon pound cake, a box of Godiva chocolate, and a bottle of pills—specific for menstrual cramps.

My heart soars at his thoughtfulness. "Thank you."

He nods and kicks off his shoes, and it's then I notice he's no longer in his business suit but in a pair of gray sweats and a T-shirt. He must've stopped by his place to change. He climbs over me, onto the bed, and rests his back against the headboard. "So, what are we watching?"

I hand him his coffee and click on Netflix. "Only one of the best shows ever…"

AT SOME POINT, DURING THE THIRD…MAYBE FOURTH episode of *Hart of Dixie*, I must conk out because sometime later, I wake up to Ben still watching the show, only he's a lot further along. My head is in his lap, and his fingers are combing through my hair.

"Good morning," he says with humor laced in his tone.

I sit up next to him and grab the bottle of water to wet my parched throat. "How long was I asleep?"

"A few hours. How're you feeling?"

"Okay...I'm sorry—"

"Stop, you have nothing to apologize for. I enjoyed watching you sleep until you shifted onto my lap. I can't remember the last time I took the day off and relaxed. It's been nice."

His phone goes off with a text, and he reads it before typing out a reply. "Brody will be home soon. They're expecting some heavy snow to come through this evening, so they canceled practice. Why don't we go over to my place, and I'll order dinner in for all of us?"

"That sounds good, but I need to take a shower first."

I rinsed off earlier, but I need a good scrub down and to wash my hair.

"I can get on board with that." Ben waggles his brows playfully. He edges off the bed and pulls his shirt over his head.

"Wait, you're joining me?"

He pauses, his shirt already off and his fingers dipped into the waistband of his pants, ready to push them down. "Is that okay?"

"Yeah, I guess, but I'm on my period," I remind him.

"So? What does that have to do with us taking a shower together?"

"Umm...Well, for one, we can't have sex."

Which is kind of the entire purpose of our arrangement.

"We *could*..." he points out. "But that's not why I want to shower with you."

Without any further explanation, he finishes undressing and saunters into the bathroom, leaving me standing and staring at his sculpted ass and back. My God, the man is sexy.

"Sav, let's go!"

His words snap me out of my mental drooling, and I join him in the bathroom. He already has the shower turned on, and the steam is billowing over and fogging the mirror.

As I watch him, completely naked, move around my bathroom

with ease, I hold back from getting undressed, suddenly self-conscious.

When he notices, he sets the towels on the sink and stalks toward me. "Raise your arms."

I do as he says, and my shirt comes off. Since I'm without a bra, my breasts are exposed, and despite the warm air, my nipples harden. He glances down, and a look of lust crosses his features.

"You're so beautiful," he murmurs, reaching for my sweats and tugging them, along with my underwear, down my legs.

Once I'm naked, he kisses me softly, making me squirm under his touch.

"I need to use the bathroom," I mutter when the kiss ends.

As if he knows why, he nods and steps into the shower to give me some privacy.

After I'm done, I join him in the shower. It's not a big area, but there's enough room for us to fit comfortably.

I stand under the spray, wetting my hair and body, and then move over to wash my hair. Before I can grab the shampoo, though, he stops me.

"Turn around," he says, pumping some shampoo into his hands. I do as he says, and then a second later, his fingers land on my head. He massages the soap into my scalp, and it's probably one of the best things I've ever felt in my life.

When I sigh into him, my back hits his front, and he presses an open-mouthed kiss to the top of my shoulder, sending a spark of desire through my body.

"Rinse," he tells me in a soft yet demanding tone.

Once my hair is soap-free, he squirts the conditioner into my hair, then proceeds to massage my scalp all over again.

My eyes close as I get lost in the relaxing feeling of his fingers. All too soon, he finishes, though, and I rinse my hair out.

As I'm reaching for the body wash, he grabs it first, his eyes locking with mine, making his intentions clear.

I consider telling him that's too intimate, too much, but he's already squirting the rose-scented liquid into his palm and rubbing his hands together.

Not needing to be prompted this time, I turn around on my own. His hands start on my neck and shoulders, kneading the tension knots out.

Then he descends, massaging my arms and back. It's so relaxing I damn near fall asleep standing. While he works his way down my thighs, avoiding the apex between my legs, I wonder if other men are like this...this attentive and caring. Neil sure as hell wasn't.

Ben turns me around, so we're facing each other.

"What's wrong?" he asks, his brows dipping in concern.

"How did you know?"

"I could feel your entire body tense."

I sigh. "Sorry, I was just thinking about my ex-husband."

His brows fly up to his forehead, so I quickly explain. "You're being so nice, and I was wondering if this is how it's supposed to be. When I got my period, Neil would complain I wasn't pregnant and that he'd have to deal with days of my emotional roller coaster. A lot of times, he would work late..." I flinch, realization dawning on me. He would come home late. He was probably screwing someone else during that week.

"Neil's an asshole," Ben says flatly. "I don't know what other men do, and to be honest, I've never done this with another woman before, but..." He swallows thickly. "I've also never felt like this before."

Before I can question what he means by that, his mouth is on mine, kissing me, devouring me. It's not sweet or soft, but hard. As though he's trying to tell me something he can't voice through words. His tongue plunges past my parted lips, tasting, caressing.

My hands slide up his wet chest and snake around his neck. His hands grab my ass, lifting me. My legs wrap around his waist, and my back hits the cold wall, sending a chill up my spine.

Ben reaches between us and finds my clit. He strokes and massages it, and my body bows against his, grinding and silently begging for the relief I know is coming. With a couple more strokes, I let go, flying high as my entire body trembles in pleasure.

"That's it, baby," he murmurs against my lips. "Fuck yeah, come for me." He doesn't stop coaxing my orgasm out of me until I've completely come down.

He gently sets me onto my shaky legs, which feel like Jell-O, making it hard to even stand.

But when I glance down at his erection, all thick and veiny and protruding outward proudly, my wobbly legs are forgotten as I drop to my knees so I'm eye level with his dick.

"Savan—" he begins, but his words are cut off the moment my mouth wraps around his shaft.

I take him all the way in, sucking and licking, working to get him off. It doesn't take long until he's coming down my throat, his fingers tangled in the back of my hair and his head thrown back as he groans through his climax.

Once I've milked him completely dry, swallowing every last drop, I stand. His eyes pry open, looking hazy and satiated, and he pulls me into his arms, crashing his mouth against mine for a quick yet punishing kiss.

"That is *not* why I wanted to shower with you," he says, a boyish grin splayed across his lips.

CHAPTER EIGHTEEN

BENJAMIN

We finish our shower, then get out and dry off. I get dressed in her room, leaving Savannah to handle her woman business in the bathroom.

The shower didn't go as planned, but I can't lie and say it didn't go better. Any time I'm with her, I can't get enough. I just want to touch her and kiss her and fucking be with her.

When she asked if other men treat their women the same way I was treating her, I couldn't be anything but honest when I told her I didn't know because I was never like this until her. It's her—she makes me want to take care of her, be there for her.

She steps out of the bathroom in nothing but a towel, and I have to remind myself—specifically my dick even though it just got plenty of attention thanks to her perfect mouth—to chill out. She's not feeling well, and the last thing she needs is me constantly attacking her because I can't seem to keep my hands off her.

Once she's dressed—in a pair of sweats and a shirt that reads, *"When a Southern woman says 'Oh hell no,' it's already too late"*—we head up to my place. We're on the couch with Savannah tucked into my side, deciding what to order, when Brody plows through the door like a tornado, throwing his bags on the floor.

He stops in his place and eyes us. "So you guys finally started dating, huh?"

"What? No!" Savannah squeaks out.

At the same time, I say, "Not yet."

Brody barks out a laugh. "You guys might wanna figure that out."

Savannah moves to the other side of the couch like my touch is suddenly contagious.

"There's nothing to figure out," she says through clenched teeth, glaring at me. "Tell him…Tell him we're just friends."

"You don't have to pretend for me," Brody says. "I'm not a kid, and I'm okay with you two dating. Hell, I'm okay with you getting married. It just sucks my mom couldn't find someone nice too." He shrugs and walks through the living room, already pulling his phone out of his pocket. "I'm calling Sariah. Let me know when dinner's here."

The second his door closes, Savannah bolts to her feet. "What the hell was that?"

"That was my kid," I say, knowing full well that's not what she was referring to.

"Ben…" she warns.

"I've actually been meaning to talk to you." When she takes a step back, I stand as well. "I know we agreed to no strings, but—"

"Don't do this."

"Savy." I sigh, stepping toward her. She takes another step back. "Things have changed."

"No, nothing has changed!" she whisper-yells. "You promised me no strings. You said you were a man of your word."

"That was before…"

"Before what?" she barks, her chest rising and falling in quick succession.

"Before I started to fall for you."

"No…No. No. No. You promised!" Tears fill her eyes and quickly spill over, shattering my heart.

This isn't what I had in mind when I imagined telling her I want to be with her.

"You promised, Benjamin!" She throws her arms in the air. "I need to go."

Before I can beg her not to leave, she's out the door, slamming it behind her. I'm stuck in place for a few seconds, unsure what to do, when Brody makes his presence known.

"What are you waiting for? Go after her."

Shit, he's right. I run out the door and down the hall, catching her while she's waiting for the elevator. Tears are running down her face, and she's sniffling loudly.

"Savannah, wait," I call out when the elevator opens. I sprint in front of her and block the doors. "Please talk to me."

"There's nothing to talk about."

"Yes, there is." I close the space between us as the doors close since nobody got in. "Over the past several weeks, my life has changed drastically. From Brody moving in, to meeting you. When I agreed to no strings—"

"You didn't agree," she hisses. "You offered."

"I did, and at the time, I had every intention of keeping it that way. I've been single for the past fifteen years and have had zero interest in anything more…until you."

"You don't mean that," she whispers. "You think you do, but you don't."

"I do." I cup her face in my palms. "When we hang out, I can't stop touching you, needing to be close to you. When we're not together, I miss the hell out of you. I'm always wanting more…more of your smile, more of your laughter. You make me a better person. You make me want everything I never thought I wanted."

"You don't know what you're saying," she breathes shakily.

I use my thumbs to wipe the tears from under her eyes, hating she's so upset. "When you thought you might be pregnant, I didn't freak out, and when you got your period today, a part of me was sad."

"Stop it," she begs. "Don't do this. You might think you want more, but this isn't who you are, and when you change your mind, you're going to break my heart." Her voice cracks on the last three words, and I vow at this moment to never let them be true. "Please…if you care about me at all, stop saying this stuff. We can cut the sex out of it and be friends."

"I don't want to be your friend." My hand moves to the back of her head, entangling my fingers in her hair. "I want you, Savy. All of you. Your mind. Your body. Your heart."

"No." She shakes her head back and forth emphatically. "You can't have me because I don't want you."

My heart drops at her admission.

She doesn't want me…not the way I want her.

Did I read this all wrong?

"I tried to pretend I was okay with all of this," she says. "Bri told me stringless, emotionless sex would be good for me. And I thought she was right. I'd been so focused on trying to create a perfect life that I forgot to focus on me…on my wants and needs. But this…" She points back and forth between us. "This isn't who I am. And as much as I want *you*, I want to find love more. And not just love…I want it all. The doting husband, the crazy kids. The cliché white picket fence. I want a home that's filled with toys and family and love and laughter."

A choked sob breaks up her words, momentarily stopping her from speaking, and I use that moment to cut in. "And I can give you all that if you give me a chance."

Her eyes go wide. "But that's not what you want. You said so yourself. It's why you left Paola. Why you stayed away from Brody all these years."

"I was scared," I admit. "And she tricked me. She lied and manipulated me. But you're not her, and I'm not the same guy I was back then. For so long, I told myself this was how it had to be, and by keeping every woman at arm's length, it made my decision easy. But then you walked into my life with your Southern accent and crazy shirts and Starbucks coffee and your goddamned fluffy boots on *my* treadmill, and everything changed."

She laughs a watery laugh, mumbling, "It's not your treadmill," and I know I have her in my grasp.

"I don't want to allow my fear of history repeating itself to keep me from being with you. My mom was sick, I know that now, and even though my dad loved her, he didn't get her the help she needed. But that won't be us. I won't allow that to be us." I lock my eyes with hers, silently pleading for her to understand. "I want everything you want, Sav. The family, the house…And I want it all with you."

With my fingers in her hair, I tilt her face up slightly. "Now, the question is, do you want it with me?"

After several long as fuck seconds, she answers me with a single nod, but that's not enough. "I need to hear you say it. Do you want it with me?"

"Yes," she breathes. "I want it with you. The house, the babies…Brody…I want it all with you."

Fuck, this woman. Of course she includes my son, and that only solidifies what I've known since I admitted to myself that I was falling for her: She's the one. She's the goddamn strings attached to my heart.

My mouth crashes down on hers in a quick but bruising kiss. "I'm going to give it all to you," I murmur against her lips. "Every goddamn thing."

We stay in the hallway kissing for several minutes until my phone chimes with an incoming text, breaking the moment.

> **BRODY**
>
> I'm starving! There's no food here.

I turn the phone around so Savannah can see it.

"C'mon, let's go back in," she says with a laugh. "I'm hungry too. I'm craving some Mexican. Oh! And chocolate cake."

"You got it." I kiss her one more time, then take her hand in mine and guide us back to my place. When we open the door, Brody pops his head out of the kitchen.

"Oh, good. I thought I was going to have to eat like a sandwich or something."

Savannah snorts out a laugh. "You poor thing."

Brody's eyes descend to our adjoined hands. "Looks like you guys figured it out."

"We did," I tell him. "Savannah and I are dating."

"And how did you come to that?" he asks with a smirk, turning his attention on Savannah. "Did my dad ask you out?"

Savannah giggles. "He did."

"Good job, Dad." He walks over and pats my shoulder. "Looks like dating isn't just for teenagers." Little shit. "Now that we got that handled, what's for dinner?"

"Do you need any help at the office?" Brody asks, closing his now empty box that held his mountain of nachos—chicken, cheese, beans, sour cream, piled high on a shitload of tortilla chips—that looked like it was meant for three people.

The kid is like a damn bottomless pit, and not only does he eat a shit ton but he also practically inhales it, leaving me to wonder if he even tasted his food.

"Why?" I ask, stabbing a piece of my cheesy grilled chicken and extending it toward Savannah so she can take a bite.

Her plump lips slide the food off my fork, and she moans in appreciation.

She couldn't decide between chicken and steak. I told her just to order both, but she didn't listen, and the second she eyed my food, I knew she wished she had.

I offered to switch with her, but she shook her head, insisting she was fine with what she got. *Liar.* She's eaten half my food through my feeding her while we watch some chick flick she picked out that she's cried through.

"Valentine's Day is coming up, and I want to buy Sariah something, and umm ..." He shrugs. "Maybe take her to dinner and a movie."

Savannah grins wide. "You're so sweet. What do you want to get her?"

"I guess it depends on how much money I can make between now and then."

"I'm sure we can find something for you to do. Maybe you can clean the bathrooms," I joke, making Savannah slap my chest.

"Be nice," she says, opening her mouth to take another bite of my food. Brody laughs, having noticed as well that she's eaten more of my food than her own. "Do you have somewhere, in particular, you want to take her? First dates are important. They set the tone for the entire relationship."

Brody's eyes go wide. "Umm. .. I don't know. I haven't thought that far ahead, and her parents are kind of strict, so I don't even know if they'll let her go out with me."

"We're having a Valentine's Day party at Lush," I mention. "You're too young to attend, but if you're okay with double dating with your old man, we can have dinner there."

"Who are you going out with?" Savannah sasses.

"You." I pull her into my side so I can kiss her temple.

"Funny, I don't remember being asked." She leans forward and grabs her glass of wine, taking a sip.

She sets it down, and I tip her chin to look into her ocean blue eyes. "Savannah Cartwright, will you be my valentine?"

A mischievous grin curls her lips. "Hm ..." She taps her chin in mock thought. "Exactly what does being your valentine entail?"

"For starters, dinner at Lush." I kiss the tip of her nose. "Followed by an evening of dancing and drinking." I peck her cheek and lean in so only she can hear my next words. "And afterward, a night in my bed." A shiver wracks her body, making me chuckle.

"You guys are gross," Brody says with a gagging sound. "I'll have dinner with you guys since Sariah's parents are more likely to let her go if my parent is there, but try to tone it down a notch, will you?"

"Hey, don't act like you don't kiss your girlfriend by your locker," I taunt.

He stands and shakes his head. "I do, but not in front of my dad. So about making some money ..."

"We'll figure it out." I'm sure I can give him something to do to earn some money.

"Thanks, Dad."

He throws his trash away, then disappears into his room, leaving Savannah and me alone.

"Want another glass of wine?" I ask, seeing hers is empty.

"No, thanks." She yawns. "I'm exhausted. I think I'll head home—"

"Let's finish the movie first," I suggest, not ready for her to leave yet.

She yawns again but agrees, and I pat my lap so she can lay her head down.

I click the movie back on, and within minutes, the sound of her soft snores fills the room. I pull my phone out, checking and replying to a bunch of emails I neglected today.

Then I check my calendar for the rest of the week. I do all this one-handed while I use my other one to play with her hair.

"Is Savy okay?" Brody asks when he comes out of his room a couple of hours later. The movie has ended, and the screen is paused.

"Yeah, she's not feeling well."

"Is she sick?"

"No, she's on her period." I could lie, but what's the point? He's fifteen and has to learn about this shit sooner or later.

Brody's nose scrunches up. "Oh. Sariah said when she's on hers, she cries a lot."

I chuckle. "Yeah, it makes women emotional." Savannah shifts slightly, snuggling closer to me. "You done with all your homework?"

"Yeah. Sariah's mom said she can go to dinner with us."

"What about the movie?"

"Only if you guys come ... but I know you have that party afterward, so..."

"I don't have to be there the entire time. I won't be at any of the others. I'll make a quick appearance, and then we can go to the movies if that's what you want to do."

His face brightens. "Yeah? That'd be cool. Thanks."

"No problem. Get ready for bed. It's getting late, and you need to get up early tomorrow."

"I'm gonna jump in the shower."

"All right, if I'm not here when you get out, I'm walking Savannah home." As soon as I wake her up ... which is hard to do when she's sleeping so peacefully.

"Or she can just spend the night," Brody suggests, shocking me. "It's not like Mom doesn't have that asshole living with her."

"Watch your mouth." I side-eye him. "Why don't you like Ted, anyway?"

He's made several digs at the guy, and his mom mentioned they used to fight. I don't know the guy, but I'm not sure how I would feel if Brody didn't like Savannah.

"I just...I just don't like him," he mumbles. "But Mom loves him so..." He shrugs. "I'm just glad I don't have to live with him anymore ... as long as you're here."

"I'm not going anywhere," I assure him. "But at some point, you're going to have to see your mom, and not just when he's out of town." We have fifty-fifty custody, but she's always had him the majority of the time because of my dumb choices. "Maybe we should sit down and talk to your mom—"

"No!" Brody barks. "Just leave it alone, please."

Something more is going on, but I don't know what it is.

"What about your therapist? Would you consider talking to him about it?"

We still have three and a half more years of him being home until he goes to college, and there's no way his mom will let him avoid staying at her house that long.

He averts his gaze, looking past me. "I guess."

Not wanting to push him, I leave it at that for now. "All right. Go jump in the shower. You have school in the morning."

"Unless it snows enough for schools to cancel," he says as he walks down the hall toward his bathroom.

Once he's gone, Savannah rolls over onto her back and looks up at me. "I don't think I like that Ted guy," she says, obviously having heard at least that part of our conversation.

"Yeah, me neither," I agree, dipping my face to kiss her. "Want to spend the night? Unlike Ted, Brody likes you and said he doesn't mind." I waggle my brows, making Savannah smile.

"As tempting as that sounds, I think it's best if I sleep at home. All my stuff is there, and I think we should take it slow...not just for us but for Brody too. He's been through a lot, and he might be okay with it, but it doesn't mean we should take advantage of that."

"You're amazing," I tell her, kissing her when she sits up. "I'll walk you home."

"Such a gentleman." She grins, kissing me back.

CHAPTER NINETEEN

SAVANNAH

"Wow! Look at you," Brianne says, walking into my room. "Benjamin isn't going to know what hit him."

I turn around and glance at myself in the mirror, taking in my appearance. Since the Valentine's Day party at Lush is a black-tie affair with a red, pink, and black theme for the occasion, I'm dressed in a bright-red velvet minidress that's covered in shimmering sequins and ruching at the waist to accentuate my curves.

The front dips low, showing off the swells of my breasts while keeping it classy with long sleeves, yet it has an off-center slit up the side.

My dirty-blond hair is down in waves with one side pinned back behind my ear. Since it's been snowing on and off, I'm wearing red suede closed-toe heels with an ankle strap.

Not wanting to wear a dress bought by another man, I bought this dress for tonight during Brianne's and my shopping trip. She needed something new as well, so we made a day of it. It was nice since we haven't had a lot of girl time between dating and working.

"Me?" I say back. "Look at you."

Brianne went with a sexier, shorter, more formfitting blood-red dress, and she looks amazing. Her hair is up in a tight ponytail with the ends spiraling down her back, and her lips are a matching matte crimson while mine are a bright red glossy color.

"We do look gorgeous, don't we?" She grins. "Benjamin picking you up?"

"Yeah, he and Brody should be here soon. We're going to pick up Brody's date and then head to Lush."

"I can't believe how much he's changed in such a short time. Although, it shouldn't surprise me."

"Why is that?"

She shrugs. "I guess I'm just learning that when the right person comes along, it doesn't matter if it's hours, days, or weeks...if they're the one, they're the one."

"Are you trying to say Marcus is the one?"

Since the night they left together from the club, they've been inseparable, but she hasn't mentioned how serious they are.

"Yeah," she says with a smile. "I think he is. What about you and Benjamin? Is he the one?"

I think about her question for a few long moments before I answer. "It's hard because at one point I thought Neil was the one, but looking back, it was actually the *idea* of him that I was caught up in. You know? The idea of getting married and being in love and having a family. I didn't think about the fact that he wasn't actually the kind of person I wanted to spend my life with.

"So, this time, I'm trying to be more cautious and pay attention to the details. I told Ben I wanted to take things slow, but it's hard when everything he does and says seems so perfect. I think in the back of my mind, I'm waiting for the moment he does something wrong so I can convince myself he isn't the one for me."

"You can't do that to yourself," she says. "If you keep waiting for him to mess up, he'll eventually prove you right. Nobody is perfect, and one day he *will* say the wrong thing, *do* the wrong thing. But that doesn't mean he isn't the one for you. It just means he's human."

A knock on the door signals one of our dates is here, halting our conversation.

"We need to have a girls' day soon," Brianne says. "Facials, pedis, manis, the whole nine yards so we can get some good girl talk in. Our shopping trip wasn't enough."

"That sounds perfect."

Another knock and she playfully rolls her eyes. "We better get that. Don't want to keep them waiting. They might die from impatience."

I grab my sparkling silver clutch and my overcoat with a laugh and follow her out to the foyer.

She swings the door open, and standing on the other side is Ben, dressed to the nines in a black suit, complete with a bright red bowtie that matches my dress, holding a huge bouquet of roses.

His hair is cut short on the sides with the top slightly longer and gelled messily in the way guys do to make it look like they just rolled out of bed yet still look perfect.

His facial hair is trimmed short, and he's sporting a grin that conveys every ounce of emotion he feels—lust, want, need, desire.

We still haven't had sex since he took me against the wall that morning at the gym. Between my period and work and Brody, we haven't found the time to be alone. I'm hoping that changes soon.

"Happy Valentine's Day," he says, stepping over the threshold. "You look stunning."

He presses a kiss to the corner of my mouth so he doesn't ruin my lipstick, then hands me the flowers that are already in a vase.

"Thank you. You look ... well, like your usual handsome self."

The man wears a suit every day. I do have to admit that tonight, his suit seems sharper, making him look extra sexy.

It's then I notice Brody standing there, also dressed in a suit and holding a bouquet of pink tulips. Dressed similarly, with his hair also freshly cut, he looks so much like his father.

"New suit?" I ask. "It looks great."

"It's a tux," Ben corrects. "Suits are for work. Tuxes are for romantic nights out with your woman ... and weddings." He winks playfully, making me laugh.

"Oh, I'm sorry," I say, sarcasm dripping in my words. "Your *tux* looks great."

Brody chuckles. "Dad said every man needs a tux just in case. It's tailored to fit me."

The pride in his voice makes my heart soar. They've come a long way in a short amount of time, and that makes me so happy.

"You both look extremely handsome in your tuxedos. Let me put my flowers in the kitchen, and then we'll go."

I'm filling the vase with water at the sink when a pair of strong arms encircle me from behind, and a masculine, fresh scent I would recognize anywhere hits my senses.

"That dress looks fucking delectable on you," Ben growls, kissing the side of my neck. "If I don't get you alone soon, I might combust."

I giggle at his dramatics, set the flowers on the counter, turn the water off, and twirl around, remaining in his arms. "Well, maybe if you're a good date, I'll *consider* letting you take this dress off me later." I kiss him chastely on his lips. "We wouldn't want you to combust now, would we?"

"No, we definitely wouldn't want that." He runs the back of his knuckles down my cheek and sighs. "Thank you for going along with this double date tonight. I know Valentine's Day is supposed to be romantic and—"

"Whoa, stop right there." I cover his lips with my fingers that are freshly painted—bright red to match my dress. "Being a father should come first, always, and you choosing to go on a double date with your son tells me more about you than any romantic gesture ever could. That alone secures your spot in my bed tonight."

He chuckles softly and shakes his head. "I don't know what the hell I ever did to deserve you, but I need you to know how thankful I am to have you."

After saying goodbye to Brianne, who assures us Marcus is on his way up and they'll see us later at Lush, we head out.

Parked in front of the sidewalk is a sleek all-black stretch Hummer limo Ben rented for the occasion.

Apparently, Brody didn't even know about it because he freaks out and takes a million selfies in front of it—all of which I'm sure will end up on social media.

Ben also has him take a few pictures of us, and then we take off to pick up Sariah. Her house is on the way, so it doesn't take long, and once we arrive,

Brody jumps out with his bouquet in his hand and runs up to her front door to knock.

"We should take a couple of pictures," I tell Ben as I watch Brody wait for someone to answer the door.

"Or I can use this time to give you this." He pulls a small black box out of his pocket. "I was helping Brody pick out his gift for his girlfriend when I saw this and thought of you...of us."

I open the top and nestled inside the felt bedding is a white gold or maybe platinum pendant with a beautiful diamond in the center. It looks like it's a knot of some sort, but I'm not sure why. Or what it means. Maybe it's just something pretty.

When I glance up, silently asking for him to explain, he takes the box from me and pulls the pendant out, letting it dangle from the delicate chain. "Turn around."

I do as he says, lifting my hair up so he can clasp it on. The pendant lands on my chest just above the swell of my breasts.

"It's a love knot," he explains. "It's made up of two strings that are tied together to form one knot. Each string represents us. When we first started this, we agreed to no strings, but now everything is different, and those strings have come together to form a knot. Alone, they're fragile and easy to break, but together ..." He locks eyes with me, and my heart thunders in my chest. "Together, they're strong and can withstand anything."

"Ben, this is so beautiful," I choke out. I've never been given a gift with so much thought and meaning put into it before. "Thank you."

I entwine my fingers around his neck and connect my mouth to his, wishing we were alone so I could show him just how much this gift means to me.

The ride to Lush is filled with casual conversation. While we met Sariah at Brody's birthday dinner, she was quiet for much of the time around so many people.

Tonight, though, she's chatting away, and I can see why Brody likes her. She's cute and bubbly and funny, and the way she talks about and looks at Brody is so sweet.

When we arrive at the restaurant, it's busy with everyone arriving for dinner and the Valentine's Day party. Outside, there's a black carpet where a photographer is taking professional photos of the couples, and since it's a high-traffic area for celebrities, several paparazzi are camped out, watching for anyone they can get their eyes on.

The four of us get our picture taken together and then separately as couples. Ben is given a QR code where we can view and purchase the images once they're uploaded.

We arrive at the hostess stand, and she greets us, recognizing Ben. She immediately walks us back to our table in a quiet area of the restaurant.

There are red, pink, and black balloons in the corner, and a small vase of roses and candles decorate the table. I glance around and notice the other tables don't have all this, which means Ben had this done in advance.

It's crazy that he's spent the past several years not in a relationship because he's naturally good at it. He pays attention to the details, which is probably why his business ventures are so successful. He's put all his energy into that instead of his relationships.

"This is beautiful," I murmur, kissing his cheek. "You really set the bar high."

He chuckles—no doubt remembering when I told Brody not too

long ago that the first date sets the tone for the entire relationship—and takes my hand in his, threading our fingers together.

Dinner is fun, and the food is delicious. Brody and Sariah are adorable together, and when Ben tells them that we have to run upstairs for a few minutes to make an appearance before we take off to the movies, Brody asks Sariah if she'll dance with him, not caring that nobody else in the restaurant is dancing.

We take the elevator to the second floor, and then Ben guides us through the club. The area is filled with large heart-shaped balloons, and the band is playing a slow, seductive number that couples are on the dance floor swaying to.

As we make our way through the crowd, several people stop Ben to say hello. He also makes it a point to seek out a few people, introducing me as his girlfriend and asking them if they're having a good time.

It's the second time I've seen him in business mode since we've met, and a lot like the day in his office, he's attentive to each person he speaks with while also being unemotional and detached. He's completely different than the Ben I've grown to know, and I know this is the man who's spent the past fifteen years building up his successful business.

When we finally arrive at a roped-off area housing a group of about fifteen people, I notice they're everyone we know. Lucas and Laura are slow dancing in the corner. Amalia and her husband are sitting at a table, holding hands and talking.

My eyes land on Scott, who thankfully seems to be on a date since he has a woman sitting sideways on his lap. He texted me once after our date, and not wanting to lead him on, I told him there wasn't a connection. I told the same thing to Toby Jennings when he texted me—after Ben and I made the decision to date—and asked me to dinner.

I find Brianne standing and talking to a girlfriend of hers I've met once while Marcus has his arms wrapped around her from behind, his chin resting on her shoulder. We lock eyes, and she leaves the person she's talking to, to come over and hug me.

"What happened to your double date?"

"They're downstairs dancing while we make a pit stop. Ben wanted to come up before we head to the movies."

"Hey," Amalia says, giving her brother a one-arm hug because he's holding my hand and not letting go. "The event is running smoothly. I've already checked in with the other locations, and everything is going well."

"Of course it is," he remarks. "You're running it. I wouldn't expect anything less."

His sister lovingly rolls her eyes before her features turn serious. "Have you heard from Dad? Gerald and I have some news, and I wanted to tell you both at the same time, but he hasn't returned any of my messages."

Ben frowns. "He's probably busy with the quarterly reports due soon." But as he speaks, I can see it in his features that he's worried.

"Yeah, maybe," she says, not sounding like she agrees. "But, um…he hasn't been in his office all week."

"What do you mean?" Ben's back goes ramrod straight.

"I stopped by, and his secretary said he hasn't been in all week."

"That can't be right…" He pulls his phone out and hits a few buttons, then puts it to his ear. A few seconds later, he hits end and pockets it. "He's probably out with some woman. It's Valentine's Day. I'll give him a call tomorrow and get it sorted out. What was it you wanted to tell us? Is everything okay?"

Amalia's lips curve into a huge grin, and Gerald wraps his arm around her. "Everything is perfect. Gerald and I found out we're expecting a baby!"

"Holy shit," Ben says, letting go of my hand and pulling his sister into a hug. "Congratulations!"

"Thank you. The timing probably isn't the best with the restaurant and—"

"What? Stop. We'll handle it. Family first. This is awesome news."

Amalia's eyes go wide as though she's shocked he's said that. While Ben shakes Gerald's hand and congratulates him, Amalia steps closer to me and wraps me in a hug.

"Thank you," she murmurs. "Thank you for giving my brother back to me." When she pulls away, her eyes are glassy, but she's smiling brightly.

She turns back to her brother, and he asks her how far along she is, but I don't hear her response because Brianne tugs me gently to the side, giving me a knowing look. "Are you okay?"

"Of course I'm okay. I'm not so unstable I lose it every time someone announces they're pregnant."

"I know, but it's okay for it to hurt. I just don't want to see you bottling it up."

I give her a hug, loving that she cares enough to make sure I'm okay. "I promise you, I'm okay. I'm focusing on what I do have these days and not on what I may never have…Like an amazing job and a best friend like you…and Ben."

"Oh my God," Brianne whispers. "You're in love with him."

My gaze goes to Ben, who's talking to his sister but looking at me with adoration in his eyes, and that makes my heart swell.

All those years with Neil and not once did he ever look at me like that. And because I never experienced that look, I didn't know it was missing…until now.

"Yeah," I admit, "I am."

CHAPTER TWENTY

BENJAMIN

AROUND THIS TIME LAST VALENTINE'S DAY, I WAS BALLS deep in some woman I met at a party at one of my clubs for a quickie in the office. I couldn't tell you her name or even what color her eyes were. Once we both got off, I threw the condom away, zipped up my pants, and then we parted ways.

I went back to my place and spent the rest of the evening getting lost in my work. That was the norm for me. The occasional hookup. Working too damn hard. Not being enough of a father to even know what my son was doing on a day supposed to be about love.

This year is different because not only do I have Brody but I also have Savannah. We've dropped Sariah off, and Brody has headed up to our place to, I'm sure, call Sariah so they can continue their evening on the phone.

I'm currently standing in front of Savannah's door, staring into her azure eyes as I thank her for tonight. For going along with the double date. For showing me that there's more to this life than faceless, meaningless sex and that it's okay to let someone in.

"Why does it sound like you're saying good night?" she asks

with a soft laugh. "You don't really think we're going to end tonight out here, do you?"

She opens the door and tugs on my lapels, pulling me over the threshold. "Bri texted me and said Marcus booked a room for them tonight, so we have the place to ourselves." She waggles her brows playfully.

"I'm sorry I couldn't book a room—" I start, feeling bad that I couldn't give her the romantic night she deserves.

Of course she cuts me off, not wanting to hear any of it.

"Stop. Tonight was perfect. The dinner and then the movie. The way you shared your popcorn with me. I don't think I've even been on a real date before like that. It was nice." Her lips curl into a smile that I swear could light up even the darkest of rooms.

She pushes me gently onto her bed so I'm sitting on the edge and she's standing in front of me. "But you know what will make it even better?" Instead of answering her own question, she unzips her dress on the side, pushes the thin straps down her shoulders, and lets the material pool at her feet, leaving her in some sexy as fuck red lingerie.

"Did you buy these for tonight?" I ask.

Running my finger over the swell of her breast, I watch as goose bumps appear along her flesh.

"I did," she breathes, already squirming in anticipation. "You like?"

"I more than like."

I pull both of the straps down, exposing her perfect tits. Her areoles are a dusty pink, and her nipples are pointed and hard, begging for my attention.

I glide my hands down the curves of her hips and over her plump ass, pulling her close to me. She comes willingly, groaning when I wrap my lips around her nipple and swirl my tongue around the beaded tip.

I trail my mouth over to her other nipple, giving it equal attention, while Savannah runs her fingers through my hair.

As I kiss and suck on her sweet flesh, I can't help but compare the intimacy of this moment to where I was a year ago. I can't imagine ever going back to being with someone I don't have this intense connection with.

I lift her to change positions, placing her on the edge of the bed, on her back, with her thighs spread for me.

She arches her back to unclasp her bra and drops it to the floor once she slides it off. Her breasts fall slightly, exposing the pendant around her neck.

"It's starting to feel a bit one-sided." She pouts, nodding toward my still clothed body.

When I don't move quick enough, she sits back up and reaches to undo my bowtie, throwing it to the side.

Piece by piece, she helps me remove each article of my clothing until I'm only in a pair of black boxer briefs.

"That's better," she breathes, pressing a soft kiss to the center of my torso.

I drop to my knees, so I'm eye level with her satin-covered cunt, and press a kiss to her mound, taking a moment to inhale her scent.

When I glance up at her, I find her on her elbows, staring down at me with awe and lust in her eyes, and I know this woman is it for me. I can feel it. I want nothing more than to worship her every day for the rest of my life.

I tug her underwear down, revealing her neatly trimmed hair, and kiss her again. Everything about her is perfect. Separating her legs farther, I lick up her center, making her gasp. She tastes as good as she smells, like the best addiction.

I get lost in her pussy, licking and sucking and eating her raw. In her sounds, every whimper of pleasure. I work her up until she's trembling under my touch, begging for a release. I push two fingers into her, and she explodes, screaming my name.

Needing to be inside her, I push my briefs down and crawl up her body, kissing every inch of her flesh I can get my lips on. Our mouths unite, tasting, caressing, nipping. She wraps her legs around my waist, and I sink into her tight warmth, our two bodies becoming one.

After we've both found our release and are lying in bed, Savannah's resting her head on my chest with her body wrapped around me like a warm blanket, and the mood seems to grow somber.

It's getting late, and I have to go back to my place soon. I hate the thought of having to sleep apart from Savannah. She's become a necessity in my life, and every time we're apart, I crave her.

But she won't spend the night with me, wanting to provide stability for Brody, so I doubt she'd be up for moving in with me—and holy shit, I can't believe I just suggested that in my head like it's no big deal, when we've only been dating for a short time.

The truth is, I want her all the time, and if she was willing to move in with me, I'm positive Brody would be on board with it. But in order to get there, I have to take baby steps with her…Start off small…But how do I get her to spend the night with me without spending the night?

And then an idea hits me…

"Let's go away this weekend." People take trips all the time. It's not technically spending the night if we're away, right?

"What?" She lifts her head. "Where?"

"To my house in Miami Beach."

"Miami? Don't we have to like…make flight reservations?"

"Something like that. We'll use the plane Sharp and Fields Enterprises share."

Her eyes go wide. "You own a plane?"

I chuckle. "With someone else. With all the flying I used to do, it was worth it. Now that I'm home, though, and don't plan to travel as much, I should probably reassess."

"What about Brody?"

"He'll be ecstatic. I promised to teach him how to drive, and the house in Miami has my Maserati. We can fly in tomorrow and spend the weekend, then fly home Sunday night.

"It might be too chilly to go in the ocean, but the pool is heated, and"—I lean forward and nip her bottom lip—"it's three stories. My room is on the bottom floor, and Brody's is on the top. We'll have plenty of alone time."

She looks like she's trying to think of an argument, but when she can't come up with one, she grins and nods. "Okay, let's do it."

Hell yes! Two steps forward.

"SLOW DOWN. IS YOUR FOOT MADE OF LEAD?"

The damn kid is going to get a ticket before he has a license. Is that even possible?

Brody side-eyes me but lets off the pedal. "Hilarious coming from you. Mom once said you got two tickets on the same day."

Fucking woman…Of course she did. And she isn't lying. It was our freshman year of college. Lucas and I rented a kick-ass McLaren for a weekend away with our girlfriends.

The women were pissed because even though it was a four-seater, it was small as fuck, and we made them sit in the back while we reenacted *Fast and the Furious* the entire drive.

I got pulled over twice during that drive in two separate cities. By the time we made it to the hotel, Paola was so mad that she refused to sleep in the same bed with me and banished me to the couch.

"I was young and dumb."

"And so am I." He shrugs, making Savannah laugh from the back seat.

When I showed her the small collection of cars I keep here since it has a decent-size garage, I expected her not to care—most women don't—but she shocked the hell out of me by knowing what each one was and arguing which cars and trucks are better.

Since she's a Southern girl, she prefers American muscle over foreign. While I would beg to disagree, it was a turn-on to hear her talk cars. Apparently, one of the guys she grew up with in foster care was a huge car freak and taught her everything she knows.

"Reckless driving will get you killed," I tell him seriously. "You're fifteen and just learning. You want to drive fast, you do it on a track where it's safe."

"Oh! Can we do that?" Savannah squeals. "I've always wanted to do that. Go like two hundred around a track."

Fuck, I love this woman.

The internal admission has me swallowing thickly because as much as I'd like to say those words were just a figure of speech, the truth is I mean them…It's probably too soon, but it doesn't change the fact that I mean them.

I glance back at her in the rearview mirror. Her hair is messy, and her cheeks are stained pink from having the windows down and the cold wind blowing in. She's never looked as beautiful as she does right now.

Unable to help myself, I pull my phone out and snap a picture of her. She pouts playfully but doesn't hide.

"A friend of mine owns a track a few hours outside of the city. We can go one day for sure."

Both she and Brody whoop in excitement.

"Make a left at the stop sign," I tell him so we can head back to the house.

After we arrived this morning, we spent the day alternating between the beach and pool. When everyone agreed we were sunned out, I told Brody we would go for a drive before I take Savannah out to dinner.

I asked Brody if he wanted to go, but he said he'd rather hang back, order in a pizza, and talk to his girlfriend on the phone.

I'm almost positive the two of them see each other more on the phone than in person. Not that I'm complaining. Virtual dating means he can't get into too much trouble—at least none that will result in diapers or antibiotics.

We pull into the driveway, and Brody jumps out, already calling one of his friends to brag about driving.

"What'd you think?" I ask Savannah, opening the back door to help her out. "Not bad for a foreign car, right?"

"I guess." She grins, sliding out. Because I didn't move, her body is flush against mine. "I think I just prefer something a little... manlier." She glides her hand across the sleek paint job. "I've always wondered what it would be like to make out in the back seat. Too bad this back seat is too small."

I lift her and push her against the side of the vehicle, and her legs wrap around my waist. "You want to make out in the back seat?" I growl against her lips. "I'll buy whatever the fuck car you want, but I guarantee we'll be doing a lot more than just making out."

My mouth crashes against hers, and my tongue delves between her parted lips, making her groan. We kiss for several minutes with her body grinding against mine, seeking pleasure.

"I want you now."

Her words create a haze in my brain, and the next thing I know, I'm walking us away from the car and over to the side of the house where there are no windows or doors that Brody can see out of and a huge fence with tall shrubbery, giving us the privacy we need.

Her back hits the wall, and she pushes her dress over her hips, giving me easier access. In seconds, my shorts are unzipped, her bikini bottoms are shoved to the side, and I'm inside her, filling her completely.

As I fuck her frantically, driving into her over and over again, hard and fast, she peppers kisses all over my face, nipping along my jawline.

"Oh. My. G—" she begins as her climax overtakes her. Not wanting to risk anyone hearing, I slant my mouth over hers, swallowing down her screams as she comes, squeezing the fuck out of my dick and bringing forth my own release.

When we both come down, she sighs, dropping her head onto my shoulder. "God, that was so good."

I pull out and set her down, and she glances down then up at me with a horrified expression on her face. "You realize we keep forgetting to use protection, right?"

"Yeah, I know." I pull my shirt off and use it to wipe the cum dripping down the inside of her thighs. Fuck, that's hot as shit.

"The chances of me getting pregnant are slim, but—"

"There's a chance...I know." I lock eyes with her. "But I don't care."

Her eyes go wide. We haven't discussed her getting pregnant, aside from me telling her I didn't want kids when we first met and me comforting her when she got her period.

But I've been thinking a lot about it since the day she told me there was a chance she could be pregnant. I thought I'd flip my shit —not at her, because I knew it wasn't only on her, it was on us both —but just at the idea of doing the whole dad thing all over again.

I'm so close to Brody turning eighteen, and Paola and I have made it through without anything bad happening, like what happened to my mom.

Yet when she told me she could be pregnant, my first thought was seeing her swollen with my baby. Of us discussing baby names, decorating a nursery... raising the baby together. And I knew something in me had changed. I'm no longer the same guy I was back then. She's changed me, changed what I want in life, in my future.

"But Ben," she says. "Getting pregnant is forever."

Yeah, it is ... which is exactly what I want with her because what I thought earlier in the car definitely wasn't a figure of speech. And before I can second-guess myself, I find myself saying exactly what I was thinking.

"I love you." But as the words leave my mouth, they don't feel like they're strong enough to describe the way I feel for Savannah, so I continue, trying to fully express the way I feel. "But more than that, I never want you to leave my sight."

Her eyes bug out at my admission, and I fear I'm about to fuck everything up. But since I've already started, I figure I might as well keep going.

"The way my body is constantly drawn toward you is like nothing I've ever felt. I crave you, desire you, need you. When you're not with me, I want you to be. You've come to own so much of my heart, and while the thought of a woman holding that kind of power over me used to scare me, with you, it makes me feel stronger and more alive."

I palm the side of her face, letting the words flow now, not over-thinking what I'm saying. "I love you, Sav, and being with you makes me feel complete. I thought building my empire did that. I thought with every club I built, I would feel more fulfilled, but now I can see the difference, *feel* the difference.

"Those three words don't feel like nearly enough, but since they're what people use to express themselves, I need you to know that I love you so damn much, and yeah, having a baby is forever, but I'm okay with that because if it's up to me, you and me ... we'll be forever."

Tears fill her eyes, and I worry I've said the wrong thing, or maybe it was at the wrong time. Or fuck, maybe it was too much too soon. But then a smile curls at the corners of her lips, and I breathe a sigh of relief.

"I love you too. And forever sounds really freaking good."

CHAPTER TWENTY-ONE
SAVANNAH

"I THINK I PICKED THE WRONG PLACE TO LIVE."

I sink my toes into the cool sand and stare up at the bright moon hanging in the sky. I don't know the exact temperature here, but it's warm enough to have my feet in the water wearing a jersey dress while still cool enough that I'm not sweating.

After we finished eating a delicious dinner at a cute little seafood restaurant that overlooks the Atlantic, we stopped on our walk back to Ben's beach house to sit and watch the sunset. One of the things I love about Ben's place is that it's within walking distance to several shops and restaurants.

"You want to stay here?" Ben asks, his warm, supple lips kissing the side of my neck.

I'm sitting between his legs, and he has his arms wrapped around my waist, holding me tight. I can't remember the last time— if ever—I've felt so safe and loved.

"Just say the word." He nips the bottom of my earlobe. "We can stay as long as you want."

I know he's only joking, but the thought of staying on this beach with Ben with no end date is kind of tempting. It's not that I don't love my life, I do. But I also love the moments when we're in our own little bubble.

"As much as I—" My words are cut off by the sound of his phone ringing from inside his pocket.

"Hold that thought," he says, pulling his phone out. "It might be Brody." When he glances at it, he hums. "I don't recognize the number. Probably spam."

"You should get it just in case."

"Yeah." He hits answer. "Fields." He listens for a moment, then, "Yes, this is Benjamin Fields." Another pause. "Yes." I can't hear what's being said, but Ben's entire body tightens in response. "How long ago?" He pushes away from me and stands, so I do the same. Something is wrong. I can feel it. He asks a few more questions and then says, "I'm on my way. Thank you," before hanging up.

"Brody?"

"No. My dad." He clenches his jaw. "He had a heart attack while he was at home. He was able to call the ambulance before he lost consciousness. When they got there, he wasn't breathing. They performed CPR, and he's alive, but he's in a coma."

"Oh, Ben." I wrap my arms around him. "I'm so sorry."

"We have to go." I can see his brain is in overdrive. Much like when he's in business mode, he's become detached. "Luckily, the jet is here, ready to go for tomorrow." He types away on his phone. "I'll call the company we use and see if they have someone available to fly us back tonight."

We speed walk back to his house, and on the way, he confirms a pilot and calls his sister to let her know the little bit of information he was given while demanding she stay calm because the stress won't be good for her pregnancy.

When we get back, he tells Brody what's happened. We pack quickly, and Ben has an Uber waiting to take us to the airport when we walk outside.

He's quiet during the entire drive, as well as the plane ride to New York. Once we land, he insists Brody and I take a taxi home while he heads straight to the hospital. It's almost eleven o'clock, and even if his father can have visitors, visiting hours won't start again until the morning.

"Shit, would you mind staying at my place with Brody?" he asks at the last second just before I close the door. "His mom isn't home yet and—"

"Hey, stop. Go be with your dad. Don't worry about us. I have Brody."

He dips his head into the vehicle and kisses me. "Thank you."

Luckily, Brody has his key on him, so we can go to Ben's place when we get home.

Using Ben's bathroom, I take a quick shower to rinse off and then change into my pajamas, and after telling Brody good night, I lie down in Ben's bed. It's the first time I've been in his bed, and it feels weird to be in it without him. I don't want to bother or distract him at the hospital, so I only send him one quick text to let him know we're home.

Then I call Brianne to let her know about Olivier, so she can let her brother know since they're best friends and their fathers are friends.

I pull up a book on my Kindle app in an attempt to read myself tired, but after I've read the same line no less than a dozen times, I give up and pull up my social media. I never go on it, but I need a distraction. I notice a couple of messages so I click on them and find one from Lois.

Ugh. Not exactly the distraction I was going for. I consider deleting it, but my curiosity gets the best of me. It figures she would message me on here since I blocked her and Neil after they both texted, trying to apologize.

> Savy, I saw your posts, and it seems you've moved on and are happy. I'm hoping this will mean you are ready to forgive me. I miss you.

I roll my eyes and am about to block her when I change my mind.

> Lois, yes, I forgive you. You saved me years of being in a horrible, loveless marriage by sleeping with my husband, and for that, I thank you. With that said, you and I will never be friends again. I wish you the best. - Savannah

A bit petty? Sure...but it still feels good.

I can see when she reads it—like she was already on the app—and I quickly block her so she can't respond. The other messages are spam, so I delete them and then log out.

I'm not sure how long I toss and turn for, but eventually, sleep must come because the next thing I know, I'm waking to a pair of strong arms encircling me from behind and the masculine scent of Ben as he kisses my bare shoulder.

"Hey," I croak out, turning to face him. He's still dressed in what he was wearing last night, and blackish purple circles are under his eyes. "How's your dad?"

He shakes his head, and I tense, fearing the worst. "He's alive," he says, making me sag in relief. "But it's not good. Because of the lack of oxygen to his brain, he slipped into a coma. The doctor said as of right now, it could simply be a matter of his body healing, but if he doesn't come around in the next couple of days..."

His words trail off, but he doesn't have to say them for me to know. If he doesn't wake up soon, it could mean never waking up.

"He's going to wake up," I tell him with every ounce of positive energy I can muster. "Did you see him?"

"For a few minutes. My sister was there too with Gerald. But visiting hours aren't until eight o'clock, and because he's in the ICU, only one person can go in, and they limit the amount of time you're there. Nobody under eighteen."

"I'm so sorry."

I wrap my arms around his torso. The words are so pointless and won't change anything, but I don't know what else to do or say.

"If he hadn't called for help, he would be dead on his floor, and nobody would even know," he murmurs. "I could tell something's been wrong with him. He looked tired. I asked him about it because he's seemed off lately, but he blew off my concerns, telling me he loves me and that he's proud of Amalia and me. I should've pushed and made him go see a doctor. If I would've—"

"You can't play the what-if game. It's a waste of time."

He nods. "I just...fuck." His eyes turn glassy. "I don't know what I'll do if I lose him. He's..." He swallows thickly.

"He's your dad," I finish for him. "Don't think the worst." I run my fingers down his cheek. "You'll go back first thing in the morning and speak with the doctors to figure out a plan."

Ben rolls us over so I'm on my back, and he's hovering over me. "Thank you for bringing Brody home." His lips brush against mine once, twice, before he deepens the kiss, his tongue caressing my own. "I need to be inside you. I need to just...*fuck,* I need to get lost in you for a little while."

His tone is pleading, his eyes begging me to help him momentarily escape. He's scared. He's already lost his mom, and now there's a chance he's going to lose his father as well.

I glance over his shoulder to make sure the door is closed, and when I see it is, I reach between us and pull his dick out. With my fingers wrapped around his thick shaft, I stroke him up and down, working him until he's nice and hard. He groans softly at my touch and dips his face, kissing along my collarbone.

As we kiss and touch, we shed our clothes, and then once Ben checks and sees that I'm wet and ready, he slides into me slowly, gently.

He frames my face with his forearms and nuzzles his own into the crook of my neck, gliding in and out of me at an unhurried pace —doing exactly what he said: getting lost in me.

We make love, and then Ben wraps me in his arms, falling asleep with his face still buried in my neck. I want to get cleaned up, but I don't move, not wanting to wake him. He's been through a lot tonight and, if the fates aren't in his favor, will be going through more in the near future.

At some point, I doze off, only to wake up to him sliding into me again. This time, he fucks me quick and rough. He doesn't kiss me —instead nipping at the sensitive flesh between my neck and collarbone—and there isn't any foreplay. Ben always makes sure I get off first. It's as if he was drawn to me in his sleep and is barely awake. He doesn't last long before he finds his release and then falls back asleep.

This time, since he's sleeping on his stomach and not on me, I do get up and jump in the shower. After I'm dressed, I tiptoe out to the kitchen, finding it's almost seven in the morning. I make a pot of coffee and whip up some pancakes, bacon, and eggs.

I'm just finishing up when I hear Ben's phone ringing. I pad into the room and find him sitting on the edge of the bed with his head hanging down. My heart plummets into my stomach. This can't be good.

Closing the space between us, I kneel in front of Ben. He looks up, his eyes filled with unshed tears, and I know something is very wrong.

"He's gone," he whispers. "He's gone."

There are no words to say, so I do the only thing I can do and wrap my arms around him, hugging him as tight as I can while he cries against my chest.

Brody must hear him because he steps into the doorway, his eyes knowing.

On the way home last night, he told me that even though his dad was gone a lot, his grandfather always made it a point to visit with him and check in on him.

But in the past couple of months, Brody hasn't talked to him as often. He was worried he wouldn't get a chance to make sure they were okay.

"Come here, sweetie," I tell him, opening my arm.

Ben glances up and chokes back a sob. "Fuck...Brody."

Without saying a word, Brody joins us on the bed, and for the next several minutes, I hold my boys, wishing I could make this better for them. I've never known what it's like to lose someone I love.

Both my parents abandoned me. And I've never had anyone else in my life close enough to miss, let alone mourn...until now.

I try to imagine what it would be like to lose Ben or Brody, but just the thought of it happening causes my heart to clench in my chest, knocking the oxygen from my lungs.

"I love you," I murmur to them both, needing them to know.

Watching how quickly Ben and Brody went from laughing at the beach to crying over Olivier makes me realize how uncertain life really is, and at any moment, those you love can be ripped away from you.

THE NEXT FEW DAYS PASS IN A BLUR OF EMOTIONAL chaos. Ben gets lost in planning his dad's funeral while Brody stays close to me. I try to be there for Ben, but the more I push, the more he pulls away.

We sit together at the funeral, but afterward, he takes off on his own and doesn't return until the next day. He doesn't even notice I'm there, and he reeks of alcohol.

When I call him, asking if he wants to meet for lunch or dinner, he tells me he's busy dealing with work.

I go to the gym the following morning, but he doesn't show up.

And the next evening when Brody tells me that his dad never came home, I head over to his place to stay with him, explaining that his father is grieving and we just need to give him some time.

"Can I move in with you?" Brody asks one night after we've had dinner and are sitting at the table while he finishes his math homework.

"What?" I ask in confusion.

"When my dad leaves, can I move in with you?"

"Brody…" I cover my hand with his. "Your dad isn't leaving. He's grieving. But he'll get through it. He just needs some time."

He nods but doesn't look like he believes me. "Okay, but if he leaves, can I move in with you? I don't…" He swallows thickly. "I really don't want to move back in with my mom and Ted."

"It's not going to come to that. I promise."

Ben isn't going anywhere. He said he wasn't. He told me he loved me and wanted a future with me. He's reconnected with his son. He wouldn't leave after all that…*Right?*

CHAPTER TWENTY-TWO
BENJAMIN

ONE MONTH LATER...

"I DON'T GIVE A SHIT WHAT IT SAYS! I NEED YOU TO handle it, and—" My words are cut off by a knock followed by Savannah walking through the door.

"I could hear you yelling from the lobby," she says, coming to stand next to me.

"Well, I wouldn't be yelling if my employees would do their damn job."

Savannah flinches, and I feel like an asshole because she doesn't deserve that. I've been on edge since my dad died, feeling as though I've been pushed into the middle of the ocean with a weight attached to my ankle.

I'm drowning, and no matter what I do, I can't come up for air. But regardless of how I feel, neither she nor my assistant deserves to be spoken to like that.

"I'm sorry," I tell her, taking a calming breath. "I just have a lot going on right now—"

"I brought lunch." She holds up a brown bag. "How about you

take a break to eat, and then you can go back to yelling afterward?" she says dryly.

I do a double take at her words. They sound like a joke, yet her face shows she's dead serious.

My assistant, of course, uses the moment to make her escape.

"I was actually in the middle of—"

"Working, I know, and it will *still* be there after lunch. But right now, you're going to sit your ass down and have lunch with your girlfriend, who brought lunch for her and her boyfriend. The same damn boyfriend she misses very much." Her words start off strong, but by the time she gets to the end, her voice is cracking, right along with my goddamn heart.

I cut across the room and pull her into my arms. Her shoulders slump, and her head drops against my chest.

"I miss you," she murmurs. "I know you're grieving, and it's going to take time, but I miss you and so does Brody."

"Baby, what are you talking about?" I tip her chin up, confused as hell. "I'm right here."

"Your body, yes, but your head...your heart...it's like you're lost, and I'm getting scared," she whispers. "Every day, it feels like you pull further away, and I'm terrified I'm going to lose you."

Her phone goes off, and she quickly checks it, types back to whoever it is, and then pockets it.

"Who was that?" I ask.

"Brody."

"What did he say?"

"He said he wanted to make pizza for dinner."

"Oh, well, I don't know if I'll be home. I have a shit ton to do and—"

"Nobody planned for you to be," she snaps. "That's the problem. You're here." She backs out of my arms and spreads her own. "All the time."

"Excuse me?"

"Nobody planned for you to be home. Just like you haven't been home a single night in the past month before midnight, if you come home at all. And when you do come home, you're back here at the crack of dawn. And you're not even going to the gym."

"What are you talking about?"

I think back to the past several weeks. Yeah, I've been dealing with the shitstorm my dad left me, but…

"When's the last time we had sex?"

I try to remember, but I can't.

"Ben, are you going to leave?" she asks softly, hesitantly. "Because Brody asked, and if you are, I need to know."

Her words are the sword that cuts through the fog in my head. I've been so lost in my own grief that I've blocked everyone and everything out, focusing on what I can do without even thinking… work. And in doing so, I've pushed away the two people who mean the most to me.

"Fuck, Sav. No. No." I lift her by her ass and carry her over to my desk, not giving a shit about anything but showing her that I'm sorry and that I'm not going anywhere.

I pull her shirt up and kiss my way down the center of her chest. Pushing the cups of her bra down, I take one of her pert nipples into my mouth.

"Ow." She jumps slightly.

"You okay?"

"Yeah, it's just been a little while."

"Too long," I agree, bringing my mouth to hers. "I'm so sorry," I murmur against her lips, needing her to know that. Needing her to understand.

I break our kiss to give her breasts some more attention. The harder I suck, the louder she groans, begging me for more.

She hikes her skirt up and frantically grabs for my pants, unbuttoning and unzipping them quickly.

Within seconds, her legs are spread, her underwear is moved to the side, and I'm thrusting into her cunt that was made for me.

Fuck, I've missed this woman. What the hell was I thinking

pushing her away? *I wasn't*…and instead of her letting me, she pushed back, bringing me back to her.

Every day since my dad's death, she's made sure I'm fed, leaving me food on the counter, taking care of my son when I was too fucked up in my grief to do it myself.

For the past month, she's stayed at my house, slept in my bed, and not once given up on me.

She was afraid I was going to leave, and I need her to know that's never going to happen. She's it for me. The woman I want to spend the rest of my life with.

She should never go a single day without knowing that, without knowing how much I love her and how much she means to me.

I find her clit and massage it in small circles until her body is trembling under my touch, her cunt contracting and choking my dick.

I lose myself in her, burying my face in her neck, inhaling her sweet scent, tasting her warm flesh. She's mine. And I'm hers. And fuck if she'll ever doubt that shit again.

I lift my head and look into her satiated gaze. There's so much I want to say, but now isn't the time. Not with me buried in her pussy anyway. So instead, I kiss her softly, keeping us connected for a little while longer.

"I love you," I murmur against her lips when our kiss comes to an end.

Her entire body sags in relief, and I hate myself for allowing her to doubt that for even a second.

"No matter what happens, I'm not going anywhere. I'll always be here."

She nods but doesn't say anything back, and that's okay. I fucked up this last month. Put my grief above her and my son. It's going to take time, but I'll show them that I'm not going anywhere. They're my number one priority, and I'll make sure they know that.

After we clean up, Savannah grabs the bag of food and sets it on the table, handing me a box and a can of soda and placing hers in front of her.

We're sitting across from each other, but I need to be closer, to touch her and feel her. I can already feel my head starting to fog up again with shit about Dad, and I can't let that happen.

I walk over to her and lift her off her chair, grabbing the box of food, and bring it with us to the couch, where I situate her on my lap.

"What are you doing?" She laughs, the beautiful sound hitting my heart.

"That's better." I give her a quick kiss. "You were too far away."

She opens the box of food, the smell of chicken lo mein wafting in the air, and scrunches her nose. "Ohh, I think it's bad." She closes the box back up. "We must've had it sitting too long when you distracted me with your dick."

It doesn't smell bad to me—in fact, it smells delicious—but when she drops the box onto the table and brushes her lips against mine, rearranging herself to straddle my lap, all thoughts of food evaporate.

After all, Savannah is my favorite thing to eat.

"FUCK."

I slam my laptop down and glance at the time. It's after six, and I need to get going so I can make it home in time for dinner. Savannah and Brody are making pizza—Brody's favorite thing to make—and I'll be damned if I miss it again.

"I've walked in on you cursing twice in one day. Do you want to talk about it?"

My gaze swings to the doorway, and I find Savannah standing there leaning against the doorframe.

"I was just about to leave. Aren't you and Brody making dinner?"

"We were supposed to." She walks farther into my office. "But it's the last day of school before spring break so he's going to the movies with his friends, and we're going to make pizza tomorrow night. And before you freak out, he asked me because he's been worried about bugging you."

"Which shouldn't go through his head," I argue, feeling like shit. "My son should be able to come to me about anything at any time. We were finally getting somewhere, and now it's like I've pushed us backward twenty damn steps."

"No, you didn't. You were grieving. You lost your dad suddenly. Nobody expects you to just bounce back." She walks around my desk, and I grip the curve of her hips, pulling her in front of me. "We'll get through this...together."

"I didn't even realize Brody had spring break coming up." I sigh in exhaustion, feeling like a damn failure. "His mom texted she'd like to see him, and now it makes sense. He's avoiding her again because Ted's home, but she's done not seeing him.

"She wants him to go to her place for a few days. She must know he's going to be on break. I can't let him hang out at the house alone, so I'll probably have him go there or come to work with me."

He's going to be pissed, but there's nothing I can do. I'm sure as hell not leaving my fifteen-year-old alone to get into all sorts of trouble—even if he's been behaving lately.

"I actually took the week off to hang out with him," she says, shocking the hell out of me. "We can come have lunch with you, and maybe you can take a day off, and we can do something fun."

"You took off work?"

"Yeah, I hope that's okay. I didn't mean to overstep. You've just been kind of out of it and—"

"Whoa, stop. I just can't believe you would do that. Thank you." I reach up and kiss the tip of her nose. "I'd say we should go away, but I'm swamped. My dad..." I swallow thickly, hating what I have to say next. "My dad must've been sick because he left me in a bind.

None of the books are current, and he handled everything. .. and with quarterly reports due ...”

Savannah frowns. "Let me help you.”

“What?” I heard her, but she already has a job.

“Ben, I took the week off anyway. I can help you sort out the mess, and we can go away for a few days.”

Her face lights up, and even if I thought it was a horrible idea to leave right now, there's no way I can say no to her. Because while I should be here, handling the mess my dad left me, Savannah and Brody need me more.

“All right. Let's do it. If you don't mind.”

“I don't. You can show me everything tonight since Brody won't be home until ten, and I'll get it all sorted for you next week.”

“Well, in that case, there's only one thing left to discuss. Where do we go for vacation?”

CHAPTER TWENTY-THREE

SAVANNAH

"Nope, it's not happening." I shake my head. "You go, and I'll safely stay right where I am...with my feet firmly on the ground."

Ben and Brody laugh.

"C'mon, Sav," Brody whines. "It's not that bad. Trust me, you're going to have fun."

"That's what you said about the Tower of Terror! I almost died. That freaking elevator ..." I shiver in remembrance. "The way it went down and my body went up!" I shriek. "Nope. Not happening."

More laughter.

"You'll be belted in tight," Brody argues.

"Yeah, because it goes fast and upside down, and did I mention fast? You go, and while I'm waiting for you, I'll sit my ass down and eat one of those delicious Mickey Mouse ice creams ... and maybe a pretzel." Mmm ... yeah, those sound yummy.

"You're going," Ben says, grabbing my hand and pulling me toward the long line. "We'll sit next to you, and I'll hold your hand.

And when you have fun, and you will, I'll even go on it with you again."

"Yeah, let's go," Brody adds. "We didn't fly all the way to Orlando so you could go to Disney and Universal for the first time and not ride all the good rides."

"Fine." I huff, knowing he's right.

When we discussed where to go away, and Ben and Brody learned I've never been to a single theme park, they insisted that's where we go.

This is our second day and fourth park, and all the other ones were great, but of course they saved the scariest ride for last.

"Besides," Brody says. "Tomorrow is Universal and Islands of Adventure, and the roller coasters there are way faster."

Ben elbows him in the ribs, making Brody grunt in pain.

"They get faster than this?" I hiss.

"You'll be fine. Let's go. And afterward, I'll buy you an ice cream and pretzel, and we can go find some more animals to take pictures with."

Brody snorts out a laugh, and I glare. "Keep it up, and I'll make you take more pictures with all the princesses again."

The line goes slow, and finally, we make it to the front, where it lists off the millions of reasons you shouldn't ride this ride and what will happen if you do.

"Great, you see this?" I point at the sign. "This is their way of saying, 'If you die, it's not our fault.'"

Both guys laugh.

"It's only for people who have heart trouble, problems with motion sickness, or are pregnant," Brody says. "Are you any of those?" He quirks a playful brow, not knowing that there's one thing on this list I wish I were.

"No," I murmur. "I'm none of those."

As if Ben knows what just went through my head, he pulls me into his side and kisses my temple.

It's finally our turn to get on the ride, and after meeting a fake

Aerosmith, we're prompted to get into the fake stretch limousine, which will take us to the fake concert—if we don't die on the way.

Once we're locked into place, Ben's hand finds mine, squeezing it so I know he's there. The music blasts into our ears, and then we rocket off into the dark.

The second we hit the first turn, I'm screaming my head off, but they were right. It's fun! We're jolted left and right and upside down. Blurs of neon signs fly by while we jam out to some rock 'n' roll, and what feels like seconds later, we come to a stop—the ride over.

"So, what'd you think?" Brody asks, wearing a shit-eating grin on his face.

"I think that was freaking awesome, and we should go again!"

"Told you!" Brody says, fist-bumping his dad.

We go on the Rock 'n' Roller Coaster two more times before we call it a day and head back to the hotel. Ben booked us a cool room where we can watch the fireworks from our balcony, so he suggests we watch them tonight.

Like every day when we get back, we all go to our rooms to shower the day off, but unlike every other time, Ben says he needs to handle some business and leaves me to shower alone.

Once I'm clean and in comfy pajamas, I head out to find Ben and Brody talking softly.

"Everything okay?" I ask, making them both look over at me startled.

"Yeah, go ahead and head out, and we'll be right out," Ben says.

"Okay, but hurry." I open the French doors and head outside. "They always start promptly at nine o'clock." I glance at my phone and see it's almost time.

"We'll be right out," he says again.

It's a cooler day in Florida, in the high seventies, which compared to New York right now is like heaven. I inhale the fresh air and am staring up at the sky, waiting for the first explosion to go off when the French door creaks open. I'm expecting them to join me against the railing, so I'm confused when I glance over and find both of them standing behind me.

"What are you guys doing? Get out here."

But instead of moving, Ben extends his arm, popping open a tiny black box and exposing a ... "Is that..." No, it can't be.

"The past few months have been the best of my life," Ben begins, forcing my gaze to snap from the gorgeous ring to him. "Between Brody moving in with me and meeting you, my life has changed significantly, and I can't imagine ever going back to the way it was before.

"When we were in my office, you asked if I was moving, and I realized I never made it clear to you and Brody that I'm not going anywhere ever. I said I wasn't, but you need to see it for yourself. You both are my life. And while a ring can't force someone to stay, it symbolizes my commitment to you."

He gets down on one knee, and my heart pounds against my rib cage as tears well up in my eyes. "Savannah Cartwright, will you do me the honor of wearing my ring and spending the rest of your life with me?"

"And me," Brody adds with a shy shrug. "Well, until I move out and go to college." Ben grunts, making Brody laugh. "It would be really fuck—freaking cool if you would be my stepmom."

"So, what do you say?" Ben asks. "Marry me and get both of us?"

"Yes," I whisper, tears of happiness sliding down my cheeks. "Yes, I will marry you." I look at Brody. "And I would love nothing more than to be your stepmom."

Ben pushes the ring onto my finger and then stands, wrapping me in his arms and kissing me while he twirls me around. When he sets me down, Brody scoops me up into a hug, making my tears fall even harder.

The first explosion of the fireworks go off, but I barely notice them, too focused on what's in front of me—love, friendship, happiness... family.

"YOUR MOM WANTS YOU TO VISIT."

"And I don't want to."

We're on the plane ride home, and I'm lying with my head in Ben's lap, half-asleep, listening to Ben and Brody talk.

"We have shared custody."

"And I'm fifteen. I don't want to go. I told her to let me know when Ted isn't home, and then I'll come by."

"What did he do that made you hate him so much?" Ben asks, his tone is filled with concern.

Brody goes silent for a beat, then says, "He's just an asshole."

The plane shakes, hitting some turbulence, and my stomach does a flip-flop, making me tighten my body.

"You okay?" Ben asks.

"Yeah, I just felt ..." Before I can finish my sentence, the plane shifts and dips, and I fly up, darting to the tiny bathroom.

I make it there just in time to expel my entire breakfast and the coffee I consumed less than an hour ago.

I'm perched over the toilet when Ben arrives less than a minute later. He pulls my hair into a ponytail and rubs my back while I get it all out.

Once I'm done, and my stomach is groaning in pain, he hands me a warm washcloth to wipe my mouth with.

"Thanks."

I stand and flush the toilet. Grabbing a disposable toothbrush they keep on hand, I brush my teeth and then gargle some mouthwash.

"There's a storm so the rest of the trip might be rocky. Why don't you go lie in bed?"

"Will you lie with me?" I waggle my brows.

"Of course."

Thankfully, the rest of the flight is spent with us in bed cuddling and not with me cradling the toilet.

"This doesn't make any sense."

I go through the numbers for the fourth time, already knowing what I'm going to find but wishing somehow, they would change. Unfortunately, numbers don't change. They're constant. Two plus two always equals four.

I take a sip of my water, and my stomach gargles.

When I woke up this morning, I wasn't feeling well, so I skipped breakfast, but now I think I'm feeling sick from not eating. I briefly wonder if maybe I'm coming down with something.

Needing a break from staring at the screen, I make myself some toast and coffee, but the second the Keurig begins to brew and the scent hits my nostrils, my stomach roils, and I end up in the bathroom with my face down in the toilet.

"Savy?" Brody calls out. "You okay?"

"Yeah! I think I have a stomach bug. You feeling okay?"

"I'm fine." He steps into the doorway. "Do you need anything?"

"No, I'm going to take a quick shower. Can you text your dad and ask him if he can bring dinner home? I don't think I'll be up for cooking."

"Yeah, sure."

After I take a shower and throw on some comfy pajamas, I head back out to the couch to go over the numbers again.

I'm in the middle of running them again when a wave of nausea hits me, and I wonder if it's the stress of what I'm going to have to tell Ben that's making me sick.

"Dammit, this can't be right," I mutter to myself.

"What can't be right?" a masculine voice asks, making me jump.

"You're home early."

Ben smirks. "I am, and I've brought food"—he holds up a pizza box—"and roses for my beautiful fiancée."

Butterflies warm my belly as I take in the pizza and gorgeous pink flowers in an elegant glass vase.

"You were so caught up in whatever you were doing, you didn't notice me come in." He drops the pizza onto the table and sets the flowers down, then comes over to sit on the couch next to me, pulling me into his arms.

"I missed you today." He brushes his lips against mine. "It was weird going all day without you."

"You probably shouldn't be this close to me," I warn. "I think I'm coming down with something."

"Yeah, Brody texted me that you were throwing up." He smirks. "I'll take my chances."

"Thank you for the flowers."

"You're welcome." He glances around. "Where's Brody?"

"In his room."

He nods then kisses me harder, making me moan. His tongue darts into my mouth, the scent of cinnamon hitting my senses. I gag slightly and back up.

"What's wrong?" he asks, concern etching his features.

"I think I'm a little…or a lot nervous to talk to you, and my body is reacting to the stress."

His brows come together. "Does it have something to do with what you were intently focusing on when I got home?"

"Yeah." I sigh. "I spent the day sorting out your books, and…" I take a deep breath. "Ben, I've run the numbers several times, and you weren't wrong. You're missing a lot of money. Several thousand."

"So my dad messed up…"

"No, he didn't mess up." And this is what I've been dreading telling him. "He was stealing from the company."

Ben's face jerks back like he's been smacked. "Excuse me? What did you just say?"

"I started going through the books for Lush, New York, but in doing so, I found several errors that didn't make sense. So, to double-check them, I had Owen send me the information for your other properties."

"You called one of my employees behind my back?"

"I didn't want to have to tell you what I suspected until I knew for sure. You've taken your dad's death so hard and—"

"Of course I've taken his death hard," he barks. "He was my dad, my only parent left, and now he's gone."

"I know," I say, trying to remain calm, but my emotions are getting the best of me, and I can feel myself on the verge of crying. "After going through the numbers, I found that *someone* who has access to your business accounts has been skimming off the top for several months."

"This can't be right." He sets me onto the couch and stands. "My dad wouldn't steal from me."

I was afraid he would say that, so I open my laptop and send him my findings. "Over the course of six months, your dad moved thousands of dollars to his personal account. The exact figures are in the report I just sent over."

"You're wrong," he deadpans, not even considering what I'm saying. I know he's hurt right now, but I made sure I had all the facts straight, and eventually, he's going to have to deal with it.

Fortunately, his business is thriving, which is why he didn't notice it missing until he went to run the reports.

His dad knew what he was doing, taking a little bit from each account so a red flag wouldn't be raised.

When I spoke to Owen, though, he told me he did notice, but when he tried to speak to Olivier, he was brushed off.

"I'm not wrong. I double- and triple-checked, and honestly, I kind of resent you accusing me of being wrong. Either you don't trust me, or you don't think I'm capable of doing my job. Either way, that's not okay."

"All I'm saying is that you could very well be mistaken. Hell, you told me you couldn't conceive, yet here we are, a few months later, and you're pregnant. So if you could be mistaken about that, maybe you're mistaken about this too."

It takes a moment to wrap my head around what he's just said, and once I do, I take a step back, trying to get a handle on this new information. "I'm not..." I shake my head. I can't be. .. We tried for years, and it never happened. I'm broken.

"When's the last time you had your period?" Ben asks. "You've been throwing up, certain smells make you sick, and your body, especially your breasts, are sensitive. It doesn't take a rocket scientist to put it together."

"No...I..." Fuck, am I pregnant? I try to think back to when I got my period last, but my brain isn't working. Too much is happening at once, and all I want to do is cry.

When Ben quirks a knowing brow, my blood boils over, and I snap at him. "Even if I were, that has *nothing* to do with the fact that your dad stole from you, and instead of listening, you're accusing me of lying about it."

Hurt and confused and needing some space to think about everything that's just happened, I bolt out of Ben's place without looking back.

It's only when I get to the elevator that I realize I'm without any shoes or keys or hell, even my cell phone. I've been staying at his place for so long that everything of mine is there.

Praying Brianne is home, I get on the elevator and press the button for our floor, all while blocking everything out that was just said. If I think about it, I'm going to lose it.

When I knock on the door, Brianne opens it, confused. "Did you lose your keys?"

The second her eyes lock with mine, all the emotions bubbling to the surface spill over, and I throw myself into her arms.

"I think I'm pregnant."

"What?" She gasps. "That's amazing." She backs up and looks me in the eyes. "That's amazing, right?"

"Yeah, it would be, if my fiancé didn't just accuse me of lying about his dad stealing from him."

Her eyes go wide. "Oh, shit. Come sit down. I think we're going to need an impromptu girls' night, complete with ice cream and tea, because it seems you have some spilling to do."

CHAPTER TWENTY-FOUR

BENJAMIN

"Fuck!"

I pound my fist against the closed door and then, without thinking, swipe a bunch of shit off the table.

When the vase holding the flowers explodes against the wood floor, shards of glass flying every which way, I release a harsh sigh, feeling as though that's the perfect representation of my life at this moment—fucking shattered.

This can't be happening. She was supposed to find the issue in the books that my dad left behind. She was *not* supposed to tell me my dad—my own flesh and blood—was stealing from me. It doesn't make any sense. He worked for me for years and was paid way beyond his pay grade. He has no reason to steal from me. She has to be lying. *She wouldn't be the first woman to lie to me.*

I'll be damned if I allow her to destroy my family and disgrace my father's name. But even as the thoughts emerge, I internally cringe because deep down, I know that's not who Savannah is. She doesn't lie or trick or play games.

I saw the look on her face when she told me, and it was clear it hurt her to say the words almost as much as she knew it would hurt me to hear them.

My thoughts go back to the weeks leading up to my dad's death...The way he was sneaking around and hiding where he was going. I tried to ask him what was wrong, but he refused to confide in me.

"Pizza here?" Brody asks, stepping out of his room and snapping me out of my thoughts. He looks around at the sight of destruction, then glances at me. "Where's Savy?"

"She left."

"What happened?" He walks over and picks the pizza box up, setting it on the table and opening it. Because it was closed, the pizza is still intact, just a little jostled.

"We got into an argument."

He nods and picks up several of the roses, carrying them into the kitchen.

"Leave it," I tell him. "I'll clean it up." It's my fault, after all.

"I got this. You can go."

"Go where?"

His eyes meet mine. "Find her and fix whatever you broke." He holds up the flowers. "I'm assuming these were meant for her."

Dammit, this kid. He's never looked or sounded so old...or wise.

But...

"It's not that simple," I tell him as my phone rings out.

I grab it from my jacket pocket, hoping it's Savannah, only to find it's my sister. She's been down since Dad's death, and with her being pregnant, I don't want to ignore her call. I hold up a finger to Brody, indicating to give me a minute, then take the call.

"Hey."

"Hey," she says back, sounding worried. "Mr. Jeffreys called. He said he's been trying to get ahold of you, but you're not taking his calls. If you need me to handle it..."

I sigh in exhaustion. Mr. Jeffreys is the attorney our dad used to create his will. I should've met with him immediately following Dad's death to sort out his affairs, but I've been putting it off.

"I'll give him a call right now," I tell her, not wanting to cause her more stress.

"Okay. How are you?"

"I'm okay. You?"

"I'm all right. I haven't seen you in a while. I was thinking you, Savy, and Brody could come over for dinner one night."

"Yeah," I choke out. "I'll let you know."

My phone beeps in my ear, and hoping it's Savannah, I tell her I'll get back to her soon, then switch over without looking at who's calling.

"Benjamin." I cringe at the sound of Paola's voice. Shit, I should've checked to see who was calling.

"What's up?"

"I would like to see my son. You're back from your trip, so can you please have him come see me?"

"He has an issue with Ted..." I begin as the sound of a phone goes off.

Brody picks it up from the coffee table and shows it to me. It's Savannah's. She left it here. Guess she won't be calling. He answers it and walks into the other room.

"Hello?" Paola snaps, reminding me I'm still on the phone with her.

"Yeah. Brody doesn't like Ted, and I think—"

"Ted isn't here," she says, cutting me off. "We're actually not together anymore. I've ended our engagement."

"Really?"

"He..." She clears her throat. "He cheated on me. It's over. He's out of town, with his mistress I imagine, but once he returns, he'll be getting his shit and moving out."

"Sorry," I tell her, unsure of what else to say. We might not be friends, but she's still Brody's mom.

"Thanks. So do you think I can spend the weekend with him?"

"I'll speak to him, but I'm sure that can be arranged." Plus, it'll give me time to sort my life out.

We hang up just as Brody is walking back out. "Your mom wants to spend the weekend with you. And before you argue, she and Ted broke up."

Brody's eyes widen. "Seriously?"

"Yeah. Are you okay to go over there for a few days?"

"Yeah."

"Who was on the phone?" I nod to Savannah's phone still in his hand.

"Bri. She's coming by to grab Savy's stuff. She said she tried to call you, but it kept going to voicemail."

"I had a call on each line."

"Why is she coming to get Savy's stuff?" he asks, glaring at me.

"Because she doesn't live here," I explain dumbly. "She's been staying here while I was dealing with my dad's death, to be here for me and you. But she doesn't live here."

"That's stupid. You guys are getting married. She might as well just stay here. And she wouldn't need her shit if you two weren't fighting." He drops the phone onto the coffee table. "Fix it," he says before turning to go to his room.

"You didn't eat," I mention.

"Not hungry." He waves his hand over his shoulder. "Guess I'll get ready to go to Mom's."

"I JUST WANT TO TALK TO HER."

"Not happening." Brianne blocks the door like a fucking guard dog. "She needs some space. You hurt her."

I know she's right, but at the same time, I need to talk to her. I was in shock by what she said. I never should've lashed out at her, and I definitely shouldn't have pointed out that she's most likely pregnant the way I did either.

When Brianne came and got her stuff, I tried to get her to let me see Savannah, but she wasn't having it, and since it's the weekend, I can't even catch her at work.

I've sent chocolates and flowers and her favorite pineapple pizza, but she still won't talk to me. I fucked up, but damn, I just need a chance to fix it.

"I've given her two days. I just want to talk to her."

"And when she's ready to talk to you, she knows your number."

She slams the door in my face, and I hang my head against the door in frustration. My phone rings, and I pull it out, hoping it's Savannah, but it's not.

"Lucas, what's up?"

"Nothing. Laura is having a girls' night with her friends. Just calling to see what you're up to? Want to grab a drink?"

"I'll meet you downstairs."

I'm not really in the mood to drink, but being alone in the condo last night sucked. There was a time when I loved the silence, but now, it just feels lonely as fuck. No Brody playing his loud as hell video games. No Savannah binge-watching her stupid shows. I used to revel in the quiet, and now I despise it.

"Congratulations on your engagement," Lucas says when he sees me.

"Thanks. How'd you know?"

Savannah and I haven't had time to discuss doing an engagement party since it just happened. Hell, we haven't even discussed when she wants to get married and what kind of wedding she wants. Then again, at this rate, there won't be a wedding.

"My sister told me. I haven't seen Savy all week since she's on vacation." He smirks, and I know something sarcastic is about to come out of his mouth. "Never thought you'd be engaged before me."

And there it is. "Never thought I'd meet a woman like Savannah."

He nods in understanding.

We spend the next few hours at Erwin's, a hole-in-the-wall bar around the corner we frequent, drinking and shooting the shit. I'm probably a good four, maybe five scotches in when my phone rings.

It's late, after three in the morning, and it's Savannah. Something in my blood turns cold with worry.

"Sav."

"Ben, I need you to come home."

"Where are you?"

I'm already standing and throwing down a couple of bills.

"I'm at your place...with Brody."

"I thought he was with his mom."

What the hell is going on?

"Just come home, please."

CHAPTER TWENTY-FIVE

SAVANNAH

ONE HOUR AGO…

"Mmm, so good."

I take a bite of my Phish Food ice cream as my favorite episode of *One Tree Hill* plays. It's the one where Nathan admits to Haley that even though he hated her leaving him to go on tour, he kept every article and photograph of her.

They're standing in the rain, yelling at each other, and then he kisses her with such passion, goose bumps prick my skin and tears fill my eyes, making it hard to see the screen.

I let out a choked sob as I scoop another bite of caramel-choco-late-marshmallow goodness into my mouth.

"I want a love like that," I say out loud, shoveling more ice cream into my mouth. When I dip my spoon in, and nothing comes out, I glance down and see the container is empty. "Figures."

I drop my spoon into the container. "Looks like my *fiancé* isn't the only Ben fucking with my heart."

"Are you talking to your ice cream?" Brianne asks with a laugh.

She must've just gotten home from Marcus's place. I told her she doesn't have to babysit me, but she's insisted on sleeping here for the past two nights.

"Yeah." I shrug, owning my craziness. "I was just pointing out that I've been heartbroken by two Bens in the past two days."

She quirks a brow. "Well, there's more of that Ben in the freezer."

My mood perks up. "You bought me more?"

"I did, but you can only have it when you talk to the other Ben."

My mood plummets.

"I think I'm done with both of these Bens." I drop the container onto the nightstand with a huff.

Brianne rolls her eyes. "You are not. You're just emotional and hurt, and cranky because you're refusing to take a pregnancy test and find out if Ben was right and knew you were pregnant before you did."

"Whatever," I grumble as my phone rings.

I grab it, ready to hit ignore, thinking it's Ben again. But when Brody's name shows up, I pause my show and answer it. No matter how mad and hurt I am at Ben, I'll always be there for Brody.

"Hey."

"Savy, I, umm, I need you." Brody's voice is nothing more than a whisper. Something is wrong.

"I'm here. Where are you?"

"I'm outside the building."

I don't understand why he's out there instead of at his dad's place, but it doesn't matter.

"I'm at my place. Do you want me to come down, or do you want to come up?"

He's silent for a few beats before he says, "I'll come up. Wait, are you alone?"

I glance at Brianne. I should tell him she's here, but something tells me he might not come up if I do.

"Yeah, I'm alone. I'll come unlock the door."

"Okay."

He hangs up, and Brianne quirks a brow. "It's Brody. Something is wrong, and he needs to talk to me. Can you, umm, hide in your room?"

"I'll do you one better and go back to Marcus's, but if you need me…"

"I know. Thanks."

I hug her, then throw on a bra and leggings before walking her out so I can meet Brody at the door.

"I saw Bri at the elevator," he says, walking in.

"She's going to Marcus's. She was on her way out when you called."

He nods, and his gaze connects with mine, and it's then I notice he has a swollen eye like he's been punched.

"What happened?"

I step toward him to check it out, and he takes a step back, shaking his head. "I…I didn't know who else to go to." His hazel eyes, identical to his father's, meet mine. "I know I have my dad, but…"

"Hey, I'm here. Come sit down."

He follows me over to the couch, and we have a seat. I give him a few moments to gather his thoughts before I ask him to talk to me.

"I like girls," he starts, confusing me because I know he does—hence him dating Sariah—and I'm not sure where he's going. "But I also think I might like guys."

I nod but remain quiet since I'm sure there's more to come, and I want to let him get it all out.

"Shit, this is so embarrassing," he mutters, scrubbing his hands over his face.

"No, it's not. Whatever you have to tell me, I'm not judging."

He releases a harsh sigh. "One night I was in my room watching…porn." His cheeks tinge pink, and I have to swallow down my smile because it's so normal, but I can imagine how embarrassing it is for a teenager to admit. "I clicked on a video, and it was of a girl and some guys. The guys, they were…" He meets my eyes, no doubt praying I understand so he doesn't have to explain.

I nod my understanding, and he continues. "I was curious, so I found some with more guys. I was watching it when Ted barged into my room drunk. My mom was asleep. He liked to watch sports and drink after she went to bed. A lot of the time, he would pass out on the couch."

A lump, the size of a bitter lemon, fills my throat as I pray to every God what he's about to say isn't what I think.

"He, umm, he called me a queer and shit, and I told him to get the hell out. Every time he would get drunk, he would talk shit, but I ignored him. I didn't tell my mom because I didn't want her to think I was gay. I don't really know."

"I get it," I tell him. "But there's nothing wrong with it if you are."

"Yeah," he breathes. "His taunting kept getting worse, and then one night, he told me if I want to find out if I liked guys, he could show me."

He clears his throat and looks down, refusing to meet my eyes as he says the next part. "He started unbuttoning his pants, telling me he could fuck me, and I would know if I was gay."

Needing to remain strong for Brody because he's trusting me with this, I swallow down the bile of anger burning my throat, patiently waiting for him to continue.

He glances up and looks at me, his eyes sad. "My mom used to say she was lonely, that my dad left her and she had to raise me alone. I didn't want to ruin her happiness."

Oh no. His getting into fights was his cry for help. He just didn't know how to handle it. It's why he never goes with his mom since he moved in with his dad.

"I don't know your mom, but I can tell you that there's no way she wouldn't want to know what Ted was doing. I saw her at dinner that day, and she loves you. What he did is wrong…so damn wrong."

"They broke up. My mom said he cheated. She didn't tell me that, but I overheard her crying to her friend on the phone."

I feel like what he's telling me is a lead-up to more, so I simply nod and wait.

"She said he moved out, so I went with her for the weekend. I was pissed at Dad for upsetting you and making you leave."

"He didn't make me leave."

"Whatever. He still upset you. I told him to fix it."

Oh, my heart.

"I guess Ted wasn't supposed to come back to get his stuff until later," Brody says, changing gears, "but he showed up tonight while my mom was asleep. He saw my light on because I was playing my PlayStation and came in. He started calling me names and shit, and then he tried to kiss me.

"I pushed him away and tried to leave, but before I could, he punched me in my face. I hit him back, and he hit his head on the edge of my bed. When I left, he was knocked out cold."

"You did the right thing. What he did is wrong and illegal on so many levels."

He nods in understanding. "I just didn't know where to go. I don't want to hurt my mom and my dad. What if I am gay?" The nervous look on his face damn near breaks my heart.

"Has your dad ever indicated he would be upset if you were?" I don't want to tell him he wouldn't care if he's nervous because of something his dad has said in the past.

"No." He shakes his head to emphasize his answer. "But I mean, he's always been about women. He even owned strip clubs."

"So? You're right. Your dad isn't gay, but that doesn't mean he would care that you are."

"True. I guess I just choked."

We're silent for a few minutes before I say what I hope he will understand. "We have to tell your dad."

He nods. "Yeah, I know. But can you be there, please?"

"Didn't you hear what I said?" I quirk a brow. "*We* have to tell your dad. I'll be there for you every step of the way that you want me there."

After I throw on a pair of shoes and a sweater, we go upstairs to his dad's place. Since Brody has a key, we go right in, but Ben isn't there. I'm not sure where he is, so I pull my phone out and dial his number. He answers on the third ring.

"Sav." His voice fills my belly with butterflies. I've missed him so much. But right now, we need to focus on Brody and fixing this situation.

"Ben, I need you to come home."

The second he walks through the door, he can tell something is wrong, and before he freaks out, I stand and walk over to him.

"Stay calm," I whisper when I hug him.

He nods into my hair and hugs me back.

The three of us have a seat in the living room—Brody next to me and Ben across from us—and then Brody begins telling his dad the same story he told me.

And even though I've already heard it, I'm almost positive my heart breaks all over again.

CHAPTER TWENTY-SIX

BENJAMIN

I'm going to kill him. Fucking kill him. As soon as I've explained to my son how much I love him and don't give a shit if he's gay or bi or a goddamned unicorn, I'm going to kill that motherfucker.

"You're not going to kill him," Savannah says calmly, making me frown. *Shit, did I say that out loud?* "I can see it all over your face, but you're not going to kill him because if you do, you'll end up in jail."

Not wanting to lie to her—because I am most definitely going to kill him—I look at my son, so I can focus on the important part here.

"I don't care if you're gay. I don't care who you like, who you fuck…You're my kid, and I'm proud of you."

He sighs in relief. "I don't really know."

"And you're fifteen. You have plenty of time to figure it out. I know I haven't been around as much as I should've been, and that's all on me, but you need to know I don't care.

"If you decide you're straight and marry a woman, great, but if you decide you're gay and marry a guy, that's great too. Either way, I'll be at the wedding."

I stand and open my arms. When he walks over, I give him a hug as tight as humanly possible, needing him to know I mean every word I say. "I love you, Brody, no matter what."

"Love you too, Dad."

We separate, and I catch Savannah wiping tears from her eyes.

"What now?" Brody asks.

"Now, I go kill that fucker."

"No, Dad, please don't," he says. "Mom already broke up with him, and technically, he didn't do anything except call me names and try to kiss me. I don't want to turn this into a thing. Please."

Fuck. Unfortunately, he's right, and since there's no proof of anything other than him punching Brody, there isn't anything we can do. Thankfully, he's here and safe, and nothing physically happened to him.

"All right, I'll respect your wishes on it, but we have to tell your mom, and if he's anywhere in the vicinity, I can't guarantee I won't lay his ass out."

We call his mom, waking her up, and she comes right over. As Brody tells her, she cries, blaming herself for not seeing what was happening right under her roof and for him feeling he couldn't come to her.

Once he's done, I tell her she can crash in my guest room. I'll call a locksmith in the morning to have her locks changed and help her move his shit out of the house.

Savannah hugs Brody goodbye, telling him she loves him and is about to leave when I stop her. "We need to talk. Please."

"I know, but not tonight." She glances over at Brody and Paola. "Tonight, they need you."

"COFFEE AND LEMON POUND CAKE, YOUR FAVORITE." I hold up the cup and bag, hoping it will be the key to Savannah letting me in.

After making sure Ted and all his shit was gone from Paola's house, I could tell Paola was completely distraught from everything and needed some time alone, so I spent the day with Brody, going to breakfast and then hanging out and playing video games, just focusing on him.

When I offered to let him stay home from school, he told me he wanted to go, so I confirmed his weekly appointment with his therapist and assured him we'll get through all of this together.

Ted might be gone, but there's no way Brody is past what happened that easily…But he'll get there, and I'll be there every step of the way.

Since he took off for an early football practice, I ran to the coffee shop and snagged Savannah's favorites in hope of catching her at home before she left. I should probably wait until after work to talk, but I can't go another minute without apologizing for the way I treated her.

Savannah eyes the goods, then sighs, snatching them from me and letting me in. "Only because I'm craving coffee and sweets."

She sits on the couch, still in her pajamas, and takes a sip. "Mmm…so good. I read if I'm pregnant, I can only drink like one cup a day. This is going to be a long nine months."

"If you're pregnant?"

"I haven't confirmed it yet."

"Why not?"

"Because I was mad you knew before me." She shrugs a single shoulder. "And I was kind of scared that if I was, I'd be doing it on my own." She takes another sip of her coffee to keep herself busy, but I take it from her, wanting to see her face, needing her to look at me.

"You're not going through anything alone." I take her hand in mine. "I was shocked by what you told me, and I reacted wrong, but

I love you, and that hasn't changed. And neither has me wanting to marry you and have a family with you."

"Did you find anything out about your dad?"

"No, not yet. But I know you wouldn't lie to me. I don't know why he was stealing from me, and I'm afraid to find out. He's gone, and even though our family went through a lot, we came out okay, and we were close. What if what I find out makes me see him in a different light?"

"True, but like you told Brody. You're family, and I don't believe he could've done anything to make you love him any less."

I want to believe she's right, but it's hard when you don't know what you're dealing with.

"Will you come with me?"

"Where?"

"To my dad's. His attorney needs to meet me there to handle his estate and assets. I've been putting it off. If I'm going to find any answers, it would be there."

"Of course," she says with a soft smile. "Why don't you see if he can meet us after work?"

"All right, but before we go to work, there's something we need to do."

Her brows dip in confusion.

"Sav, you've been wanting a baby for years. How is it not killing you not knowing if you're pregnant?"

It's been in the back of my mind every other damn second since I put the pieces together.

"I told you why. Plus, I think I wanted you to be there. I really thought I was broken. It feels like it's almost too good to be true."

"Or…" I bring her hand up to my lips and kiss each of her knuckles. "It was meant to be."

"IF YOU'RE NOT PREGNANT, IT'S NO BIG DEAL," I TELL HER as I watch her nervously pace the bathroom.

It turns out Brianne had already bought tests, so finding out was as easy as her peeing on a stick.

Once she did, she began pacing. Back and forth. Back and forth. And when I saw how nervous she was, it hit me.

What if I'm wrong and she's not pregnant—and I just put it into her head that she is. She's going to be devastated, and it's all my fault.

Shit.

"Sav, did you hear me?"

"Oh my God!" She grabs the stick and waves it in the air. "I'm pregnant!" She thrusts the test toward me so I can see the word PREGNANT, then throws herself into my arms. "Thank you. Thank you. I can't believe it." She steps back, tears flying down her cheeks. "I've wanted this for so long, and now I have it, and it's all thanks to you."

Jesus, this woman. She's actually thanking me for mistakenly knocking her up when I should be the one thanking her.

"Sav, you've got it all wrong," I tell her, palming her face and wiping away the liquid from her cheek with my thumb. "When I met you, I was broken and hanging on by a thread..." I finger her necklace—the one with the love knot. "I was going through life, but not actually living. Until I met you. It's me who should be thanking you."

"No." She shakes her head and kisses me softly on the lips. "It's like you said when you gave me the love knot. We were both broken, hanging on by a thread. But together, those strings formed a strong knot that will withstand the test of time."

She presses her lips to mine again, this time deepening the kiss, and I thank whoever was responsible for that annoying fucking treadmill. Had it not driven me nuts, I might never have given this Southern-accented, coffee-loving, weird T-shirt-wearing woman, who holds my heart in the palm of her hand, a second glance.

EPILOGUE

SAVANNAH

THREE MONTHS LATER...

"THAT'S THE HEAD...AND THE HANDS...THOSE ARE THE feet...and oh! It seems your baby is not at all shy. Those little legs are spread wide." The doctor laughs, glancing at Ben and me. "Are we finding out the sex?"

"No," I say, giving her the answer Ben and I agreed on. Life only has so many surprises, so we decided to wait until our little alien is born to find out—yep, you read that right, our baby's nickname is Alien.

Brody took one look at the ultrasound pics, having never seen any before, and said it looked like I was carrying an alien. Of course Ben thought it was hilarious, so, for the past three months, we've called our precious little miracle an alien.

The doctor goes about taking measurements, explaining the baby's right on schedule growth-wise, then we listen to the heartbeat.

Ben squeezes my hand, knowing I get choked up every time I hear it. He surprised me with an at-home doppler so I could listen to it any time I wanted. The fear of this being my only pregnancy, since it was so hard to conceive the first time, has me enjoying every step of this pregnancy—from weekly baby bump pics to journaling how I feel, I'm not leaving anything out.

"Everything looks good. Here are some pictures." She hands us a strip of black and white images. "And you can view the video on the portal. You can check out and schedule your next appointment for four weeks from today."

"Thank you."

After I get dressed and check out, we head out. I scheduled the appointment late in the afternoon so we could take the rest of the day off.

When Ben tells his driver a different address, I look at him confused. "We're not going home?"

"We are."

That's all he says before he pulls his phone out and goes about checking his emails. I'm a little annoyed that he's being so short with me, but I chalk it up to him being busy, so I use the time to track my progress this week and then look up some more baby names.

We can't seem to agree on a single one, so I like to make lists and send them to Ben. He then goes through them, commenting on each one and why that name isn't good. Some of his answers are actually kind of funny—like Luke for a boy reminds him of *Star Wars*, and apparently, he's traumatized from when he read *Charlotte's Web* as a kid and the poor spider died, so Charlotte was also nixed.

Twenty minutes later, we're out of the city and going down a less congested area. The longer we drive, the bigger the houses get and the farther apart they sit.

"Hey, Ben. Did you plan to stop somewhere?"

He glances up quickly and looks around. "Yep."

I wait for him to elaborate, but he gives me nothing. "Care to share where?"

"Nope." He goes back to looking at his phone, and I snatch it from him.

"Hey, where are we going?"

He chuckles at my annoyance. "Patience. You'll see." He leans over and kisses my cheek, and I sag against him.

A few minutes later, the driver stops in front of a gorgeous two-story colonial-style home with cute country-style shutters, a large wraparound porch, a decent-sized front yard with actual green grass, and a white picket fence.

When I see a for sale sign in the front, my heart pounds in my chest. "Ben..."

He smiles and opens the door, edging out and then taking my hand to help me.

"I believe I promised you a white picket fence," he says, walking us up the U-shaped drive.

His words, confirming what I was thinking and hoping when I saw the sign, cause me to choke up with raw emotion. I'm engaged to a man I love, and we'll soon officially be a family.

My hand that's not entwined with his goes to my belly—we're adding to our family. And he's gotten me my white picket fence.

Ben grabs the lockbox, types in a code, then pulls the key out, unlocking the door. We step inside, and it's completely empty, like the most beautiful blank canvas.

I can instantly imagine Brody and Ben laughing with each other in the living room while they play video games, family meals at the dining room table. I glance to the left and see the massive kitchen, and thoughts of making homemade pizza with Brody—and one day our little alien—come to mind.

We walk through the house and out the back door. There's more grass—the perfect size backyard to hold a swing set and maybe even a pool—with more white fence.

We go back in, and he walks me through more of the downstairs —including the spacious master bedroom and en suite bathroom.

There are five bedrooms, three bathrooms, and a large library upstairs that can double as an office.

"Brody and I came to see it the other day, when you were working late, to make sure it looked the same in person as the virtual tour," Ben says, standing in the middle of the library. "It's actually not too far from his school and only a thirty-minute drive into work.

"I was thinking we could make this an office, and once the baby comes, we could work from home a few days a week. I haven't put an offer on it yet because I wanted you to see it first. See if you can picture yourself living and raising a family here. So, what do you say, Sav, want to fill this home with me?"

I attempt to tell him yes, but my emotions get the best of me, and I choke out a sob, tears blurring my vision.

"Yes," I finally get out. "I most definitely would love to fill this home with you."

BENJAMIN - SEVEN YEARS LATER

"You did it!" I wrap my arms around Brody and pat his back. "I'm so damn proud of you."

Today is his college graduation. He earned a business degree while spending the past four years working for me and learning the business.

When he told me he wanted to follow in my footsteps, I wanted to make sure my footsteps were worthy. So over the past several years, I've worked—with the help of my wife—to make Fields Enterprises a place where people want to work and are comfortable coming to me.

When I finally met with my dad's attorney, I learned he was in debt—bad. He had depleted all of his assets, his cars were being repossessed, and his house was under foreclosure.

He was always the type of man to handle shit himself, never wanting to talk. He did it with my mom when she was sick, refusing to get her help, and then again with us when he was going through whatever he was going through.

Not wanting it to continue with me, I've made it a point to make sure my door is always open, and my family and employees know they can come to me at any time.

"You know what this means, right?" Brody deadpans. "I'm one step closer to becoming the next CEO of Fields Enterprises."

I glance at my very pregnant wife as she beams with pride at Brody while holding our six-year-old son's hand—we named him Olivier, after my dad—and I chuckle. "Yeah, that's exactly what it means."

With Savannah expecting again—something we weren't sure would ever happen again since we decided not to go to a fertility clinic but instead let nature take its course, or not—I'm ready to settle down and work fewer hours. I have baseball games to coach, and with our little girl on the way—it's not confirmed, but I think she is—I imagine we'll have our hands full with her.

"I'm so proud of you," Savannah says, giving Brody a hug.

"Thanks." He roughs up Olivier's hair. "One day, you'll be walking across that stage."

Olivier dodges Brody and laughs. "I don't wanna go away. I wanna stay home with Mommy."

"Let's see if you say that in a few years," Brody tells him.

Brody didn't go away to school, but he did move out, wanting to live in the city, which to Olivier is like living on another planet.

After Paola gives Brody a hug, telling him congratulations, we head out to meet everyone for dinner to celebrate.

We arrive at the restaurant and are brought back to the private dining room where our friends and family are waiting for us since the university only allowed four tickets per graduate.

Everyone stands, congratulating Brody on a job well done while the kids run around, catching up with each other.

Savannah comes over and wraps her arms around me from the side, her head dropping against my chest. "I love that sound," she says, tightening her arms.

"What sound?" I glance down at her. "All I hear is a bunch of people talking and kids screaming and laughing."

"Exactly. It's the sound of love...of happiness...of family." She tips her face up and presses her lips to mine. "It's a sound I'll never tire of hearing."

BONUS EPILOGUE

SAVANNAH

"Okay, everyone. It's go-time!"

The wedding planner herds my bridesmaids out the door and then turns back to me. "Once Brody gets here, meet us by the entrance."

I give her a nod while double-checking my makeup in the mirror. I'm reapplying my lip gloss when there's a knock on the door, followed by, "You ready?"

Brody stands in the doorway. Dressed sharply in a black tux, he reminds me so much of his dad. It's crazy to think in less than a year he'll be off to college.

My thoughts go back to last year, when Ben was insisting that we figure out when and how we were going to get married. I had postponed it once, saying I wanted to wait until I wasn't pregnant. And then again, after our son was born, wanting to lose some baby weight so I would feel good about myself in my wedding dress.

Only when the time came to plan the wedding, I wasn't sure if having an actual wedding was the best idea…

"All I'm saying is that we could go to the courthouse and get married." I shrug, refusing to make eye contact with Ben because he'll know I'm full of shit the second our eyes lock.

My fiancé knows me too well.

"And I'm saying I wouldn't mind that if I believed for a second that's what you actually wanted." Ben pinches my chin and turns my face so I'm forced to look at him. "But I don't believe that's what you want."

"I already had a wedding. I don't need another one."

"The wedding you told Aunt Amalia you hated?" Brody asks, walking straight to the fridge. He grabs a bottle of water and downs it, then leans over the counter.

"I don't know what you're talking about," I mutter even though I did tell her that. Only I thought nobody heard.

"Yeah, you did," Brody retorts. "You said, 'Make sure you plan the wedding you want so you're not stuck in a wedding planned by your egotistical, selfish husband and mother-in-law.'"

I glare at Brody. "That is not how I sound."

Ben laughs. "But is that what you said?"

I sigh. "It is, but I was just trying to explain to her that she shouldn't let her in-laws plan it for her. She was upset about Gerald's mom wanting to have it at a church, and Amalia wanted to have it at the Botanical Garden."

Thankfully, she listened to me, and she and Gerald were married in a beautiful Botanical Garden in upstate New York.

"Because you were speaking from experience," Ben says. "Because your douchebag ex and his parents planned your entire wedding."

"Yeah," I admit begrudgingly.

"Savy." Ben palms my cheek. "Do you want to get married at the courthouse or do you want to have an actual wedding?"

"I want to have a wedding but…"

"But what?"

"When Neil's mom was planning the wedding, she made sure there was no aisle because she didn't want me to have to walk down it alone. She acted like it was my fault that I was an orphan, and she was embarrassed that I wouldn't have my dad to walk me down the aisle."

"Fuck her," Ben scoffs. "You can walk down the aisle by yourself, and fuck anyone who has a problem with that."

"I know," I mutter. "But the thought of doing that…after she said it. I don't know." I shrug. "I know I shouldn't care what anyone thinks, but the thought of standing at the end of an aisle by myself…"

"I can do it," Brody offers.

"What?" I look over at him in confusion.

"I'm not your dad, obviously," Brody says. "But you're like a second mom to me…hell, if we're honest, you're more like my first mom."

Since everything went down with Ted, Paola has kind of retreated. She goes out often, goes away with different guys, and she never asks Brody to go over to her house anymore. I think she's punishing herself for not seeing the type of person Ted was and allowing Brody to be in that position. But instead of pulling Brody closer, she's pushed him away. To the point where their relationship is nonexistent.

I hate that for both of them, but I know firsthand that unless someone wants to be a parent, nobody can make them.

So, when we moved to the new house, Brody of course moved with us, and we've created a life here as a family. Six months ago, we welcomed Olivier Fields—named after Ben's father—and Brody has taken to being a big brother like a fish to water. And in turn, we've gotten closer.

"I appreciate that," I say to him, "but—"

"I'd love to walk you down the aisle," Brody explains. "Sure, it's the dad who usually does it. But who says it has to be?" He quirks a brow, holding his phone up. "It says here that anyone can walk you down the aisle."

"Brody," I choke out, his words catching me off guard. "Are you sure?"

"The purpose is to give the bride to the groom," he reads from his phone. "So I don't see why I can't walk you down the aisle. It's just a symbolic way to wish the couple good health and happiness. And I'm fucking thrilled that you're about to marry my dad."

Before he can finish his sentence, I'm out of my chair and around the counter, pulling him into my arms. "Thank you," I cry. "I know you don't get it. You're too young. But this means the world to me."

"It's no big deal." Brody shrugs.

"It is to me." I pull back and kiss his cheek. "It means everything to me."

"Bahahahaha!" The sound of Olivier's cries through the baby monitor has me taking a deep breath and wiping my tears.

"I better go get him."

"I can do it," Brody offers. "I've been so busy with school, I haven't spent much time with him. Now that I'm out of school for the summer, I get to spend some time with my little bro. You guys plan the wedding. I'll get it."

Before either of us can argue, Brody retreats from the kitchen.

"You heard him," Ben says. "Let's plan a wedding."

"Thank you again for doing this." I walk over to Brody and kiss his cheek gently, so I don't get makeup on his face.

"Savy." He shakes his head. "Walking you down the aisle is the least I could do. After all, it was you who brought my dad back to me. Gave me a home and a family. I love my dad and my mom...I mean, she's going through shit, and I hate that we're not close, but I still love her. But it was you who saw past the immature kid with a cigarette in his mouth. If it weren't for you, I don't even want to think where I'd be. You brought our family together, and I'm damn lucky that I'll get to call you my stepmom."

"Stop it," I choke out. "You're going to ruin my makeup."

Brody chuckles. "Sorry."

"I know stepmom is the politically correct term, and I know you have a mom, but please know that you're not just my stepson. You might not be my blood, but I still consider you my son."

"Savannah!" the wedding planner whisper-yells. "C'mon, you're up."

"Coming!" I yell back as Brody extends his arm for me to take.

"C'mon, Mom," he murmurs softly. "Let's go *officially* make you a Fields."

BENJAMIN

"You look stunning." I hold my wife in my arms while we dance in front of our family and friends. "If I wasn't so hell-bent on getting us out of here and consummating our marriage, I would insist you walk back down that aisle again."

Savannah throws her head back with a laugh and I memorize that sound. I find myself doing that often. Memorizing her features even though I get to spend the rest of my life with her.

Take her walking down the aisle, for instance. The way her dress fit, snug around her body, plumping her breasts up, the soft smile spread across her face while approaching me on my son's arm, her blue eyes looking into mine as she recited her vows, promising to love me forever, will be engrained in my head and heart forever. Today was the day I married not only the love of my life and best friend but my soulmate.

"I think once was enough." She leans in and presses a kiss to my lips. "But I am looking forward to peeling this tux off of you later."

I spin her around and when we get near the edge of the floor, our one-year-old son yells out, "Mama! Dada!" waving his tiny hand from where he sits on his brother's lap.

"I owe you so much," I tell her, pulling her tighter into my arms. "Had you not strolled into that gym, I don't even want to imagine where my life would be without you."

"Well, it's a good thing you never have to," she says, kissing me again. "Your strings are tied to mine for life, and there's no getting this knot out."

"There's no one I'd rather be tied to than you."

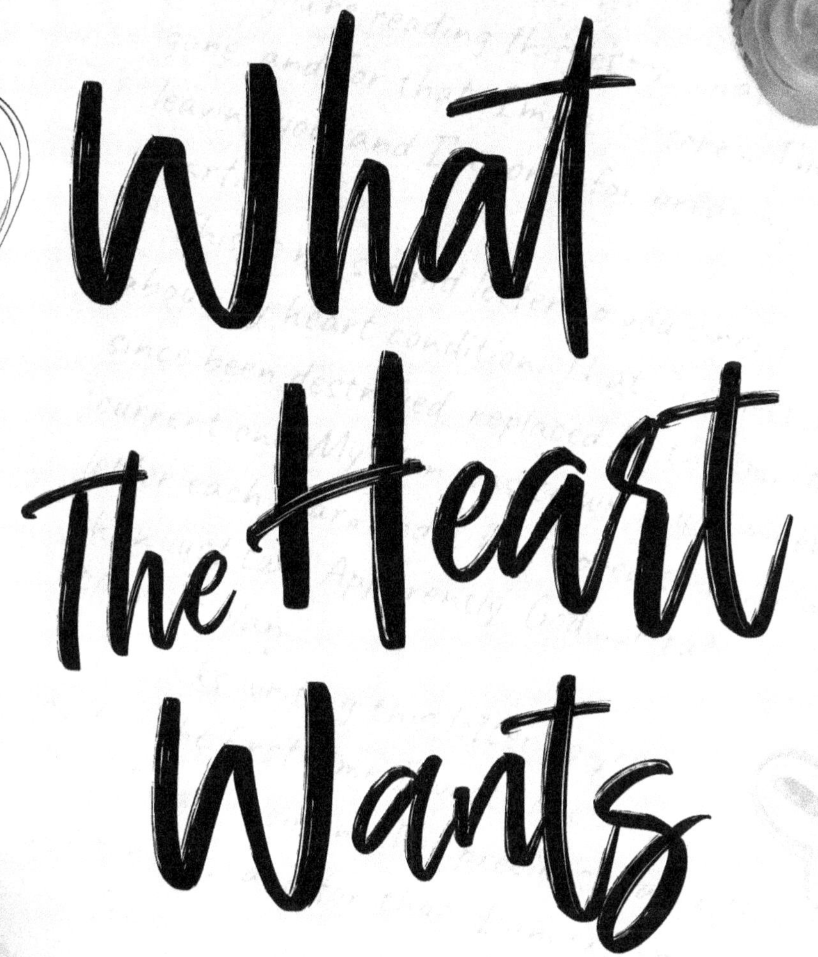

What The Heart Wants

And my heart wants them both...

"DO YOU HEAR THAT?" I WHISPER, LISTENING FOR ANY sound outside our bedroom. My question forces my husband's eyes to open. He was already half awake, thanks to me asking him the same question a few minutes ago, but since it's only five in the morning, he was probably hoping I'd fall back asleep.

Peter shakes his head and smiles as he pulls me toward him. "I don't hear anything," he says, giving me a soft kiss. My belly erupts with butterflies, the way it always does when my husband kisses me. It's been that way since the first time he kissed me ten years ago.

Without breaking our kiss, he rolls us over so I'm on my back as he hovers above. "Merry Christmas, Aubs," he murmurs against my lips as he pushes his groin against me.

I wrap my arms around his neck, fully on board with some early morning sex, when the noise I've been waiting for finally arrives.

"Mommy! Daddy! Santa came!" Evie shrieks. Two seconds later, she and her brother, Miles, burst into our room, both of their faces lit up with excitement.

"There's a gazillion presents!" Miles says as Peter rolls off of me, groaning even as he breaks into a smile. He's already switching to dad mode.

"We musta been sooo good," Evie adds.

"The best," I agree.

"Go check it all out, and your mom and I will be right there," Peter tells the kids, who nod and race out, their tiny feet padding across the tiled floor.

"To be continued," Peter says, kissing me softly.

After using the bathroom, we head out to the living room, where we find the kids attacking their stockings, candy and small toys strewn about, while they wait for us to open presents.

Peter plops onto the couch and pulls me down with him, wrapping his arms around me and kissing my cheek. "All right, who's opening the first gift?" he asks with a huge smile on his face.

"Me!" both kids exclaim.

We pass the morning with the kids opening present after present. Peter is a culinary professor, and I work at my grandma's bakery, so we're not rich by any means, but we love the holidays and always make sure to put money aside to make them special.

"Mommy, this one says your name," Evie reports, bringing the small gift over to me. "Look…" She thrusts it at me. "It has an M for Mommy."

"You must've been really good," Miles says. "Rory said mommies and daddies don't get presents because they're too old." Rory is Miles's best friend in his preschool class.

"Oh, your mom was very good," Peter says with a knowing smile. "Open it."

I take the box from Evie and unwrap it, a little giddy since Peter and I agreed not to exchange gifts this year due to money being tight. Inside the flat box are several pieces of paper. "What did you do?" I ask as I read the words over and over again.

"It's a two-week trip to France to study with some of the top culinary chefs," Peter says, making me gasp in shock.

"Pete…" My heart thumps wildly in my chest. "How did you…? How can we afford this?"

He lifts his hand and cups the side of my face. "I used my connections at work. You leave in three weeks, and I'm using my time off to stay with the kids."

I look over at our four-year-old twins. I've never been away from them that long. But this opportunity is once in a lifetime. "Thank you. You're the best husband ever."

His smile stretches across his face. "I love you, Aubs. I just want —" His words are abruptly cut off, his features suddenly twisting into a pained expression. His eyes meet mine, a strange mixture of shock and…fear?

"Pete, what's wrong?" I ask, confused.

"I…I think…my…chest…heart," he stammers.

He clutches his chest as I try to piece together his words. His chest…His heart…"Pete…"

"Daddy, what's wrong?" Evie asks, toys forgotten.

"Daddy, does your belly hurt?" Miles asks.

"My heart," Peter repeats, and it finally clicks. *His heart!* "Something's wrong…" He looks from the kids to me, and my own heart feels like it's about to stop beating. This can't be good.

"Kids, go play in your room for a few minutes. Daddy isn't feeling well," I tell them, trying to keep my voice calm so they don't freak out—which is damn hard to do since on the inside, I'm the one freaking the hell out.

The kids, evidently too worried and scared to argue, run off.

"Bree, I need you to call 9-1-1." Peter's face is ashen, and his voice is breathy, like it's hard to even speak. I grab my phone from the end table and then do as he says and call the emergency number. As I'm telling them all that I know—my husband is having chest pain and says it's his heart—my eyes stay on Peter, praying they get here quickly. I'm giving them our address when Peter looks at me with tears in his eyes, mouthing *I love you.*

His eyes close, and I scream into the phone to hurry. They ask me to stay on the line, so I put them on speaker, so I can use two hands to grab my husband's shoulders and try to wake him up. "Pete, please, wake up. Help is on the way. Just hang in there…"

His body jerks slightly and then goes still, and I don't know how I know, but I *know* his heart is no longer beating. I can feel it, as if my own is connected to his. As if our souls are one and he's taking mine with him.

I lay my head on his chest, trying to hear something, even the faint *thump, thump* of a heartbeat, but there's nothing.

"Pete, please don't do this," I cry, begging my husband to come back. Unable to sit and do nothing, I try to press my palms against his chest like I've seen them do in those doctor shows.

But nothing happens.

The paramedics arrive, and everything from that point is a blur of chaos. They try for so long to resuscitate him, but it's clear he's already gone. My husband—the love of my life—and my children's father, isn't going to wake up. As realization settles in, I break down, sobbing uncontrollably. One of the paramedics pulls me into her arms to comfort me while another explains that they will be transporting Pete to the hospital since that's standard procedure.

The paramedic asks if there's someone she can call, and that's when I remember our kids are here. I pull out of her embrace and run into Miles's room first, where I find both kids huddled together, my son's arms wrapped protectively around his sister. Both are crying softly, and when they look up at me, I can see it in their eyes —*they know.*

But still, I say it—more for me than them. As if I need to say and hear the words to accept that they're real. "Daddy's gone," I tell them, dropping to the floor and pulling my babies into my arms. "He went to heaven," I choke out.

The kids and I sit together in our silent, tear-filled grief for God knows how long, until my grandma shows up for our traditional Christmas breakfast.

"What's wrong?" she asks, concern etched in her features. "Was the ambulance leaving from here?" From the time I was five years old, my grandma—or as my kids refer to her, Nana—raised me as her own when my parents were deemed unfit. Since grandpa had passed before I was born, it was always just the two of us up until the time I met Peter.

"Nana!" Evie cries, getting up and running to her. "Daddy's gone!" She throws her tiny arms around her great-grandma's neck and sobs. "His heart hurt him, and he went to heaven."

My grandma's eyes meet mine, liquid filled to the brim, and I nod in confirmation before my own tears well up again and I hide my face in Miles's neck, wanting to go to sleep and wake up to find all of this was a nightmare.

Bree,

If you're reading this letter, that means I'm gone, and for that, I'm so, so sorry. I'm sorry for leaving you, and I'm sorry for breaking your heart.

This is my second letter to you since finding out about my heart condition. That first letter has since been destroyed, replaced by this most current one. My plan was to write you a new letter each year, and I had hoped to write more than just two. Apparently, God...or fate...had a different plan.

It sucks writing this letter to you as much as it sucked the first time I wrote one, but it means that I was given another precious year with you and our kids, and for that, I am extremely grateful.

I know what you're thinking...What heart condition? When I first experienced some exercise-induced symptoms, I mentioned it to my doctor and he had me go in for testing. Once my heart condition was confirmed, I debated telling you—and it tore me up not to—but I didn't want you to have to carry the weight of my diagnosis on your shoulders. I expect you're angry with me for keeping you in the dark, but every day, I had to live with wondering when my last day would come, and I didn't want you to live with that same fear.

If it's any comfort, please know, it's a rare heart condition and not genetic. Our babies are safe. But if you want to get them tested for your own peace of mind, I've included everything you'll need to know, including my doctor's information.

I have so much I want to say to you, but I'll start with how much I love you. You are my entire world. You and our kids. The day I saw you baking in the kitchen at school, your eyes filled with such passion, I knew you were "the one." I shouldn't have felt that way since you were so much younger than me, but still, despite the age difference, despite you being my student, I knew you were the woman I would one day create a life with. And as I write this letter, I can't help thinking about our life together. Every step of the way, you've made me the happiest man in the world. From you agreeing to go on a date with me, to moving in together, to getting engaged, to saying I do, and then giving me the two most beautiful, amazing babies.

Bree, I need you to know that you made me so damn happy. Every day, my world has been brighter, happier, better because of you. And not just as my wife, but as my best friend, my soul mate, and as the mother of my children. My favorite thing to do—besides being inside you (sorry, but I can't write a goodbye letter without mentioning that)—is to watch you with Miles and Evie. Your patience and kindness and the way you love and care for them is such a turn-on. As I'm writing this letter, Evie has an ear infection, and you're, of course, lying with her in bed, soothing her and making sure she's okay. Because that's what you do...take care of us. Every day, since the moment I made you mine, you've taken care of our kids and me.

Your heart is so big and full of love, and I feel like the luckiest man to be loved by you. To be kissed by you, to be touched by you. To share this life with you for as long as I have. There's no one I would rather have spent my life's journey with than you. I HATE that if you're reading this, it means our journey has been suddenly cut short, but please know, I have no regrets, because I got to live the BEST DAMN LIFE with you by my side.

Even though I'm gone, I need you to promise that you will continue to share your big heart with others. You're still so young, and you have so much love to give. Please don't close yourself off to all of life's possibilities. I know that as you read this letter, the soil that's covering my casket is still soft, and you're not close to thinking about moving on. But this is my only opportunity to say what I need you to hear: Once you're done mourning, I want you to move on. It took my mother twenty years after my dad passed to carve out a new life for herself, and I hated that for her. That she spent all those years alone. The day she met Stephen, is the day she finally allowed herself to give her heart to another man. And that is the day I saw my mom happy again for the first time since she lost my dad.

I don't want that for you. Or for our kids. I want you to find love. Love hard and let yourself be loved in return. Find a man who is deserving of your big heart and let him love you, Aubs. Because you deserve to be loved. My biggest fear is that you'll end up alone, and I want so much more for you. My second biggest fear is that our kids won't have a father figure in their lives. You know I lost my dad when I was ten, and I missed him so much. Please know that if you find someone who loves you and our kids, you have my blessing to move forward and create a life with him. Get married, have more babies, BE HAPPY.

Along with this letter is the information for a savings account I set aside that will cover the funeral costs and replace my income for a little while. It isn't much, but it should be enough so you can keep working at the bakery with your grandma, doing what you love.

I'm so sorry that you now have to do it on your own, but it makes me feel a little better to know you have your grandma and my mom and stepdad. Let them help you.

I have two letters I'm including for the kids. I hate that they're so young and probably won't even remember me, but I know you'll tell them about me and show them pictures, so they'll know how much I loved them and never wanted to leave them.

Fuck, writing this letter sucks, but I imagine it's not as hard as you reading it. Please don't hold on to your anger towards me for not telling you. Please understand that I was protecting you. I love you so damn much, and it feels like, no matter how long this letter is, my words will never be enough. Just know that you are my world, and I would've given anything to still be here with you and our babies. And when you're feeling alone, read this letter and look at our photos to remind yourself of the incredible love we once shared. As long as you hold a piece of me in your heart, I will always live on, just as I will live on through the beautiful babies that our love created.

I love you, Bree.

-Pete

CHAPTER ONE

AUBREE

"You are going to have the most amazing time!" I pull my son into my arms and hug him tightly, hating that for the first time, he and his sister will be away from me for most of the summer, and not just for the night. "I love you and I'm going to miss you like crazy."

"Mom, I love you, and I'll miss you too, but you're going to hug me to death." Miles chokes his words through a laugh that sends my heart soaring. Nothing is better than the sound of my children laughing, especially when you've lost as many loved ones as I have. Every smile, every laugh, every moment feels like a precious gift— one that can be taken at any moment.

I mentally shake myself, refusing to go there.

"Sorry," I say, loosening my hold on Miles. "Be good for Grammy and Papa, okay?"

"I will," he says with an eye roll that makes him appear more like a teenager than the almost nine-year-old he is.

"If you need anything, call me," I say to Evie next, who nods in understanding. "I love you more than red velvet cupcakes," I tell my baby girl, pulling her into a hug that damn near rivals the one I just gave Miles.

She giggles, hugging me back. "I love you more than chocolate fudge brownies."

Reluctantly, I let her go and take a deep breath, knowing they're in good hands with my in-laws, Beatrice and Stephen. They have a vacation home in Florida where they'll be spending the summer, and this year, since it's the first summer since my grandmother passed away, they've offered to take the kids with them so they won't be bored at the coffeehouse.

I told them I could put them in camp—although it would be tight money-wise—but the kids really wanted to go to Florida, and as much as I hate the thought of not seeing them for such a long time, I couldn't say no. Not when they were beyond excited. I can't really blame them since their grandparents' vacation home is directly on the beach. They also have a pool and hot tub, and they'll be spending a lot of time sailing everywhere aboard their yacht. Beatrice also told them that if, at any time, they feel homesick, she would bring them right back home to me.

"Thank you for taking them," I tell Beatrice, now giving her a hug.

"You don't have to thank me for spending time with my grandbabies," she says. "Enjoy the bit of time to yourself," she murmurs. "Take a bath, read a book, go out with Lacey, have fun...*Get laid.*"

She winks, and I choke out a watery laugh at her last demand—at the fact that my sixty-five-year-old mother-in-law is telling me to have sex, and it's not the first time she's suggested it.

"I'll definitely take a bath and read a book," I tell her pointedly.

She sighs, knowing the getting laid part isn't going to happen, despite her suggesting it every time we talk. I get she wants me to honor Pete's wishes and move forward, the way she finally did after her husband passed away, but it took her twenty years...It hasn't even been five years since Peter passed away. It's not that I don't ever plan to move forward with my life, but I'm just not ready yet.

With one last hug to the four of them, they get into the town car and take off for their summer adventure, leaving me standing here, wondering what the hell I'm going to do without my babies all summer long.

"You okay?" Lacey, my best friend, asks, wrapping her arm around me for a side hug as we watch my entire world drive away.

"When did they grow up?" I choke out, feeling like my heart's in the car with my kids. "Only yesterday they were just learning to walk and talk, and now they're leaving me for the entire summer like it's no big deal."

"They'll have a blast," she reminds me. "And they'll always be your babies. But they are growing up, and it's okay to give them some room to grow and experience."

I sigh, knowing she's right. Ever since we lost Peter, I've kept them close, probably too close, but when you watch your husband die in front of you—and four years later, your grandma dies from a heart attack—you tend to realize just how fragile life really is. Even though Peter said the condition wasn't genetic, I still had the kids evaluated, not wanting to take any chances. Thankfully, as of now, they're both healthy with no signs of heart problems, but it doesn't stop me from worrying.

"How long is Sammy gone for, again?" I ask as we walk toward the back door of the coffeehouse. Sammy is Lacey's fifteen-year-old son—she and her husband, Samuel, got pregnant our senior year of high school. It was a shock, but they handled it better than I would have at that age. That's for sure.

"Football camp is for four weeks, but once he gets back, he'll have practice every day. Which means..." Lacey grins mischievously. "It's you and me all summer, since my darling husband is eyeballs-deep in a project he's working on and won't be coming up for air any time soon." Her husband is an architect and from what she's told me, an amazing one at that.

"Don't even think about it," I say, giving her the side-eye, already knowing where she's going with this.

"What?" she says innocently.

"You know what. Did Beatrice put you up to this? I swear the woman is more determined to get me laid than I am."

Lacey cracks up. "She also gets laid more than you do."

"Truth." I cringe, not wanting to think about my in-laws' sex life.

We head back inside Heart's Coffeehouse and Bakery—our family surname of "Heart" prominently on display. It was my grandparents' pride and joy, left to me when my grandma passed away. She and my grandfather opened it just over fifty years ago and lived in the apartments directly above it, both of them running it together until a tragic car accident claimed his life.

With the coffeehouse being my grandparents' favorite place to be, I practically grew up here, and now, since it's *my* favorite place, my kids have grown up here as well. Just like my grandparents, the kids and I live in the apartments just above the bakery.

After Peter died, I couldn't keep the home we owned, at least not without stretching myself too thin. And, if I'm being honest, I couldn't handle the constant onslaught of images resulting from that fateful morning. So, we moved into one of the apartments above the coffeehouse, allowing us to be close to my grandma, while also enabling me to take the money I made off the sale of the house and put it into savings. It was also convenient since I have to be here in the early mornings and evenings several times a week to bake and open the shop. Since my grandma passed away, Lacey has taken over opening in the morning so I can get the kids to school. When they say it takes a village, they really aren't kidding, and I'm extremely fortunate to have the best village helping me raise my kids.

Lacey bumps my shoulder with hers. "So, I was thinking…after we close, we could get dressed up, put on some makeup, and go out to Wine and Dine. Make it a ladies' night out."

I internally groan, even though I knew this was coming. And

since I know that Lacey isn't going to drop it until she gets me out, I decide to get it over with. "Sure," I tell her. "Sounds good."

She squeals in delight. "Yes! We're going to have so much fun. We should go shopping too, since I know your wardrobe could use a major overhaul."

I glare her way. "Now you're pushing your luck." I hated shopping before I had my kids, but now, with my curvy mom bod (Okay, fine, it's not *all* from my kids. Some of it is because I love sweets and spend most of my time baking and trying new recipes) shopping is my least favorite thing to do. It's not that I hate my body—I'm okay with having curves, but it's hard to shop for clothes when it feels like everything that's cute is meant for a size three.

"Fine." She raises her hands, waving the metaphorical white flag. "But we should still go shopping soon."

The rest of our day is spent serving customers. The coffeehouse offers all types of drinks, as well as freshly baked goods. I make a variety of items, depending on my mood, and once we sell out, that's it. Because Heart's has been around for so long, we stay busy and almost always sell out before it's closing time.

Lacey and I run the front together, and I have a couple college students come in for a few hours every morning to help with the rush—and sometimes in the afternoons—if I have something to do. Since all the baking gets done ahead of time, when it's three o'clock, all we have to do is clean before we lock up.

We agree to meet at Wine and Dine at eight o'clock—which means I'll be up early tomorrow to get some baking in since I won't get it done this evening—and then Lacey takes off to get ready.

After enjoying a nice, hot, quiet bubble bath, I video-call my kids to check on them. Of course, they answer with huge smiles on their faces, telling me they've arrived—which I already knew since Beatrice is amazing and has texted me every step of the way—and are heading to the beach house to get settled in. I remind them to behave and tell them that I love them before I let them go, promising myself that I won't be that annoying helicopter parent.

Until now, neither of them had been given electronics, but since they would be away—and I was freaking out—Beatrice bought them each an iPad as an early birthday present, so we'd be able to video-call and message all summer.

After spending a few hours getting lost in a romance novel, I search my closet to find something to wear. All the way in the back, I find a dress I haven't worn in years, but when I give it a good look, and memories surface from the last time I wore it—for Peter's and my five-year wedding anniversary—I hang it back up and go with a pair of jeans and a flowy top, throwing on heels at the last second, so Lacey won't completely kill me.

With my blond hair blow-dried and thrown up into a high pony-tail, and a bit of makeup donning my face, I head out to meet Lacey. It's a warm night in New York, so I grab a taxi and let it take me the mile to the bar we're meeting at.

She's already seated when I arrive and has ordered us a bottle of wine to share, along with a couple of appetizers to munch on. The live music is chill, and with the glass of wine in my hand, I relax and enjoy myself.

"Thank you," I tell her as we eat, drink, and sing along to the music. "You were right. I needed to get out."

She smiles softly and pats my thigh. "That's what best friends are for."

A few minutes later, she nods toward a table of guys glancing our way. "See anyone you like?" She waggles her brows playfully. "I bet you can have your pick."

"Nope." I shake my head without giving them a second glance. "I'm good right here."

She lets out an exasperated huff but, thankfully, drops it.

We hang out, ordering a dinner to split, along with another bottle of wine, and once we're tipsy and full, we get up and dance to the music. It feels good to let loose. Until masculine hands grip my hips, and a warm breath leans in too close. "Can I have this dance?"

I turn around, backing out of his touch. He's taller than my five-foot-six, maybe six feet, dressed in a typical New York-style corporate suit, clean shaven and good looking, but when I look at him, I feel nothing. No butterflies, no chemistry. Nothing. Not like how I felt the first time I locked eyes with Peter. When I knew at that moment, before any words were even spoken, that he was the one.

Some people think I'm full of it. They don't believe that a person can know they've found the one without speaking, but I know how I felt, and I know Peter felt the same way. And I don't care that everyone thinks I should move on—that even my late husband wants me to move forward. I refuse to settle for anything less than what I felt with my husband. And if that means I end up alone for the rest of my life, then so be it. I know what it feels like to be in love and to be loved, and I would rather be alone than feel anything less.

"No, thank you," I tell him politely.

He opens his mouth to argue or perhaps to accept my response, but I shake my head and walk away before he gets the chance to do either.

I feel Lacey at my back, silently chastising me for turning the guy down, but she doesn't comment, knowing it won't change my mind.

"I think I'm ready to head home," I tell her, taking a sip of my wine. "It's getting late, and I have to get up early."

"Okay," she says, smiling sadly at me. "Sam is going to swing by to pick me up. We'll give you a ride home."

"Thanks."

An hour later, I'm home with a clean face, heel-free, and in my pajamas. With the kids gone, the house is quiet—too quiet. And like the masochist I am, I pull up the videos on my phone and watch the ones from when Peter was alive—Halloweens, birthdays, trips to the park. I skip over the Christmases, unable to watch those. Even nearly five years later, it's still too hard to think about the holiday.

My heart both hurts and soars as I watch him laugh and smile. When I finally cry myself to sleep, I dream about him and the life we were supposed to have together. And like every dream I have about him, he's there, telling me, *showing* me how much he loves me. When my alarm clock goes off in the morning, I wake up cold and alone, wishing I could close my eyes and go back to sleep, so I could be back in his warm embrace, where I belong. Because even though I'm not ready to move on, some days I really hate being cold and alone.

CHAPTER TWO

HAYDEN

office," Carly, the receptionist who handles everything on our floor, says over the intercom. "And, fair warning, he's in a ripe mood," she adds wryly, making me chuckle.

"Thanks, I'll be right there."

I finish the email I'm typing to the property appraiser's office and then close out of the program, taking a deep breath to mentally prepare for whatever my father needs to speak to me about. I consider texting my sister to ask if she knows what's going on, but ever since Dad announced he's retiring at the end of the year and will decide then who will be stepping into his shoes as the new CEO, my sister's competitive streak has taken over. Instead of working together, she thinks we're competing against each other.

"Hayden, did Carly tell you that I needed to see you?" my dad asks, walking into my office not even thirty seconds later.

"Yeah, I was just about to come see you."

Since he's now dropped into the visitor seat on the other side of my desk, I make no move to get up.

"I need you to put whatever you're working on to the side and handle the wellness center project," he says, getting straight to the point.

"You know I'm in the middle of the—"

"And now you're handling *this*," he says, cutting me off. "Whatever you're working on, give it to someone else or put it on hold. This takes priority."

I sigh in annoyance, then remember something…"I thought Gretchen was handling the wellness center." At our Monday morning meeting, my older sister said she had it all under control. And since her main goal in life is to convince our dad that she should be given the CEO position, she would never agree to hand a project as important as this one over to me. She practically begged to be given the lead on this project.

Dad clears his throat. "She is…"

"So you want me to go behind her back?" I raise a single brow in question. "If Gretchen finds out, she's going to be pissed." My sister is the most competitive person I know, and my moving in on her project will be the equivalent of starting WWIII.

"If we don't close on the deal soon, Atwater Investments will pull their backing," Dad explains. "Your sister fucked up, and I'm going to deal with her later, but right now, we need to save this deal."

I nod in understanding. "All right, so what's the issue?"

Dad spends the next thirty minutes getting me caught up to speed. According to him, the building owner passed away recently, and his son inherited it. When he put it up for sale, not wanting to deal with it, we put in a bid so we could build a state-of-the-art wellness center and spa.

In order for the deal to go through, though, the tenants had to agree to be bought out of their leases, and all have done so, except for one. And since New York is all about the tenant's rights, we can't move forward without the agreement of this tenant.

"If it's only one tenant, couldn't we just finalize the sale and, once the tenant's lease is up, not renew it?" I ask the obvious question. How long could the lease be for? The standard length is one year.

"The lease is for ninety-nine years," Dad says, shocking the hell out of me.

"I'm sorry, what?" I choke out a laugh. "Are you serious?"

Dad glares, not seeing the humor in this like I do. "There are forty-nine years left. I need you to make the tenant see reason. I don't care what it takes. If we lose the contract with Atwater, our reputation will take a huge hit. You know how big of a player he is in the game."

Not to point out the obvious but..."Shouldn't this have been handled *before* you guys put in thousands of man-hours and dollars toward this project?" Rule number one in real estate is to have all your ducks in a row before you bring a deal to the table. Something like this should've been considered beforehand.

"I thought it was," Dad growls. "Gretchen said it was under control, but it clearly wasn't. And then she hid it from me, thinking she could handle it even though she was in over her head. If it hadn't been for the building owner following up and me being given the call by mistake, I wouldn't even know about the issue."

"Did you try to speak to the tenant?" In my entire life, I've never seen my dad not get his way, ever.

"Of course, I did."

"And...?" I prompt.

"And it ended with the cops being called and me being cited for trespassing and harassment."

I hold back a laugh, imagining all this going down. "And you think I'm going to magically convince this person to break their ninety-nine-year lease?"

Dad scrubs his palms over his face, then leans over the desk and locks eyes with me. "Yes, I do. Because if you do, come December, you will be the new CEO."

And now, he's got my attention.

"Just like that? If I get this tenant to let us buy out their lease, you're really going to retire and appoint me the new CEO?" Dad has claimed he's going to retire several times now, but it never ends up happening. He's too much of a control freak to hand over the reins.

"Yes, you handle this, and the position is yours." He extends his hand for a shake, and I meet him halfway.

"Consider it done."

Sucks for Gretchen, but her fuckup is my gain. And it *will* be my gain because at the end of the day, there isn't anything I won't do to ensure that I'm the CEO of Shea Real Estate Investments. I've been dreaming of this and working my ass off for it my entire adult life, and nothing will stop me from achieving my dream. The thought of one day taking over and finally being out from under my dad's thumb—being able to run things my way—is the only thing that keeps me going.

After Dad sends the files over, I spend the rest of the day combing through everything, so I'm prepared. You never go into a battle without knowing your enemy, and since this tenant is the only thing keeping me from becoming the new CEO, she's now my number one enemy.

I WALK UP, AND MY EYES ARE IMMEDIATELY DRAWN TO the pastel pink and yellow awning with matching tables and chairs outside. Across the top reads Heart's Coffeehouse and Bakery: Coffee And Treats Made From The Heart. There's a line curving around the corner, and as the door opens and closes, I catch a whiff of the addictive aroma of espresso mixed with something…sweet.

I had planned to go in and speak to the owner, but since it's so busy, I get in the back of the line to check the place out. The line moves quickly, and once I'm inside, a few people away from the counter, I assess the situation. The walls, a pink and yellow floral pattern with some green mixed in, remind me of visiting my grandma at Martha's Vineyard when I was a kid. It's clear the shop hasn't been updated in years, yet it's clean and inviting—also like my grandmother's home.

Damn, I miss that woman. She was probably the only sane person in my family.

The tables and booths are occupied by people drinking coffee, eating sweets, and conversing. When I step up to the counter, an assortment of pastries, muffins, and cupcakes line the inside of the display—all of them looking freshly baked and mouthwatering.

When I glance up, bright-blue eyes meet mine, accompanied by a soft smile. "Good morning, what can I get you?" When I hear her melodic and mesmerizing voice, I forget where I am and what I'm doing for a second.

"Umm," I choke out, mentally shaking myself out of the trance this woman—from her voice and smile alone—has put me in.

You're here for a reason, I remind myself. To speak to the owner and convince her to let us buy her out of her lease. "Are you the owner?"

Her smile widens, and two dimples make an appearance. If I thought she was beautiful before, I was wrong. The woman is down-right gorgeous.

"That would be me," she says. "I'm Aubree Heart. How can I help you?"

I open my mouth to tell her I have business to discuss with her, but the words won't come out. I'm too enraptured by her looks, by her smile, and by those goddamn dimples. It's like some weird spell has been cast over me.

After a few awkward moments, she laughs, the sound hitting me like an arrow straight to my fucking chest. *Holy shit, what the hell is wrong with me?* Is the coffee laced with something strong enough that the smell alone is causing me to have some strange out-of-body experience?

"Have you been here before?" she asks. "If not, I can make some recommendations..."

Someone behind me clears their throat, and I realize I'm holding up the line.

"Can I, uh, get..." I glance at the display but can't really focus. My head is fuzzy. "Uh, a dozen cupcakes...and...a coffee?"

"Sure. Any particular flavors?"

"Any is fine."

As she rings me up—and I stare at her like a dumbass—I notice that she doesn't have a ring on her finger, and from my research, she isn't married. My gaze moves to her heart-shaped face. I wonder what it would feel like to kiss her, what her plump and shiny lips would taste like. Is she a quiet kisser, or would she make sweet little sounds as I nibble on her lips? Her blue eyes meet mine as she hands me the box of cupcakes and my coffee, and I get lost in their warmth. With my order in hand, I'm forced to move to the side, so I head out, wondering what the hell just happened.

I spend the rest of the morning researching the business, the property...the owner. From the little I could find, her grandparents opened the coffeehouse fifty years ago, and after they both passed away, she inherited it. She also lives in the building, which means she's not only the business owner but the damn tenant—a fact I missed when I initially researched her. Her apartment lease is up in six months, so that's not the issue. It's the forty-nine-year lease on the business that's the problem. By the time I'm done and ready to head back to Heart's, my head is back on straight, and I have my priorities in order. Nothing will stand in the way of my future—not even a gorgeous, blue-eyed, twin-dimpled woman.

THE SECOND I STEP INTO THE COFFEEHOUSE, AUBREE greets me with those damn blue eyes and dimples. I quickly glance around and see that the shop is empty, which is what I was hoping for by showing up ten minutes before they closed.

"Hey, you came in this morning, right? Coffee and cupcakes. Were they so good you're back for seconds?" She winks playfully as she wipes down the counter, and my dick, like the traitor it is, stretches behind my slacks.

"Actually, I was hoping I could talk to you." I step toward her and reach out my hand. "My name is Hayden—" I begin, but before I can finish what I'm trying to say, a woman flies around the corner, moaning like she's being fucked. Only instead of a man between her legs, there's a brownie between her fingers.

"Oh my God, Bree. These brownies are seriously the best thing I've ever had." When she realizes Bree isn't alone, she laughs. "Sorry, but seriously, these are so good. Want to try one?" She grabs one from the case and puts it on a napkin. "They're Bree's new recipe." She hands it to me over the counter. "Prepare to be blown away."

I take the brownie and tear a piece off, popping it into my mouth, and holy fuck, she isn't wrong. The chocolatey goodness practically melts in my mouth.

"Right?" the woman says knowingly. "I'm going to bring some home for my husband. One bite of this, and I'm soooo getting laid." She waggles her brows, and Aubree slaps her playfully.

"Sorry about her," Aubree says, her cheeks tinting an adorable shade of pink. "We try to keep her hidden in the back, but sometimes, she escapes."

I chuckle at their banter. "It's all good."

"So are you back for another coffee?" she asks after a beat. "We're about to close, but I can whip you up something."

"Actually, I was wondering if you'd go out with me," I blurt out, shocking the hell out of myself.

Aubree's eyes go wide, and her friend chokes on the brownie she's inhaling. I consider backtracking since that's not why I came here. Instead, I find myself waiting for her answer, telling myself by going out with her, I can get close to her and see where her head's at.

"That's very sweet," Aubree says, yet I can already tell by her tone that there's a but coming. "But," she continues, smiling sadly, "no." She shakes her head. "You seem very nice." Since she doesn't know me, she can't possibly know whether I'm actually nice, so I know she's only saying that to let me down gently. I consider pushing the issue, but when I notice her eyes are a bit glassy, filled with what looks like genuine sadness, I nod and bow out.

"No worries," I tell her, and then to save face, I add, "Could I get a couple of coffees and brownies to go? They really are good."

She nods and then goes about getting my order ready while her friend rings me up. Once I have the drinks and food, I give her one last smile, then head out, wondering, not for the first time since I met this woman, what the hell has gotten into me. Until now, I've never had an issue separating work from my personal life, but something about this woman fucks with my head.

It's for the best. Had she agreed to go out with me, it would've blurred the lines. I need to keep my head on straight and figure out how to convince her to let us buy her out of this ridiculous lease, so my dad will appoint me the new CEO. That's been my goal since I was old enough to go work with him. It kept me motivated through four years of college and getting my real estate license. It's what's driven me the past eight years since I've graduated, and I have been working my way up, proving I'm capable of running Shea Real Estate Investments. Every day when I deal with my dad's shit, I remind myself there's a light at the end of the tunnel. I have a goal.

So then why the hell does her turning me down feel like it's not for the best?

Fuck.

CHAPTER THREE
AUBREE

"WHAT THE HELL IS WRONG WITH YOU?" LACEY SMACKS my arm and glares. "That man was hot with a capital H and wanted to take you out."

"I'm not read—" I begin, but the look in Lacey's eyes has me closing my mouth without finishing my thought.

"Bree…" She sighs. "You know I love you, right?"

I nod, mentally preparing for what she's about to say, knowing she won't hold back. She never does.

"It's been almost five years since you lost Peter, babe. And since then, I've watched you be both mom and dad to Miles and Evie, giving them damn near every ounce of you. And then, after Grandma Violet passed away, the little bit of you that was left went into this coffeehouse."

"That's because I'm all they have," I point out on the defense. "And this coffeehouse…" I wave my hand around to emphasize my point. "It's what pays the bills, keeps my kids' bellies fed, and a roof over our head. Pete is gone, my grandma is gone…All I have is *me*. My kids depend on *me*."

"And I get that," she says softly, "but at what point are you going to live for yourself? Get out there and date again?"

"I did date."

"You went on one date," she says, hitting me with a pointed look. "Two years ago."

"And it sucked." I pout, remembering how badly the date went.

"It was one date," she repeats. "And then you gave up. What's the point of any of this"—she waves her hand in the air—"if you're not happy? If you're merely going through the motions instead of actually living?"

"I am happy," I mutter.

Lacey pulls out her phone and taps away on it, and a few seconds later, she turns it around. And the image—the two smiling faces—on display, damn near has me stumbling back.

"This is you happy." She taps on the screen with her manicured nail. "When you were with Peter, you were happy. You were in love. Now, you're just existing. And as your best friend, I hate that for you."

As I stare at the picture, missing my husband something fierce, raw emotion clogs my throat, and I know she's right. I haven't been living. "I miss him," I whisper, wishing I could pull him out of that photo, wrap my arms around him, and seek comfort in his warm embrace. I try so hard to pick up the slack, to make up for being my children's only parent, but I'm tired. I miss having a partner, someone to be by my side, to hold me and kiss me and love me. I'm mentally exhausted and emotionally drained. But more than that, I'm lonely.

"I know you do," Lacey says, pocketing her phone and pulling me into a hug as tears fill my lids and slide down my cheeks. "But he didn't want this for you. He told you that himself. He wants you to find love."

I sigh into her hold. "Okay."

"Okay?" She pulls back and looks at me curiously as I swipe the tears off my face.

"Yeah, the next guy who asks me out, I'll say yes." It'll be hard to move forward, but I have to start somewhere because I don't want to feel like this forever.

A triumphant grin spreads across her face. "Oh, Bree, I am so holding you to that."

I roll my eyes, hiding how nervous the thought of actually going on a date makes me. "Whatever."

"Sam and I are going out to Le Petit tonight," she says, changing the subject. "You should join us."

As much as I appreciate the invite, the last thing I want to do is get dressed up, so I can play the third wheel on her romantic date with her husband because my best friend loves me and doesn't want me to be alone.

"I appreciate it, but I think I'm going home to soak in the tub, crack open a bottle of wine, and finish reading my book."

"Oh, look at you," she mocks. "Living on the edge."

CHAPTER FOUR
BRODY

"Damn, what's this brownie laced with? I can't stop eating it." I shove another bite into my mouth and wash it down with a sip of the equally delicious coffee—rich and creamy, strong but not too bitter. Sweet but not overly so…perfect.

"Wouldn't doubt it," Hayden, my roommate and best friend, mutters. "How the hell am I supposed to convince the owner that she needs to let us buy out her lease, which will mean closing down her coffeehouse, when she makes shit as good as this?"

He pops a piece of brownie into his mouth. "And you should've seen her." He groans and drops backward, looking up at the ceiling. "Gorgeous and sweet. Blond hair and blue eyes. Dimples, bro." His eyes lock with mine. "She's beautiful and sexy and fucking adorable all at the same time."

I chuckle at Hayden, never having seen him act like this before. We've been friends since elementary school—only being separated during high school when his parents sent him to boarding school— and have shared an apartment since our freshman year of college, so I've seen plenty of women come in and out of his life, but I've never seen him act like this before—especially not after only talking to her a couple of times.

"You ask her out?" He glares my way, and I bark out a laugh. "You struck out."

"It's for the best." He shrugs, playing off the rejection. "She's business, and the last thing I need is to mix business with pleasure."

My phone goes off with a text from my stepmom, Savy.

> MOM
>
> We miss you! Dinner tomorrow night? And bring Hayden.

"Dinner tomorrow night at my parents'?"

"Sure," he says. "Maybe I can pick your dad's brain as to how I should handle this lease situation."

"So that's all she is? A work complication? You're not going to try again?"

"Nah." He takes a sip of his coffee. "I need to focus on the endgame. Plenty of other fish in the sea."

I eye the box of brownies. "Maybe I'll stop by the coffeehouse and pick up a dessert. I bet Savy and Penelope would love some of these brownies." Both my stepmom and sister have major sweet tooths.

My words, of course, get Hayden's attention, but before he gives anything away, he schools his features. "You can do whatever you want."

"Like ask her out?" I taunt.

"Go for it. But don't be surprised when the only thing you leave with is a box of brownies."

"WELCOME TO HEART'S. WHAT CAN I GET YOU?" THE second my eyes land on the woman—the one with the blond hair, blue eyes, and sexy as fuck dimples—I know this is the woman Hayden was referring to...and holy shit, he was dead-on. She's beyond gorgeous. When I mentioned asking her out, I was only messing with Hayden, but now, it's on.

"A half-dozen brownies..." I eye the display, checking out the delicious sweets. "A few of those cupcakes..." I point at the vanilla ones my younger sister will love. "And your number," I say, giving her my panty-dropping smile women can never turn down. Forward much? Maybe. But I know what I want, and in the business I'm in, having the confidence to back up the brains is the difference between those who dream and those who achieve.

Aubree—or Bree as it's mentioned on her name tag—splutters. "Excuse me?"

"Brownies, cupcakes, your number...in any order." I extend my hand. "My name is Brody Fields, and I want to take you out."

Another woman—who appears to be around the same age as Bree—yeah, I'm going with Bree since we'll soon be on a personal level—chokes on whatever she's drinking.

"Did you put him up to this?" Bree hisses at her friend, her hands going to her hips. "This is not—"

"I swear, I didn't." Her friend raises her hands in a placating gesture.

Bree turns back around to look at me. "She didn't tell you to ask me out?" Before I can respond, she leans over the counter and whispers, "Did she pay you?"

I quirk a brow in confusion while her friend barks out a laugh. "I can honestly say she did neither." Why the hell would this beautiful woman need someone to buy her a date anyway?

Bree glances back at her friend, who shrugs, then, with a sigh, she looks at me. "All right, I'll go out with you," she mutters, making her friend snort out a laugh.

When my brows rise, wondering what the hell is going on, she flinches. "Sorry," she says, perking up slightly. "If you don't want to go out with me anymore, I'll understand."

"Oh, no, you don't," her friend says. "He asked you out, so you're going out with him." She rips a piece of paper and scribbles something across it. "This is Bree's number. Text or call to make plans. She's going out with you."

I look at Bree, who almost looks sick at the thought of going out with me. Did I forget to brush my teeth this morning? I glance down, and I'm dressed in one of my usual suits. I recently got a haircut, and I shaved a couple of days ago, so I'm not too shabby.

"Here are your treats," her friend says. I glance down at her name tag and see her name is Lacey. "Don't forget to call or text." She hits me with a pointed look, and as I walk away, I can't help but wonder what the hell just happened.

It's been twenty-four hours since Bree, er, I guess her friend, gave me her number, and I've considered whether or not to call. On the one hand, she's gorgeous, and I'd love to take her out, but on the other hand, she didn't seem all that into it. It was almost as if her friend was forcing her to go out with me.

I'm not a playboy by any means, but I've been told I'm a good-looking guy. I've never had a problem drawing the attention of the opposite sex—or in my college days, the same sex. (What can I say? I'm an equal opportunist.) So I'm not really sure what to make of what happened back in the coffee shop with Bree. If it was her or me…Guess there's only one way to find out.

I pull out my phone and type out a message, then erase it. Then after a few minutes, I glance at the clock and see it's just after noon, so the coffeehouse is still open. Without second-guessing myself, I let my assistant, Hillary, know I'm leaving for a late lunch and head out of the building with my laptop bag in hand. Since the coffeehouse is several blocks from where Fields Enterprises is located— the headquarters for the investment company I own with my dad and run—I grab a cab. Thank goodness I didn't walk because we're not even halfway there when the sky opens and rain covers everything it touches.

I'm checking a few emails on the way when one comes in from Bill, my CFO, informing me of an issue he's having with a contractor handling one of our renovations. I email him back that I'll video-call him as soon as I get to where I'm going. When the cab stops, I swipe my card and then dart out into the rain, jumping over the puddles to get inside where it's dry.

The door chimes as I step inside and glance around, immediately recognizing Bree, whose eyes widen when she realizes who's just entered. The place is almost empty, save for what looks like a couple sitting in the corner chatting quietly.

"Hey," I say, smiling at her. "Can I get a coffee and a croissant, please?"

Her brows pucker, no doubt confused as to why I'm asking for food and a beverage instead of discussing our date. Usually, I'm not one to play games with women, but something tells me this particular woman is different, which means I'll need to handle her differently.

"Sure," she chokes out.

Once I have my coffee and pastry, I grab a seat at a table and pull my laptop out of my bag, powering it on. Out of the corner of my eye, I see her watching me, but I pretend I don't notice as I type in my password and click on the video chat.

Bill's face has just come over the screen when a throat clears. "I'm sorry, but this is a laptop-free coffeehouse," Bree says, looking slightly uncomfortable.

"A what?" I ask.

"Laptop-free," she repeats, pointing at a sign sitting atop the table.

This table is laptop-free.

Reading, conversing, and daydreaming are encouraged.

"Hey, Bill, I'll have to call you back." Without waiting for him to reply, I hit end on the call and close my laptop. "Is this for real?" I ask, perplexed at the thought that there's a place in New York City that doesn't allow one to use their laptop.

"Yep," she says, unwavering. "You can call your mom, or read a book, or you can people watch...enjoy the quiet."

Holy shit, this woman is dead fucking serious and so damn adorable. Now that she's out from behind the counter, I'm able to take her in. She's sporting a flowy top and skinny jeans. Despite the cute little frilly apron over her front, I can make out every one of her delectable curves. As my gaze ascends, taking in her thick thighs, hips that I'd love to grab ahold of and dig my fingers into, and perfect breasts, I wonder what it would take to get her to bake me some of those delicious brownies in nothing but that apron.

"All right." I lock eyes with her. "Then let's talk."

"What?" she splutters.

"Well, my mom isn't available, I don't have a book with me, and if I'm honest, the only person I want to watch is you." I nod toward the seat in front of me. "So have a seat, and let's talk."

"I..." Her eyes dart around, but when she realizes the place is dead and she has no excuse, she sighs and plops into the seat in front of me.

"I'm Brody Fields," I tell her, figuring it's best if we start over. Yesterday didn't exactly go as planned.

"I'm Aubree Heart."

"It's nice to meet you, Aubree," I say, using the name she gave me instead of the one on her name tag.

"You can call me Bree," she says as a young girl, who looks to be in her teens and wearing a matching apron, comes over and sets a cup of coffee down for her.

"Thank you," she says to the girl.

I glance over Bree's shoulder and see the woman from yesterday —Lacey—standing to the side with a wide grin on her face. She winks at me and then disappears behind the wall. Although I don't know her, I'm almost positive that was her way of saying she approves of me.

"It's a cute place you have here," I tell Bree, focusing my attention on her.

"Thanks." Pink tints her cheeks. "It was my grandparents' place before they passed away. Now, it's mine." I already know this since Hayden filled me in, but since she can't know that, I go with it.

"Are they the reason for the no laptops signs?"

Bree nods. "She hated it. Died at eighty-two years old without ever owning a single piece of technology." The way she smiles when she talks about her tells me they were close, and I wonder how the fuck Hayden thinks he's going to convince this woman to walk away from here.

"So what do you do?" she asks, eyeing my suit.

"I run Fields Enterprises. We mostly find restaurants and clubs and renovate them. We help companies that are going under save their businesses and bring them to the next level. Sometimes, we buy and sell them. Other times, we'll hold on to them when we think they'll bring in a decent profit. Once in a while, the owner will take us on as a partner to help manage the establishment for a percentage."

"Are you good at what you do?"

I bark out a laugh at her question. "I do all right," I say nonchalantly.

She looks around her bakery. "What do you think of my place? Anything you would change?"

I wasn't planning to talk business, but at this point, I'll talk about anything she wants if it means I have her attention.

As I take in the place, as I would any other potential investment, assessing it as an outsider, the first thing that comes to mind is her food. "Do you make all of your own food?"

She nods.

"Sell it anywhere besides here?"

She shakes her head.

"If you were my client, I would suggest you get your name out there. A lot of cafes and bakeries get their products from third-party distributors and would be more than willing to support a small business, especially a local one. Not only would it bring in additional income but with your company's name on the products, it'd also be free advertising."

She sucks in her bottom lip and then lets it slowly slide out. "I never thought of that."

"Most don't." I shrug. "It's why eighty percent of restaurants and clubs fail their first year in business. But from what I can see, you have quality products, and your prices are reasonable. You have a prime location with a welcoming atmosphere. You're already ahead of most of those places."

"Well, I'll have you know," she says, her face lighting up with what looks like pride. "This coffeehouse has been in business for fifty years and has no intention of going out of business any time soon." The passion and determination in her voice are such a damn turn-on. It also tells me that she knows about Shea trying to buy her out, and she isn't having it.

Fuck, Hayden is in for a fight.

Good thing it has nothing to do with me.

"So tell me about you," I say, shifting the conversation toward where I'm hoping it will go—with me asking her out *again* and her saying yes this time without it sounding like someone ran over her puppy. "When you're not baking and running this place, what do you enjoy doing for fun?"

She opens her mouth, then closes it, and then laughs softly. "That should be an easy question." She takes a deep breath as if to mentally prepare for what she's about to say. "Honestly, this bakery is pretty much my entire life these days…aside from my children."

It takes a second for me to wrap my head around what she just said. She has children. Not a child—children. Plural. As in more than one. I wait for the sirens in my brain to go off, for me to be turned off and no longer interested, but for some crazy reason, it doesn't happen.

"Where's the dad?" I ask, making her flinch. "Sorry," I tack on. "I just don't want to be encroaching on another man's woman."

My eyes go to her ring finger, and she follows my line of vision. "I'm not married," she says softly. "Well, I was, but he died." She sighs and closes her eyes. "Dammit," she hisses, her lids opening and her blue eyes shining with emotion. "I swore I wouldn't do this." She shakes her head and laughs, but it comes out bitter and mockingly. "Feel free to run any time."

Normally, had a woman spilled all that baggage at my feet, I'd take her up on that offer and run...fast and far. But once again, I have no desire to go anywhere. It's clear the woman has enough emotional baggage to fill a 747, but the only thing that comes to mind is what it would take to help her organize those bags and maybe clear some of them away.

"I'm good right where I am." I reach across the table and swipe a falling tear, catching it with the pad of my thumb. "So the other day, when I asked you out, the reason you looked like I stole your favorite cupcake was because you're not ready?"

She snorts out a laugh. "Cupcakes aren't my favorite. White chocolate chip cookies are." She waggles her brows and jumps up. A few seconds later, she sets a plate of delicious-looking cookies down.

I grab one and take a bite, and holy fuck, they're even better than the brownies. "Jesus, woman," I groan playfully. "Don't you know the key to a man's heart is through his stomach? Keep feeding me this stuff, and I'm going to beg you to marry me."

She chokes out a laugh. "I think we should probably go on a date first."

"Is that your way of asking me out?" I joke.

She sucks her bottom lip into her mouth, then lets it drag out slowly. "You're right," she says, confusing the hell out of me. Our conversation is all over the place, and I can barely keep up. "The reason I reacted so badly when you asked me out," she explains. "It's because I haven't dated since my husband died. Well, I did once, and it didn't go well at all."

I nod in understanding. "I get it. Well, I don't get it, but I do," I say, sounding like a dumbass. "I mean..." I run my fingers through my hair.

"I know," she says with a smile, saving me. "But I do want to try...if you still want to go out with me, that is. And if you don't? If the kids and the dead husband are too much, I totally—"

"I do," I tell her, cutting her off. "I want to take you out."

She releases a harsh sigh. "Well, okay, then. When?"

"Tonight."

"Oh, I—"

"She'd love to," her friend calls out from somewhere. "She has nothing to do, and her kids are out of town."

"Go away!" Bree yells back, then takes a deep breath, releasing it slowly. "Yes, I would love to go out with you...tonight."

CHAPTER FIVE
AUBREE

"That's so cool!" I grin at the fish my son holds up, his features filled with pride.

"Papa said we can cook it and eat it with dinner." Miles beams even though he's never had fish before. He's been looking forward to going fishing since we talked about the trip, and the fact that he caught something his first time has him even more excited. "We're going to go again tomorrow while the girls go shopping." He scrunches his nose up in disgust, and I laugh lightly.

"We're gonna get our nails done too!" Evie yells from next to her brother, side-eyeing the fish.

"That will be fun. I can't wait to see the color you pick," I tell her.

The buzzer goes off, indicating someone is asking to be let up, so I say good night to the kids with a quick "I love you." Even though it's only six o'clock, I'm not sure when I'll be home tonight. Brody wouldn't give me any details about our date. All he said was to dress comfortably, and he would be here at six to pick me up.

Which doesn't fit with the Brody Fields I Google stalked earlier today. I know, I know…I sound like a crazy person, but you can't be too careful these days, and with me being a widow who lives alone with her kids, I wanted to make sure the guy taking me out isn't some nut job. I couldn't find much about his personal life, aside from the fact he's thirty years old and in every picture of him, he has a woman who looks like a Victoria's Secret model attached to his arm.

And if that wasn't enough, I also learned that when he said he runs Fields Enterprises, he was downplaying it. He's the active CEO and owns it with his father, who recently retired. The company is worth billions. Yes, billions.

I almost wished I hadn't looked him up because now I can't help wondering if I'm completely out of my element here and why the heck this wealthy man, who is only seen with size zeros, asked me out.

I came close to canceling a dozen damn times but didn't want to be rude. I agreed to go on the date, so I'm going.

"Hello?" I say to confirm it's Brody.

"Hey, it's Brody."

"I'm in 4D," I tell him before I buzz him up.

While I wait for him to come up, I double-check my outfit. I'm wearing a pair of skinny black jeans with rips up and down the front and a long-sleeved, floral peasant top. It's light and flowy, and paired with my heels, it can be casual or a bit dressy. Because we're in the middle of summer, I curled my hair in loose curls since straightening it is out of the question, and I put on some light makeup—eye shadow, blush, and lip gloss—to finish my look.

When I hear a knock, I grab my purse and head for the front door, my heart thumping behind my rib cage in nervousness and anticipation.

With a deep, cleansing breath, I swing the door open and find Brody standing on the other side, looking delectable in a pair of dark blue jeans and a powder blue button-down dress shirt with the sleeves rolled halfway up his arms, showcasing his muscular forearms. Our eyes lock for a moment—my blue to his hazel—and something in my stomach stirs. I tamp it down, refusing to accept it could possibly be butterflies. I'm nowhere near ready for butterflies.

But as I try to convince myself they can't be butterflies, I remember the first time I saw Pete, and I can't help but compare the two. Unlike on my last date nearly two years ago, when I felt absolutely nothing, right now, as I stare at Brody, I feel something. And that scares the shit out of me.

"Hey," he says with a sexy lopsided smile gracing his lips. "You look beautiful." He lifts his hand, and it's then I see the pink and yellow flowers in a vase. "I wasn't sure what kind of flowers you liked," he says. "So I went with the colors of your coffeehouse."

"They're perfect," I choke out as I take them from him and bring them up to my nose. The scent hits my senses—a flashback of the first time Pete took me out and brought me flowers—and I close my eyes, not wanting to ruin this date before it's even begun.

Unfortunately, when I open my eyes, Brody is frowning. "What's wrong?" he asks. "If you don't like them…"

"I do," I say, opening the door wider so he can come in while I set them on the table. "It's just that the last person who brought me flowers was my late husband." I shake my head. "I'm sorry." I sigh, hating myself for bringing up my dead husband to my current date.

"Hey." He takes my hand in his and threads our fingers together, and a spark of heat courses through my veins, igniting my body on fire. "Don't ever apologize for your feelings or for bringing him up. He was your husband and the father of your children. I can't even imagine how hard this is for you. If you're not ready…" He starts to remove his hand from mine, and instinctually, I tighten our grip.

"No," I blurt out, suddenly feeling the need to see this date through. I've come across hundreds if not thousands of guys over the years, and not one of them made me feel this way—the way Pete made me feel. "I am. I mean, maybe not completely, but I want to be ready. I know he's gone, and he told me to move on." I cringe at how crazy that sounds. "He wrote me a note. He had a heart condition, and he knew his time was limited. He knew I would struggle with moving on, so he told me in his note that he wanted me to move forward…and find love again.”

Brody nods. “It sounds like he loved you very much.” He steps closer and brings our hands up between us. “I’m honored to be part of your journey in finding love again.” He kisses the top of my hand softly, his lips lingering for a few seconds, and my breath catches. Butterflies erupt in my belly so chaotically that they’re impossible to ignore or try to deny what they are.

Butterflies—just like the ones I only ever got with Pete. That has to mean something, right?

“I, um…Let me just put these on the table, and then we’ll go.” Needing a moment to sort out my raw emotions, I break our connection and walk into the kitchen to set the flowers on the center of our kitchen table. Since the place is so small, there’s no actual dining room.

“It smells like cupcakes in here,” Brody says with a soft laugh.

“I swear the sugar seeps into my pores. I literally live and breathe that coffeehouse.” We walk back out to the living room. “I’d give you a tour of my place, but really, what you see is what you get.” Besides, I’m sure my tiny apartment is the last place this guy wants to hang out in. “My room is back there, and there are two rooms for the kids. The only bathroom is down the hall.” I shrug.

Brody scans the small living area. “I like it,” he says, nodding toward the black and white photos on the wall of Heart’s from years ago. They were taken the day my grandparents opened. “It’s cute.”

“I guess,” I mutter as he walks over to the hallway wall where the kids’ artwork is framed and hung.

“You don’t like it here?” he asks, looking at each of the drawings like they’re professionals hung in an art museum.

“I hate it here.”

“Why?” he asks, genuinely sounding interested.

“Pete and I bought a townhouse just outside the city. I loved it there. We had a small yard, so the kids had space to run and play. We even had our own bathroom. I couldn’t keep it after he passed away, so I moved here to be near my grandma. It's cheap and conveniently located near Heart's, but I hate it. Won't matter soon anyway. The building owner is trying to sell the place."

He quirks a brow, so I continue, telling him something that not even Lacey knows. If she did, she would worry, and I don't want her to worry.

"I only have six months left of my lease and then he can kick us out, which he's made clear he'll be doing. But the bakery has a longer lease, so he's pissed because I'm refusing to let him buy me out of it. His parents were good friends with my grandparents, and to ensure the bakery was secure here, they signed a ridiculously long lease, but that doesn't stop him from harassing me every chance he gets. And now, the people who are trying to buy the building have started in on me."

I huff in annoyance. "Sorry, the whole thing just makes my blood boil. They want to turn the place into a freaking spa or something. So they think I should just move my bakery elsewhere, like it hasn't been here for fifty years, and we don't have enough damn spas in the city. It's like New York is losing all of its sentimental value, you know?"

Brody nods in understanding.

"Okay, vent over," I say with a nervous laugh, wondering if Brody's trying to plan his escape. "Where should I send my payment for this therapy session?" Surely, a mock therapy session is not what he signed up for when he asked me out.

"You can vent any time, no charge," he says with a playful wink as he flicks his wrist to check the time. "But we do need to get going, or we'll be late." He steps toward me and takes my hand in his, once again entwining our fingers—and *once again,* those damn butterflies make an appearance.

We're so close that I catch a whiff of his cologne—a bit smoky like cedar wood. "You smell good," I say because apparently, I lose my filter when I'm around this man. "What is it?"

"Tom Ford," he says, his eyes filled with heat meeting mine. He leans in close, and I think he's going to kiss me—and crazily enough, the thought doesn't freak me out like it probably should—but instead, he bypasses my mouth and goes straight for my neck, the tip of his nose gliding across my flesh as he inhales deeply. "Just as I thought," he murmurs. "Sweet, just like you." My heart races as heat floods my body. And then, he backs up, taking the warmth with him—and like the crazy person I'm apparently becoming, I want to beg him to come back and keep me warm.

"You ready for our date?" he asks.

"Yeah," I whisper, willing my heart to slow down. We haven't even left for the damn date, and I'm already completely taken by this man. The way he smiles, the way he listens, the way he smells…My gaze goes to the way he's still holding my hand. I never thought I'd be okay with another man holding my hand, yet with Brody, it feels right. I feel comfortable and don't want to break the connection.

With his fingers still laced with mine, we head out and into the elevator. When we step onto the sidewalk, Brody guides me over to an expensive-looking burnt-orange SUV and opens the door for me. Once I'm in, he closes the door and rounds the front while I put on my seat belt and take in the vehicle. With digital everything and a display screen almost the size of my laptop, this SUV must have cost a fortune. *Which makes sense since he's rich.*

"What kind of car is this?" I ask when he flips some red thing and presses a button to start the vehicle. I've honestly never seen anything like this before.

"A Lamborghini Urus," he says, pulling out into the traffic. "I don't drive often, but where we're going, we need a vehicle."

My brain is still stuck on Lamborghini. One night, when the kids and I had dinner with Lacey and her husband, he was talking about cars and mentioned a Lambo—as he called it—was his dream car, but since they cost hundreds of thousands of dollars, it was only a dream.

If this is the car he drives…

"What's wrong?"

"Nothing," I say quickly.

"Really? Is that why your entire body stiffened in your seat and your smile disappeared? Try again."

"It's just…" I sigh. "I'm a single mom who owns a bakery and lives in a shoebox-sized apartment."

"So?" He glances at me for a second before focusing back on the road.

"If this is the car you drive, I can't even imagine your home."

"Yeah, and?"

"And you're fit…like muscular, and you own some crazy successful business."

"Okay."

"I'm just wondering what you're doing with me when, from what I saw online, you're always seen with some gorgeous model." There, I said it. Maybe it makes me sound insecure—okay, it totally makes me sound insecure—but c'mon, there's no way I'm this guy's type.

While I wait for him to answer, he clicks his indicator on and then swerves over two lanes to pull into an open parking spot on the side of the road.

"First of all," he says, turning his body to fully face me. "Don't ever put yourself down in front of me again. You're gorgeous, every goddamn inch of you. The moment I saw you, I was attracted to you. My first thought was what it would feel like to get my hands on those luscious curves."

I gasp at his admission.

"And as far as you being a single mom goes, from what I've seen, being a parent is the hardest damn job. My dad was a single dad when he met my stepmom. He was struggling, my mom was struggling, and…" He swallows thickly. "I was struggling. Savy walked into our lives and took my dad and me in, loving us unconditionally. She could've easily said she didn't want to deal with his baggage since I wasn't her kid, but she didn't. From the moment she met me, she's treated me like her own son, and I love her like she's my second mom.

"And my mom…like you, she was a single mom, who tried hard, who cried too many times to count, and always questioned if she was doing a good job or fucking me up. We had a lot of rocky moments, but I know she was doing the best she could, loving me as much as she could.

"So please don't refer to yourself as a single mom like it's a flaw…something that makes you worth less. If anything, it only adds to your value."

He cups the side of my face and swipes a tear I didn't even realize had fallen. "Yeah, I'm well off. From what you said, you looked me up…"

"I just wanted to make sure you weren't a psycho," I choke out, embarrassed.

He chuckles. "Then you know I'm worth billions. I live in a nice home and drive nice cars. I won't apologize for that. My dad built Fields Enterprises from the ground up, and I've busted my ass every day to follow in his footsteps. But the size of my bank account isn't all I am. I hope you'll give me a chance to show you every part that makes me who I am.

"Now for the women…"

I cringe. "You don't have to—"

"My company owns a lot of exclusive clubs, which means the women I tend to meet are models. Those photos aren't of me on dates. They're at club openings. I rarely date, to be honest. I've been so focused on finding my place at Fields. Wanting to make my dad proud and earn my place in the company, I haven't had time to seriously date. I don't have a type. I've dated all different types of women. But I can tell you right now that I'm one-hundred-percent attracted to you. To every curve and dip. Those blue eyes and twin dimples…"

When his tongue darts across the seam of his lips, his eyes filled with lust, I've never felt so attractive.

"No more putting yourself down. If I didn't want to be here, I wouldn't be. And really, you're the one who turned me down the first time." He smirks playfully. "So if anyone should be insecure, it's me."

I bark out a laugh, thankful he's lightened the mood and my insecurities haven't ruined our date.

"Thank you," I tell him.

He nods and smiles. "I'm not a dating expert, but in the future, if something bothers you, tell me, please. In my business, communication is huge, and I imagine it's the same with a relationship."

He squeezes my hand, then turns around, putting the SUV in drive.

"I want to be here with you," I tell him after a few minutes. "I was reluctant to go on this date for all the reasons I mentioned, but now, I'm all in."

"Good," he says, "because I'm about to take you on the best first date of your life."

"Oh, yeah, and where is that?"

"You'll have to wait and see." He winks playfully and steps on the gas, zipping in and out of traffic as we head over the Brooklyn Bridge.

A little while later, we drive into a parking lot filled with cars. A man stops us, and Brody shows him something on his phone that he scans before we continue on our way. I wasn't paying attention, so I didn't catch a sign on our way in. As Brody finds a spot nestled between two orange cones, I glance to the right and take in the gorgeous sunset overlooking the Manhattan skyline. The sky is a breathtaking mix of oranges and pinks, and I can't help but grab my phone out of my purse and snap a couple of pictures. During the day, New York is chaos, but right now, looking out at the water, it looks so calm and beautiful.

I have no idea where we are or what we're doing here until I see the gigantic screen hanging across a large building.

"A drive-in?" I ask in excitement. I didn't know something like this even existed in New York.

"Yep." He turns off the car, and we get out. I follow him to the back of the vehicle where he pops the trunk and pulls out two lawn chairs and a cooler that I assume is filled with food and drinks. I expected him to take me out to eat, maybe to a movie, but this is so thoughtful and different.

"I brought dinner and snacks," he says once we've set up our chairs. "I wasn't sure what you liked, so I brought a variety."

"What movie is playing?" I ask as the commercials start.

"*Pretty Woman.*"

I can't help the grin that spreads across my face. "That's one of my all-time favorites. I haven't seen it in years."

Brody pulls out a bunch of finger foods, a bottle of wine, and a couple of bottles of water, and we spend the movie eating, drinking, and softly talking. The movie is as good as I remember, and his company is perfect. When the credits roll, I wish the night wasn't over.

"I was thinking we could go for a walk," Brody says as if he can read my mind.

"I'd like that."

We pack up and head out, and Brody drives us to a park along the water. As we walk, he holds my hand, and my stomach tightens at the gesture—something that keeps happening every time he touches me. I think about how he was right: this is the best first date I've ever been on.

"Tell me about your kids," he says, shocking me. The truth is, I only brought them up at Heart's to shock him. I thought if I dropped the kids bomb, he would run—but he didn't.

"They're with my in-laws in Florida for the summer," I tell him. "First time they've been away from me. It hasn't even been a week, and I already miss them like crazy. They're twins, eight years old and going into the fourth grade. Miles is four minutes older than Evie and takes his job as her *big* brother seriously."

Brody laughs. "I love that. I was an only child until my brother and sister came along years later. Olivier is fourteen and about to start high school. He's a huge techie and is currently working on making some gaming app. Penelope is the same age as your kids, and she's girly as hell. Loves everything pink and sparkly. I take being their older brother very seriously."

As I listen to him talk about his family, I can feel how much he loves and adores them.

"I stay busy with work," he continues, "but I try to have dinner with my family at least once a week. Everyone loved your treats the other day. I wouldn't be surprised if Savy stops in and buys everything you make."

"I've been thinking about what you said about selling my products to other stores. Would you be able to point me in the right direction? With those assholes trying to take away my livelihood, I feel like maybe I should have a backup."

Brody nods. "I can definitely help you. We can schedule a day and time to meet at my office. When—"

"Oh, no," I cut him off. "I couldn't afford you." I laugh nervously, not wanting him to think I'm trying to take advantage. "If you could just maybe give me a starting point, I would be so grateful."

"How much is the company who's trying to buy you out of your lease offering you?"

"Not enough to start over," I say honestly. "Leases in New York have gone up. What I pay a month is almost embarrassing. I'll never find another location anywhere in my price range. And even if it was enough, you can't put a price on Heart's. It's where I grew up. When my parents didn't want me, my grandparents took me in. I was raised in that coffeehouse. It's where I felt safe and loved and learned of my passion for baking. It's where I found out I got into culinary school. Where Pete proposed. Where my kids had their first birthday."

I swipe the fresh tears from my face, hating that I keep getting so emotional around this guy. "I'm sorry," I say not for the first time. "Dating should be fun, and I keep making it *not* fun."

"Stop," he says, pulling me toward him until our bodies are almost flush. "I'm having a great time. And I love that you already feel comfortable enough to talk to me, to confide in me. I've had plenty of superficial, but with you, I see something beyond the surface, something deeper."

His eyes lock with mine and then glide slowly down my face, landing on my lips, and I know what he's thinking because I'm thinking the same thing. He wants to kiss me. But he's not sure if he should since I'm all over the place and this is our first date. And had someone asked me if I would be okay kissing on the first date, I would've said no, but now, my answer is yes.

Reading my thoughts, again, he murmurs, "I really want to kiss you."

"So do it," I breathe out.

His eyes ascend back to mine. "You sure?"

"Yes." I swallow thickly. "I want you to kiss me."

He doesn't have to be told twice. One of his hands lands on the curve of my hip, and the other cups the side of my face. He's a good half-foot taller than me, so he dips a little, and then his mouth connects with mine. The kiss is gentle at first, his lips brushing against mine. His tongue darts out, slowly gliding along my bottom lip, and I think he's tasting me. His lips are the perfect mix of soft and strong, and when his tongue slides into my mouth, he tastes sweet, like the red wine we were drinking earlier, mixed with the icing from the cupcakes we had for dessert. Butterflies once again erupt in my belly, and I want to both squeal and cry because butter-flies were supposed to be only for my husband, but now there they are, flying around for Brody over and over again.

After a few seconds of gentle kissing, he deepens the kiss, and my hands move between us, pulling on the front of his shirt, wanting him closer, as my tongue joins in, tangling with his. His hand glides up my side and cups the other side of my face, and I get lost in everything that is Brody Fields. His taste, his touch, the way our mouths meld together and move against each other as if we're perfectly in sync.

When the kiss ends, he sighs softly, his forehead resting against my own as we both catch our breaths. "I had a really good time tonight."

"I did too," I tell him, meaning it. Lacey wouldn't be thrilled to know that I'm already falling for the first guy I've gone out with. But I can't help it. I didn't realize how much I missed those damn butterflies until I felt them again after all these years. I know I barely know him, but I want to get to know him. I want to kiss him, talk to him, and go on more dates.

Now, I just have to hope Brody wants that too.

CHAPTER SIX
BRODY

I'VE NEVER TAKEN DATING SERIOUSLY. SURE, I'VE BEEN on plenty of dates over the years, but none of them meant anything more than me having a good time. Aside from my family and Hayden, nobody has meant anything to me. When I was fourteen, my dad met Savy, and I felt real love for the first time. I saw the way someone acted when they put you first and considered your heart in the equation. My mom loves me, but her love has always been misplaced. She puts money and status and whatever guy she's dating first. Hell, even now, she's living in Florida with husband number four. I haven't seen her in years, and she's okay with that.

But Savannah Cartwright—now Fields—was different. She was the first woman to show me what love looks like. She was the first woman I gave my heart to, and she kept it safe, always putting me first. I watched her unconditionally and selflessly love my dad and me—and later, my brother and sister. I told myself I would never settle for a love that's less than what Savy gave us—still gives us.

So yeah, I've dated, but I've never taken it seriously because not one woman I've met has given me an inclination that she could love me the way Savy loves my dad and my siblings and me. Until now.

I dropped her off at her front door, promising to call her tomorrow. That was two days ago, and I can't get her off my mind. Our date was perfect, the conversation flowed, the kiss was mind-blowing, and the chemistry was off the charts. Unfortunately, I don't think she felt the same. Because when I called and then texted, she never answered or responded.

"Still haven't heard back from her yet?" Hayden asks, sitting at the table across from me, dressed in his suit with his espresso in hand.

"Nope." I drop the phone onto the table like it offends me. "I really thought there was something there." I shrug, playing it off. "Oh well, another one bites the dust."

"I'm going to see her later," he says, leaning back. "I've put together a better offer for her, as well as a list of available storefronts she could lease and move her bakery to."

"She won't go for it. That bakery means everything to her. She told me all about the *assholes* trying to rip it out from under her." I glare at him even though I know it's only business, and it's clear Bree doesn't want anything to do with me. She might not have felt the connection, but I did, and even though there's obviously no future for us, after listening to her, I hate what Shea's trying to do to her.

"Hey, man." He lifts his hands. "It's just business."

"You really think when you get there, you'll be able to separate shit and go through with it, ask her to give up the only thing she has left of her grandparents, the business that provides for her and her children?"

"She has kids?" His brow furrows together.

"Yeah, eight-year-old twins. A boy and a girl."

"Huh," he says, looking lost in thought.

"What?"

"I just thought learning that would be a turn-off, but for some reason, I can totally see it, and it only makes her hotter."

I want to talk shit, but he did find her first, and I know exactly what he means. I never thought I'd be attracted to a single mom who owns a coffeehouse, but I am…big time.

"All right, I gotta go," he says. "I'm stopping by there on my way into the office. If all goes as planned, the papers will be signed by the time I leave, and she'll have some money in her pocket. Then I'll be on my way to being appointed the new CEO of Shea Real Estate Investments. My dad will finally retire and leave me the hell alone."

CHAPTER SEVEN
AUBREE

"ARE YOU SERIOUSLY CHECKING YOUR PHONE AGAIN?"

I slip my phone back into my apron pocket and avoid Lacey's glare. "I was seeing if the kids had texted." Lie. I was checking to see if Brody texted or called. He hasn't. It's been two days since our date, and I haven't heard from him. I shouldn't be as hurt about him not calling as I am, but I really thought something was there. Apparently, my lack of experience means I misread the signs, and while I felt something, he obviously didn't.

The bell chimes, and when I glance up, I find the guy from a few days ago standing in front of me. He's dressed in another tailored suit and is carrying a briefcase in one hand. His brown hair is messy, and his face looks like it hasn't been shaved in a few days. He's as good looking as the last time he was here—when he asked me out, and I turned him down—only right now, instead of his green eyes being filled with warmth, they're lacking any emotion.

"Welcome back," I say. "What can I get you? It's probably too early for a cupcake," I joke. "But I made some orange cranberry muffins that, if I must say so myself, are to die for."

He opens his mouth to speak, then closes it. Open. Close. He does this a few times before he shakes his head and chuckles, then mutters something under his breath.

"Is everything okay?" I ask.

"Yeah, sorry," he says. "I'll take a coffee and a muffin, please."

"Sure thing." I ring him up while Lacey gets his drink and Caroline, the college student working this morning, gets his muffin.

He pays, and I hand him his drink and food. Only, instead of walking away, he says, "Eat with me."

"What?"

"It doesn't look like you're too busy yet. How about you grab a coffee and one of the to-die-for muffins and sit with me?"

Since we're between the early morning and late morning rush, I say, "Okay, give me a minute."

"Sure, I'll save you a seat." He winks playfully, and the action hits me right between the legs. Jesus, it's like a levee has been opened, and the water pours through so quickly, I can't shut it fast enough.

"He's totally going to ask you out again," Lacey says once he's walked away.

"And?"

"And you need to say yes! He's sexy as hell and clearly likes you."

"What about Brody?" I hiss. "Isn't that like cheating?" I glance over at where Hayden sits casually at a table, watching me with interest in his eyes.

"You went on one date with him," Lacey deadpans, forcing my attention back on her. "And he hasn't even called."

"I know." I sigh. "But he did kiss me."

"That's hardly a marriage proposal," she deadpans.

I can't help my flinch at the mention of marriage. "I'm never getting married again."

Lacey's face softens. "My point was, if he wanted to lock you down, he would've called or texted. He didn't. There's nothing wrong with putting yourself out there and playing the field. You're a young, single woman. If that guy asks you out"—she nods toward Hayden—"say yes."

"I'll think about it," I mumble. "But I already turned him down once. I doubt he'll ask again."

Lacey shakes her head. "One day, you'll see how beautiful you are. Peter thought you were a goddess. I don't get why it's so hard to believe other men would feel the same way."

"Pete also fell for me when I was young, skinny, and before I was a mom."

"And now, you're a grown woman, have a body filled with the most perfect curves, and have two amazing kids."

Since I can't argue with that, I push my insecurities aside and grab my coffee and muffin so I can join Hayden.

"Sorry about that," I tell him. "Just had to go over a few things with Lacey."

"No worries," he says with a sexy, easygoing smile. "This muffin is delicious." He tears off a small piece and pops it into his mouth, then washes it down with a sip of his coffee. My gaze goes straight to his Adam's apple, watching as it bobs when he swallows. For a moment, I wonder what it would be like to place my lips there and feel it move.

Holy shit! What is wrong with me?

As if he can hear my crazy thoughts, his emerald eyes meet mine, now filled with enough heat to catch this place on fire.

He leans forward, his eyes not leaving my own. "Go out with me," he says. "I know you said no before, but all I'm asking for is one date. One chance to show you a good time." His attention moves to my lips briefly, then back up to my eyes. "And I think we could have a good time."

The area between my legs tightens, and it takes everything in me not to squirm in my spot. "Okay," I say before I can second-guess myself. "One date."

A slow, seductive smile curls at the corners of his lips. "Tonight."

"Tonight?" I squeak out.

"Yeah, tonight. Before you have time to change your mind."

I snort out a laugh and shake my head. "Okay, tonight."

He pulls a pen out of his briefcase and hands it to me, along with his napkin. "Write your number down, and I'll text you later with the details."

I do as he asks, then slide it back to him. "I better get back to work," I say, noticing the late morning rush is beginning.

"That muffin was delicious," he says, gathering his food and drink as we both stand. "Sweet with the perfect mix of tart." He steps toward me, and I catch a whiff of his scent—warm with a hint of spiciness, like being wrapped up in a blanket in the middle of winter while sitting in front of the fireplace. "I'll see you tonight," he murmurs, leaning in and kissing my cheek. Only instead of it being a quick peck, his lips linger, warming my skin, and those damn traitorous butterflies make an appearance.

Jesus! This can't be happening again.

"Have a good day," he says once he pulls back and his eyes meet mine. "I'll see you tonight."

"Holy shit," Lacey says once he's gone. "I couldn't hear anything that was said, but the look in his eyes...and the way he kissed your cheek before leaving." She fans herself dramatically.

"Tell me about it. I'm going to need to find time with B.O.B. before our date tonight, so I don't risk jumping his bones," I mutter, referring to my battery-operated boyfriend.

Lacey barks out a laugh. "Forget B.O.B. You need to get laid, and if it's with that sexy man, that's even better."

"I am not sleeping with anyone on the first date. I let Brody kiss me and look where that went...nowhere. This time, I'm making the guy earn the kiss. And if he wants to sleep with me, he'll have to prove he wants more."

"More...like marriage?"

"No," I quip. "More like...I don't know! Just more."

I stare out the window, thinking about how my body reacted to Brody and then Hayden. "I think there's something wrong with me."

"Why?" Lacey asks, concerned.

"Pete was the only guy to ever give me butterflies. Didn't matter who it was, how charming or good looking they were, nobody could cause butterflies to attack my belly but him." I shake my head in frustration. "It doesn't make any sense. I thought they were a sign, like it meant Pete was the one."

"And you're concerned because talking with Brody and Hayden didn't give you butterflies?"

"No, I'm concerned because they appeared several times with Brody and then again with Hayden."

CHAPTER EIGHT
AUBREE

Buzzzzz

"Hello?"

"Hey, it's me, Hayden."

"Hey! I'll be right down."

Since I let Brody up, I'm meeting Hayden downstairs this time. It's clear that whatever happened on my date with Brody didn't go as well as I thought, so I'm doing the opposite. Instead of venting and talking about my kids and coffee, I'm going to keep it light and fun. And instead of googling him, I'm going to get to know him the old-fashioned way. I'll let him tell me about himself instead of snooping and finding shit about him that will cause me to feel insecure. Not exactly the safest route to take, but I'm going with the whole ignorance is bliss and all that jazz.

Tonight, since Hayden called and said he's taking me out for dinner, I'm wearing a storm-gray maxi dress. It's short-sleeved and flows almost to my knees, paired with faux alligator print heels. My hair is down again but braided on one side around my face. I went bold with a smoky look around my eyes to match my dress and blood-red matte lipstick on my lips. It's been a long time since I've dressed up and put makeup on like this, and I must admit, I feel pretty—and like a real adult.

When I step off the elevator, Hayden waits for me. He's no longer in a suit, but he's dressed up in a striped, black button-down, sleeves rolled to his forearms that give Brody a run for his money, and matching black slacks. But unlike Brody, Hayden's sporting ink on his arms, giving him more of a bad-boy vibe.

As he watches me walk toward him, his eyes light with interest, and I've honestly never felt sexier in my life. Maybe I am curvy, and maybe I have put on some weight since I had my kids, but between Brody's words and the way Hayden is looking at me, it's clear they both find me attractive. So it didn't work out with Brody...Lacey's right—I'm young and single, and it's time I act that way. Have a little fun.

"You look stunning," Hayden says, leaning in and pressing a soft kiss to my cheek. "You hungry?" he whispers in my ear, making me wonder if his question is a double entendre.

"Starved," I tell him.

"Perfect."

He escorts me to an awaiting SUV, where he opens the back door and slides in after me. There's a driver in the front, and he takes off to wherever we're going once we're in.

"How was the rest of your day?" Hayden asks conversationally.

"Good. Busy. People love their caffeine and sugar."

He laughs. "I don't blame them. After drinking your coffee, my stash at home tastes like shit."

"Guess you'll have to come in more often," I say, shocked by my easy flirting.

"Guess I will."

The drive to the restaurant is quick, and once we arrive, Hayden takes my hand in his and guides us inside. The name of the restaurant is Lush, and while I've heard of it since it's extremely popular here, I've never been. For one, I couldn't afford it, and two, it's not somewhere you take your kids.

"Mr—"

"Please, call me Hayden," he says before she can finish. "For two."

"Right this way," the hostess says, bringing us to a table situated outside on a terrace. Since we're the only ones out here, it's private and quiet, aside from the soft music playing above us.

"Wow," I breathe, staring out at the city. The setting sun provides a breathtaking view. "I've lived here my entire life, and sometimes, I forget how beautiful the city can be."

"I agree," Hayden says. "It's a view worth memorizing." But as he says the words, his eyes never leave me.

"Thank you for giving me a chance," he says.

"It wasn't that I didn't want to go out with you," I admit. "I just wasn't sure if I was ready to date."

"And now you are?"

"Yeah, I am."

"Good," he says with a nod.

After we peruse the menu and order our drinks and appetizers, he says, "Tell me about yourself."

Because I don't want to scare him off the way I did with Brody, I stick to the surface. "Well, as you know, I own a coffeehouse and bakery. I inherited it from my grandparents after they passed. Baking is my passion, and coffee is my addiction." I wink playfully, and he chuckles.

"There are worse things to be addicted to."

"True. What about you? What are your passions?"

He flinches slightly, and it's so quick that I wouldn't have seen it if I wasn't watching him. "Work, mostly. I work for my dad. He has high expectations, so most of my time is spent trying to reach them."

"That doesn't sound like much fun," I say honestly.

"No, not really, but I love what I do. And I'm hoping to take over one day, and when I do, I'll change shit so it's a better place to work. I'll be a better boss to work for."

"That sounds like a good plan."

"So when you're not baking those addictive brownies and cupcakes, what are you doing?"

"When I have the time, I love to read and take bubble baths. I enjoy going to wine tastings. One day, I'd love to do one of those tours. You know, the ones where they show you how it's all made."

"And you step on all the grapes?" Hayden adds, making me laugh.

"Yes! That would be so cool."

"What else?"

"Umm, when the weather permits, I love going to the beach, and on rainy days, I enjoy baking and trying out new recipes. When my kids—" I stop mid-sentence, realizing too late what I just said. I try to think of how to backtrack, but there's no way without sounding like an idiot.

"When your kids…?" he prompts. "You have kids?"

"Yeah." I clear my throat. "I have two."

"Any reason you didn't mention them earlier?"

"Truth?" When he nods, I continue. "I recently went on a date, and I thought it went good, actually, better than good." I cringe, feeling bad that I just said that to the guy I'm on a date with. "But he never called afterward, so when I went over how the date went, I thought maybe I went too deep too fast and scared him off. So tonight, I was trying to be less deep and more carefree. But the truth is, my life is kind of deep. I'm a widowed single mom. I lost my husband almost five years ago, my grandma shortly after, and now I'm raising my eight-year-old twins on my own. Until this week, I had only been on one date since my husband passed away, and it was horrible, making me not want to date at all…And there I go again," I groan, "word-vomiting my entire life."

I stop talking to take a breath, and also, to see if there's anything he wants to say—like nice knowing you, but I gotta go. But when I look at him, he's smiling softly.

"First, I'm honored to be on your short list of dates. And second,

I want to know everything about you, including your kids. Any man who truly wants to get to know you, spend time with you, have a *future* with you, will be okay with you having kids and understand that the three of you are a package deal. And if he doesn't get that, he's not worth wasting your time on."

I release a sigh, finally relaxing. "Thank you. I think I needed to hear that. My kids are my life. They're away with my in-laws for the summer, and it's taking everything in me not to drag them back home." I laugh lightly, and Hayden joins.

"Where are they?"

"Florida. The kids and I are close with my late husband's parents. They're all the family we have left. They took them to their vacation home. They live on the beach, near a pier, and have a boat. My kids are in saltwater heaven."

Our food arrives, and we continue to talk while we eat. Hayden tells me a little about his family. His parents are married but not close. He believes the only reason his mom stays with his dad is for financial stability. He has one older sister, who also works with him, but they're not close either because they're both vying for the same position. She's married but doesn't have any kids because she's too busy with work.

"My true family is my best friend and roommate," he says as we finish our dessert. "We've been friends since we were kids, only separating during high school when my parents forced me to go to boarding school."

"That sounds horrible."

"It was, but in our family, it's tradition. My dad went, my sister went, so of course I went. When I returned, my dad wanted me to go to school where he went—Yale. But I drew the line and went to NYU. Graduated with honors and then went straight to work for my dad."

"Sounds like you're just as married to your job as your sister is."

"I was," he says simply, "but recently, my priorities have shifted, and I find myself wanting more." At that word, my thoughts go back to my earlier conversation with Lacey, when I told her I wanted *more*. Could it be possible that the second guy I've been out with could be the one? I shake the thought from my head. No, that's crazy. And besides, I thought that about Brody and look how that ended.

Hayden stands and extends his hand, knocking me from my thoughts. "Dance with me?"

I place my hand in his, and he pulls me up so our bodies are flush against one another. My hands glide up his chest and encircle his neck, and his slide down my sides and settle on my lower back. We sway to the music as the chemistry sizzles between us. I consider resting my head on his chest, wanting to hear his heartbeat and smell his scent, but as his eyes stay locked with mine, I can't bring myself to break the connection.

"I could dance with you all night," he murmurs, drawing me closer. "You feel perfect in my arms." He twirls us around, and my back hits the brick wall. His hand ascends into my hair, and he tilts my head back. "Tell me I can kiss you, Bree. Tell me I can feel what your lips feel like, taste you…"

My breath hitches, and I nod. I'm about to verbalize my permission, but before I can get the word out, Hayden's mouth is on mine, his lips coaxing my own. His tongue pushes between the seam of my lips to taste me, and when I suck on his tongue, wanting to taste him back, he groans into my mouth. When his fingers tighten around the strands of my hair to the point it's almost painful, a zap rushes through my body and straight to my core.

Our kiss turns fervent, desperate. Our mouths fuse, our tongues dueling with each other. My hands lock around Hayden's neck, and with one hand, he lifts me off my feet, pinning me against the wall. My legs wrap around his waist, and I grind myself against his hardness, wanting more…needing more.

And then he breaks the kiss, his eyes meeting mine. "Fuck, Bree. I knew you'd taste good, feel even better, but…" He shakes his head. "You're as goddamn addicting as those brownies you make."

I can't help the laughter that bubbles up, and then I realize I'm in his arms, my heat rubbing against his stomach, and I go shy.

"Don't do that," he says, gripping my underside and pushing me farther against the wall so our bodies are closer. "Don't go shy on me, now." He kisses my lips softly, and butterflies swarm my belly. "That kiss was hot as hell, baby, and if I were any less of a gentleman, I wouldn't have stopped. But I don't just want tonight with you. I want tomorrow and the next day..."

"More," I breathe. There's that damn word again. The one that's both exhilarating and scary at the same time. Both exactly what I crave and am afraid of.

"Yeah, I want more," he says.

I nod in understanding and untwine my legs. He reads my silent request and puts me down. "I..." I swallow thickly. "I don't know what I'm capable of giving you," I admit truthfully. Sure, the kiss stirred something deep inside me, made my heart pick up speed, made those damn infamous butterflies appear, and I have no doubt I'll be spending some time with B.O.B. later tonight, thinking about this kiss, but I also felt like this about Brody a few days ago. I told Lacey earlier I wanted more, but the truth is, I'm not sure if I'm ready or if I'm even capable of more.

"Until this week, I hadn't really dated in over four years, and before that, I was with my husband for almost ten, and he was my first real boyfriend...my first and only everything. I want to put myself out there, but I need to take things slow."

Hayden nods. "I just want a chance to get to know you. See where things go. We can take it slow, no commitments or strings. Keep it casual."

I find myself relaxing at his words. "That sounds good."

CHAPTER NINE
BRODY

"Where the hell have you been?" I ask, glancing up from my laptop as Hayden strolls through the door with the biggest Cheshire cat grin spread across his face.

"Out to dinner at Lush…with Bree."

That gets my attention. I slam my laptop closed and cross my arms over my chest. "What were you guys doing there? Celebrating her signing away her coffee shop?"

"Fuck you," Hayden quips, his smile disappearing.

"Wait a second." I stand, suddenly pissed off and jealous, but mostly pissed off. "Are you telling me you went on a fucking date with Bree tonight?"

"And if I did?"

"Then I'd say you're a dick because you know damn well this isn't going to end well."

"I'll figure something out," he says with determination in his voice.

I shake my head and scoop up my laptop so I can head to my room. Before I get halfway down the hall, he calls out my name, so I turn around.

"For what it's worth, I don't think she got your calls and messages."

I quirk a brow.

"She mentioned you tonight. Didn't say your name, but I knew she was referring to you. Said the guy she went on a date with and thought she hit it off with, never called her. When I was asking her about herself, she tried to keep it light and not mention her kids, but it slipped, and when I asked her why she tried to hide them, she said she thought maybe shit got too deep too quick with you because you never called, so she was trying not to make the same mistake with me."

"That doesn't make any sense." I called and texted, and she never responded. "Why are you telling me this?" I ask. "You obviously like her, and now that I know, you know I'm going to go to Heart's and talk to her."

He nods. "Yeah, I know." He sighs. "I really like her, but it was clear in the way she spoke that she really liked you too. Yeah, I want her, and tonight was amazing. She kisses like a fucking dream. And she's so damn sweet and sexy."

"Yeah, I know," I agree. "I tried to play it off like her not answering me wasn't a big deal, but the truth is, I haven't been able to get her off my mind. It's taken everything in me not to go to Heart's and ask her what went wrong because I honestly thought everything went perfectly."

"I get it," Hayden says. "And after hearing her tell me about her late husband, I would give anything to be the next guy she gives her heart to, but I want her to choose to give it to me. To give it to the man she's fallen in love with, and if that man is you, I couldn't live with myself knowing the only reason she didn't choose you is because of a miscommunication."

"So you're okay with me going there and asking her out on another date?"

"Yeah. I told her we'd take shit slow. She was with the same guy for years, so she needs to date. She deserves to get out there and find herself, find the man who she wants to be with."

"And if it's me?"

"Then I'll be happy for you." He shrugs. "But it might be me."

"Until she finds out that you're trying to steal her coffeehouse from her," I point out, joking but also serious. "Then I'll be there for her." I wink playfully, lightening the mood.

Hayden chuckles. "And when she finds out that you've known all along?"

"Nah, that shit has got nothing to do with me."

"Doesn't it, though? You know about it…that makes you guilty by association."

"Fine, then I guess I'll tell her what I know."

"You wouldn't dare," he growls. "I said I'm going to handle it."

"Your dad won't stop until he removes her from that property."

"If she won't sell, he doesn't have a choice. I'll just have to convince him that we're better off finding somewhere else to build the wellness center."

Holy shit. This sounds nothing like the Hayden I know. "You really fucking like her."

"Yeah, I do."

"Okay." I nod. "Maybe you can pull that off." Hayden is nothing if not determined and stubborn as hell when he puts his mind to something. "But you don't think she's going to be pissed when she learns the only reason you met was because you were planning to convince her to sell her family's fifty-year-old business?"

"And once she learns we're roommates, you think she's going to let that go?" he volleys.

"No, I'll have to grovel like crazy," I admit with a smirk. "But at least I'm not the man trying to singlehandedly destroy her life. There's no way she'll pick you over me."

"I guess we'll just have to wait and see," he says. "May the best man win."

"Oh, I plan to…" Because the prize—it's her goddamned heart, and I have every intention of it becoming mine.

"Welcome to Heart's! How can I…?" The second Bree sees it's me, her words fade away, and her eyes narrow into thin slits, telling me what Hayden said was the truth. For whatever reason, she thinks I didn't call or text her.

"What do you want?" she asks, popping her sexy hip out and dropping her hand onto it.

"You."

"Obviously not, or you would've called or texted."

"I did." I pull out my phone and open it up to the thread where my messages went unanswered. "But you didn't respond. Which is why I'm here. Any reason you didn't reply? I mean, if you didn't want to see me again…"

"I did," she says, shaking her head. "I thought you didn't. I never got a single message or call from you. I swear." She pulls out her phone. "What's your number?"

I give it to her and a few seconds later, my phone rings. Only her name doesn't come up, but a number that's almost identical to hers, aside from one digit. "It's a one."

"Huh?"

"The last digit. I thought it was a two." I open her contact and show her before I slide my phone into my pocket. "I had a good time with you, and I called the next morning to see if you'd like to go out again. When you didn't answer, I left a voicemail. Then later, I texted…twice, but apparently I wasn't calling or texting *you*. I should've come by sooner, but I figured it was your way of saying you didn't want to see me again."

"I would've responded," she says. "I thought you not calling was your way of saying you didn't want to see me again. I know things got kind of...deep. I was venting, and then I dropped the kid bomb and that I googled you. And for a second, I went all woe is me..." She laughs nervously. "Honestly, I wouldn't have blamed you for running for your life."

"I'm not running anywhere," I tell her. "Unless it's toward you." I wink playfully, and she throws her head back with a laugh.

"Go out with me tomorrow?" I could take her out tonight, but tomorrow is Saturday, which means, if I go for tomorrow, I'll get the whole day with her.

My question sobers her up. If I didn't know she went out with Hayden last night, I'd think she was reluctant to go out with me, but because I know what she doesn't, I recognize the guilt. She likes us both.

"We're not like dating, right?" she asks, then cringes. "It's just casual, getting to know each other?" Ahh, so she's trying to justify dating us both. Fuck, she's so innocent and adorable.

"Yeah, casual."

"Okay," she says, smiling softly. "Then I'd love to go out with you."

"Perfect. I'll pick you up at nine? Is that too early?"

"No, I'm a morning person. Should I dress a certain way?"

"Whatever you're comfortable in. We'll be doing some walking." She mentioned on our date the other night that she loves to try out different bakeries, and since we discussed her possibly putting her products into other businesses, I think the perfect date could be checking out various places.

"Sounds good." She grins, her twin dimples popping out, and I wish I didn't need to get to work so I could spend the day just staring at her. But since I have a business to run, I head to the office after buying a coffee and muffin.

I spend the morning going through a bunch of emails, dealing with a contractor who's pissing me off, and having a meeting with the architect I have handling the new club that Hayden and I are partners in.

"Mr. Fields," my assistant says, "your lunch is here."

"Perfect. You can bring it back. I'm free."

"How'd the meeting go?" Hayden says, walking through the door a few minutes later with our lunch in his hands. He sets it down on the table I have in the corner of my office. "I told Hillary I'd bring it back for us so she could head out to lunch." He takes our boxes out while I finish my email and hit send.

"Good." I shut down my laptop and go over to the table to join him. We try to have lunch together a couple of times a week since we're working on several projects together. "Everything is on track, and the grand opening is scheduled as planned."

"Nice," he says, opening his box of food and digging in. "I'll need the income from this place to replace my current income."

"What?" His tone is light, indicating he's joking, but something underneath says he's also serious.

"I met with my dad today and tried to pitch finding a new building for the wellness center. Even came prepared with several other options. Some better than the current building. But he's so damn stubborn." He spears his noodles with his fork. "I don't know what I'm going to do." His eyes meet mine, silently begging for advice. Even though we're at odds over Bree, he's my best friend, closer to a brother, so I'll always put him first.

"What do you need from me?"

"I don't know." He sighs. "I just...I really like her. We're going out Sunday."

I laugh softly.

"What?"

"Nothing...It's just, well, we're going out tomorrow."

He shakes his head and chuckles. "That must be why she said she couldn't do tomorrow."

"Yep, so what are you going to do about your dad? Because you know she isn't going to agree to be bought out."

"For now, I'm going to drag shit along. If she won't sell, there's nothing I can do. He's just pissed he isn't getting his way."

"This could mean your sister gets that position."

"Yeah, hence me saying I need the income," he deadpans. "Because there's no way I'm working for her. She'll let the position go straight to her head." He mock shivers. "I'd rather quit than work for Gretchen."

"You could always come work alongside me," I tell him, not for the first time. His family issues are nothing new, something I've been listening to for as long as I've known him. I don't know why he puts up with them, except maybe he feels like he has something to prove, which is such bullshit because he's a thousand times better at what he does than his sister and dad combined.

"Yeah? Will that offer still be on the table when Bree chooses me?"

I snort out a laugh. "Hey." He glances up at me. "You're my brother for life. No woman will ever come between us, not even sexy as fuck women with curves for days, mesmerizing blue eyes, and the most perfect dimples."

"Remember that time in college when we fucked that server? What was her name?"

I know exactly who he's talking about, but I couldn't tell you her name. "Started with an M, I think."

"Maybe," he says, leaning in and looking at me. "And then the other chick from our business class."

"Lauren, I think."

"Lina," he corrects.

"Fuck, I can't remember. That shit was a long time ago."

He sucks his lip into his mouth, obviously thinking hard about something, and I stop eating to give him my full attention. "What if Bree were willing to be with both of us?"

For a split second, I can picture it. Her riding me from on top while I suck on her nipples, massaging her clit. Hayden pounding into her from behind, gripping those luscious hips.

It wouldn't be the first time we've shared a woman. During freshman year, shit got crazy, and somehow, we ended up having a threesome with the server at the local pub we frequented. It was the hottest thing I'd ever experienced.

After that night—and word got out about what we did—women practically lined up at our door, wanting both of us. After being with a few women, I confided to Hayden that I thought I might be bi. I was scared that he'd run, but instead, he pulled his shirt over his head and said, "Let's find out." I learned that night that while being with a guy could feel good and natural, I preferred the female body over the male.

After we graduated and moved into our condo, we both got busy with work, with being adults, and our threesomes stopped. I've been with a few women over the years, but none of them have held my attention. Until Bree...

"She'd never go for it," I tell him. "Besides, I want more with her. More than some hot threesome. I want her heart."

"Same," he says, forking his food into his mouth and dropping the subject.

CHAPTER TEN
AUBREE

"Hey, you!" I wrap my arms around Brody's neck for a hug. It's Saturday morning, and I'm excited about our date. It will be the first time in a while I'm not at the bakery, but Lacey promised she had it all under control. Since I didn't have any plans last night, I baked everything for today and tomorrow so I won't have to bake any more until tomorrow night or Monday morning.

Lacey mentioned that since my social life has picked up, I should consider hiring another part-time baker, but I'm not ready to go there yet. Sure, we're steadily busy, but in a few months, we'll be evicted, and I'll have to find us somewhere to live. Somewhere way more expensive than what I'm paying now, which means I need to save every extra cent I have.

"Mmm, you smell like cupcakes," Brody murmurs, making me laugh.

"That's because I baked last night and went in early this morning to get things situated. I swear, no matter how much I shower and scrub myself, the scent lingers."

"I like that you smell like cupcakes." He leans in and glides his nose across my neck, sending a rush of desire through my body.

"You know what I'm wondering, though…" He places a soft kiss on the sensitive area just below my ear. "If you *taste* like cupcakes."

"You've already tasted me," I breathe, remembering our kiss at the end of our date.

"Yeah, your lips, but I want to know if *all* of you tastes sweet."

His words cause the area between my legs to clench and my skin to heat as I imagine him exploring every inch of my body to find out. "We better go," I say, my voice coming out raspy. It's messy enough that I'm dating two guys. The last thing I need is to add sex to the mix.

Brody chuckles but doesn't argue, and we head out on foot. He pulls his phone out to check something and then guides us to wherever we're going. While we walk, we talk, and I enjoy our conversation as we get to know each other. We keep it light, focusing on our favorites, like our favorite food and drink and song. And I find that we have a lot in common.

When we end up at Shell's Bakery, I give Brody a confused look.

"You mentioned you like to check out bakeries. This one sells products from outside distributors. I was thinking we could check a few out today and see if maybe you can picture your products being sold at any of them…or all of them."

His admission causes me to choke up. He thought about our conversation, looked into the bakeries that outsource, and planned a day so we could check them out together.

"Hey, if this isn't something you're interested in," he begins, mistaking my tears as sad.

"No, it is. The tears are because…" I laugh a watery laugh. "I keep trying to keep it light with you, but it always ends up going deep."

"I'm okay with deep," he says. "Talk to me."

"For the past few years, even though I have my kids and Lacey and my in-laws, I've still felt alone in a lot of ways. Like I'm trying to do it all on my own, and most days, I feel like I'm doing okay, but other days, it feels like I'm failing. And then all this stuff came up with the building being sold." I sigh, closing my eyes for a moment to get myself together before opening them back up and looking at him. "It just feels really good to have someone in my corner. To think about me. It makes me feel a little less lonely."

Brody grips the curves of my hips and pulls me toward him. "You're not alone, Bree. If you let me in, I'd love to be here."

He presses a soft kiss to my lips that ignites a fire in my belly. "Now, how about we go check out the bakery? See if she needs those addictive brownies of yours?"

"Are we almost there yet?" I ask for the millionth time, cringing when I realize I sound like my kids. But in my defense, Hayden won't tell me anything, not even a single clue, and we've been driving for well over an hour.

"Soon," he says with a lighthearted laugh, squeezing the top of my thigh. We're in his Porsche SUV, which isn't quite as luxurious as Brody's Lambo but just as techie and pretty.

"Did you have a good day yesterday?" he asks, making conversation. My thoughts go to Brody and our day together. We hit up a dozen bakeries, taking notes on each one and gathering info so I'd have it all to make a decision. It was fun checking out each place and comparing it to mine. I even got a few ideas I'd like to implement at Heart's.

Afterward, when we were both full and wired from all the coffee and treats we ate, we went for a walk through the park and stopped at the lake in the middle to sit and chat. After a fun and relaxing day, I didn't want the date to end when Brody walked me to the door. I considered calling Hayden and canceling because that's how into Brody I am, but when I tried to dial the number, I couldn't do it. When he showed up this morning, I was relieved that I didn't because even though I like Brody, I also like Hayden.

The thought causes my stomach to roil. I've never dated more than one guy at a time, and I hate that I'm doing it now. At some point, I'll need to pick one, but I can't imagine pushing either one away.

"Bree?" Hayden says, knocking me out of my thoughts.

"Huh?"

He chuckles. "I asked how your day was yesterday."

"Oh, right." I swallow thickly. "It was good. Productive." There… not the complete truth, but not exactly a lie either.

"How about yours?" I ask, focusing the attention back on him.

"It was all right. Spent the day getting caught up on work."

I spot a large wooden sign that reads Brookstone Vineyard and Winery and gasp.

"A winery?" I shriek. "Are we going to a wine tasting?"

"Not just a tasting," he says as we drive along a dirt road surrounded by hundreds, if not thousands of acres of vineyards. "We're going to tour the vineyard, learn about how it's all made, then make some of our own. Then we'll do a wine tasting with lunch."

"Stahhhhpp!" I throw my arms around his neck and smack a kiss on his cheek. "This is amazing!" I pull back and glance at Hayden, who's smiling softly. I told him while we were at dinner that I loved going to wine tastings and would love to go on a tour one day, and he listened. *Just like Brody listens.* I shake my head to dispel the thought of Brody while I'm on a date with Hayden.

"Thank you," I tell him, after clearing my throat—and trying and failing to push the guilt away.

When we arrive, we're greeted and then taken on a tour through the vineyards. Afterward, we get to pick out our grapes, then, with bare feet, we stomp them! It's so much fun, and I'm shocked when Hayden willingly joins in without me having to ask —or beg. Once our grapes are crushed, we rinse off our feet, where Hayden lifts me against the side of the barn wall and kisses the hell out of me until I'm a panting mess. We're forced to separate so we can finish drying off and head to lunch. Since Hayden is driving, he only has a sip of each wine, leaving the expert testing to me.

"How are your kids doing?" he asks while we eat.

"They're good. Miles caught a fish, and Stephen, my father-in-law, told him they could cook it. Of course, my kids have never had fish before…" I roll my eyes, and Hayden chuckles.

"How'd that go?"

"Miles said the next fish he catches, he's letting it go because it's a waste to kill something that tastes that gross." I pull out my phone and show him the pictures Beatrice sent, watching to see if he's bored, but with every picture, he comments and asks questions.

"Evie looks just like you," he says when I swipe to a picture of my daughter dressed in cute pink pajamas holding a doll that looks identical to her. Apparently, there's a store where you can buy a doll with similar features, and Evie's looks like her twin.

"She has her dad's eyes," I say without thinking.

Hayden glances up at me. "Do you mind if I ask what happened?"

I'm about to say I already told him when I remember I didn't talk to him about Pete—it was Brody. Dammit, I'm such a shitty person. I seriously need to choose one of them, but it's so hard when they're both so freaking amazing.

"He had an issue with his heart and passed away on Christmas morning. It will be five years this Christmas."

Hayden frowns and nods. "How long were you together?"

"Not long enough," I say, hating that I'm getting emotional. "Almost ten years. He was my first real boyfriend, my first…everything. I thought he'd be my last, but life doesn't always work out according to plan." I clear the emotion out of my throat and take a sip of my wine. "That's actually why I turned you down when you asked me out. I haven't really dated since he passed away."

"What made you change your mind?"

"My best friend, Lacey. She reminded me that Pete wanted me to move forward and find love again. And I can't exactly do that if I don't ever put myself out there."

"Makes sense." He takes my hand in his. "I'm glad you changed your mind, Bree. I really enjoy spending time with you and getting to know you."

"I am too," I admit truthfully.

The rest of the meal is delicious, and after I mention which wines are my favorites, Hayden surprises me with a bottle of each one.

The drive home is filled with conversation, and when he walks me to my door, our kiss turns heated. I'm forced to stop it from going any further, making me realize I can't keep doing this. It isn't fair to either guy—or me—to keep everyone at arm's length. I need to choose. The problem is, I have no idea how to.

"Have sex with them both."

"Are you out of your mind?" I glare at Lacey. "I am not having sex with both of them."

"Why not?" She looks at me like I'm the crazy one. "Whichever one is better in bed is the one you choose. Life's too short to be stuck with a man who's shit in bed."

"It's bad enough I'm dating them both behind their backs. I'm not having sex with them too. That would make me a seriously horrible person."

"So you're, what, going to keep dating them both forever?"

"No. I'm going to pick one. It's just hard. They're both so damn perfect," I mutter, feeling like an even worse person for complaining that I have two amazing guys who have both made it clear they really like me.

The problem is, it's been almost three weeks since I've started dating Brody and Hayden, and I'm nowhere closer to figuring out which one to choose. After my date to the vineyards with Hayden, I went home and made a pro/con chart, but for every good thing about Brody, there was one for Hayden. And crazily enough, neither one has done a damn thing that I can put on the con side. I'm sure it's because I've yet to spend the night with either of them, and we're still in the early stages of dating, but there isn't a single flaw that I can name that would put one ahead of the other. They're both pretty damn perfect, which would be great if I didn't need to find a reason to choose one over the other. And with every date they take me on, they only get that much more amazing.

"Whatever." Lacey shrugs. "If you want to take the moral high road, that's up to you. Just seems like it would be a *horrible* waste not to try them both out."

"Try what out?"

My eyes go wide in shock, and I spin around to find Brody standing at the counter, dressed sharply in his business suit sans tie.

"I was just telling Bree that it would be a horrible waste not to try out her new chocolate chip cookie recipe with white and milk chocolate chips," Lacey says, not missing a beat. "I mean, how can she possibly know which one tastes the best if she doesn't try them both?"

"If I try every variation, I'll get sick," I say dryly, asking myself why I'm even arguing with her.

"Not if you just take a *small* bite of each," Lacey says with a smirk.

"I agree," Brody says, "and if you need a taste tester, I'm your man."

Lacey snorts out a laugh, and I shoot her a quick glare. "On your way to work?" I ask, stepping out from behind the counter and away from my best friend's nosy behind.

"Yeah, thought I'd grab a coffee and a muffin and…" He pulls me into his arms and leans in to kiss the corner of my mouth. "I was thinking we could do dinner and a movie tonight…at my place."

My stomach sinks. Shit, at his place? Where there's privacy and a bed. How the hell am I supposed to keep him at arm's length if we're alone behind closed doors?

"Ummm…" I look up into his sexy hazel eyes and want to say yes, but I can't. "I can't," I say. "I have plans." Technically, it's not a lie since I plan to spend the night figuring my shit out. It's gone too far, gotten out of control, and I need to decide before I go out with either of them again.

His gorgeous smile disappears, and my heart clenches in my chest. "All right. Well, what about Sunday?"

"Can I let you know?" I say, not wanting to make any plans until I know what I'm going to do.

"Sure."

Lacey gets him his coffee and muffin, and then with a soft kiss that makes my knees weak, he heads out. The door has only just closed when it reopens and in walks Hayden.

My gaze swings over to Lacey, and her eyes go wide because, holy shit, that was close.

"There's my favorite baker," Hayden says, encircling his arms around my waist and kissing me. "You having a good morning?"

"Uh-huh," I say, my heart beating a million miles an hour.

"I was thinking we could do dinner and a movie tonight…at my place."

I hear Lacey laugh and then try to cover it up with a fake cough.

"I actually can't," I say. "I have plans tonight."

When Hayden's face falls, similar to Brody's, it solidifies that I have to make a decision tonight. We can't go on like this for another day. I'm going to decide tonight, and tomorrow, I'll let them both know. Then I'll be honest with whoever I pick and tell him about the mess I've gotten myself into.

CHAPTER ELEVEN
BRODY

I STARE AT MY PHONE, TRYING TO FIGURE OUT WHAT THE hell he's talking about. Shouldn't he be gloating since he got to Bree first? We agreed that whoever got her to say yes to the date at our place would get to claim the condo as our own since we both can't bring her there. When she told me she couldn't hang out tonight, I assumed it was because Hayden got to her first.

Instead of texting him back, I call him.

"Yeah, yeah, I know. Stay away tonight," he mutters. "I really thought I got there first. You must've fucking ran there, asshole."

"I did run," I say with a laugh. When we discussed it this morning, we agreed we had to ask her in person. Whoever got there first gets to bring her back to our place and the other person has to find somewhere else to hang out. I don't think either of us has ever gotten ready for work that fast in our lives. "But I thought you got there first. Bree told me she couldn't make it tonight."

"Really? She told me the same thing," he says.

We both sit on the phone in silence for a few minutes before I say what I'm pretty sure we're both thinking. "Could she be dating someone else?"

"No way. Every day, she's either with you or me. When the hell would she have the time to date a third guy?"

"True," I agree. "Maybe she has plans with Lacey."

"Maybe. I'm going to ask her out for Sunday since we have that thing tomorrow night."

"I already did that, and she said she'd let me know," I say.

"Well, damn."

"Yeah. Lunch later?"

"Of course," he says. "Order Thai."

"We had Thai on Tuesday."

"Fine," he groans. "Korean barbecue."

"All right, see you then."

CHAPTER TWELVE
AUBREE

"PLEASE, PLEASE, I'M BEGGING YOU." LACEY CLASPS HER hands together and dramatically gets down on one knee.

"What?" I ask, only half paying attention. I've been stuck in my head, trying to figure out who I'm going to pick. Unfortunately, even after twenty-four hours, a new pro/con chart, a bottle of wine, and a long bubble bath, I'm no closer to figuring it out.

"Did you not hear anything I've said?"

"I'm sorry. I'm lost in my thoughts."

She frowns. "Still trying to figure out which guy to choose?"

"Yeah." I sigh. "I know it makes me sound horrible, but I really like them both."

"It doesn't make you sound horrible. You're human, Bree. And I love that you're opening your heart up again."

"And now I have to hurt someone else's...and my own." Tears fill my lids, and I try—and fail—to blink them away.

"Oh, Bree," she says, pulling me over to a table to sit down since the shop is quiet at the moment. "This was supposed to be fun and carefree. An introduction back into the dating world." She wipes a falling tear. "What the hell happened?"

"I suck at carefree," I mutter with a pout. "I'm falling for both of them. Like I really like them both." I sniffle. "And now I have to pick one, and I can't do it."

"Oh, sweetie." She hugs me. "You were just supposed to put yourself out there."

"Well, I did, with both of them, and I can't choose. Brody is so sweet and loves to have fun. And I enjoy talking business with him. Remember how he took me to look at all those bakeries? And our date at the drive-in…"

Lacey nods.

"Oh! And I forgot to tell you, the other day when your allergies were acting up, and you couldn't come in? He came by to see me, and I was so busy, I couldn't talk, but instead of leaving, he came around behind the counter and helped me." I choke up at the thought of having to break up with him.

"And then there's Hayden. He's such a good listener. Well, really, they both are. But like the other day, while we were out, Miles messaged and asked if I would go fishing with him when he got home. That night, Hayden texted me a list of the perfect piers that aren't too far away. And he loves wine like I do. We had so much fun at the vineyards.

"Ugh, and the way they kiss. Brody is passionate yet gentle and playful, while Hayden is a bit more intense. I have this connection with Brody. We can talk for hours, and it's just so comfortable, and with Hayden, the chemistry is so hot. Well, it's hot with both of them…" I sigh, my body heating up at just the thought of being with either of them.

"Wow," Lacey says, shaking her head. "You've really fallen for them both."

"I know." I groan. "It's only been a few weeks, but I can't imagine not being with either of them. How the heck am I supposed to break up with one of them?"

"I don't know," she says. "I wish I had a better answer for you, but I honestly don't know what you should do. When I fell for Sam,

I knew he was the one, but there was only him." She takes my hand in hers and squeezes. "Just remember to follow your heart. It won't steer you wrong."

I release a harsh breath and nod, wishing it were that easy. "So what were you begging me for?" I ask, changing the subject.

"Sam is making me go to the grand opening of Silk tonight, and you know he'll spend the entire time talking business. I was begging you to come with us, so I'll have someone to hang out and talk with."

"The strip club?" I've heard her talk about it on occasion. Her husband is the head architect on the renovations project to turn what was once a seedy strip club into something more...high-class. I'm not sure a strip club of any kind can be considered high-class, but who am I to judge since I've never been to one?

"It's also a steakhouse," she points out.

"With naked women dancing," I volley, scrunching my nose. Again, I'm not judging, but that's not exactly where I want to spend my Saturday night.

"The food and drinks will be delicious. Sam says even the women dancing are the best, and that it's not trashy. It's a playground for the obscenely wealthy. He wants me there, and I can't say no since I'm his wife, but I'd really love it if you would go with me so I'm not alone. All the wives and girlfriends will be there, and I never fit in."

Her face drops, and the saddest pout graces her lips. I groan, knowing I'm going to agree to go because when she does that shit, I can't say no.

"Ugh, fine. But I have nothing to wear."

"Eeep! Yay! Thank you!" She throws her arms around me. "We can go shopping after we close. My treat since you're doing me the favor."

I STARE AT THE TEXT, WANTING SO BADLY TO SAY YES, BUT instead, I close out of the message thread and drop my phone into my purse. I told myself until I figure out which guy I'm picking, I won't be seeing either one, but it's so hard when I miss them both.

Jesus, how did I get myself into this mess? To go from having no one—feeling lonely and wondering if I would ever be able to move on—to caring about not one but two sexy and sweet guys?

My taxi pulls up to the front of Silk, and after paying him, I get out, so I can head down the black carpet to where the bouncer stands, letting people in. Since I needed to get ready, and Lacey's house is nowhere near mine, I insisted we meet here. There was no reason for them to drive all the way over to get me, only to go back up to where Silk is located.

As I walk across the carpet, with several photographers and

paparazzi snapping pictures of everyone, I've never been so grateful to Lacey for buying me this dress. It's a long-sleeved, black-laced skater dress with a plunging neckline that shows off my curves in the best way, hiding my flaws and accentuating my assets. So that I'm comfortable yet stylish, I went with my favorite lace-up front stiletto heeled mesh boots. It gives me the sexiness and height without killing my feet. I kept my hair down and straightened it, something I rarely do since it's so thick and takes forever to straighten. Then I went heavy on my eye makeup, giving myself a smoky look. I must admit, I look good, sexy even. For the past few years, I've been down on myself and my curves, but being with Brody and Hayden has given me my confidence back, especially when they both look at me like they want to devour my body every time we're around each other.

"Aubree Heart," I tell the bouncer, giving him my maiden name since I started using that shortly after Pete died. The kids have Westley—which was his last name, but I found it too hard to explain when people would ask if I'm married or divorced, and I'd have to explain I'm a widow. I'll always be Aubree Westley-Heart, but it just hurts less to go by Aubree Heart.

After showing him my ID, he lets me through, and I head inside toward the hostess desk, checking out the inside on my way. It's all mahogany wood mixed with dark reds and gold accents.

"Good evening," the hostess says, smiling politely. She's standing behind the hostess desk, so I can only see her from the waist up, but she's in all black with only a tiny bit of cleavage show-ing, and her makeup is on point. She's gorgeous and not what I expected. "How may I help you?"

"I'm here for—"

Before I can finish my sentence, Lacey calls out my name, saun-tering toward me, dressed in a sexy little red number complete with matching red lipstick and red heels. The color pops against her pale skin and black hair.

"We need to talk, now," she says, her tone serious.

"Okay, can we get a drink first?" I ask as I let her guide me into the club-slash-restaurant. I gotta admit, the place is the perfect mix of elegance and sexiness. As we walk through, I notice the plush booths have high backs, giving each one an intimate feel. Women dressed in black leather cheeky bottoms, lacy black tops, and heeled stiletto boots are dancing on the poles erected in the center of several small round stages spread across the floor.

I stop to watch as one woman does some spin and then somehow flips upside down before she slides down the pole only to do another spin.

"I always assumed pole dancing would look trashy," I whisper to Lacey, "but these women make it look like an art." I nod toward the woman I'm watching, who's now gliding around the pole like she's performing and not in the middle of stripping.

"From what I've heard, these women take classes several times a week."

"We should take pole dancing lessons," I tell her, shocking both of us. "I can't imagine doing anything close to what that woman is doing, but I bet it'd be fun."

"I'm down," she says. "But right now, we need to talk."

She grabs my hand and guides us toward where I assume the bathrooms are since that's where women tend to talk. I'm so intrigued by this place. I'm glancing around when I see a guy who looks a hell of a lot like Brody, standing at the bar talking to…"Wait, is that…?" Holy shit, it is! Brody is here, and he's talking to…"Is Brody talking to Sam?" I tug on Lacey's hand, preventing her from walking any farther as my gaze locks on Brody.

As if he can sense me, he looks past Sam, and his eyes land on me. His features morph into a look of shock, obviously not expecting to see me here. But after a quick second, the shock wears off, and his eyes trail down my body, drinking me in. Based on the way his gaze turns heated, he likes what he sees. He says something to Sam, then sets his glass down and starts stalking toward me like a man on a mission.

"Brody knows Sam?" I whisper to Lacey without taking my eyes off Brody. He's dressed in a suit, but unlike his usual corporate ones, this one is sharper, more expensive looking, and he's actually wearing a tie. It's blood-red and matches the color scheme of the club.

"He does," Lacey says as Brody approaches. "And so does H—"

"Bree?"

I twirl around since the masculine voice calling my name isn't Brody, and my heart stops. I suck in a harsh breath as I take in Hayden, who's standing only a few feet away from me. He's also dressed to the nines in a suit, only his shirt is black, and his tie is gold.

When I glance back to see where Brody is, I bump directly into him. He catches me so I don't fall, and then I back up slightly, watching as the two men I've fallen for come face-to-face.

My blood drains from my body.

My heart kicks into overdrive.

My skin turns cold and clammy.

"What are you doing here?" Brody asks as I quickly glance at Lacey, who looks almost as nervous as me. And then it hits me—this is what she needed to tell me. They're both here.

"I..." I begin, but the words won't come out. I fucked up. I made a horrible decision to date two men, and now I've been caught. I need to own up to it, admit what I've done, and bow out gracefully. This isn't who I am—well, it's not who I was. Apparently, it is who I am now.

A cheater.

Regardless of how casual it was, despite the fact that I've kept them at arm's length and haven't done anything more than kiss them.

I'm a cheater.

"You look beautiful," Hayden says, leaning in and kissing my cheek. "This dress…Jesus, it's like it was made for you. I had no idea you'd be here tonight. Are you here with someone?"

My eyes dart to Brody, who seems to be waiting patiently for me to answer and, for some crazy reason, despite the fact that Hayden just kissed me, he doesn't look mad.

Why the hell doesn't he look mad?

"She's here with me," Lacey says since I've yet to answer. "My husband is Samuel Powers."

"Oh, shit," Brody says, shaking his head. "I had no idea. He always talks about you, but I never put it together."

"He was a huge asset to the renovation of Silk," Hayden adds, joining in the conversation. "The man has talent, that's for sure."

Wait a second. They both know Sam? How is that possible?

"Are you talking about me?" Sam says, coming over and putting his arm around his wife. "It looks like you've met my better half and her best friend. I was planning to introduce you, but you ran off," he says to Lacey, kissing her temple. "Have introductions been made?"

"I actually know her," Brody says. "She works at Heart's with Bree."

"Oh, you know Bree?" Sam's confused gaze flits back and forth between us.

"I do. Her coffee and pastries are the reason I've had to double my gym time." Brody winks at me, and butterflies swarm in my chest, reminding me how I feel about him, and also what I'm about to lose.

"You're telling me." Sam laughs, completely oblivious to what's about to go down. "I'm torn between begging Lacey to bring sweets home and not allowing them in the house. They're a damn addiction."

"The best addiction," Hayden adds, making Sam turn his attention on him.

"You know Bree too?" Sam says, then adds, "Well, that makes sense since you two are practically joined at the hip."

"Who's joined at the hip?" I blurt out in confusion. He can't be referring to...

Sam laughs. "Brody and Hayden." He looks from one guy to the other. "They own this place together...and are best friends and roommates."

My body stiffens. "You're..." I breathe, glancing at Hayden. "You're..." I swallow thickly, my eyes going to Brody. This can't be happening. I've not only been dating two guys, but I've been dating best friends. I'm pretty sure I just moved from horrible person to worst person alive.

"We are," Hayden says softly.

Before I can respond, a beautiful woman, who clearly works here based on her attire, comes over and says, "Welcome to Silk. You can have a seat at any of the booths, and someone will be by to serve you shortly."

"Thank you," Hayden says, then turns his attention to me. "Bree, why don't you sit with us?"

I glance at Lacey, silently begging her for help. "I'm here with Lacey," I choke out.

"Well, then, Lacey, Samuel, would you guys like to join us at our table?" Hayden asks them.

Sam nods with a smile. "We'd love to."

Hayden takes my hand in his, and I should probably pull away, but I'm too in shock, too confused, too...*freaking the hell out* to do anything but let him guide me over to a circular table surrounded by three moon-shaped plush booths.

Hayden slides in, taking me with him, and then Brody slides in after me, making me the cream in the most awkward Oreo sandwich ever. Lacey and Samuel sit in the booth to the left of us, leaving one booth open, but a few seconds later, a couple comes over and introduces themselves as Lucas and Brianne Sharp. Apparently, Lucas is Sam's boss and owns the architecture and construction company where Sam works.

When the server comes over to take our drink orders, I order a double rum and Coke. The girly drinks aren't going to cut it tonight if I have to be squeezed between the two men I'm dating at the same damn time. Lacey eyes me with curiosity and confusion, silently asking what the hell is going on.

I simply shake my head since I have no idea while several questions flit through my brain. Are they aware I've been dating them both? Are they okay with it? And the one that I get stuck on is if they were okay with it, why didn't they say something? That one gets my hackles up. Sam mentioned they're roommates and best friends. We talked for weeks about everything—my kids, our jobs, our families—yet not once did either of them mention the other.

And then a horrible thought crosses my brain, one that has me feeling as though I'm going to puke: Was I nothing more than a game to them? Did they plan this out? It can't be a coincidence that they both came into Heart's and asked me out. And if they're as close as Sam insinuated, there's no way they never discussed who they were dating.

This entire time while I've been freaking out, have they known I was dating them both? The thought has me tensing in my seat, and I'm suddenly more pissed than apologetic.

Hayden must notice because his hand moves to the top of my thigh as he leans in and squeezes it. "We'll talk later, okay? Right now, just enjoy the night. The food is to die for."

"But…" I breathe, wanting answers to my questions. Before I can voice that, though, Brody's hand lands on my other thigh, forcing my words to be cut off.

"You look gorgeous," Brody murmurs, kissing the sensitive area just below my ear. "All night, we've wished we could've invited you. And then, to see you, dressed in this sexy as hell dress and those heels, walk through the door. Fuck," he groans. "It's like a fantasy come true."

We…Oh my God, he said *we*. They know. They've known. They were in on this, and I had no idea.

The server returns with our drinks, and I down mine in one go, needing the liquid courage to get through tonight. Brody chuckles, then orders me another, and I let him, not wanting to make a scene. Tonight is important to Sam. Lacey told me this was a huge project for him, and there are talks about him being promoted.

While I sip the second drink slower, everyone at the table talks about the club and their hopes for it, then eventually moves on to discuss other business. Since I don't really have anything to add, I sit quietly, which is probably best because while the guys talk and I drink, both massage circles into my exposed flesh. And when the appetizers arrive, their hands ascend under my dress and get dangerously close to the apex of my legs. I should push them away, but my common sense is clouded by my arousal.

But when Hayden's fingers brush my center, I snap out of it, shoving both their hands away. "I need to use the restroom," I announce louder than necessary, making everyone look my way.

I catch Hayden's smirk as he shifts out of the booth so I can escape and take a moment to find my bearings.

I'm not looking behind me as I flee, so I don't realize both guys follow me until I'm almost to the bathroom. Brody calls my name and grabs my bicep, pulling me into a door marked PRIVATE.

The second the door closes, and I see we're in an office, I spin around and glare at both of them. "You knew…the entire time I was dating you both, you both knew, didn't you?" My tone is a mixture of anger and hurt because even though I'm mad, I'm also hurt.

"Was this all just a game? Date the fat chick and see who she picks?" I ask, hating the insecurity in my voice. "Did you laugh after every date? Compare notes? How much did you bet?" I accuse.

"Fuck no," Brody says, stepping toward me first. "This wasn't a game. We're both attracted to you. We want you just the way you are." His hand cups my cheek, and for a split second, I relax into his touch before I back up, needing answers.

"How long have you known?"

They glance at each other, something silently being said between them, before Hayden answers. "The entire time."

I gasp. "And you said nothing." I shake my head. "This whole time, I've kept you at arm's length, trying to choose one of you, hating myself for dating two guys at the same time, feeling like the most horrible person in the world, and you knew and said nothing?"

"You are *not* a horrible person," Brody says. "We both really like you and care about you and…" He sighs. "We were okay with you dating us both."

"For how long?" I cry. "Would you have let this go on forever? What would've happened when I picked one of you? What would you have done then? You're roommates and best friends! You would've brought me back to your place and introduced me to the guy I broke up with?" I hiss, tears burning behind my lids. I know I brought this on myself by dating them both, but they knew and didn't even say a word.

And now, I have no choice but to end things with both of them.

"I didn't see either of you last night or confirm plans for the future because I've been stressed out thinking I needed to choose. It hurt my heart to imagine not being with either of you, and now, because of what you did, I have to lose you both."

"What? Why?" Hayden approaches, but I put my hand up to halt him in place.

"Why?" I screech, traitorous tears falling as the reality of the situation hits me. I've been falling for two men, and now I'm about to lose them both. "Because you're best friends, and I can't pick between you without hurting the other person or myself!"

When both guys try to come closer, probably to comfort me because I'm now full-on crying, I stop them. "I have to go," I mutter through my tears, darting past them and out the door.

Hell-bent on getting away, I completely forget to let Lacey know I'm leaving until I'm in a cab and on my way back to my apartment. I send her a message that I'm not feeling well and will talk to her tomorrow—Sunday is her day off, but I have no doubt she'll be in to get the scoop. Of course, she asks if I'm okay and offers to come over tonight, but I tell her I just need to be alone.

After getting undressed, I run myself a hot bubble bath, turn off my phone, and try to get lost in my current book. Unfortunately, my heart hurts too badly, and my brain won't shut off, so instead of reading, I close my eyes and try—and fail—not to cry, wishing I wouldn't have listened to Lacey. I thought I could do casual, and instead, I ended up with my heart broken by not one but two guys.

CHAPTER FOURTEEN

HAYDEN

"We fucked up."

I nod in agreement as we both stare at the doorway where Bree just fled through.

"She called it a game."

"It wasn't a fucking game," I argue.

"I'm pretty sure I said something along the lines of 'May the best man win.'" He sinks into the chair behind the desk, and his face falls into his hands.

"A game would imply we were playing with her. I can't speak for you, but I wasn't playing. I like her a hell of a lot, and my intentions were never to play her but to keep her."

Brody lifts his head to look at me. "And you think I was playing? I told you I like her. But we both can't keep her, and right now, I'm almost positive she doesn't want either of us."

"She wants us," I disagree. I could see the way she looked at us, reacted to our touch. "She's just upset because we betrayed her, but we can explain ourselves and get her to listen."

"And then what? We convince her to keep dating us both? To choose one of us? You going to be okay when she picks me?" Brody looks at me with his serious face, telling me he's not being a smart-ass. He means what he's saying. "Because I can tell you right now, I'm not letting her go without a fight."

"That's how we got into this mess in the first place." I sit across from him in the visitor seat, and we sit in silence for several minutes, both of us lost in our own thoughts.

"It's too bad we both can't be with her," Brody says with a humorless chuckle, suggesting the same thing I said a while back. At the time, he said she'd never go for it and that he wanted more than a threesome, but now that we know she likes us both and we feel the same…

"What if we—"

My phone rings, cutting me off, and thinking—and hoping—it's Bree, I slip it out of my pocket and click answer without checking to see who it is. Big fucking mistake.

"Hayden, how are you?"

"Dad, hey, what's up?"

I glance at Brody, who grimaces.

"I was calling to check on the situation."

I roll my eyes. He knows tonight is the soft opening of Silk, and I'll be busy with that. Still, because I partnered with Brody outside of the company, with my own money, he's bitter as fuck and will do anything to interrupt my night.

"I'm handling it," I tell him, the same thing I've been telling him for weeks.

"Handling it would mean she's signed over the lease. Nothing's being handled."

"It takes time." Time to figure out how to convince him to find a new property to build the wellness center on.

"I think we need to meet tonight to go over what exactly you're—"

"Dad, I'm in the middle of something. We can meet Monday morning at the office. I gotta go."

Without waiting for him to reply, I hang up and pocket my phone.

"Deal still going through?" Brody asks.

"It's not happening."

He scoffs. "Does your dad know that?"

"He will, once I figure out how to steer him toward a better option. Once I do, he'll let it go." At least I hope he will.

"Your dad isn't going to let this go," Brody says as if reading my mind.

"He's not going to have a choice because Bree isn't going to sign, and there isn't anything he can do about it."

"And what about your position?"

"It's not going to come to that," I say. "I'll make sure of it. Now back to what we were talking about. Why can't we?"

His brow furrows. "What?"

"Before my dad called, you said it's too bad we both can't just be with her. Why can't we? All the women we fucked in college loved it. Some preferred it."

"Yeah, horny as fuck college students. Bree is a grown woman and a mother."

"And I'm not saying we tag-team her like we did in college." I lean in, the craziest—yet best—idea hitting me. "What if we both date her instead of her choosing?"

Brody gives me a confused look, so I explain. "You're my best friend. We've known each other for over twenty years. We've lived together for over ten. Hell, I've even fucked you. I know you better than anyone, and you know me better than my entire damn family. Would it be such a stretch that when we finally find a woman who we both like, it's the same one?"

Brody sits up straighter, his sign that he's giving this some thought. "So you're proposing a poly relationship?"

"Why not?" I shrug. "We won't be the first. Plenty of people do it...including families with kids. Hell, I think there's a show or two about it. I'd like to think we live in a society where people are more accepting of nonconventional relationships. But if not, who cares?"

"And what if she doesn't go for it? What if she only wants one of us?"

"Then the other person walks away, and our friendship stays intact. We're stronger than that. At the end of the day, I only want you to be happy, and I know you want the same for me. If that means I'm not in the equation, then I'll bow out."

Brody nods. "I agree. I want her and getting to share her with you is a fucking bonus. But if she ends up only wanting you, I want you both to be happy." After a few beats, he laughs softly. "Are we really going to do this?"

"We have to be one hundred percent on board with this. Can you see yourself spending your life with Bree, me, *and* her kids? Sharing a house, sharing a woman? We're obviously not there yet, but if *we* can't see it, if *we're* not sure, we shouldn't propose it to her."

Heat sparks in Brody's eyes, and I know he can see it all the same way I can. Our future with Bree. With her kids. Hell, maybe even some kids of our own with her. Coming home to her, spending our lives with her.

Now we just have to make her see it too.

CHAPTER FIFTEEN
AUBREE

Brody and Hayden,

While I'm upset at what you did by not telling me that you knew I was dating you both, I am not without fault, so I want to apologize. Until you two came along, I had only gone on one crappy date since Pete passed away. And before him, I only had one boyfriend in high school, so I'm not extremely experienced in the world of dating.

When you both asked me out, I wasn't quite ready to move on yet, but Lacey convinced me to get out there, so I did with Brody, but then he had the wrong number, and I assumed he didn't want to see me again, so I agreed to go out with Hayden. And then Brody came in. I never meant to date you both, and I wasn't trying to pull one over on either of you, but somehow, it happened. I kept telling myself I would pick one of you, but the more I fell for you both, the harder it became. I've spent so much time trying to pick, and I can't.

When I met my husband, the first time he looked at me, I got butterflies, and the same thing happened with both of you. At first, I thought maybe the butterflies were a lie, that they didn't mean what I thought they meant. But then I realized they were accurate. It would be my luck that when I moved on, I would fall for not one but two guys.

The fact is, I could see a future with both of you. I know it's early on, and anything could happen, but I wouldn't continue to date someone I don't see a future with. Who I can't imagine introducing to my kids. That is why I was so hurt when I found out you guys are best friends and roommates.

It was one thing to pick one of you when you didn't know each other, but now that I know you're friends, I can't do it. And that hurts because I went from having two amazing guys who I was enjoying getting to know to having no one. And I feel like if you would've been honest, my heart could've been saved because I would've stopped seeing you both a long time ago. But you weren't. And now, I have to end things with both of you. I truly wish you both the best, and I'm sorry for my part in all of this.

xo Bree

I HIT SEND ON THE GROUP CHAT, FIGURING IT'S BEST TO message them both at the same time—since I don't have their emails—then exit the thread. It's been eighteen hours since I found out I was not only dating two men but two best friends, and my heart still hurts. Yeah, I'm mad that they hid it, but I'm more hurt than anything because they let me get to know them and care about them both, and now I have to be without them both, which sucks.

After closing up and thanking Jessica—who is in culinary school and loves to bake—for opening this morning and handling all the baking when I realized I was in no place to open the shop myself after crying all night, I head home.

I call my kids and chat with them for a little while—telling them no less than a dozen times that I miss them—and then decide to throw on my pajamas and make the rest of the day a wallow day. Tomorrow, I'll wake up, ready to move on, but today I need to wallow with a pint of ice cream and an ugly cry book. As I'm grabbing my e-reader from the bathroom where I left it last night, there's a buzz from the intercom. Assuming it's Lacey coming to check on me, I buzz her in and unlock the door, swinging it open so she can come right in.

Only it's not Lacey who enters, but Brody...and Hayden, both dressed in a pair of jeans and a T-shirt, somehow looking sexier casually dressed than they did in their tuxes last night.

"Do you always blindly let strangers up and unlock the door so they have access to you?" Brody chides as they stroll in like they own the place.

I shake my head, shocked and confused as to why they're here. "I thought you were Lacey," I stammer. "She texted me that she would be by this afternoon."

"Text her that you have company," Hayden says, taking my hand in his and guiding us toward my couch. "We need to talk."

"Umm..." I shake my head again, watching Brody close and lock the door.

"In the future, you need to ask who's at your door," Brody says.

"What if it were a kidnapper or a sex trafficker, or someone coming to rob you?"

"Umm…" I repeat because *what the fuck?* "Did you get my message?"

They both nod.

"We did," Hayden says, "but we don't agree or accept it."

"What?" I choke out with a baffled laugh.

"We're not going to apologize for both of us dating you," Brody says, sitting on the coffee table in front of me while Hayden sits beside me. "Dating you was the best decision we've made. Should we have told you? Yeah, and that's on us, not you. In the beginning, we honestly thought you'd pick one of us. When you didn't, we both fell for you, and since neither of us was willing to give you up, we accepted that we were both dating you."

"And we don't want to stop," Hayden adds.

"So you want me to just date you both?" I choke out, wondering if this is some kind of joke.

"You said in your message you couldn't pick because you like us both," Brody says, his face deadly serious. "Well, we both like you too. And we both want to be with you."

"So the only solution is for you to date us both," Hayden says matter-of-factly.

"Until I decide?" I glance at each of them. "I'm not going to do that to either of you. That's what I was trying to do, and look how that turned out."

"No." Brody shakes his head. "We don't want you to choose…"

"Unless, at some point, you feel that one of us isn't for you," Hayden finishes. "But as long as you want us both, we want to be with you."

"We'd rather share you than lose you," Brody says, taking my hand in his and kissing the top of it. His lips are soft yet firm, and the way they linger on my flesh sends sparks through my body, straight to the apex of my legs. For a moment, I'm distracted by the way he makes me feel…until his words hit me.

"Are you insane? Are you seriously suggesting I date both of you? How would that even work? You take even days…" I eye Brody. "And you have odd." This time Hayden.

"Nothing has to change," Hayden says, taking my other hand and threading his fingers through it. The traitorous damn butterflies swarm my belly, and I silently beg them to go away. "Until you found out we were friends, you were dating us both."

"Yeah, but I also felt guilty as hell!"

"Now you don't have to feel guilty," Brody says.

As my gaze flits back and forth between them, I realize they're serious. They want me to date them both, and they're okay with it. And then, because I've apparently lost my mind, I start to think about how it would all work. Sure, we've been dating, and I haven't done more than kiss them, but eventually, things will move to the next level. "What about sex?" I blurt out.

"You want to have sex with us?" Hayden smirks playfully.

"Well, I mean…" My body heats at the thought of being with them. I imagine Brody would be gentle, taking his time to make love to me sweetly. Hayden, on the other hand, would be a bit more animalistic, devouring every inch of me. The thought of having both of them, in their own way, has me clenching my thighs in want.

"You're thinking about it, aren't you?" Brody grins. "Who were you thinking about? Me or Hayden?" The way he asks, he already knows.

"Both of you," I breathe out.

"And we both want you," Hayden says. "We talked about it, and we're okay with you being with both of us…in every way."

I'm crazy to even consider this, right? But how can I not? I want them, care about them, and they're offering a solution where I can keep them.

"So we would be in a relationship, the three of us? Or would it be separate?"

"It can be however you want," Brody says. "But we're okay with the three of us being together. It's probably too soon to talk that far ahead, but if it came to it, we're okay with sharing you completely. Living together and creating a life together."

"And what if one of you changes your mind?" Just the thought of one of them walking away has my heart sinking.

"It's not going to happen," they both growl at the same time.

"But if it does?" I prompt, refusing to let my question go unanswered. "We have to consider every possibility because the damage and hurt will affect all of us."

They both nod in understanding, but Brody is the one who answers. "We discussed all of this last night. If one of us decides to walk away or if..." He swallows thickly. "If you decide you don't want to be with one of us, that person will walk away."

I open my mouth to argue, but he lifts his hand to halt my words, continuing. "Hayden and I have been best friends since elementary school. We've been living together for over ten years. Our friendship is solid. I can promise you that while it will hurt like a bitch, whoever it is you don't want to be with will walk away without issue, and our friendship will remain intact."

"This is no different than being in a conventional relationship," Hayden adds. "Nothing is ever guaranteed in life, but we want this to work if you do. We don't have all the answers since we've never done this before, but we can take it one day at a time...together."

"I need to think about it," I say. "This is a huge decision to make. I have two kids..."

"Who aren't coming home for another month at least. That gives us time to see how it goes." Brody moves to the couch and lifts me onto his lap so I'm facing Hayden. "We know about your kids, and we look forward to getting to know them."

"And I need to think about the fact that even though you say it won't affect your friendship, there's a possibility it will. And what will people think? You both are prominent businessmen. Aren't you worried about how this will all look?"

"Is this conventional?" Brody says. "No. But it's been done

plenty of times. And I can assure you that Hayden's and my friend-ship is strong enough for this."

I'm about to respond to the friendship part of what he said when his other words—it's been done plenty of times—hit me. "Have *you guys* done this before?"

Hayden and Brody share a look, and then Brody speaks. "In college, Hayden and I hooked up with a few women together."

Holy shit! "You've had multiple threesomes?"

"We were young and experimenting. None of them meant anything, but when I was younger, I thought I might be gay…or maybe bi." Brody pushes a fallen strand of hair behind my ear and grins sheepishly. "I wasn't sure what to do or how to figure it out because I was too afraid of what people would say. My parents knew and accepted me no matter what, but the outside world can be cruel as fuck." He cups the side of my face. "One night, I was struggling. When Hayden and I were with a woman, I was so turned on, and I was afraid I was attracted to my best friend, who I knew wasn't gay. Hayden came home and said if I wanted to know if I liked guys, I needed to be with one."

"So what did you do?" I ask, invested in the story.

"I spent the night with Hayden."

I swing my gaze over to Hayden, who shrugs nonchalantly. "We meant it when we said we're best friends. I knew Brody wouldn't be comfortable being with some stranger, so I fucked him."

"So you're bi?"

"Eh, I think I was more bi-curious. Don't get me wrong, I find Hayden attractive." He smirks at his friend, who waggles his brows playfully. "But being with him made me realize that while it was good, it wasn't enough. If I never had sex with a guy again, I'd be fine with that." He glides his hand down to the curve of my hip and squeezes. "But the threesomes we had made me realize I enjoy watching people have sex. The thought of watching you and Hayden together turns me on. The possibility of getting to keep you forever and knowing my best friend is also happy and with the woman he wants to be with makes me fucking happy. And I don't give a shit what anyone thinks or says."

"I don't either," Hayden agrees. "Maybe it's because we're worth billions between the two of us that we don't have to give a shit about what anyone thinks, but I have no problem sharing you with my best friend and the world knowing it. My family isn't close, and I've struggled with whether I wanted to be with someone. I was scared to end up in a loveless marriage like my parents. I haven't been able to picture a future with any woman I've dated. The truth is, I was content just simply living with Brody and sharing my life with him. He's more than my best friend. He's my family, and the idea of being with you and him, the possibility of spending our lives together, makes me, for the first time, want a future with a woman. I would be nothing but proud to walk down the street with you...and Brody."

Oh, my heart. I should be freaking out, but the way they love and care about each other and want me to be a part of their lives makes it so hard to be anything but in awe. But the problem is that the fantasy isn't always the reality.

"I still need to think about this," I tell them. "I need to make sure I'm okay with everything going into this. I know nothing is guaranteed, but I don't want to say yes when I'm not completely sure."

"We get it," Brody says, leaning in and kissing my lips softly. My stomach knots, wanting more, but all too soon, he ends the kiss and looks at me with patience and understanding in his eyes. "If you need to talk, we're here."

As I'm nodding, wishing the kiss could continue, Hayden pinches my chin with his thumb and forefinger and turns my face toward him. His mouth crashes against mine, his tongue pushing past the seam of my lips. My body heats, and before I realize what I'm doing, I slide off Brody and into Hayden's lap. He chuckles against my lips and breaks the kiss, making me pout.

"You see that?" he murmurs. "The way you felt when you kissed

Brody and then me? You can have that all the time. You just have to say yes." He briefly presses his mouth to mine and then stands, setting me on my feet.

The guys head toward the door, and I almost beg them to stay, but I really do need to think with a clear head. And I can't do that in their laps while kissing them.

"We'll wait to hear from you," Brody says.

"But try not to make us wait too long," Hayden adds with a wink.

CHAPTER SIXTEEN

AUBREE

"Let me get this straight. You have a harem of men who want you to be with them, and you're asking me if I think you should do it?"

I roll my eyes at Lacey. "First of all, for it to be a harem, it'd have to be three or more guys with one woman. In my case, there are only two, so it would be a menage or a polyamorous relationship."

Lacey snorts. "It sounds like you're familiar with these terms. Is this the shit you read about? I might need to pick up reading." She waggles her brows, and I groan.

"Can you focus, please?"

"Sorry." She shrugs, clearly not at all sorry. "So Brody and Hayden knew the entire time you were dating them both, and instead of being mad, they proposed you continue to date them both. And you're not sure if you should. Am I following?"

"Yes." I'm also upset that they hid the fact that they knew all along, but since we all made some shitty choices, and they clearly aren't mad that I was two-timing them, I've decided to let it go. No point in dwelling on what's already happened.

"I only have one question," Lacey says seriously, her eyes locking with mine. "Will you be fucked by them both at the same time?"

"Lacey!" I hiss, glancing around to make sure her husband isn't listening.

"What?" She throws her arms up in the air. "C'mon, Bree. Just the other day, you were in tears because you thought you had to pick one and you couldn't. Only to now be told that you get *both* of those yummy men. What's the issue here?"

"The issue is..." I clear my throat. "The issue is that..." I sigh and bang my head on the table in frustration.

"The issue is that you're seriously considering it, and that scares the hell out of you," Lacey says, hitting the nail on the head.

I glance up at her. "This isn't just like a one-time threesome, Lace. They want an actual relationship. Like to date both of them." I swallow down the emotion clogging my throat. "They talked about a *future*. Like with the three of us and my kids."

"Do you like them both enough to see where it goes?"

"Yeah, I do. I mean, I know it's only been a few weeks, but..."

"But?" she prompts.

"I told you about the butterflies. I knew the moment I met Pete that he was the one. And I think the reason it was so hard to pick between Hayden and Brody was because I felt that same connection with them."

"Then what's the problem?"

"A poly relationship isn't the norm. I have two kids who lost their father. I'm trying to provide stability. Their mother being with two men is hardly considered stable. And what if this all goes wrong? Where does that leave me? Where does that leave *us*?"

"You had the perfect *stable* life with Pete. You guys did everything the right way. Dated, got engaged, married, moved in together, bought a home, had two beautiful babies. You guys were the definition of perfectly stable, yet it still ended with you heartbroken."

I swallow thickly. "We weren't perfect," I mutter.

"Pretty damn close," she says. "My point is that nothing's guaranteed." She takes my hand in hers and squeezes it gently. "So maybe it's okay to live your life however you want because at the end of the day, what's the point if we're not living and loving, even if it's not considered the norm?

"I've only met Hayden and Brody a few times, but even I can see how much they care about you. Why not see where it goes? And as far as your kids are concerned, is it so bad that they see their mom being loved by two men? I think there are worse things in life than that." She shrugs.

"And," she adds, not finished, "after losing their dad and Grandma Violet, would it be so horrible that they're loved by two more people? Because we both know Miles and Evie are so freaking lovable, and I have no doubt the moment they meet Brody and Hayden, they'll have them wrapped around their little fingers. Nobody is immune to their charm."

She finishes her little speech and stares at me patiently, waiting for me to think, but the truth is, there's nothing to think about because she's right. I learned the hard way that life is too damn short, and people can be taken from you in the blink of an eye, so it's pointless to worry about the what-ifs. I have two men I care about who want to continue getting to know me and like me enough to consider a future. Maybe it will work out, maybe it won't, but I would be crazy not to see where it goes.

"You're right," I tell her. "I would be a fool to let two men who care about me walk away simply because our relationship wouldn't be conventional."

"Exactly," she agrees. "Plus, who the hell would say no to being DP'd?"

"D what?" I look at her in confusion.

"DP'd," she repeats. When I look at her like she has two heads, she sighs. "You know, when two guys take a woman at the same time. One in her pussy and the other in her ass."

"Lacey!" I hiss, smacking her hand and shoving it away.

"What? Don't you read all those romance novels? Watch porn?

It's been like forever since you've gotten laid. You have to be using something to get yourself off."

"Yes, I read *those* kinds of books and watch porn, but I didn't know it was called that."

"Okay, so now you know. And you, my lucky best friend, get to be DP'd. I'm totally going to be living vicariously through you."

"I doubt that will be happening," I say, trying—and failing—not to think about Brody and Hayden taking me at the same time. *Jesus, that would be hot.*

"Why not?"

"For starters, my life isn't a romance novel *or* a porno. They said things would continue how they are. Me dating both of them. Although…" I trail off, remembering what they said about being with women at the same time in college.

"You should probably talk to them," Lacey says. "Make sure you guys are on the same page…in *every* way." She waggles her brows suggestively.

"You're right." I pull out my phone and send a group text, asking them if we can get together to talk. This is all complicated as it is. I'd rather figure this all out before my kids get home. That way, they aren't affected if it doesn't work out.

They both text back that they can meet me anywhere and anytime. Since I'm already out, I offer to go to them, and Brody texts back their address and that I can come over whenever I want.

"I'm going over to their place so we can talk."

"Good." We stand, and Lacey pulls me into a hug. "Just remember that the only thing that matters is your happiness. And when you're happy, your kids will be happy too. Everyone else outside your bubble can go fuck themselves."

"I don't know what I would do without your crazy ass," I tell her, hugging her back.

"Well, it's a good thing you'll never have to find out." She pulls back and winks, and I smile, despite the pain her words elicit deep inside me. She meant it as a joke, but since Pete and my grandma died, I've learned not to count on anyone to be there. Maybe it's time I start letting people in again and stop living in fear of losing everyone I love.

WHEN I WALK INTO THE LOBBY OF HAYDEN AND BRODY'S place, I'm met with an elderly gentleman dressed in a suit who greets me with a soft smile. Brody warned me that I'd have to check in with the front desk before I could go up the first time, so I'm prepared. After introducing myself and giving him my ID, he scans it. He then has me sign a couple of papers before handing me an elevator key and the code I need to input to go to their floor, which is apparently the penthouse.

"Thank you," I tell him when he hands me the key. "Do I return it here when I'm done with it or—?"

"No, ma'am," he says. "It's yours to keep. If you should ever no longer need it, we can deactivate it at the desk."

I thank him, shocked that Brody has requested I have my own key before I've even agreed to anything.

As I take the elevator up to their floor, I send him a text:

ME

An elevator key, huh? A little presumptuous, aren't we?

A text from him comes in almost immediately after mine goes through:

BRODY

More like hopeful.

Instead of responding, I get off the elevator, expecting to end up in a hallway, only to find myself standing in their foyer.

"Is that elevator just for you?" I ask as I walk deeper into their home.

"It is," Brody says, coming over and giving me a kiss on my cheek. He takes my hand in his and guides me farther inside. "Hayden is on a business call, but he'll be out shortly. While we wait, why don't I give you a tour?"

We start in the spacious living room that looks professionally furnished and decorated. With onyx hardwood floors, stylish black leather furniture, and pristine white walls, the place screams single and wealthy. A beautiful fireplace sits in the corner next to a black spiral staircase that must lead to the second floor.

"And this is the kitchen," he says as we walk into a gorgeous, state-of-the-art kitchen bigger than my entire apartment. I admire the top-of-the-line appliances, and the number of cabinets and counters are a baker's wet dream.

"We don't cook much." He shrugs sheepishly. "So it's kind of a waste, but it came with the place."

"God, I could live here," I blurt out. When Brody's brows fly up to his forehead, I quickly backtrack. "I mean, in this kitchen. Not here, like here, here. Like, I'm not trying to move in…I just really like the kitchen…" Brody snorts at my rambling, and I sigh. "I just meant that this kitchen is amazing, and if I had one like this, I'd probably bake in it all day."

"Well…" Brody steps toward me and pushes me gently against the counter. "You're welcome to bake here any time you want." With my hair in a high ponytail, he wraps his fingers around the strands and tugs my head to the side, giving himself access to my neck. "Hell, if you wanted to live here, I don't think either of us would be opposed."

"I don't think that'd be—"

Brody presses his warm lips to the sensitive spot just beneath my ear, cutting off my train of thought, my only focus now on how good his lips feel on me. He trails his tongue along my heated flesh, and I moan.

"Damn, I leave to make one phone call and miss all the fun."

I jump at Hayden's voice and try to push Brody away. Only when I reach out, he snags my hand and spins me around, so he's leaning against the counter, and I'm facing Hayden with my back pressed against Brody's very hard front.

"Sorry," I squeak out, dropping my face to look at the ground in embarrassment at having been caught with Brody.

"For what?" Hayden steps around the island and stops in front of me. "What are you sorry for?" He pinches my chin and forces me to look at him. "A part of dating both of us means you're with *both of us* in every way, and we don't get jealous." He proves his point by leaning in and pressing his lips to mine in a passionate yet quick kiss. "Fuck, I've missed those lips," he murmurs as he pulls back.

"Well, Bree here, was just saying how she wants to move in," Brody says with a laugh.

"I did not!" I smack his chest and try to get away, but he wraps his arms around my torso and holds me tighter. "I said I could live in your kitchen."

Hayden chuckles. "Have you shown her the bedroom yet? Maybe we can convince her to live in there." He waggles his brows, and I reach out to playfully smack him. Only when my hand lands on his chest, he grabs ahold of it and tugs me out of Brody's arms and into his.

His mouth crashes down on mine and his tongue darts past my parted lips, tasting me. I can't help but sigh into the kiss, wanting more. I always want more. The kiss ends all too soon, and I'm left panting like a dog in heat, wishing I could hump his damn leg.

Of course, Hayden notices. "Later," he says with a smirk. "First, we need to talk." When I pout, he chuckles. "Didn't you say you wanted to talk?"

"Yes," I say reluctantly.

The guys show me the rest of the place, and holy shit, it's incredible. I've heard about places like this, but I've never actually been in one. For most in New York, like me, eight hundred square feet and two bathrooms is considered luxurious. This place is at least five times the size of my place, with four bedrooms, three bathrooms, a loft, a gym, and two offices. The living room is huge, and their bedrooms are gorgeous, furnished with dark woods and decorated in soft browns and creams. Their bathrooms both have a spa tub, complete with jets—forget the kitchen, I could live in the damn tub! Give me a glass of wine and my e-reader, and I'd be good for life. They also have a laundry room—even though they tell me that they never use it because they get all their clothes dry-cleaned—and a dining room that's separate from the kitchen and seats six people.

My, how the rich live.

Once the tour is over, and I'm actually considering moving in here—I'm just kidding, but damn, that bathtub!—we settle in on the couch in the living room to talk. I'm sitting on the same couch as Hayden, but there's space between us, so I can focus, and Brody is sitting on the loveseat adjacent to me. Brody and Hayden have beers in their hands, and Hayden's poured me a glass of my favorite white wine.

"So what would you like to talk about first?" Brody asks, taking a sip of his beer.

"Are you planning to DP me?"

Both guys spit their drinks out at the same time, and I realize I probably should've worded that better. Whoops, too late now.

CHAPTER SEVENTEEN
BRODY

"Are you planning to DP me?"

The thought of Hayden and me filling Bree at the same time, thrusting into her pussy and ass, feeling her warmth as our cocks slide in and out, rubbing against each other through her thin walls, has my dick swelling behind my pants.

I wipe the droplets of beer I spat from my chin and set my beer down to give Bree my full attention. When she said she wanted to talk, I had no idea this was what she wanted to talk about, but I'm definitely not complaining.

"Is that what you want?" Hayden asks, moving closer to Bree. Her eyes are wide, almost like she didn't plan to ask that question, and she chews on the corner of her lip, trying to decide how to answer.

"I don't really know what I want," she says softly, her voice cracking like she's nervous. "I've never done this before." Her gaze flicks from Hayden to me. "All I know is that I really like you both, and I like dating you and getting to know you. I want to see where it goes since my kids are away and won't be affected by any of it.

"I mean, for all we know, one or both of you can change your mind." She shrugs like it's not a big deal, but the way she frowns says the idea of one of us walking away would upset her, telling me she cares more than she's leading on. She's just scared and nervous to let us in, which is okay, because this is new, and we have plenty of time to chisel our way into her heart.

"We're not going anywhere," I tell her, confident enough that I can speak for Hayden, based on the conversations we've had about this recently, "but as a businessman, I know that actions speak louder than words, and it's going to take time to prove how we feel."

She nods in understanding, then clears her throat. "I think it would be good if we just see where things go, take it one day at a time, but, um...I was thinking..." Her neck and cheeks tinge pink, and I hold back my chuckle, not wanting to make her feel uncomfortable since whatever she's trying to say is probably sex-related. She proves me right when she finally finishes her sentence. "I think we should all get tested. I'm on birth control, and I haven't had sex since my—since Pete passed away..." She trails off, her lips forming a slight frown at the mention of her late husband. "But if we're all going to be sexually active, I want to make sure we're safe...and..." She takes a deep breath, then releases it, her eyes descending. "If you change your mind, I would really appreciate it if you'd break up with me before you sleep with someone else."

"Not happening," Hayden says, "but I agree."

"Same," I add. "But we get it. Trust is earned over time." I lean forward and squeeze her knee, and she looks up at me. "Don't be embarrassed to talk to us. Neither of us has been in a relationship like this either. But we want to try because it's worth it if it means we get to be with you."

"Do you have any more questions?" Hayden asks.

"No, not right now, but I do have one thing I want to say." She looks at me, then Hayden. "I don't like that you kept the knowledge that you were both dating me from me. I know I was in the wrong to date you both, but I was confused and unsure how to handle it. You flat out kept it from me. I don't want things kept from me anymore, and in the future, if I'm unsure of something, I'll talk to you. I'm not a dating expert, but from my experience while being married, communication is important."

I glance at Hayden, who flinches, obviously at war as to whether he should mention the sale of the building to her. His gaze meets mine, and he shakes his head, silently telling me to keep my mouth shut before he glances back at Bree and nods in understanding. We'll have to have a conversation soon because I'm not risking losing Bree over this bullshit. If what he's saying is true, and his dad doesn't have a leg to stand on, then it won't matter that she knows.

"It won't happen again," I tell her.

She breathes a sigh of relief. "Thank you."

Hayden's phone goes off, and he checks it, groaning. "I have to head into the office," he says. "There's an emergency with one of the properties, and I need to handle it, or my dad will have my ass."

Since he's moved closer to Bree during the conversation, he takes her chin and presses his mouth to hers for a quick kiss. "I'm so damn happy that you're giving this a chance," he murmurs against her lips before he stands to head out.

Once he's gone, and it's just Bree and me, I ask her if she's eaten dinner, hoping to spend more time with her.

"No, I went over to Lacey's after work and was going to eat with her and Sam but ended up coming over here."

"Do you have any plans tonight?"

"That depends," she says with a sexy smirk that makes me want to pick her up and carry her to my bed and get lost in her. "What are we doing?"

"We can go out to dinner...or we can order in and watch a movie."

"I choose the second option."

I cross over to the couch she's sitting on and lift her into my arms so she's sitting on my lap. Wrapping my arms around her waist, I kiss her gently and revel in her taste. "I was so scared you were going to tell us no," I admit, pressing my forehead against hers.

"I definitely have my reservations," she admits, "but I looked it up online, and it's actually quite common. There's a lot to consider, but for right now, I just want to continue getting to know you both."

"I like the idea of that." I kiss her again, but this time, instead of pulling back, I deepen the kiss, stroking her tongue with my own. My hands grip the curves of her hips, and I lift her to straddle my lap. We kiss like this for several minutes—tasting, coaxing, and learning each other's bodies. Until Bree's phone rings in her pocket, and she jumps back slightly.

"It's my kids," she says. "Can I…umm?" She glances around.

It takes me a second, but before she can finish her question, I put two and two together. "You talk to them, and I'll order us food." I give her a chaste kiss. "Italian, Thai, Japanese…?" I list a few choices she's mentioned she loves.

"Mmm, Thai sounds good. I love shrimp Pad Thai and chicken fried rice. Oh! And some spring rolls."

"You got it." I lift her off me and set her on the couch. The phone has stopped ringing, but as I walk out of the room to give her some privacy, I hear her call them. A second later, two excited little voices sound throughout the house followed by Bree saying hi and how much she misses them. Instead of walking away, I stop to watch and listen as she talks to them, every word and gesture filled with love. The way she listens with patience and sounds genuinely excited over everything they say reminds me so much of my step-mom, Savy.

My heart swells at the thought.

When Miles says he misses her, she asks if he'd like for her to visit. He tells her that would be awesome and then goes over every-thing he wants to show her once she's there. When he mentions going fishing, she tells him that once he's home, they can go fishing around here, naming several piers they can go to. Miles cheers and says he's going to look them up. His voice is replaced with her daughter's, who tells her all about their trip to the zoo and how much she misses her.

Not wanting to eavesdrop more than I already have, I head to my office. Once I'm done placing our order, I open my laptop to check some emails while I wait for Bree to finish. I'm responding to my CFO regarding some budget questions when Bree knocks on the doorjamb, leaning against it. I hit send, then close my laptop.

"Sorry about that," she says. "Once they start talking, it's hard to get them to stop."

"C'mere," I tell her, rolling back in my chair slightly.

She pads across the room, barefoot, and I note how adorable her bright pink toes are—the same color as her coffeehouse. When she stops next to me, I pull her in front of me, pushing my laptop out of the way so I can lift her onto my desk. She spreads her legs, setting her feet on the arms of my chair. I roll between her thighs and wrap my arms around her waist.

"You never have to apologize for talking to your kids," I tell her. "Hayden and I meant it when we told you that we understand they're a package deal. I know firsthand how important the relationship between a child and parent is, and I also know what it feels like to be loved by someone who isn't biologically related to you. I met Savy when I was fourteen and mad at the world, and it was her acceptance, her motherly love—when she wasn't even dating my dad yet—that helped me get through some rough shit.

"One day, when you're ready, I look forward to meeting and getting to know them. And the fact that they're your kids is enough to already have me caring about them."

Her eyes turn glassy, and she wraps her arms around my neck. "Thank you. You have no idea how much that means to me. My kids are my entire world, and I think a part of why I never dated was because I was afraid of how it would affect them as well as whoever I'm dating, especially after the one date I went on went so badly the moment I mentioned I was a single mom.

"When I was younger, no matter how quiet and behaved I was,

my mom always yelled at me. And her boyfriends hated me. I spent years living in fear of being a bad kid until she took off, leaving me with my grandma."

My heart breaks at her words, and I find myself holding her tighter while she talks, loving that she's letting me in.

"When Pete said he wanted to have kids, I was scared he wouldn't want them once they were born. And when I found out we were having twins, I freaked out. He kept telling me to calm down, but I was so scared the house would be too messy, the babies would cry and wake him up and he'd be upset. Babies are loud and messy, and as they grow up, that doesn't change."

She smiles a watery smile and I wipe the tear that leaks out and trails down her cheek.

"And did he prove otherwise?"

"He did," she says, her smile widening, those sexy as fuck twin dimples popping out. "One day, he had enough of me walking on eggshells. He followed me around all day and wouldn't let me do a single dish or clean the house. When the twins would cry, he'd get them. By the end of the day, the house was trashed, the worst I'd ever seen it. I was exhausted and started to pick up, but he stopped me and said this was what a lived-in home looked like and that he loved everything about it. He made me go to bed with the house the way it was, and while I was sleeping, he cleaned it."

Another tear slides down her face. This time, I can't help myself when I lean in and kiss her cheek, where the liquid sits, darting my tongue out and tasting the saltiness. "I hate to see you cry," I murmur, "but I love that you're sharing with me. Pete sounds like he was a great man, and he was right. This place…" I jut my chin out, referring to Hayden's and my home. "It's clean, almost sterile, because it's barely lived in. That's how my dad's places always were too until he and Savy moved in together. They created a family together, and the home they live in looks lived in. And neither of them would have it any other way."

I kiss her lips, licking the salty liquid that's landed there. "Any man who deserves you will accept your children, noise, crying, screaming, lived-in home, and all. Even if you decide tomorrow that you don't want Hayden or me to be those men, don't ever settle for anything less."

The food arrives while we're talking, so we separate long enough to eat, but once we're done, I pull her against my side so we can pick a movie to watch. She selects the one she wants—a chick flick about a nerdy girl who ends up falling for the popular guy—and then, after giving her a shirt and boxers of mine so she'll be more comfortable, we settle on the couch with her snuggling into my side.

As she watches the movie, laughing at the funny parts and sniffling at the sad, half of my attention is on the movie, but the other half is on her—on the way she fits perfectly into my side, the way she smells sweet like vanilla, how, when I massage her thigh, needing to touch her in some way, her skin is soft and smooth.

About halfway through the movie, Bree yawns, but when I ask her if she's tired, she shakes her head. Less than twenty minutes later, though, her soft snores are heard over the movie, and I know she's fallen asleep. I should probably wake her up and offer to take her home, but the idea of her sleeping in my home, in my bed, is too enticing, so I carefully lift her into my arms and carry her to bed, loving the way she looks there, like it's where she belongs.

She barely stirs, and once she's under my blankets, she nestles her face into one of my pillows, sighing contentedly before her breathing evens out. Once I know she's asleep, I head back out to the kitchen to get the food cleaned up before I join her in bed.

I'm putting the last of the dishes into the dishwasher when I hear the elevator doors slide open, and Hayden walks in, looking worse for wear.

"Everything okay?" I ask, closing the dishwasher and then leaning against the sink.

"Yeah. One of the investors for the wellness center was threatening to pull his funding. They're getting antsy."

"So what are you going to do?"

He scrubs his hands over his face and sighs. "I put together a presentation of other options, properties that have better locations, are cheaper, and will bring in a higher profit. I've requested a meeting next week and hope that they'll agree to let Bree's building go."

"And if they don't?"

"Then I'll have to flat out tell my dad it's not happening. But regardless, I'm going to tell Bree the truth after this meeting. I just want to have all the information before I do, so I can be completely honest with her."

I sigh in relief. "Good. The last thing we want is to push her away over this shit."

"Where is she?" he asks, glancing into the living room. "Did she go home?"

"Nah." I grin at the thought of where she is. "She fell asleep, so I carried her to my bed. She's there now, and I'm about to join her." I wink, knowing it will get a rise out of him.

He shakes his head and chuckles. "All right, well, I'm gonna go shower and get some sleep. You guys have a good night?"

"Yeah," I tell him as we head toward our rooms. Originally, the place only had one master bedroom, as most homes do, so after we bought it, the first thing we did was turn the guest room into a second master bedroom and add an en suite bathroom since we have another two bedrooms upstairs.

"She confided in me that she was scared to date again because her mom and her mom's boyfriends were always shitty and made her feel like she was unwanted and could never do anything right. She was scared whoever she dated would feel that way about her kids."

Normally, I wouldn't spill someone else's business, but Hayden and I spoke, and since we're in this together, we agreed we wouldn't keep shit from each other where Bree's concerned—we both want her to be happy.

"What about her husband?" Hayden asks tightly, assuming the worst.

"He put her at ease, refused to let her feel like that, but I think she's afraid most guys won't be like him. Especially since the one date she went on before us turned to shit after he found out she was a mom."

"We'll just have to prove her wrong," he says with a shrug.

We stop in the doorway of my room, both of us looking in at a sleeping Bree. The city's lights shine through the blind slats, lighting up her face like a halo over an angel.

"She looks so sweet lying there," Hayden says softly. "I want her here...her and her kids. I don't even know them, and I want them here with her. I could never imagine having a family, didn't want that shit...didn't want to be anything like my parents. But fuck, she's a goddamn game changer. I saw a pregnant woman walking down the street, and my first thought was *what would Bree look like carrying our babies.*" Hayden chuckles under his breath. "I think I've lost my mind."

"Nah," I say, looking over at him. "I think it's called falling in love, and I'm pretty sure I'm right there with you."

Hayden swallows thickly. "It's too soon for that, though, right? I mean, it's only been a few weeks. Shouldn't it take months...even years to fall in love?"

"I'm not sure," I say honestly since I've never fallen in love. "But my dad and Savy fell hard and fast. It couldn't have been more than a few months before he was asking her to move in."

Hayden nods. "Do you think she'd mind if I slept on the other side of her? I don't want to make her feel uncomfortable, but she's right there, and I miss her."

"I don't see why not. It's not like we're going to touch her or anything. We're just going to sleep."

CHAPTER EIGHTEEN

AUBREE

MY INTERNAL ALARM GOES OFF EVERY MORNING AT FOUR, whether I have to go in to work or not. I have to go in this morning since I chose to stay with Brody to have dinner and watch a movie instead of baking last night.

Wait a second. Brody…

My eyes pop open, remembering I never went home last night, and come face-to-face with a sleeping Brody. His face is calm, serene even. My thoughts go back to the last man I slept in bed with—Pete—expecting to feel some sort of guilt, but surprisingly, the only thing I feel is content and happy and, for the first time in a long time, carefree. Until I remember one minor detail: Hayden's sleeping somewhere in this house, and he probably saw Brody and me asleep in here. My heart drops, guilt crushing my good mood. I'm not sure how I'm going to find a—

There's a stirring behind me, and then fingers grip the curve of my hip, cutting off my thoughts. When I turn around, ready to scream, I find the man I was just thinking about. Hayden's hair is messy, there's a bit of stubble on his face, just as I like, and his features are etched in concern.

"Hey," he rasps, his deep voice filled with sleepiness. "I was, uh...I was going to dip out before you woke up so you wouldn't know I was here." He cringes at his words. "It's just, well, you looked so beautiful sleeping, and Brody didn't think it would do any harm..." He sighs when I don't say anything. "Did I fuck up?"

I love that he cares—that they both think about my feelings. I considered, for like a second, that this could all be a game, but once I thought about it, about their actions, I knew that was just my fear and insecurities talking because everything these two men have done these past few weeks has shown me that they genuinely care.

"No," I tell him, moving toward him so we're closer and don't wake Brody up. "I was just feeling guilty for being in bed with Brody while you were sleeping somewhere else." His hand glides down my side and around to the globe of my ass. "I like you both being in here. I don't..." I swallow thickly. "I don't like having to choose. I like you both."

He leans in and gives me a soft kiss, which isn't the norm for him. Sweet is usually Brody, while rough and passionate is all Hayden. "We don't want you to choose. We want you to be with us both, and if that means the three of us share a room, we're completely okay with that. You're running the show. Whatever you want to happen will happen."

"I like this," I admit, glancing back at Brody, who's still asleep. "Being here with both of you...I wish I didn't have to get out of bed and get ready for work." My hand comes up and slides under his shirt, stopping at each of the ridges of his hard abs.

"So quit your job and stay in this bed forever," he jokes. "I can promise we'd make it worth it."

"Fuck yeah, we would," Brody says from behind me, making me jump slightly. Suddenly, the front of his body presses into the back of mine, but before I can say anything, Hayden's mouth attacks mine in a punishing, passionate kiss. His fingers delve into the back of my hair, deepening the kiss, as Brody peppers soft kisses along my neck and exposed shoulder.

I groan into Hayden's mouth, and he deepens the kiss, his tongue darting out and finding my own. Since his fingers are still threaded in my hair, I assume it's Brody's hand that slides down my thigh and calf. Instinctively, I lift my leg, hooking it over Hayden's and giving him access to between my legs as we continue to kiss. I have no idea what I'm doing or where any of this is going. One minute, I was getting up for work, and the next, I'm sandwiched between two guys—no, not two guys—*my guys*. They're mine. The thought sends a chill down my body, making me visibly shudder.

"You okay?" Hayden asks, pausing the kiss.

"Yes, I'm good," I murmur against his lips. "Kiss me."

He doesn't have to be told twice. His mouth is back on mine, kissing, tasting, stroking. Between his mouth on mine and Brody's lips and hands on me, my body feels overstimulated in the best way possible. It's been years since I've been touched like this, and I had no idea how badly I was craving it. Like eating a cupcake without having anything to drink. I was dying of thirst, and these guys... they're the coldest, most refreshing glass of milk.

Hayden moves me onto my back, breaking our kiss, but before I can argue and beg him to come back, Brody's mouth is on mine, his tongue pressing past my parted lips, not even caring that Hayden's mouth was just there.

Hayden's lips trail along my neck, and then he tugs on my earlobe. "Can we make you come, baby?" he murmurs. His question causes my thighs to clench and my body to squirm.

"Yes," I breathe without breaking the kiss with Brody.

My answer causes Brody to kiss me harder, his tongue to delve deeper. My hands come up and run along the back of his shaved head, tugging on the short strands on top, as Hayden disappears from next to me. The boxers Brody lent me along with my underwear slide down my legs, leaving me naked from the waist down.

"Fuck," Hayden growls, spreading my legs wider. For a split second, I consider closing my legs, not wanting him to see all of me —and trust me, there's a lot of me—but at that moment, Brody kisses me harder, sucking on my tongue, and all insecure thoughts are lost to his touch.

Hayden's fingers separate me, and then his tongue slowly glides up my center, and I groan into Brody's mouth.

"Fuck," Hayden repeats again, only this time he adds, "she tastes so damn good, man."

Brody growls against my mouth, nipping at my lips. He breaks the kiss and looks into my eyes. "When he's done, I'm getting a taste." His mouth crashes against mine in a very un-Brody-like way, and I groan as Hayden licks and sucks my clit. It's been too long, and I come quickly—so quickly, if I were a man, I'd probably be embarrassed.

Colorful sparks explode behind my eyelids, and my body shakes in pleasure as my orgasm overtakes me. I'm still soaring high above the clouds, lost in my pleasure when I notice Hayden has replaced Brody, which means…

A single digit enters me, and Brody hisses, "Jesus, you're so wet."

"You gotta taste her," Hayden says, pulling my shirt over my head. Our eyes lock briefly, and I take a deep breath, knowing he's going to look at me and what he's going to see: naturally large breasts that aren't perky anymore, thanks to breastfeeding two babies for a year, and a soft stomach marked with stretch marks from carrying them almost full-term.

But this is me, and I can't change who I am. Nor would I want to because those *flaws* are part of being a mom, and I wouldn't change that for anything in the world.

Hayden's eyes leave mine, trailing down my body, stopping at my breasts and then my stomach. I watch with bated breath, waiting for the disgust to take over his features. I might've only looked Brody up on Google, saw the images of him with all those women, but I have no doubt Hayden's been with his fair share of beautiful women.

"You're so gorgeous," he says, his finger running over my nipple.

"So damn perfect." His finger skims down the center of my chest, along my stomach, over my stretch marks, and stops at the apex of my legs. I release the breath I was holding, my heart swelling at his words—so damn perfect. Nobody's perfect, not really, but I love that he sees me as such.

He sticks a finger inside me and then pulls it out as Brody says, "You were right. She tastes delicious." Brody's lust-filled eyes lock with mine momentarily before he goes back to licking and fingering me.

"Taste yourself," Hayden says, bringing his glistening digit up to my mouth. Without thought, I part my lips and then wrap them around his finger, sucking on my essence—a mixture of sweet and tangy—not giving a shit how dirty this is.

"Good, right?" he prompts, removing his finger.

I swallow thickly and nod, watching as he takes his wet finger and trails it down my throat and back to my breast. He pinches it hard, and I squirm at the pleasure-pain that shoots through my body. His face dips and latches onto my nipple, biting and sucking on it roughly, while reaching across to my other one and pinching the hardened tip.

Between Brody pleasuring me and Hayden giving attention to my breasts, my second orgasm climbs higher and higher until it hangs on the precipice. With one more lick and another bite, I fall off the edge, screaming as my climax crashes through my body, sending me flying high once again.

"Best way to wake up," Hayden says, kissing my lips. I moan into his mouth, wanting more. But all too soon, he breaks the kiss, and it's Brody's turn to kiss me. With the taste of me on his lips, my body tightens, and I'm turned on all over again.

As if he can read my mind, Brody chuckles. "Later, sweetness. Right now, you need to get to work." His words have me springing into action. I grab my phone from the nightstand, where Brody must've placed it, and see it's almost five o'clock.

"Shit!" I hiss, jumping off the bed. "I'm late. I need to get to the shop, and I haven't baked anything yet." I search for my clothes from yesterday and find them folded neatly on the dresser. Snatching them, I run into the bathroom and quickly do my business and then get dressed. I'll have to work in this because I won't have time to shower and change by the time I take the subway home.

"Hey, slow down," Brody says when I walk out. He's dressed in a T-shirt and jeans. "I can drive you to your place."

I sigh in relief. Usually in the city, driving anywhere wouldn't be faster, but since it's still early, him driving me will definitely get me home quicker.

With a quick goodbye to Hayden, Brody and I head out. It's once we're in his SUV that it hits me. While I came twice, neither of them got any.

"What's going through that beautiful mind of yours?" he asks, once again somehow realizing I'm lost in my own head.

"You and Hayden didn't..." I nod toward his crotch. "You didn't...get off."

He smirks and shrugs. "That was about you. Tasting you and making you come were enough for us. Did you enjoy being with both of us?" His words come out nonchalantly, but something in his tone, mixed with the way he's biting his lip, tells me he's nervous about my answer.

"I liked it," I admit truthfully. "I liked waking up to both of you, and I liked both of you pleasuring me at the same time."

"That's a lot of likes," Brody jokes.

"Well, I *liked* it a lot."

"What about love?" he asks. "Could you love it?"

I briefly wonder if his question is meant as something more. If he's asking if I'm capable of loving him—loving them. Up until recently, the thought of falling in love again seemed like an impossibility, but now..."Love is definitely a possibility," I tell him honestly.

A beautiful smile stretches across his face, but he doesn't say anything else.

When we arrive at my place, I give him a quick kiss, then head inside my shop so I can get to baking. The day flies by. Jessica comes in and works beside me, and when Hayden texts, asking if I want to play hooky and go to the beach with him tomorrow, I ask Jessica if she'd like some extra hours. She excitedly says yes, so I text Lacey to let her know I'm taking the day off.

LACEY

Holy shit, did someone steal my best friend
and replace her with someone fun?

ME

Haha

LACEY

Seriously, that makes me so happy.
Everything will be handled. You have a good
time, and Tuesday, be prepared to tell me all
about your day.

CHAPTER NINETEEN
AUBREE

THE HOURS FLY BY. HEART'S STAYS BUSY ALL MORNING, and we sell out of almost all the pastries before noon. When it dies down, I tell Jessica she can get out of here since I can close on my own. She and Lacey will be opening together tomorrow, but since I got all the baking done this morning, it will be easy for them.

Assuming that I'm spending the night at my place, when the clock strikes three, I lock up and am ready to head upstairs to shower and order in dinner when my phone chimes with a message from Hayden:

> HAYDEN
>
> I miss you and can't wait until tomorrow to see you. Pack a bag and spend the night?

For a second, I consider telling him that's not a good idea, that we should be taking things slow, but my heart—and libido—win out, and before I can second-guess myself, I text back

> ME
>
> okay.

After packing my clothes and bathing suit, I lock up and head downstairs.

I'm prepared to walk to the subway, but I quickly learn I won't have to because sitting in the no-parking zone is Hayden, waiting for me in his fancy car.

He jumps out of it and, like a gentleman, takes my bag and opens the door for me. With a kiss on my lips, he closes the door for me and rounds the front, getting in and taking off.

"How was work?" he asks conversationally. It's such a simple question, but it makes me smile. I didn't realize how much I missed mundane things like that until now. With Pete gone, I went through the motions and didn't focus or dwell on what I'd lost, needing to stay numb to get through each day and be there for my kids. I stopped thinking about what I needed and wanted. But now that I'm allowing myself to feel again, it's as if the light has been shined down on me, and I don't want to go back into the dark.

"It was good. Jessica is happy to be opening tomorrow. She's a culinary student and loves to bake. I don't hand over the reins enough."

"Nothing wrong with delegating, especially if it means you get to enjoy your life a little more."

When we arrive, Brody sits in the living room, staring at his laptop. "Yeah, we can discuss this tomorrow," he says, glancing up and smiling at me. He must be talking to someone from work.

"Hey, Brody!" a woman calls out. "Dinner Friday night?" Okay, maybe it's personal...

"Yeah, sounds good. I was thinking I'd bring someone..."

"Could it be whoever just walked in that you're grinning at like a fool?" the man says.

Brody laughs. "Yeah..." He nods for me to join him, but I shake my head.

"C'mere," he says, grabbing my hand and pulling me down so I'm almost sitting on top of him. I glance at the screen and see a man, who looks to be an older version of Brody, with the same color hazel eyes and brown hair—only his strands have a bit of salt and pepper sprinkled in—sitting in a chair with a gorgeous, younger woman on his lap. She has blond hair and blue eyes, and the sweetest smile on her face.

"Savy, Dad, this is Bree Heart. Bree, these are my parents."

I wave, slightly overwhelmed and a little embarrassed at meeting them like this. "Hi," I squeak out.

"Oh, aren't you beautiful," Savy coos, a slight Southern twang laced in her words.

Her husband chuckles. "What my wife means is that it's nice to meet you, Bree."

"Yeah, that." She giggles, playfully slapping her husband's chest. "Please tell me you'll be joining Brody Friday night." With the look of hope in her eyes, I can't say no.

"Sure."

"Good." She claps excitedly. "Where's Hayden? Tell him he better be joining you guys."

I cough lightly, wondering how this will go down, but Brody doesn't miss a beat. He says he'll make sure Hayden's there before telling them good night and telling his dad that he'll see him in the morning.

"You work with your dad?" I ask when he ends the call. I thought he said he ran the company.

"He's more or less retired, but I trust his opinion and judgment, so I go to him when I need business advice. He's going to sit in on a meeting tomorrow morning with a potential new client."

"Guess you won't be going to the beach with Hayden and me tomorrow, then." I pout playfully.

"Someone's gotta work," he growls playfully, lifting me into his lap so I'm straddling his thighs. He tucks my hair behind my ear and kisses me softly, his tongue running across the seam of my lips. My body comes to life, and I clench my legs in want. His hands descend, landing on my butt, massaging the globes, and I moan into his mouth, grinding myself against him. Lost in the kiss and the way he's touching me.

Until there's a throat clearing, and I jump, remembering Hayden is the one who picked me up. "Shit, sorry," I mutter, trying to scramble off Brody. I swing my leg around, so I can slide off his lap, but he holds me to him, not letting me go.

"What are you saying sorry for?" Hayden asks, raising a brow as he sits next to us.

"Umm…" I glance between the two of them. "I just thought… well, you picked me up. I shouldn't be kissing Brody when it's your time."

Brody's brow furrows. "Sweetness, there is no *his time* or *my time*. It's *our* time. Kiss whoever you want, hang out with whoever you want. We promise, neither of us will get mad or jealous."

I glance at Hayden to see if he agrees, and he nods. "This is new for all of us," he adds. "But you never have to worry about us getting upset over who you want to spend time with."

"How is Friday night going to work?"

Hayden glances at Brody, who says, "We're having dinner with my parents."

"Ahh, well, they won't care," Hayden says like the idea of telling Brody's parents that they're dating the same woman is no big deal.

"Seriously?" I look at Brody.

"They love and accept me the way I am. Besides, they're probably in shock that I'm even dating a woman serious enough to introduce to them. This whole time they've probably been waiting for me to tell them that I'm really dating Hayden," he says with a laugh.

"It'll be fine," Hayden says, grabbing my legs and setting them on his lap. He pulls my shoes and socks off and then starts to massage my feet and ankles. "Why don't we order dinner and watch something? I'm starved."

While the guys discuss what to order, I sink back against Brody's chest, enjoying the foot massage from Hayden. When you're on your feet ten-plus hours a day, your feet take a beating.

Once Brody's ordered a pizza, he asks if there's anything in particular that I want to watch. Since I don't watch much TV, I let them choose. As the show starts, Brody's fingers trail down my arm and land on the top of my thigh while Hayden continues to massage me. He's moved on from my feet and is up to my calves and shins now, and I can't help the groan that escapes when he hits a particularly sore area.

"Feel good?" Brody rasps, making me open my eyes and look at him. His face is close to mine, his eyes burning with desire. I glance at Hayden, who's looking at me with a similar expression, and my insides tighten, wanting to please them the same way they pleased me.

"Really good," I breathe, glancing from Brody to Hayden as I muster up the courage to do what I'm considering.

When Hayden taps my leg, silently conveying to lift so he can remove my shorts, I shake my head and remove my legs from his lap. His brows knit together in confusion, and Brody's does the same when I slide off his lap and onto the floor between the two of them.

They're close enough that I don't have to choose, so I reach for each of their pants at the same time, undoing their buttons and zippers. It's been years since I've pleasured a man, and never two at the same time, so it doesn't surprise me that my hands shake as I reach into their pants.

They're both hard, and when I wrap my fingers around their shafts to pull them out, I find they're both long and thick. My mouth waters at the thought of taking them into my mouth. Pete always preferred sex over oral, and once the twins were born, we didn't get much time to ourselves, so I didn't get to do it often, but something about making a man come apart with my hands and mouth made me feel powerful.

"Bree," Hayden whispers, glancing down at my shaky grip on his shaft. "You don't have to do this."

"I want to," I murmur. "I want to make you both feel good."

They both nod, and Hayden moves closer to Brody, so I don't have to reach as far.

"I've only been with one guy," I admit. "So if I suck at this…" I laugh humorlessly, but neither of them joins in.

Instead, Hayden grips my chin and lifts it to look at him. "None of that insecurity bullshit," he demands. "We're in this together, and whatever you do is more than we expect."

I nod in understanding, even though I know he's only saying that to put me at ease. They're red-blooded males in their late twenties who've had several threesomes. There are expectations there, whether they want to admit it or not. But I appreciate what he's doing.

Hayden leans down, and his lips crash against mine in a punishing kiss that has me whimpering into his mouth. As he kisses me, I stroke their shafts, taking them from hard to granite. Using the beads of pre-cum, I create more friction until my hands are sliding easily up and down.

When Hayden breaks our kiss, Brody palms my face and kisses me softly, tenderly. I could kiss them all night, but what I really want is to make them come, and not just from my hands alone.

Gently, I end our kiss and then lean over, taking Brody's cock into my mouth first while I continue to stroke Hayden. My tongue swirls around his fat mushroom head for a few beats before I open wider and take him all the way down my throat. He curses under his breath, and the area between my legs dampens, loving that I'm doing that to him. That my mouth is doing that to him.

Not wanting to ignore Hayden, I slide my mouth slowly off Brody and switch to Hayden. When I take him into my mouth, my teeth scrape along the skin of his shaft, and he curses as well, confirming what I already know about him—he likes it rougher.

I glance up at him through my lashes, wanting to see his face, and our eyes lock. "Jesus, Bree. I want to fuck your mouth so badly."

"So do it," I taunt, wanting that as well.

When he doesn't take me up on it, I glide my mouth back down his cock, scraping his skin again, until his thick head hits the back of my throat, making me gag slightly.

The action is enough to spur him on.

His fingers thread through the back of my hair, and he begins to fuck my mouth savagely, taking every bit of pleasure I have to offer him. I reluctantly release Brody's dick so I can use Hayden's knees to keep my balance as I take every inch of him into my mouth, letting him control the situation.

All too soon, he's warning me that he's going to come, and I'm silently insisting that he keep going. With a few more thrusts that have my eyes watering, he pushes my head down and stills, spilling his hot seed straight down my throat. It tastes horrible, but I swallow every bit he gives me.

When he releases me, I take a deep breath and glance up at him, finding his lids hooded over, completely satiated, just how I wanted him. He grips me by the back of my neck and fuses our mouths together for a hot, quick kiss, not caring that I still have his cum on my tongue.

When we part, I crawl over to Brody, who's taken over lazily stroking himself and waiting patiently.

"I loved watching you," he says, reaching over and wiping under my eyes. "Taking Hayden's cock like that. Fuck, you looked so damn hot." His praise causes a new kind of heat to spread through my veins, warming me from the inside.

I get onto my knees and lick my way up his shaft, starting at the base and ending at the engorged head. Knowing he's gentler, I give it a sweet kiss, then suck it into my mouth. He groans and the backs of his knuckles tenderly drag down my cheek in approval.

With the care that Hayden doesn't want or need, I take him all the way into my mouth, then glide back up, swirling my tongue around the head once again. I continue to do this, over and over again, until Brody's legs are shaking and he's warning me that he's close. Just like with Hayden, I don't stop. Instead, I increase my speed and suction my cheeks, and seconds later, Brody explodes in my mouth. This time, though, it doesn't go down as easily as it did with Hayden, and I have to quickly excuse myself to go spit it into the sink before I gag and throw up. While I'm in there, I use the restroom and then brush my teeth.

When I return, the guys are standing in the kitchen with the pizza that must've been delivered while I was in the bathroom.

I glance at Brody, feeling bad that I couldn't swallow it. "Sorry about that," I mutter, a bit embarrassed.

"What the hell are you sorry for?" He cuts across the kitchen, his eyes narrowed. "That was without a doubt the best head I've ever gotten, and I've tasted cum before and that shit's gross."

His admission has me laughing. "It totally is," I agree, grabbing a slice of pizza and taking a bite.

CHAPTER TWENTY

HAYDEN

Playing hooky with Bree means getting up at the crack of dawn and getting my shit done, so I can take the day off. But as I lie in Brody's bed, where the three of us fell asleep last night—after giving Bree a couple of orgasms that left her sated and barely able to keep her eyes open—it's hard as hell to pry myself from this bed.

Bree's sleeping on her stomach, facing me. Her blond hair is splayed out across the pillow and the sheet is only covering her lower half, exposing her creamy back. She's snoring softly and her plump lips are making a perfect O shape, reminding me of the way she sucked Brody's and my dick last night.

She's gorgeous, but more than that, she's sweet and funny and down to earth. She's the complete opposite of the women Brody and I have dated, yet she's perfect for us. The way she's shy and reserved, yet trusting and open—

"I can feel you staring," she rasps, cutting off my thoughts. She scoots toward me, laying her head into the crook of my shoulder and throwing her arm over my torso.

"I can't help it," I admit, not caring that the next words out of my mouth make me sound corny as hell. "I could stare at you all the damn time."

She laughs softly and snuggles closer against me. "Do it quieter so I can sleep," she jokes.

I'm supposed to get up, get some work shit done, but I lie here instead, trailing my fingers up and down her back as I listen to her fall back asleep. I lean in and smell her hair—because I've officially turned soft—and sigh at the vanilla scent. She always smells sweet, like she was made to be in a bakery.

"You're such a creeper," Brody whispers through his laugh, obviously having caught me sniffing Bree's hair.

"How the hell does she always smell like a damn cupcake?" I whisper back, shaking my head.

"She's too sweet for her own good."

"Truth. You sure you don't want to join us at the beach?"

"Nah," he says. "I have a meeting this morning that I can't miss."

After watching her sleep for a few more minutes, I carefully shift out from under her so I can get ready and get some stuff done. If I'm going to convince my dad and the other investors that we're better off forgetting about the building Bree lives in, I'll need to make a compelling argument because the first time I brought it up, my dad wasn't buying it.

I'm working in my office when Bree comes padding in a few hours later, freshly showered and dressed in what looks like a bathing suit cover-up and flip-flops, holding a cup of coffee and a muffin in her hands.

"Breakfast," she says with a smile, setting it down. She goes to retreat, but before she can get away, I snag her by those luscious hips and pull her back toward me.

"You bake these this morning?" I ask, breaking a piece off and popping it into my mouth. It's banana and practically melts in my mouth. I swallow it down with a sip of the iced coffee she brought, and it tastes better than anything I've ever made, which makes sense since she does this for a living.

"Yeah," she says. "I used the ingredients you guys had on hand. The only fruit you have are bananas."

"A man could get used to this." I break another piece off and push it past her lips.

She chews and swallows, then asks, "Used to what?"

"For one, waking up next to a beautiful, naked woman…" She blushes, her cheeks and neck turning an adorable shade of pink, and I note to make her blush more often. "And then being made coffee and homemade muffins. Keep it up, and Brody and I will be begging you to never leave." *Hell, we're already considering it, and she's only spent the night twice.*

"Very funny. You almost done?"

"Yep." I close my laptop. "I'm ready to go."

"A WOMAN COULD GET USED TO THIS," BREE SIGHS, repeating the words I said to her earlier as she sips a fruity beverage our cabana boy just brought her.

When we arrived at the beach club I booked for the day and were taken back to the cabana I rented that's located directly on the private beach, complete with a huge couch, a double lounger, a mini fridge, and a television, Bree asked, "Is this for us?"

I nodded, and she looked around, perplexed, then added, "Well, damn, when you do the beach, you go all out, huh? I was proud of myself for remembering to bring a blanket we could share." Then she reached up and encircled her arms around me, murmuring, "Thank you," while peppering kisses all over my face.

"I want you to get used to it," I tell her, squeezing her thigh. "My hope is you'll get so used to it that you'll never leave."

She sets her drink on the table and turns toward me. "I don't need any of this," she says, her tone serious. "I appreciate it, but I don't need it. I've been happy my entire life, laying a blanket in the sand and lying across it. The only thing I want is to find someone who wants to lie on that blanket with me. Who loves my kids and me, and wants to create a life with us. I want someone who will stand by me and be my best friend. The rest is just a bonus."

At her words, a ten-ton weight of guilt settles in my gut, and I vow to meet with my dad tomorrow to discuss the situation. I can't keep hiding this from her, and the sooner I tell her, the better it will be.

"What about *two* men who want to lie on that blanket with you? Who want to love you and your kids? Who want to stand by your side?"

She smiles softly. "I'd feel like I won the damn lottery."

"You should've taken me to my house. I have sand in places sand should never be in, and I need to take a shower."

"Which is exactly why I brought you here instead," I tell her, lifting her over my shoulder caveman style and slapping her ass.

"Hayden!" she shrieks. "Put me down!"

I ignore her, carrying her to my bathroom, and then set her down once we're both standing in the open shower that could easily fit several people. I turn the hot water on, and it immediately waterfalls down on us.

"Better take off your clothes, so you can get all that sand out," I say, waggling my brows as I pull my shirt off and throw it to the side.

Her eyes rake down my chest and over my abs, landing on indents that dip into my shorts. When I push them down my thighs, my soft dick falling flaccid against my thigh, she sucks her bottom lip into her mouth. Some guys would be embarrassed for a woman to see him soft, but since I know I'm a decent size, I couldn't care less. Besides, if Bree keeps looking at me the way she is, it'll be hard soon enough.

"Your turn," I tell her.

"Eh, I'm good." She shrugs. "I happen to like the sand where it is," she says, her eyes hinting at a bit of insecurity hidden behind her playful tone.

"Bree..." I step toward her and lift her chin. "I've already seen you naked, and every single inch of you is perfection."

"It's different in the heat of the moment. You focused more on getting me off than on my rolls and stretch marks." She sighs. "In the light of day, I'm far from perfect. Meanwhile, you and Brody look like that. It's hardly fair," she says, pouting.

"And now...I sound like a whiny, insecure little girl." She groans, throwing her head back.

"Stop." I chuckle, gliding my hand down her side and settling it on the curve of her hip. "There's nothing wrong with being insecure. We all have our flaws and doubts, and we live in a social media-driven society where pictures are photoshopped.

"But I need you to understand that you're perfect just the way you are. I mean, fuck, you carried and then gave birth to not one but *two* babies at the same time."

I grip her chin with my thumb and forefinger, and she opens her eyes. "When I look at you, all I see is your beautiful face." I kiss the corner of her mouth, and she sighs into my touch.

I lift her shirt halfway, silently asking permission to remove it, and she takes over, slipping it off and dropping it onto the shower floor. She's still in her bathing suit, so I pull the straps down her arms, then push it down her body until the material is on the floor, next to her shirt, leaving her completely naked.

"I see your perfect breasts." I tweak her nipple, and she expels a soft gasp.

I trail my fingers down her front, along her soft stomach with a few stretch marks. She flinches when my hand stops and settles there. "I've never dated a woman who's had kids before, but I can honestly tell you that seeing those marks for the first time on a woman was a fucking turn-on. I've yet to meet your kids, but I love listening to you talk about them. A huge part of what makes you, *you* is that you're a mother, and I can already tell you're a damn good one. The only thing I see when I look at those marks is strength and love."

I guide my fingers downward to her neatly trimmed pussy, loving that she willingly spreads her legs for me. "You're perfect, Bree," I tell her, shoving two fingers inside her, silencing the loud moan that escapes her with my mouth. "Brody and I want you...all of you, just the way you are." I finger-fuck her hard and rough, kissing her the same way until she's coming apart around my fingers. When she sags against the wall, I pull my fingers out and lift her, ready to fuck her right here in the shower. I've been dreaming about how it will feel when her tight cunt grips my hard cock.

"Wa-wait," she breathes just before I enter her. "I..." She swallows thickly. "I can't do this."

Stunned, I set her down and back up. "Is everything okay?" I ask, confused as hell.

"Yeah...I'm sorry. It's just..." She rolls her lips against her teeth. "I can't have sex with you."

"Okay, you're not ready yet? That's all you had to say." I tuck a couple of wet strands behind her ear. "I'm okay with waiting. We're doing this at your pace."

"It's not that." She flinches. "I know you guys said we're in this together, but I feel like whoever I have sex with first is who I choose. And I don't want to choose. I want you both equally." I almost laugh, but then I realize she's being dead serious, and holy fuck, does it do shit to my heart because she wants us both...equally. Her words solidify Brody's and my hope that we can somehow make this shit work.

"Then you won't have to choose," I tell her, kissing her so she knows I'm not mad and completely understand.

"And how will that work?"

"I don't know yet," I tell her honestly, "but we'll figure it out… together."

"WHERE'S BREE?" BRODY ASKS, DROPPING HIS BRIEFCASE onto the table.

"She had to go by the coffee shop to close up. The woman who was supposed to close had a family emergency."

"She coming back here when she's done?"

"She didn't say. I think I'll go by there and surprise her. Take her out to dinner. You wanna go?"

"Can't. I have a proposal I need to finish. Try to convince her to come back here after dinner." He grabs his laptop and sets it on the table. "Did you guys have a good day at the beach?"

"Yeah." I grin, recalling how sexy she looked in her one-piece bathing suit. It might've covered all the important parts, but it still clung to every curve and was low-cut, showing off the swells of her breasts. Fuck, when I peeled it off her body in the shower, I've never been so damn hard in my life. Which reminds me…

"She wouldn't have sex with me."

Brody's brows hit the top of his forehead. "She's not ready yet? That's okay. We can give her all the time she wants…"

"Actually, she is ready. But she said she doesn't want to choose. She's worried whoever she has sex with first, the other person will feel like she didn't pick them. She said she wants us both equally."

Brody's face splits into a grin. "She's so damn perfect."

"Yeah, she is. So what do we do?"

"We choose for her." He shrugs.

"So how do we do that? And if you suggest some bullshit like flipping a coin, I'm going to punch you in the face."

Brody throws his head back with a laugh. "Nah, that's for little kids. I was going to suggest rock, paper, scissors."

CHAPTER TWENTY-ONE

AUBREE

MY HEART SWELLS AT HER THOUGHTFULNESS.

I have no idea when I'm going to visit, and the thought of leaving Brody and Hayden sucks. But I'm missing my kids something fierce. This is the longest I've gone without them, and I don't think I can last much longer without hugging and kissing them, despite the fact that I know they're having the time of their lives.

A thought pops into my head—maybe I could ask Hayden and Brody to join me. We could make it a long weekend since the Fourth of July is coming up.

No. I mentally shake my head. It's too soon for that. And them meeting my kids at my in-laws is not the time or the place.

I'll go by myself, spend time with my babies, and then when I come back, spend the rest of the time they're away with Brody and Hayden, making the most out of my temporary kid-free situation.

I'm going through my closing procedures when the door chimes, and in walks Benitez Russo, the building owner and bane of my existence.

"The answer is still no," I tell him, continuing to wipe down the tables.

"Why do you have to make this so difficult?" he says, walking a few feet in but not more, knowing he's not welcome in my coffeehouse. He might own the building I live and work in, but I can't stand him. His father was such a good man, but he's unfortunately nothing like him, which is why Benitez never came around until Sal passed away. Since he was his father's only child, it makes sense he left everything to him, but it sucks because now I have to deal with him.

"Take the money, Heart," he spits, calling me by my last name like he always does. "It's more money than this shitty place will ever bring in."

"I've said it before," I say, moving on to the next table, refusing to give him more attention than necessary, "and I'll say it again. My business isn't for sale. In six months, I'll be moved out, but Heart's Coffeehouse and Bakery will still be here. If you don't like it, take me to court." We both know he'll lose, which is why he hasn't done it yet.

"Now if you'll excuse me, we're closed." I glance up and glare at him, making it clear it's time for him to go.

"Fine, but this isn't over," he says, heading back toward the door. Before he can open it, though, the door swings open, and in walks a sexy-looking Hayden, dressed in a black T-shirt and dark wash jeans, the same clothes I left him in a few hours ago.

"What are you doing here?" I ask, pleasantly surprised. When he dropped me off earlier, we didn't make any plans for tonight.

He opens his mouth to answer, but before the words come out, Benitez says, "Hopefully to talk some sense into you."

I'm confused by his words, but when I glance at Hayden, he doesn't look confused. Instead, he looks...shocked and almost scared.

"Mr. Shea, it's good to see you," Benitez says, extending his hand to shake Hayden's.

Shea...that can't be his last name. That's the last name of the asshole I kicked out and called the cops on for harassing me when he wouldn't leave after I told him under no circumstances would I let him buy me out so he can turn this building into a stupid spa.

No, that can't be Hayden's last name because his last name is... and then it hits me. I don't know his last name. How the hell do I not know his last name? Brody's is Fields. Hayden's is...

"What's your last name?" I blurt out.

Benitez looks at me like I've grown two heads, but I ignore him.

Hayden swallows thickly. "I can explain."

"Is your last name Shea?" I ask, needing him to tell me it's not. Needing for the thoughts now swirling through my head to be wrong. "Is it?" I bark.

"Of course—" Benitez begins, but I cut him off.

"Get out. Now!"

He rolls his eyes. "Good luck," he says as he exits, leaving Hayden and me alone.

"Is your last name Shea?" I ask again, hearing the shakiness in my voice. "Is your dad..." I swallow thickly, not wanting to finish my question but knowing I have to. "Is your dad Joseph Shea?"

"Bree," he breathes, a pained expression on his face. "Please let me explain."

"Answer my question."

"Please—"

"Answer it!"

"Yes, that's my last name, and yes, Joseph is my dad, but it's not what you think."

Oh, my God. My heart cracks behind my rib cage as I think about the past few weeks, how we met…When he came in here and asked if I was the owner.

"When were you going to tell me?" I ask, getting choked up at the thought that everything between us has been a damn lie. From the moment we met, he had an agenda, and it wasn't to date me.

"Can we sit down and talk, please?" he asks slowly like I'm a rabid animal he has to be cautious around.

"I don't need to sit. I need you to answer me. Did you know your dad is trying to get rid of my coffeehouse so he can build a freaking spa here?"

He nods, and my stomach roils.

"And when you came in here the first time, was it to convince me to sell out?"

Another nod, and it takes everything in me not to throw up.

"Get out."

"Bree, please." His eyes, now glassy with emotion, beg, but I can't hear him. I don't want to hear him. I'm too hurt. I feel too betrayed. And then it hits me.

"Does Brody know?"

"Bree, please."

His non-answer tells me everything I need to know—they both know.

"Get out, right now. We're done."

"Bree—"

"Out! Now!" I yell, stalking toward the door and swinging it open.

His gaze darts back and forth between me and the door, debating whether he should listen. Thankfully, he does, and with a sigh—and a piece of my heart—he walks out the door and out of my life.

CHAPTER TWENTY-TWO
HAYDEN

"I fucked up. Bad," I tell Brody when he answers the phone. "She found out about my original motives and demanded I leave, saying it's over."

Brody curses under his breath but thankfully doesn't pull an 'I told you so.' "What are you going to do?" he asks, raw emotion seeping through every word. We might've agreed that we would walk away if Bree only wanted to be with one of us, but we both know that this lie by omission will be the reason we lose her if I don't fix it. We both knew about the situation. And based on her question regarding Brody, Bree knows too.

"There's only one thing I can do. I'm going to tell my father once and for all that it's not happening. Then I'm going to beg Bree for forgiveness." I pull into the underground garage where my parents live and turn off the engine. "I'll let you know how it goes."

We hang up, and I head up to my parents' place, already learning from Carly that he's working from home this afternoon. I ring the doorbell, and a minute later, my mom opens the door with a glass of white wine in her hand. The woman always has a damn drink in her hand.

"Hayden," she coos, opening the door and kissing my cheek as I walk in. "To what do we owe this pleasure?"

"I'm here to speak to Dad. Is he in his office?"

She nods. "Since you're here, you should stay for dinner."

I nod noncommittally since I have no idea how this conversation will go.

I find my dad in his office, typing vigorously on his laptop. When I walk in, he glances up, then does a double take. "Son, I heard you took the day off. Everything okay?"

"Yeah, I need to talk to you, though." He removes his glasses and sits back, giving me his attention. "Aubree Heart isn't going to let you buy her out of her lease. She's emotionally attached to it, and no amount of money you can offer will change her mind. I have a list of other properties that I would like to present, and I'd like your support on this—"

My dad holds up his hand. "Benitez said he saw you there a little while ago. Said it looked personal. Is there something you want to tell me?"

I was afraid that asshole would run to my dad. "We're dating. Well, we were before she found out my part in all of this." Though, technically, since I never once spoke to her about selling out, I don't really have much of a part in any of it...But that doesn't matter since I knew and kept it from her.

Dad nods. "Everyone has momentary lapses in judgment. You're young and still have a lot to learn. Starting with not choosing pussy over business. But now that it's over, and I'm assuming you've learned your lesson the hard way, you need to handle this."

His words grate me, the way he callously refers to Bree like she's something of insignificance when she means so much more to me than that.

I release a calming breath. "She's not just pussy," I tell him, needing him to understand. Wanting to give him the benefit of the doubt. "I care about her. She's become someone important to me.

She's not going to sell, and I'm not going to ask her to. We need to figure out another option."

His eyes widen fractionally before he schools his features, shaking his head. "How the hell do you expect to run a company when you can't separate business from pleasure?" He stands, towering over me. "Either you convince her to sign over that goddamn lease, or you can kiss that CEO title goodbye."

I stare at him, wondering how in the hell I was raised by someone so emotionally detached. His son, his flesh and blood, just told him he cares about someone, and his only response is to threaten me.

"I quit." The words are out before I even realize what I'm saying, but I don't regret them. For years, I've given this man every damn part of me, but it's never enough. It's never going to be enough.

"You don't mean that," he says, looking stricken like he never imagined I could say such a thing.

"I do." I stand, ready to be done with this conversation. "I quit. Gretchen can have the CEO title."

As I'm heading toward the door, he calls out, "You're making a big mistake. Think about what you're doing. Take some time off to rethink this. You're about to throw away your entire future for a woman."

"I know exactly what I'm doing," I tell him. "And she's not *just* a woman. She's the woman I can see spending my life with. Goodbye, Dad."

After saying bye to my mom, I take off. I don't call Bree, knowing she won't answer. Instead, I go home so I can talk to Brody, and we can figure this out together. When I walk through the door, he's pacing the floor. He looks up at me. "How'd it go?"

"I'm unemployed." I chuckle humorlessly.

His eyes widen. "He fired you?"

"Nah, I quit after he told me to stop choosing pussy over business, even after I told him I care about Bree. Fuck him."

"You don't need him," he agrees. "You only worked for him because of familial obligations. Now you can come work with me." He grins, and I shake my head. On several occasions, Brody's asked me to come work with him, but he's right. I felt like I owed it to my dad, to my family, to work for the family business, even though he never appreciated me. I kept hoping if he could let go of the reins, I could take over and turn it into a place I wanted to work at.

"We'll see," I say with a smirk. "I think I'm going to take a few weeks off. Use that paid vacation I never fucking use."

Brody chuckles. "Makes sense. And while you're off, you can beg Bree to take us back."

"Us?"

"I tried calling and texting, and she sent my ass to voicemail and didn't respond to my messages. She's lumping me into this shit, and you need to fix it."

"She asked if you knew. I didn't confirm, but I think she put it together since we're close. I'm sorry, man." I clasp his shoulder. "I'm going to do everything in my power to make this right."

The first thing I do is text Bree, asking to talk, hoping maybe she's calmed a little. When she doesn't reply, I look up a common "I'm sorry" flower and then order a bouquet of blue hyacinths to be sent to her immediately.

Since I know that won't be enough, I wait for the confirmation that she received them, and then I go over to her place since I know she's home. I slip in with someone else so she can't deny me access and then knock on her door.

Without asking who it is, she swings the door open, her eyes widening in shock, telling me she was expecting someone else.

"I don't want to talk to you," she says, ready to slam the door in my face.

"Please, just give me a few minutes."

"I don't have a few minutes," she says, sniffling. "I thought you were the car service."

"Car service to where?" My heart beats like a drum in my chest. *Where the hell would she be going?*

"To the airport," she answers robotically. "I'm going to visit my kids for a few days. I miss them."

She's running. This isn't good.

"Please don't do this," I say, stepping toward her.

She takes a step back. "Go visit my kids?"

"No, *run*. I fucked up. I know I did. But Brody wasn't a part of this."

"He knew and didn't say a word. He's guilty by association." She grabs the handle on her suitcase and pops it up. "I gotta go."

She pushes me out the door and locks it behind her, ignoring me the entire time. I follow her to the elevator, unsure what to say but too scared to let her go—like when she gets into the car it's going to be the end of us when we've only just begun.

With that thought, fear drives what I do next. Reaching out, I press the emergency stop button, halting the elevator.

"What the hell are you doing?" she yells over the blaring alarm.

"Please don't go," I beg again, crowding her in the corner. "Please don't get in that car and get on the plane with the purpose of running. I know I fucked up, but fuck, Bree…" I shake my head, tears pricking my lids. "I care about you so much, and I never meant to hurt you."

"But you did," she says so softly I can barely hear her over the alarm. Tears slide down her cheeks like twin waterfalls, and it feels as though I'm at the bottom, drowning in her emotions. "If you care about me, you'll let me go. You hurt me, and now I'm done."

"I'm afraid if you go, this is the end," I admit out loud. "You're the best thing to happen to me. For years, I was only focused on work, and it wasn't until I met you that I realized I'd been going through the motions. You walked into my life, and suddenly, I can see an entire future I never considered before."

"Then you should've thought about that." She presses the button, and the ringing stops, the elevator continuing its descent.

When the doors open, she stalks out before me, and I follow her out the door and to the car, wishing I could kidnap her and hold her hostage, so she'd be forced to listen and let me make shit right. But life doesn't work that way, and as she gets into the car without so much as a glance back at me, I know she's done. And as the car drives away, I watch Bree take my heart—and Brody's—with her.

CHAPTER TWENTY-THREE
AUBREE

"Mommy, you're here!" Evie runs toward me, and I kneel, scooping her into my arms for a hug. "I missed you so much." She kisses me and pulls back. "You're not going to make us go home, though, right?"

I bark out a laugh. "Is home so bad?" I joke, setting her down.

"No, I love home," she says, warming my heart. "But Grammy and Papa are going to take us to see the dolphins, and I really want to go."

"That sounds like a lot of fun, and no, I'm not going to *make* you go home. I just really missed you and your brother and needed some really good hugs and kisses."

Evie's smile spreads across her face. "I'm the best hugger and kisser ever!" She throws her arms around me again, pulling me down to her level, and with each kiss she peppers on my cheeks and nose and chin, my broken heart heals a little more.

"You are definitely the best hugger and kisser ever," I agree, kissing her back, my throat filled with raw emotion.

"Mom!" Miles yells, running out to join us. "Sorry, I was fishing with Papa." He hugs me tight and gives me a chaste kiss on my cheek. "Wanna go fishing with me?"

"She's going to play dolls with me," Evie argues.

"I can do both, but first, why don't we go inside, so I can say hi to Grammy and Papa?"

"Fine," they both groan.

Since it's already late, we hang out and catch up for a little while, and then, with the promise that I'll get up early and go fishing with Miles and then spend the afternoon playing dolls with Evie, I put the kids to bed, reading them a chapter in their Harry Potter book that Beatrice has taken over reading to them every night.

Since Beatrice and Stephen are early sleepers, they show me to my room, which overlooks the ocean with a balcony attached to it, and then wish me a good night.

With the house quiet, I change into my pajamas, grab a glass of wine from the fridge, and then head out to the balcony to read, hoping to escape.

The romance novel I'm reading is about a couple who've been friends since they were little. They spent a heated night together, and a couple of months later, when she finds out she's pregnant, he doesn't remember because he was addicted to drugs and high the night they spent together.

With every page I read, as he works hard to make things right but continues to screw up because he's broken, my heart cracks a little more, hoping the heroine will see how much he loves her, how much he wants to be better for her…for himself.

I get lost in the words, in the story, and the next thing I know, I'm flipping to the epilogue with tears pouring down my cheeks, so happy that despite all the trials and tribulations they faced, their love was strong enough to get them through it. It wasn't easy, sometimes it was damn hard, and the odds were against them, but no matter how many times they messed up, they kept fighting for each other, for their love.

My thoughts go back to earlier…to Hayden begging me to let

him explain. He accused me of running, and he wasn't wrong. I didn't give him a chance to talk because I was too hurt to listen. I told him and Brody that in order for us to work, we have to communicate, yet at the first sign of trouble, I refused to do just that.

Were they wrong for hiding it from me? Yes. Do I have the right to be upset? Hell yes. But one thing I learned a long time ago from being married is that nobody is perfect. The fact is, Hayden never once mentioned me selling out my lease, and when Brody and I discussed business and I mentioned it to him, he didn't try to sway me one way or the other. If they had ill intentions, wouldn't they have hinted at something by now? We've been seeing each other for several weeks now.

As if they can sense me thinking about them, my phone goes off, and when I check it, it's a text from Brody in our group chat.

> **BRODY**
>
> I know shit is fucked up right now, but I'm lying in bed, and it's not the same without you. I just need you to know that. I miss you so damn much. I hope you arrived safely and are enjoying your time with your kids, but I miss you...

Along with his text is a selfie of him lying in bed with a bit of light streaming in, probably from the hallway light since they leave it on. His hazel eyes are staring at the camera, his face covered in scruff since he hasn't shaved in a few days. His lips are tipped up slightly, but not enough to call it a smile, and his features almost look...sad.

My chest aches at the thought of him hurting. I care about him and Hayden, and even though I'm hurting, I don't want them to hurt. Regardless of how it all shakes out, we need to talk. I need to listen to them and then decide. Running isn't how things should be handled.

ME

> I arrived safely, and it felt so good to hug and kiss my babies. Miles is taking me fishing in the morning, and then Evie and I are going to play dolls. I miss you too. Both of you.

I hit send, knowing Hayden will see the text.

BRODY

> You don't know how much those words mean to us. Enjoy your trip, sweetness. When you're ready to talk, we'll be here.

I tear up at his words, wishing I could be in two places at once. Hating that I left without talking to them. But right now, I need to focus on spending time with my kids. They made it clear they're having a good time and don't want to come home yet, which means I only have a few days with them before I need to get home to run Heart's while they stay for another few weeks.

ME

> Thank you. Good night.

BRODY

> Night xo

TUESDAY MORNING

BRODY

> Morning, I hope you have fun fishing. Catch something big!

ME

> <<insert picture of Miles and me holding a huge fish>>

BRODY

That's quite the fish! Good job.

ME

Thank you. Miles caught it and was so proud.

TUESDAY NIGHT

BRODY

<<insert photo of empty bed>> Missing you
like crazy.

ME

<<insert picture of wineglass filled with white
wine>> Miss you too.

ME

Miss you, Hayden.

HAYDEN

Miss you so much more.

WEDNESDAY MORNING

BRODY

Hey, sweetness. Just thinking about you.
Hope you have a great day with your kids.

ME

<<Insert picture of Evie, Miles, and me at the
beach in our swimsuits, eating watermelon>>

BRODY

You look beautiful, and your kids look just
like you.

ME

Thank you.

WEDNESDAY NIGHT

BRODY

Good night, sweetness. Sweet dreams.
<<insert selfie of Brody lying in bed>>

ME

Good night. <<insert selfie of me lying in
bed>>

ME

Good night, Hayden.

HAYDEN

Good night, beautiful.

THURSDAY MORNING

BRODY

<<insert picture of coffee from Heart's>>
Coffee is delicious, but you taste better.

BRODY

Lacey says hi. <<insert picture of Lacey
sticking her tongue out at me>>

ME

> Nothing tastes better than coffee...Tell Lacey hello and that I'll see her soon.

THURSDAY NIGHT

I check my phone several times while sitting outside sipping my wine and reading my book, but nothing comes through, and I wonder if something is wrong, or maybe Brody's busy. Hayden has only texted after I texted first, and I know it's because he's trying to give me the space I asked for. I'm checking my phone for the millionth time when Beatrice knocks lightly on the door to let me know she's here.

"You don't have to knock," I say with a laugh, gesturing for her to join me. "It's so nice out here. I don't know how you ever go back to New York. I've considered moving here several times," I joke.

Beatrice sits in the chair next to me. "We've considered it. Especially with Stephen retiring this year, and we plan to stay here more often, but we'd miss our grandkids and you too much." She smiles softly at me and then takes a sip of her wine that she brought out with her.

"How are you doing?" she asks after a few moments of silence.

"I'm good."

She side-eyes me. "Let's try again, and this time, you be honest."

I sigh, hating that she knows me so well and wishing I could hide my emotions better. "I met someone." I clear my throat. "Actually, I met two people."

Her brows kiss her forehead in surprise. "Well, damn, when you commit to something, you really go all out, huh?" She waggles her brows. "So why are you so down?" Her eyes widen, and she leans in. "Was the sex bad?"

"No!" I splutter.

"So it was good?"

"No." I shake my head. "We haven't had sex."

"Okay. So, what's wrong?"

"The two guys I met…I've fallen for them both."

"Oh, is that why you've been distant? Are you struggling with who to date?"

"No." I down my wine in one gulp, needing the liquid courage to say what I need to say next. "I actually don't have to choose. I'm dating them both…and they know. It was their idea."

I hold my breath, waiting for the judgment to come, but instead, a huge smile spreads across her face, and she says, "This sounds like a romance novel I read recently. Which one was it?" She snaps her fingers, deep in thought. "Shoot, I'll have to look it up later."

I snort out a laugh and shake my head, grateful to have such an amazing mother-in-law.

"In all seriousness," she says, "do they treat you good?"

"They treat me like gold," I admit, then I spend the next several minutes telling her all about Brody and Hayden. How we met and how I quickly fell for both of them. Then I explain about the building situation—at least the little bit I know since I haven't spoken to Hayden yet.

"At first, I was hurt and ended things, but then, once I was away from the situation and able to think, I realized I was acting prematurely, and I need to hear them out."

Beatrice smiles. "Remember that time when you and Pete first moved in together, and you asked him to throw the clothes into the washer, and he grabbed the wrong clothes and turned the entire load pink?"

I laugh, remembering it all too well. "It was our first fight." I was so mad he didn't listen to what I had instructed. I was overwhelmed with school and work, and I told him he didn't care enough to listen.

"You've come a long way since then. When I met you, you were young and had a lot of growing up to do, and I loved watching you grow into an amazing wife and mother." She pats my hand. "Relationships take time and patience. And you've been out of the game for a while. It's easy to forget how clueless men can be, but just remember that when a man loves you and cares about your well-being, he'll make it right. What did Pete do the next time he turned the clothes pink?"

"He went out and bought me an entirely new wardrobe," I say with a watery laugh.

"I know it's still new with these guys, but if you're giving them the time of day, I'd bet they're good men, and if you give them a chance to explain and make things right, they will."

My phone dings with an incoming text, and I glance at it, seeing a text from Brody:

BRODY

Sorry my nightly text is so late. I had to work late so I can leave early tomorrow to drive out to my parents' place for dinner. I hope you had a fun day with your kids. Miss you.

*His parents' place for dinner…*Shit! I was supposed to go with them until I took off to Florida in an attempt to protect my heart.

"Hey, Beatrice, I was thinking of leaving tomorrow morning. There's this thing…"

She grins knowingly. "Let's look at flights."

FRIDAY MORNING

> BRODY
>
> Morning, sweetness. Hope you have a great
> day with your kids. Feel free to send pics.
> Miss you.

"You sure you don't want to come home with me?" I ask my kids again as we pull up to the airport. I already know what they're going to tell me, but I have to ask anyway.

"No, thank you," Miles says politely, making Stephen and Beatrice laugh under their breath.

"I'm gonna miss you so much, but I'm good here," Evie adds.

Stephen pulls up, and everyone gets out to say goodbye. I hug my kids tight, telling them I love them and that I'll call them once I land.

When tears prick my lids, Evie palms my cheeks. "Don't cry, Mommy. We'll be home soon, and if you miss us too much, just video call us." She kisses my lips, and I wonder when the hell my babies grew up.

The flight is only a couple of hours, and when I land, I grab a taxi to go home so I can drop my luggage off, shower, and change. Since I don't know where Brody's parents live, after I'm ready to go, I call his office and ask Hillary if he's still there, so I can figure out where to meet him. I'm hoping she'll know their address if he's already on his way.

"I'm almost positive he went home first," she says. "He usually goes home to change and drives there."

"Thank you!"

Twenty minutes later, I'm walking through the lobby of the guys' building and getting onto their private elevator. When I step inside and swipe my card, a knot forms in my stomach, afraid of what will be waiting for me on the other side. I know they miss me, but what if once Hayden explains, it means I can't be with him? What if he asks me to give up Heart's? There are so many ways this can go...

Maybe coming back to go to dinner when things are up in the air wasn't the best idea.

In my head, it was my way of telling them I want to work things out. Even when Pete and I would fight, when it came time to visit our friends or family, we would do it together because no matter what, at the end of the day, it was us against the world. Which is what I want for Brody, Hayden, and me...For it to be us against the world.

The door slides open, and when I step into the foyer, I'm greeted by a shocked Brody and Hayden. Since the elevator notifies them when someone is heading up, they knew someone was coming, but based on their expressions, they weren't expecting me.

"Hey," I say, waving shyly as my heart hammers in my chest. "Is the invitation still open for me to join you at your parents' for dinner?"

A huge grin spreads across Brody's face, and he stalks toward me, pulling me into his arms. "Hell yeah, it is," he murmurs, kissing my cheek. "Fuck, how is it that you haven't been to the bakery in days, and you still smell like a damn cupcake?" He inhales my scent and presses a soft kiss to the curve of my neck. "I missed you so much," he breathes, raw emotion bleeding through every word. "Thank you for coming home."

He sets me on my feet, and I turn my attention to Hayden, who's standing a few feet away, looking nervous. "We need to talk."

He nods, unmoving, unsure what to do, so I make the first move.

Walking over to him, I encircle my arms around his neck and kiss the corner of his mouth. "I'm hurt and upset, but I want to hear what you have to say. Then we'll go from there."

"Thank you," he murmurs, wrapping his arms around my waist and nuzzling his face into the crook of my neck. "I'm going to make this right, I promise."

CHAPTER TWENTY-FOUR
AUBREE

"You're even more beautiful in person!" Brody's stepmom, Savy, coos, pulling me into a motherly hug. "And you're right, Brody. She does smell like cupcakes."

"Savy," Brody groans, making everyone laugh. "First time I bring a woman home and you guys are determined to embarrass me."

"It's nice to meet you," his father says, leaning in and kissing my cheek. "And Hayden…" He clasps his hand, doing that half shake, half hug guys do. "What's this I hear about you finally coming to work for Fields?"

His question has me freezing in place, my gaze going straight to Hayden. We obviously haven't spoken yet, and we kept the conversation about my trip to visit my kids on the drive here, so I have no idea what they're talking about.

"Yeah," Hayden says, sounding a bit nervous as his eyes flicker over to mine. "I filled out the paperwork with HR today." He shrugs, looking sheepish.

"I know how much you wanted to prove yourself to your dad," Ben says, "but you did that over and over again, and if he didn't appreciate it and see your worth, that's his loss. Fields Enterprises is excited to have you as part of our team."

"Damn right, we are," Brody says, clasping Hayden's shoulder. "We're going to take the company to the next level." He winks at his dad, who barks out a laugh.

"You quit your job?" I blurt out, unable to contain my confusion.

Everyone goes quiet as Hayden walks over to me. "I wasn't on board with the way my dad handled business, so yeah, I walked away."

"Because of me?" I whisper so only he can hear, shocked at what he's saying.

He reaches out and tucks a wayward strand of hair behind my ear. "I would do just about anything for you," he admits quietly, causing butterflies to flutter in my chest. "I want to talk about this, but I think we should wait until after dinner, once we're alone."

I nod in agreement, then encircle my arms around his waist, resting the side of my face against his chest, needing him to know that regardless of what happens between us, I appreciate what he did for me. He holds me tightly for a few seconds, his lips pressing against the crown of my head.

When we separate, I turn around and find Brody, along with his parents watching us. Brody smiles softly, but his parents wear confusion in their expressions.

"We should probably talk," Brody says to his parents, walking over and sliding his arm over my shoulders. "Are Olivier and Penelope joining us?"

"Ollie is spending the night at his friend's, and Penelope is at a cheer sleepover, so it's just us this evening," Savy says. "Dinner's just about ready, so why don't we head into the dining room?"

"Do you need any help?" I offer, not wanting to seem rude.

"Sure," she says with a smile. "Ben, can you grab a bottle of wine?" She glances at me. "White or red?"

Since red tends to get me drunk quicker, I go with white.

"Your kitchen is gorgeous," I mention when we walk into it.

Really, their whole house is amazing, but her kitchen is similar to Brody and Hayden's—a baker's wet dream.

"Thank you. I love to cook, so Ben made sure when we bought this place and renovated that it had a decent kitchen. Do you like to cook?"

"I do," I admit. "But baking is my passion."

"I made a pot roast tonight, which the guys love, but if you ever want to make Brody and Hayden's favorite, go with lasagna. They'll devour it." She glances back and winks, and I know she knows, even though it hasn't been said yet.

"I..." I splutter, unsure what the hell to say. "I really care about them both," is what I settle on, making her stop what she's doing and face me. "I've never been in a relationship like this before, and I have no idea how it will all play out, but I truly care about them both."

"I can tell," she says warmly. "And from what Brody's said, it's obvious he cares about you. I haven't spoken to Hayden, but I can see it in the way he watches you that he's smitten as well."

"And you're okay with this?" Technically, I'm a grown woman and don't need anyone's approval, but I don't have many people in my life. I would love it if Brody's parents gave us their blessing since it's clear they're close, and I doubt we'll be getting Hayden's family's approval anytime soon.

"Brody mentioned you have two kids. Eight-year-old twins, right?"

"Yeah, they're with my in-laws for the summer. My husband passed away almost five years ago, but I'm still close with his parents."

"I didn't have anyone growing up," she admits, emotion laced in her words. "I was a foster kid, and because my parents always had one foot in the door and one out, I was never able to get adopted so I could have a real family.

"When I met Brody and Ben, I found my family, and in a lot of ways, they found their family with me. Brody might not be mine biologically, but he's my son in every way that matters. As his step-mom, as someone who loves him more than life itself, all I want is for him to be happy. And it's clear when he speaks of you and then seeing him with you tonight, he's happy.

"And Hayden…Well, he's not technically mine either, but his family isn't the best, and he spends more time here than with them." She shrugs. "It's safe to say we've unofficially adopted him, so the fact that you're making both of them happy is only a bonus."

"Thank you," I tell her, getting choked up. "Your blessing means a lot to me. I don't have a lot of people in my life, and the last thing I want to do is alienate anyone in theirs. When they suggested this, I was skeptical, but I couldn't choose between them, and after losing so many people close to me, how could I turn down two men who care about me and want to be with me?"

"Damn right," Brody says, making me jump. "It's about time you accept the fact that we both want you and that you're ours." He kisses my cheek, and I can't help the blush that creeps up my neck and face as Hayden and Ben join us in the kitchen.

"So you're all together?" Ben asks with zero judgment in his tone.

"Yeah," Brody tells him. "We both fell hard for Bree, and since she didn't want to choose, we proposed that she date both of us."

"How did you guys meet?" Savy asks, making me glance at Hayden, who looks nervous and uncomfortable. We probably should've talked about all of this before going to dinner, but we didn't have the time.

"At her coffeehouse," Brody says, not missing a beat. "I'm pretty sure she puts something in those brownies because with one bite, she had us both addicted."

"YOUR PARENTS ARE SO GREAT," I TELL BRODY AS WE WALK into their condo a few hours later. The wine was crisp, dinner was delicious, the dessert was heavenly—and I totally asked her for the recipe—but more importantly, the company couldn't have been better. They were completely open and welcoming. They asked questions but didn't judge, and when it was time for us to leave, they made Brody and Hayden promise to treat me good and bring me back soon.

"They are," Brody agrees. "I was hoping you'd get to meet my brother and sister...next time." Brody pulls me onto the couch with him and snuggles me into his side. I sigh in contentment, having missed this so much while I was away.

"I know it's late, but can we talk?" Hayden asks, instantly sobering me.

I nod and pull away from Brody, wanting to be in my right mind while we talk.

Hayden pushes out a harsh breath and sits on the coffee table in front of me. "I need you to know before I start that Brody wasn't okay with me keeping it from you, but I put him in a shitty situation, and he was stuck between a rock and a hard place."

I nod in understanding, already knowing this because he said it when I first found out, but I can respect Hayden for trying to keep his best friend out of this. When they said if I didn't want to be with one of them anymore that they'd respect it, they obviously meant it, and I can tell by the way Hayden's talking, even if he believes we're over, he's trying to save Brody from the same demise.

"The day I met you, I was sent by my father to convince you to let us buy you out of your lease," he admits. "Until I walked through the door, you were just business, but something crazy happened when I saw you...Like instant attraction." He shakes his head, smiling softly. "All business was thrown out the window, and all I wanted was to take you out on a date." He smirks. "But you weren't having it."

Brody chuckles under his breath. "She was having me, though."

He winks, and I bark out a laugh, remembering how that went down.

"Only because I made a deal with Lacey," I tell him. "After I turned down Hayden, she convinced me to give the next guy who asked me out a chance, and that was you."

Brody's features pinch together, and Hayden laughs.

"I should've walked away," Hayden says, steering the conversation back on track. "But when I went in there again to talk to you, I couldn't help myself. I had to try again, and you said yes."

He smiles sadly. "I knew it was a conflict of interest, but I kept telling myself I'd figure it out. I spent hours, hell days, finding better, more profitable properties to present to my dad, but he was hell-bent on buying you out because he's not used to being told no."

"It probably doesn't help that I called the cops on him."

Brody and Hayden laugh.

"No," Hayden says. "That definitely didn't help." He takes my hands in his and massages circles into my palms. "I never once told him I would convince you to buy out. I kept saying I was handling it, and in my head, I honestly thought I could get him to change directions. The properties I found had better locations and would be easier to get permits for. But he's stubborn, and at this point, he's only refusing to look at a different property out of spite.

"I went to him and told him that I care about you, that I'm falling in love with you, and asked him to please reconsider. When it became clear that business would always come first—even ahead of his own son—I quit."

My brain freezes at the word love. It's too soon to be falling in love, right? Yet that's exactly what I'm feeling. I'm falling for both of them…fast, and that's why when I found out about Hayden, it hurt so badly. Because it only hurts when you care.

"My dad isn't going to stop coming after you," Hayden says, his lips curving downward. "But there's nothing he can do. The lease can't be broken unless you agree, which you won't be doing. Benitez can take you to court, but he most likely won't win."

"And if he does," Brody adds. "I have the best damn attorneys on retainer that will fight him."

"We won't let them take Heart's from you," Hayden agrees, "regardless of how things end up between us."

My heart squeezes behind my rib cage at how selfless and thoughtful they are. "I appreciate that," I tell them both, "but it's not your fight. It's mine. And I won't take it lying down."

"That's where you're wrong," Hayden says. "Your fight is ours. If you'll let us fight beside you...*with you.*"

"I want you both beside me, but in order for this to work, we have to communicate honestly. I understand you didn't directly come after me, but sometime in the past several weeks we've been dating, you should've told me. I would rather find out from you than someone else. And I'd rather be hurt by the truth than be ignorant to the lie."

Both men nod in understanding. Brody pulls me into his side and kisses me softly, and Hayden moves to the couch on the other side of me. I kiss Brody for several beats, tasting his warmth and reveling in his sweetness, then I break the kiss to give Hayden some attention.

"No more hiding things," I tell him before I press my lips to his, my tongue darting out to entwine with his. He sighs into the kiss, then deepens it, as if with each curve of his lips he's apologizing over and over again. When I moan into his mouth, he lifts me by my hips into his lap.

"I'm so sorry," he murmurs against my mouth. "I promise, only honesty from now on."

"Speaking of honesty," I breathe, pulling back and glancing from Hayden to Brody nervously. "I have a confession to make." At the thought of saying what I need to say, my body heats, my neck and face no doubt turning a shade of pink. "I...I want to take things further...with both of you...but I can't choose." I already told Hayden this, but I haven't told Brody.

"I know," Brody says, "Hayden told me." I sigh in relief.

"I told her we'd figure it out," Hayden says with a wink, causing butterflies to attack my belly. I have no idea how they plan to figure it out, but I can't wait. Every time I'm with them has me wanting them more and more.

"We want to take you away this weekend," Brody says. "Any chance you can get the coffeehouse covered?"

"For how long?" I just got back from being away, and it would be kind of irresponsible to bail so soon. But at the same time, I've been busting my ass for years without taking any time off, which is why I hired competent employees.

"We'll leave tomorrow morning and come back Monday night since the Fourth of July is Sunday," Hayden says.

"You guys don't have to work?"

"Fields will be closed for the three-day weekend," Brody says.

"Where are we going?" I ask, getting excited at the idea of spending three whole days alone with them.

"We have a few options." Brody grins. "I have a beach house in Miami I bought from my parents a few years back, they have one in Montauk, and my aunt has one in The Hamptons that she's not using. Pick your place, and we'll be there tomorrow morning."

I was just in Florida, but it was to see the kids, not to go away with the guys. Would that make me horrible to be there and not see them?

"Umm…" I think, unsure which place to pick. "I don't know. You pick." I sigh. "I'm learning I have a problem making decisions," I half joke, making the guys laugh.

"That's okay," Hayden says, lifting my chin. "We're completely okay with making the decisions for you."

He leans over and, holding my chin, sucks my bottom lip into his mouth, nibbling on my flesh. "On our way, we'll stop at your place so you can pack a couple of nice outfits for going out, swimsuits for the beach, and lingerie. Or better yet, forget the lingerie. No panties either. We need easy access to that sweet pussy of yours."

CHAPTER TWENTY-FIVE
BRODY

"She's so damn sweet," Hayden says, glancing down at Bree, who's asleep across the couch—her head in my lap and her feet in Hayden's—in Fields's private jet. Since it's a holiday week-end, the only time available was early as fuck in the morning, which meant leaving before dawn. As soon as we stepped onto the plane, Bree laid down and passed out. I debated taking her somewhere closer—like to Montauk or The Hamptons—especially since she was just in Florida—but my yacht is docked at my beach house in Miami, and the thought of watching her lie out across the deck in her bathing suit made the decision for me.

"I can't believe she forgave me so easily. I was more than prepared to beg and grovel...or walk away if she asked me to." He sighs and stares at her.

"She cares about you. When someone cares, they don't just write you off. They stick around through the hard times." I can't even count how many times I messed up in my teenage years, and not once did Savy or my dad walk away. My mom, on the other hand, took off when shit got rough.

"I want to make sure this weekend is special. And not just in the bedroom. I want to make it a weekend she'll never forget. Spoil the hell out of her. Take her shopping and to the best restaurants. We should bring in a masseuse."

I laugh under my breath. "We can do all that, but you have to know she's not like that. She doesn't care about materialistic shit. If she did, she would've taken your dad's offer to buy her out of the lease. She would've walked away with plenty of money."

"True," he says, his eyes never leaving her. "I just want to show her how much she means to me, and I don't know how to do that. This is all so new. I've never felt like this about a woman before. I want to give her the entire world."

I nod and run my fingers through her hair, feeling the same way. "We will give her the world," I murmur softly, glancing at Hayden. "Starting with a weekend to remember."

"You own this?" Bree asks, her features in total awe as she stares up at the three-story house on Miami Beach.

"I bought it from my dad. He and Savy weren't traveling much after she had my sister, so they decided to buy a place closer to home. Since he owned the place outright, he priced it embarrassingly low, but it wasn't really about the money. It was about him passing my favorite getaway down to me. Some of my best memories with my dad were made here." I glance over at the huge garage that's filled with cars. "This is where he taught me to drive his Maserati." I grin, remembering how badass I felt driving his two-hundred-thousand-dollar car.

"I love that," Bree says, threading her fingers through mine. "Losing so many people close to me made me see how short life is and that the most important thing we can do is create memories. Because at the end of the day, that's all we'll have when they're gone."

"And that's exactly what we're about to do," I tell her, lifting her into my arms, bridal style. She squeals in shock, encircling her arms around me as I walk us up the sidewalk while Hayden types in the code and opens the door so I can carry her into the house. I bring her up to the master bedroom that's been renovated since I purchased it and drop her onto the king-sized bed, caging her in my arms.

Pressing my mouth to hers, I gently coax her lips apart so I can suck her tongue into my mouth, tasting her sweetness. When she moans, and her legs wrap around my waist, pulling me closer to her, I force myself to break the kiss so we don't take shit too far. That will happen tonight. But today is about spending time together—the three of us.

"Up you go," I say, dragging her to her feet. "Change into a swimsuit. We have a beach to check out."

Once we're all dressed in our beachwear, we head out. There's a pool and hot tub that I pay to be kept up, and the beach is in the distance. Bree chooses the beach first, so we walk down there and over to the cabana.

"Is this for us?" Bree asks, looking around in confusion. The beach is private, only for residents, but I rented a cabana and had it delivered this morning once I knew we'd be coming here for the weekend.

"Yep, it's all ours."

I drop our towels onto the table while Hayden pulls Bree down with him onto one of the lounge chairs. I can't help but watch as he kisses and touches her, loving on her like she might disappear at any second. I know how worried he was about losing her. I'm just thankful she's so damn forgiving. Many women wouldn't be.

"Come swimming with me!" Bree says, jumping off the lounge chair. She pulls her cover-up over her head, exposing the sexy as hell black and gold one-piece that hugs her curves. My eyes land on the swells of her breasts that are peeking out of the top of her suit and descend slightly to her pert nipples that are so hard, they could probably cut glass. Fuck, what I wouldn't give to put my—

"Actually, I think you should come here," Hayden says, hooking a hand around her hip and pulling her toward him. He must've been thinking the same thing as me because once he has her close enough, he wraps his lips around one of her nipples, then tugs on it through the thin material.

Bree lets out a shocked shriek that quickly turns into a breathy moan as Hayden sucks on her nipple. He releases it only long enough to pull her breast out of its confines, and then he's back on her, sucking and nibbling.

Unable to sit by and watch any longer, I walk over to Bree and rest my hands on her hips from behind. Her head falls back against my chest, and I gently fist her hair, tilting her head to the side and running my lips and tongue along the curve of her neck.

"Oh, God," she breathes. "Forget the beach. I want to go back to your room."

Hayden and I both release her with a chuckle.

"Not yet," Hayden says.

She releases a huff, and even though I can't see her, I imagine her pouting. "Why not?"

"Because once we get you in that room, we might not ever leave." Hayden winks playfully, then without giving her a warning, he lifts her over his shoulder.

"Hayden!" she screeches. "Put me down!"

A loud slap to her ass is his only response as he carries her down the beach and straight into the water.

We spend the day playing in the water and lounging between the sun and the shade. We walk to a small seafood restaurant for lunch, and then once Bree announces she's all sunned out, we head back inside to relax and get ready for tonight.

"Who's joining me in the shower?" Bree asks, eyeing us both seductively. Since we're determined to take her out before taking her to bed, we both shake our heads, knowing our restraint is only a small tug away from completely unraveling.

"Seriously?" She pouts. "Neither of you want to shower with me?" She glances back and forth between the two of us, and when neither of us gives in, she sighs. "Fine. I guess I'll just have to take care of myself."

She turns on her heel, and it only takes Hayden and me point-two seconds to chase after her.

CHAPTER TWENTY-SIX
AUBREE

"I can't believe you did this," I say in awe as I stare at myself in the floor-length mirror.

When we got out of the shower, where neither guy would do anything other than help me wash my body, I went to my luggage, prepared to grab one of the two dresses I had brought. Instead, I found a large black box with a fancy gold ribbon on top waiting for me on the bed. Inside, I found a crystal floral embellished Oscar de la Renta halter mini dress in my size. I'm not a fashion expert, but even I know that name.

When I pulled the dress out, I stared at it for several seconds, afraid to put it on. But when Brody came over and softly kissed my bare shoulder, telling me that he couldn't wait to see me in it, I got to work getting ready.

Since we're in hot and humid Miami, I curled my hair in loose waves and put on light makeup, not wanting it to all drip off my face. I put on the beautiful dress and matching heels and then walked over to the mirror, where I'm standing right now, staring at myself. For the first time in a long time, I like what I see.

Instead of looking like a mourning, exhausted single mom, I'm happy and glowing. Like a woman who's well rested and isn't working herself into the ground anymore. Who's falling in love...

"You deserve the world," Hayden says, stepping behind me, his warmth radiating between us. He's dressed in a pair of black slacks and a maroon button-down shirt, the sleeves rolled up to his elbows, showing off his tattoos. One day, I'm going to ask him to tell me what they mean. His hair is gelled in such a way that it looks naturally messy and sexy.

With one hand on the curve of my hip, he dusts my hair to the side and peppers a couple of kisses along my jawline. "And if you let Brody and me, we'd like nothing more than to give it to you."

My thoughts go back to the letter Pete wrote me, asking—no, *demanding*—that I find love. I wonder if he would be okay with me being with two men.

As the thought swirls around in my head, Brody appears in the mirror on the other side of me—dressed similarly to Hayden, only his shirt is royal blue. "You look stunning," he says, leaning down and kissing my cheek.

And as I look at the reflections of the two men who have quickly worked their way into my heart, I know without a doubt Pete would approve because all he ever wanted was for me to be happy and loved, and I have that in spades with these two.

"Good evening, Mr. Fields," a beautiful raven-haired hostess with bright blue eyes and blood-red luscious lips says when we walk into Harmony, a restaurant that Brody told me his company bought last year and renovated and might be selling—if the price is right.

Since he said he hasn't been here in several months, it blows my mind that this woman would know who he is, but at the same time, it doesn't surprise me because he's beautiful—with his hypnotic hazel eyes and pouty lips—in a way that goes straight to a woman's libido.

When Brody simply smiles at her and says, "Good evening" back, she takes it as her cue to move the one-sided conversation forward.

"Your table is ready." With a sensual sway to her hips that would probably draw a gay man's eyes to her ass, she walks ahead of us, and the confidence I had before we arrived diminishes slightly, wondering why on earth two beautiful, wealthy, young men are with me when they could be with her.

Until a hand slides around my waist, and I glance up to see Hayden's gaze on me while we follow the hostess to our table. He dips his head to speak close to my ear, his warm breath causing a tremor of desire to ripple through me. "I know we have to eat dinner, but the only thing I want to eat is you." My legs clench together, and I consider telling them to forget dinner so we can go back to the house.

My features must give away my thoughts because Brody chuckles softly as he pulls out my chair for me and says, "Dinner first, sweetness. Dessert afterward." He kisses my cheek and then helps me push my chair in before he moves to sit next to me while Hayden sits across from me.

Brody orders us a bottle of wine, and I enjoy it, but I don't drink too much, not wanting to get drunk. The food is delicious, and after dinner, they shock me by getting into an elevator that takes us up to a nightclub. We're escorted to a VIP booth that comes with our own server and has a small VIP-only dance floor.

After Brody orders us a round of shots and we down them, Hayden wastes no time taking my hand and leading us onto the dance floor. With the music vibrating against the walls, he pulls me into his arms and sways to the music. His hands slide down my back and land on my ass, squeezing the globes as he tugs me closer to him so our bodies are flush against one another.

Since the music is loud, we don't speak, but as our gazes and bodies meet, words don't need to be said for us to communicate.

His eyes, filled with molten lust and desire, sear into mine. His fingers dig into my flesh. And then his mouth descends on mine, our lips fusing and our tongues dancing as sensually as we are.

I'm lost in everything that is Hayden, so I don't realize that Brody has joined us until his arms band around my waist, his fingers splaying across my front. His front presses against my back, and when he moves my hair to the side and trails fiery kisses down my spine, I moan into Hayden's mouth.

"I'm ready to go back," I murmur against Hayden's lips. "Please," I breathe, needing them more than I need my next breath.

"I'm not sure you're ready yet," Hayden says. He licks the seam of my lips as Brody sucks on my earlobe, and I clench my legs together, worried I'm so turned on that I'm going to combust right here on the dance floor.

"Trust me, I am," I groan. "I'm more than ready." Hell, I'm so ready, I'm afraid the wetness between my legs will drip down the insides of my thighs.

Hayden smirks, then looks over my shoulder at Brody and nods. I can't see Brody's response, but he chuckles softly against my ear and whispers, "You sure you don't want to dance some more?"

Tilting my head to the side, I glance up at him. "I want to leave now."

His response is to grasp my chin and slant his mouth over mine. He kisses me for several seconds, exploring my mouth with his tongue before he breaks the kiss and murmurs, "Let's go."

The drive back to Brody's house feels like it takes forever. Nobody says a word, the only sound coming from the music playing on the radio. But even without anyone speaking, the clear sexual tension is so thick it could be cut with a knife.

When we arrive at the house, Brody takes my hand in his and guides me up to the bedroom with Hayden following. I gasp when we step into the room and see it's been transformed from a standard master bedroom to a romantic getaway, complete with rose petals scattered along all the surfaces. Electric candles don the dresser and nightstands, and when I walk over to the basket on the bed, I find several items, including oils and lubricants.

"How did you do all this?" I ask, taken aback that they would go through all this trouble to make tonight memorable. From the dinner to the dancing, and now this...

"We know people," Brody says with a sexy wink.

Hayden takes the basket and sets it on the nightstand while Brody brings me over to the bed, gently motioning for me to sit.

Every time I imagined having sex with one of them, it made me nervous, especially when I thought about having to choose. Right now, I'm so turned on that all I want is for one of them to be inside me. Actually, no, I want them *both* inside me. I have no idea how this will work, but I trust them when they say they'll handle it. And it's with that thought that I know I'm ready to take things to the next level.

"I trust you," I say out loud, needing them to know how I feel. Both guys stop in their tracks, and then twin smiles spread across their handsome faces.

"Good," Hayden says, "because you'll need to trust us for what we have planned."

"I do," I say firmly with a nod to accentuate my words.

Brody bends in front of me and takes my heeled foot in his hands while Hayden walks over to the corner of the room.

A few seconds later, soft music fills the silence as Brody removes my heel and then kisses the instep of my foot. A bolt of electricity races up my body and straight to my center. He removes my other heel and kisses that instep as well. Kissing my foot shouldn't turn me on like it does, but holy hell, I can't help it. Every time one of them touches me in any way, my body reacts.

"Stand," Hayden gently demands. When I do, he turns me slightly and unzips the back of my dress. The material pools at my feet, leaving me in only the cream-colored floral matching bra and panty set that leaves little to the imagination.

"Jesus," Hayden breathes from behind me. "Tell us you bought this for us."

"I did," I admit softly. After we started taking things to the next level, Lacey and I went shopping, and I bought some cute matching sets. It's been years since anyone has seen my undergarments—since I've cared about anyone seeing them—and I wanted to make sure I had some that would make me feel sexy.

"You look gorgeous...perfect," Brody says, standing. He dips his head and kisses the swell of one breast, then the other. "Lie on the bed," he murmurs, looking at me with fire in his eyes.

With my heart thumping so heavily in my chest, it feels as though my entire body is pulsating. I sit on the bed and then inch backward until I'm in the center with my head on the feather-soft pillows.

Hayden takes something from the basket and walks over to the side of the bed. "Remember how you said you didn't want to choose?" I nod. "We're taking the choice out of your hands." He shows me a black velvety-looking eye mask, and my eyes go wide.

They're going to blindfold me. Holy shit! I should probably be concerned, but I meant what I said—I trust them.

"If there's anything you don't like, you have to tell us," Brody says, kneeling on the bed and crawling over to me. "Our priority is to make sure you feel good. If you don't enjoy something, you have to speak up."

I nod, then open my mouth, quickly closing it when I change my mind about what I wanted to ask.

Brody notices immediately. "Bree, I just said you have to speak up. What were you going to say?"

I take in a deep breath to build up my courage, then release it. "I...I want to be with both of you...in every way...but..." I swallow thickly, suddenly shy and a bit embarrassed about what I'm about to admit. "I've never had anal sex before."

"Because it never happened or because you didn't want to?" Hayden asks.

"It never came up. I don't know if he wanted it or thought about it, but he never mentioned it, and neither did I." Pete's and my sex life was good, but we weren't really what you'd call adventurous. "I want to be with both of you in that way, but I just wanted you to know I've never done it before, and I read that it could hurt." I flinch, remembering the articles I read. Some said how good it could be, while others mentioned the pain.

"Your pleasure comes first," Brody says, cupping the side of my face. "We will never do anything with the intention of hurting you. Your trust means everything to us. If something hurts, you have to tell us. We won't know unless you say something. And as far as anal goes, when it's done correctly, it can feel good. I know this personally."

"You liked it?" I ask curiously. They mentioned experimenting together, but Brody said it made him realize he wasn't interested in being with a man like that.

"It felt good," he admits, glancing over at Hayden and smiling. "But it also felt like something was missing. Could I be with a guy again? Yeah. But it's not what I crave. I crave you. Your womanly curves..." He runs his fingers across my breasts and down my torso. "This sweet pussy..." His hand finds its way under the material, and he slides a finger between my lips. "I could go without dick for the rest of my life and not give a shit, but I need this pussy. I *need* you."

"What if you could have both?" I ask, unsure where the hell that came from.

Brody tilts his head to the side, so I continue. "What if you could have Hayden and me? Would you want both of us?"

"Where is this coming from?" Brody asks, his lips turning down slightly.

I feel my chest and neck and face heat, and it must be visible because Brody quirks a brow. "Umm...well..." I glance at Hayden, then back to Brody. "After you mentioned being with Hayden, I might've looked up gay porn."

Brody's brows shoot up to his forehead. "And?"

"And it was kind of hot."

Hayden snorts out a laugh.

"Did you imagine Hayden fucking me?" Brody asks, a sexy smirk quirking at the corner of his lips.

"Maybe…"

"Maybe?" he taunts.

"Okay, yes." I sigh. "I did."

"How turned on did you get?" Hayden asks, tweaking my nipple through the material. I glance down and see my nipples are hard, poking through my thin bra.

"Enough that I got myself off…twice," I admit sheepishly. "I know you said you could live without being with a man, but what if you could have both? Would you want it?"

"That all depends on Hayden," Brody says, glancing at his friend. "Hayden's one-hundred-percent hetero, and like I said, if I never had dick again, I'd be completely okay with that."

"It's something I wouldn't be opposed to doing again," Hayden says with a shrug. "I'm always down for experimenting in the bedroom, especially if it turns you on enough to make you get your-self off twice." He waggles his brows at me playfully, and my face grows warmer.

"But tonight," Brody says, "is about you. We have all the time in the world to experiment. Right now, our focus is on being with you."

"And that's exactly what we're going to do," Hayden adds, lifting the blindfold up to my eyes and securing the elastic behind my head. The lights immediately go out, and I'm drowned in the darkness.

"You ready?" Brody asks.

"For what?" I breathe.

"For us to make you feel good."

CHAPTER TWENTY-SEVEN
AUBREE

As I lie still, my chest rising and falling in quick succession, the bed dips, and then there's some shuffling. I listen intently since my vision is gone, wanting to know what's going on, unsure why the guys wanted me blindfolded.

Until my panties glide down my legs and fingers wrap around each of my thighs, spreading them open, and then it hits me—I have no idea who's touching me, whose lips are trailing soft kisses up the inside of my thigh. They did this to take the choice out of my hands. So I don't have to decide between the two of them. They did this for me because they understand and accept that I care about them both.

Raw emotion clogs my throat, and I swallow it down. Despite my eyes being covered, I close my eyelids and relax, allowing my other senses to take over.

A warm tongue slides between my folds, licking and teasing, as another tongue glides across my neck and chest. A hand slides under my back, and my bra is undone and removed. And then a mouth is on my taut nipple, sucking and biting. Fingers pinch my other nipple, rolling and tugging on it. I arch my back and moan, wanting more, *needing* more.

A tongue slides up my center and lands on my clit. At the same time, two fingers push deep inside me.

"Oh, God," I breathe, overwhelmed in the best way. "I want your dicks," I moan, my hand grabbing for the guy closest to me. When I'm met with nothing but flesh, I realize they took off their clothes.

Words aren't spoken by either of them—so I can't tell who's who —but when a hard, thick cock slides against my open palm, I know it's his way of giving me permission to participate. I can't see, but I can feel the beaded pre-cum on the tip. I use it to help lubricate his hard length, stroking him up and down, getting him even harder.

I lean over slightly, guiding the shaft into my mouth and darting my tongue out to lick the smooth head. Fingers fist my hair, and I know...*I fucking know* I'm sucking Hayden's dick.

The tongue licking my clit slows down, massaging gentle circles that have my legs clenching while the fingers—I'd bet my life are Brody's—curl upward. And then fingers pinch my nipples hard. It all feels too good, becomes too much, and with Hayden's dick in my mouth, I come harder than I've ever come in my life. I take his shaft all the way down my throat as my body spasms so hard, my legs shake, and my center clenches around Brody's fingers.

And then the fingers and tongue and cock are gone. I lie quietly, working on catching my breath while I wait to see what'll happen next.

A few seconds later, soft lips are on mine, coaxing my mouth open. There's an urgency in the kiss—desire...need. I kiss him back and am about to wrap my arms around his neck when my hands are stopped and lifted above my head, silently conveying not to touch so I can't know who is on top of me and who's next to me.

My thighs are parted more, and a hard cock enters me slowly and deeply. I groan into his mouth, taking him inside me, inch by delicious inch with nothing between us. A mouth goes to my breast, sucking on my nipple, and I realize the man who's kissing me isn't the one who's inside me.

The hands holding my own—the hands that belong to the man

kissing me—thread their fingers through mine so we're connected. I might only be having sex with one of them, but they're both making love to me in their own ways. With their lips and tongues and hands and cock.

With each languid thrust, each fiery kiss, each sensual touch, I feel every ounce of want and desire and love emanating off them. My second orgasm creeps toward the edge, building slowly, and then I fall, my body soaring through the clouds. Stars dance across my closed lids, and my inner walls grip the cock inside me like a vise. Since I don't know whose name to call out, I scream God's name in vain as my climax overtakes my entire body.

I've barely landed back on earth when the bed shifts. The cock buried deep inside me slides out, and the hands holding mine release me.

I assume it's over, and I'm about to tell them how amazing it was when hands grip the curve of my hips and flip me over like I weigh nothing. My body moves with ease, my forearms and knees hitting the mattress.

My legs are spread—and I note the cum dripping down the insides of my thighs—and then another cock enters me from behind so hard and deep, causing my body to surge forward.

Fingers gently grip my chin and lift my face upward, and then a mouth is on mine, kissing me softly, passionately. I'm so lost in the kiss that I gasp out loud when a hand slaps my ass cheek, the cracking sound filling the quiet room. And I know who's fucking me and who's kissing me. I don't need to see to feel.

Hayden fucks me hard from behind, one hand gripping the flesh of my ass and the other my hip, while Brody kisses me. It doesn't take long before another orgasm begins to work its way up. This one is different from the others. It's buried deep within me, pushing, climbing, clawing its way higher and higher.

As if Hayden can sense my struggle, his fingers slide around my hip to my front and land on my clit. Using my juices, he circles the sensitive nub, and a few thrusts later, my pussy constricts around his dick, trembling in pleasure. Hayden's movements turn erratic, his fingers on my hip dig into my flesh almost painfully, and then he explodes inside me.

My juices, mixed with theirs, drip out of me and down my legs, and when he pulls out, I break my kiss with Brody and fall onto the bed, satiated and exhausted. I don't even bother to remove the blindfold, simply content to lie here and revel in what we just did— what they just did to me.

A few minutes—or hell, maybe hours—later, the blindfold is removed, and both guys are standing in front of me, stark naked.

"So?" Brody asks. "How was it?"

I glance from him to Hayden, who's tugging on his bottom lip, and get a sense that they're nervous. As if they could believe for even a second that I didn't just enjoy everything that happened.

"When I've gotten some sleep, I'm going to demand we do that again and again," I tell them. Both their faces split into the most adorable grins, and I can visibly see they're relieved.

"But first," I say with a sigh. "I need a shower."

I slide to the edge of the bed and am about to stand when Hayden lifts me into his arms, bridal style. I screech, shocked at how easily the guys can carry me when I know I'm not light, and then his mouth is on mine, silencing me as he walks us to the bathroom.

Brody turns the water on, and once steam billows out of the shower, Hayden sets me inside on the bench.

The guys go about washing my hair and body, and I let them, still spent from the three orgasms they pulled out of me. I had no idea I could even come that many times or that sex could be that freaking good. The thought has me frowning, and Brody must notice because he bends in front of me and palms the side of my face.

"What's going through your head?" he asks gently. I'm about to tell him nothing, but before I can get the words out, he adds, "And don't say nothing. Remember what you said. In order for this to work, we have to communicate honestly."

I nod in agreement. "I was just thinking how that was the best sex of my life."

Brody grins. "The first or second time?"

I snort out a laugh because they think I don't know who went first. "The second," I say, just to mess with him. "The first guy sucked." Hayden barks out a laugh, and Brody frowns.

"I'm kidding," I tell him. "I appreciate what you guys did so I wouldn't have to choose, but I know it was you who went first and Hayden second." I frame Brody's face with my hands. "I know your touch. How you kiss. I don't need to see you to know how you feel." I look at Hayden. "You both were amazing in your own ways."

My eyes go back to Brody. "I love that I get soft and gentle with you." I run my fingers through his wet hair. "It makes me feel cherished."

I reach out for Hayden's hand, and he gives it to me, stepping next to Brody and then bending at my level. "And I love that when I'm with you, you're rough and passionate. It makes me feel desired." My gaze flits between the two of them. "You both make me feel wanted and loved. I feel like I have the best of both worlds."

"Then why did you look upset?" Brody asks thoughtfully.

"Because when I was thinking about how perfect tonight was and how amazing the sex was…with *both of you*"—Brody smirks and Hayden grins, and I roll my eyes—"my first thought was that I've never experienced sex like that, ever. And then it hit me that by thinking that, I was inadvertently saying sex with you guys was better than with Pete." I drop my eyes to my lap, hating that I'm comparing them. It's not fair to any of them.

"Hey," Hayden says, lifting my chin. "It's not better or worse. It's different. You were young, and then you guys had kids. There's nobody here to interrupt us. No stress from life. You were able to enjoy it."

With every word Hayden speaks, I fall harder for him. For the man who cares about me enough to defend my late husband, knowing how hard moving on is for me.

"So what you're saying is, once my kids are home, the sex will suck?" I ask jokingly to lighten the mood.

"Fuck no," Brody says, shaking his head. "It just means we'll be sneaking around and having quickies." He winks playfully, and I laugh, thankful for the mood shift.

"In all seriousness," Brody adds, "you're older, and you know your body better. Sex in our younger days was different and more awkward. Hayden used to come in like two seconds flat."

"Fuck you!" Hayden barks through his laughter, smacking Brody in the back of the head. "I easily outfucked you in our college days, and I'll outfuck you now."

"I'm totally game for testing this out," I say, bobbing my head for emphasis and making both guys chuckle.

"Later," Hayden says. "Right now, we need to finish showering and get some sleep. We have plans tomorrow that involve us getting up early."

"Plans for the Fourth of July?" I ask. "Where? What are we doing?"

"It's a surprise," Brody says, giving me a chaste kiss. "You'll see in the morning."

CHAPTER TWENTY-EIGHT
AUBREE

"ARE YOU FREAKING KIDDING ME RIGHT NOW?" I GASP, taking in the giant boat—no, scratch that, *yacht*—in front of us. I don't know anything about yachts, but this thing looks expensive and luxurious, and holy shit, I'm pretty sure it's bigger and definitely nicer than my apartment!

When the guys woke me up at six and said to pack for a day at the beach, I thought we were going down to the beach again. So I was confused when, instead of going out the back door, we got in the car and drove to the marina after stopping for breakfast and coffee.

I was even more confused when Brody said to wait outside while he went in to speak to someone. Hayden and I strolled down the sidewalk, checking out all the boats and Jet Skis, until Brody came back and said they were ready for us. I didn't know who *they* were until he guided me over to a beautiful yacht and said we'd be spending the day on it and would be watching the fireworks from it.

"You rented this for the entire day and night?" I ask excitedly. When I visited my kids and in-laws, we didn't have a chance to go on their boat, and this one is way the hell nicer.

"Rent?" Hayden shakes his head. "Brody owns this."

My head whips around to look at Brody. "Why do you own something that's docked thousands of miles away?"

"I usually keep it docked in New York in the summer and here in the winter, but I've been busy, so I never had it brought back to New York. Figured we could use it before the summer is over." He pulls me into his side, his lips grazing my ear. "It has a large bedroom with a king-sized bed. Have you ever fucked in the middle of the Atlantic?"

A wave of desire flows through my body. "Let's go...now." I tug on his hand, ready to board the boat while Brody chuckles, letting me pull him along.

Once we're on board, Brody gives me a tour of the bedroom, bathroom, main area that's larger than my living room, decent-sized kitchen, and last but not least, the hot tub.

"We'll be using that later," he says with a smirk.

"How are we supposed to enjoy the hot tub if you have to drive?" I ask. "Wait, can you even drive this thing? Don't you need like some special license or something?"

Brody laughs. "I have a boating license, and I can drive it, but I won't be. I've hired someone to drive us over to the island where we'll dock and watch the fireworks. He'll get a ride back, and then I'll drive it back here."

"So someone will be on board with us?" I say, my disappointment evident in my tone. So much for making use of the hot tub and bed...

"Yes, but you won't even know he's on board. He's a professional," Brody says, leaning in to give me a kiss. He goes to pull back, but my active libido has me snaking my arms around his neck and deepening the kiss. In my defense, the dam levee was holding back my sexual drive for years, and once they broke through it, years of sexual desire poured out, and I doubt there's any hope of reining it back in, especially not with these two around.

All too soon, Brody breaks the kiss, laughing when I pout. "We need to take off, and then I'm all yours," he promises, giving me one more quick kiss.

"Fine," I groan, following him out.

We find Hayden talking to a man who looks like a captain of a ship, dressed in a suit with a nautical cap on his head. He must be the man who will be driving the yacht. He shakes hands with Hayden, then Brody, and then with a polite nod to me, disappears inside.

I'm about to suggest we lie out since the pillowed area up front looks beyond comfortable when my phone rings from my bag. I pull it out and find my son's name on the screen.

"Hey, you! Happy Fourth of July!" I say when his face comes onto the screen.

"Hey, Mom!" he says back. "Guess what?"

"What?"

"Grammy and Papa surprised us with a trip to Disney!"

"Yeah!" Evie adds in excitement. "We're gonna watch the fireworks with Mickey!"

I already knew this, which made me feel better about being so close to them and not seeing them—that and when I told Beatrice I would be in town, and she could hear the guilt in my voice, she demanded I enjoy my alone time because they would be home in a couple of weeks. They're going to Disney for a few days and then beginning their journey home in an RV Stephen bought. Apparently, he and Beatrice are going to travel in it for a few months after they bring the kids home. It's something he's always wanted to do and can do now that they've retired.

"That's so cool," I tell them, loving that they're having the time of their lives with their grandparents. If not for them, there's no way I'd be able to afford to do with them what they've done this summer, especially since I'm trying to save up for a new apartment before my lease runs out. "Make sure you take lots of pictures with Mickey so I can see."

"We will," Evie says. "Are you doing anything fun today?"

"I am. A couple of friends of mine are taking me out on a big boat, and we're going to watch the fireworks from here."

"Is it big like Grammy and Papa's?" Evie asks.

"It is."

"Evie, Miles, come get your shoes on." I hear Beatrice say.

"Oh, we've gotta go, Mom," Miles says. "Bye, love you."

"Make sure you put on sunscreen so you don't burn," Evie says, sounding like me. "Love you, bye!" she says, blowing me a kiss and then clicking end on the call.

My heart swells at her motherly advice, and I suddenly get choked up, missing them like crazy even though I was just with them less than forty-eight hours ago.

I think about what it will be like when they get back...the busy days with sports and playdates. Their birthday is coming up, so I need to start planning the party—Miles wants a *Minecraft* theme, and Evie wants American Girl. It's her new obsession ever since Beatrice took her to the American Girl store. So I'm planning to get them each their own cake and let them pick out some decorations.

School starts back up in September, which means homework and school projects, more playdates...early mornings and late evenings at the bakery.

I'm not complaining. I love my life. I love my kids. I'm just wondering how I'm going to juggle it all once they're home. I was stretched thin before Brody and Hayden came into my life. How am I supposed to give them the attention they deserve while running a business and trying to be a good mom? It's easy now while my kids are gone, but how will this work when my short reprieve from reality is over? Will Hayden and Brody get frustrated? Will they decide that the stress isn't worth it?

I'm lost in my own head when Brody and Hayden walk over to join me. Brody hands me a drink and drops down to the left of me while Hayden sits on my right.

After sipping the fruity drink and taking a calming breath, I watch as the boat slowly moves forward, wishing I could shake my negative thoughts from my head.

"How are the kids?" Brody asks like he always does when I get off the phone with them.

"Good. Spending the day with Mickey Mouse." I force a smile, but I can tell Brody doesn't miss a beat when his brows furrow in concern.

"The kids will be home in a couple of weeks. Beatrice doesn't know an exact date since they're stopping along the way at various places, but she said to expect them home in the next ten to fourteen days tops."

"That's good, right?" Hayden asks.

"Yeah. I've missed them like crazy."

"So what's with the long face?" Brody asks, taking my hand in his and bringing it up to his lips for a soft kiss.

"Mother's guilt," I say simply with a humorless laugh. "I miss them, but I've also enjoyed my time alone…and my time with you two. It'll be different when they get back."

"Different, sure," Brody agrees, "but not necessarily bad."

I stifle a laugh at his ignorant optimism and nod in agreement, not wanting to get into anything deep right now. It's a beautiful day, and they've taken me out on a gorgeous yacht. I just want to enjoy myself and enjoy them.

To change the subject, I remove my shirt, revealing my tankini that does an amazing job of making my breasts look damn good while hiding my stomach. Both of their gazes zero in on my chest, and I know the conversation is officially dropped.

"Can one of you put sunscreen on me?" I ask, standing and removing my shorts so I'm only in my bathing suit top and bikini bottoms.

"I will," Brody says, snatching the sunscreen from the table.

I take a sip of my drink and set it down, then lie on my stomach, resting my head on my forearms. Brody sprays the liquid onto my flesh and then starts massaging my shoulders and arms, moving his way down to my legs. Between the rocking of the boat, the fresh breeze, and how good his hands feel on me, my eyes flutter closed.

CHAPTER TWENTY-NINE
AUBREE

"There she is," Hayden says with a warm smile. "We thought you were going to sleep the day away."

Shit, I must've been tired because I totally fell asleep while Brody was applying sunscreen to my body.

"Sorry," I mutter, rolling to my side.

"You don't have to apologize," Brody says from behind me, squeezing my hip. "I'm pretty sure we're so whipped we could watch you sleep all day."

Hayden chuckles but doesn't argue. I notice he's lost his shirt, leaving his chiseled chest and six-pack abs on display. My eyes descend and land on his happy trail that disappears into his board shorts.

"Where are we?" I ask. We're obviously outside, but the boat isn't rocking like it was earlier, nor is the wind whipping my hair around.

"In the Atlantic near the island," Hayden says. "Captain dropped the anchor and took off." His eyes meet mine, and he smirks, knowing I was checking him out.

I sit up, and sure enough, nothing but water surrounds us. I catch a couple of boats cruising in the distance, but other than that, we're completely alone.

"We're alone?" I ask, just to confirm, looking at Brody, who is also shirtless.

He nods, a slow smile tugging at his lips.

"So if I wanted to kiss you here…" I lean in and kiss his pectoral muscle. "Nobody would see me?"

"Sweetness," he croons, pulling me over him to straddle his hips. "We could fuck you right here, and nobody would know." He rocks forward slightly, and I feel his hard cock straining behind the material of his shorts.

"I don't want you to fuck me," I say, making him frown. "I want to fuck *you*. You guys were in control last night. I want to be in control this time."

Brody glances over at Hayden, who grins wide. "You want to be in control?" Hayden asks. "You got it. Tell us where and how you want us."

The thought of fully exploring both of them causes the apex of my legs to tighten. "Can we stay out here?" I ask, loving the idea of fucking them outside in the open.

"Sure," Brody says.

"I want to fuck you both…at the same time," I blurt out.

Brody chuckles. "You can do that, but if you're referring to one of us fucking your ass, we have to take it slow. Otherwise, it will hurt."

I know that, but I really want to be with both of them. "Okay, so can we work on that?"

"We can do anything you want," Hayden says, taking my hand in his and kissing each of my knuckles before moving his lips to the inside of my wrist. For a moment, I get lost in his touch, but then I remember I'm supposed to be in charge, not him, so I pull my hand away and climb off Brody.

"Lie next to Brody," I tell Hayden. He does as I say, and I take a moment to admire my two sexy as hell boyfriends.

"Take off your shorts," I say next. With matching smirks, they tug their shorts down their muscular legs and drop them next. Both of their cocks are hard, jutting up toward their stomachs, and my mouth waters at the thought of sucking them both off, so I do just that.

Getting onto my knees, I situate myself between them and start by licking the head of Hayden's cock while I wrap my fingers around Brody's shaft and slowly jack him off. I take Hayden in deeper, licking and sucking on his velvety smooth skin, and then release him, so I can give Brody the same attention.

The guys lie there, watching and moaning as I suck them both off from head to balls until they're hard as steel and leaking pre-cum, begging me to fuck them.

Since I know Brody took me first last night, after giving Hayden's cock a quick kiss, I climb on top of him and guide myself onto his cock, using his shoulders to hold myself up.

"Brody, come here," I moan, taking a moment to get used to how deep Hayden is in this position. "I want you in my mouth."

He does as I say, and with Hayden buried inside me, I take Brody's entire shaft into my mouth. It could be all the porn I've watched—yes, I wanted to know how this would all work, and I'm aware porn isn't real, but it gave me a good idea of the mechanics—but when I start swiveling my hips so I can fuck Hayden, I'm so turned on, I glance up at Brody and say, "Fuck my mouth."

Brody is the gentlest between the two, so I know he won't hurt me—not that I think Hayden would hurt me, but since this is my first time, it's probably best not to go from zero to a hundred.

Gently, like I knew he would be, he tangles my hair in his fingers and then starts to fuck my mouth, slowly sliding in and out of it.

Having him taking control allows me to focus on fucking Hayden. I gyrate my hips and glide up and down his shaft, finding where it feels the best. Hayden pinches my nipple, and I moan around Brody's shaft as my orgasm builds.

When I hit the spot just right over and over again, my walls contract around Hayden's cock, and I come hard, my screams muffled by the fact that my mouth is still filled with Brody's hardness.

Hayden takes over, his hands gripping my hips, and fucks me from underneath, finding his release at the same time Brody fills my mouth with his own. I swallow every drop he gives me and don't stop until he's licked clean.

"Jesus." Brody sighs, pulling out and stepping back. "I come in like two seconds every time I'm inside you. Your mouth, your pussy...I can't control myself with you."

Hayden laughs. "We didn't even have time to work on you taking us both."

I feel my face blush, loving that they're so attracted to me they can't hold back, especially since I feel the same.

"Let's clean up, and then we can work on that," Brody says with a smirk.

I have no clue how they want to work on it, but I'm sure as hell not about to argue.

Since the yacht has a full-sized shower, the three of us take one together. After rinsing off quickly, we head out to the bedroom to dress. But before I can get my suit back on, Brody grabs it and chucks it to the side.

"On the bed, sweetness," he says, nodding toward the king-sized bed behind me.

I back up, and when the backs of my knees hit the edge, I climb onto the mattress, inching myself toward the top until my head finds the pillows.

Hayden walks in and throws something onto the bed by my legs, and when I look at it, I find it's a bottle of lube.

"Have you ever put anything in your ass?" Hayden asks, climbing onto the bed between my legs. I should probably feel vulnerable, being completely naked in broad daylight, but the way they look at me, with such want and desire, I can't help but feel good about myself, about my body.

I shake my head, suddenly nervous and a bit excited at the thought of them filling me in every hole.

"We'll start small," Brody says, hopping onto the bed and lying next to me. He grasps my chin and turns my face toward him, curving his lips around my own. I'm so caught up in our kiss that I don't realize Hayden has spread my legs and is kissing his way up my thighs. When he parts my lips and glides his tongue up my slit, I moan into Brody's mouth. I'm sensitive from my earlier orgasm, but that doesn't stop my body from springing to life at the thought of climaxing again.

Brody breaks the kiss and trails his lips along my neck, nipping and sucking while Hayden does the same to my clit. He pushes a finger and then two inside me. At the same time, Brody sucks on the pulse point on the sensitive part of my neck, damn near sending me over the edge. But then Hayden removes his tongue from my clit, along with the pleasure.

I squirm, annoyed, and Hayden chuckles. "Not yet, baby," he chides.

"I was so close," I whine, which has Brody shaking with silent laughter as he kisses his way back to my mouth. Our lips fuse, and our tongues meet, dancing erotically. I can't get enough. I pull his face closer, deepening the kiss, and for a split second, I forget Hayden is down there until his tongue descends…down…down…down…not stopping until it reaches my ass. He spreads my cheeks wide and spears my hole with his tongue.

"Oh, shit!" I gasp into Brody's mouth as Hayden's tongue swirls around the tight rim.

Brody breaks our kiss and palms one of my breasts, tweaking and plucking my nipple while he takes my other nipple into his mouth, sucking on the hardened tip. Pleasure zaps through my body, straight to my core, and I tense up, needing to find release.

"Bree, I need you to relax," Hayden says as if I have any control over my actions at this moment.

"I need to come," I beg. "Please, make me—"

My words are cut off when Hayden pushes a single digit into my ass. At first, I'm not sure if it feels good, but then he starts moving it in and out and desire starts to build inside me.

Brody's mouth finds my neck again, and he suckles on my heated flesh. "Does that feel good?" he whispers between searing hot kisses.

"So good," I moan as Hayden's tongue goes back to massaging my clit. "Oh, God, yes, right there." Between Brody's mouth on my neck, his fingers plucking my nipples…Hayden's tongue on my clit, and his finger in my ass…my pleasure builds higher and higher until it reaches the top and then spills over, my orgasm crashing through me unlike anything I've ever felt.

Bright colors fill my vision, and then everything goes black, my body feeling like it's not even my own anymore.

When I come to, my heart is pounding like I've just run a marathon. My legs feel like Jell-O, and my pussy is still spasming. I open my lids and find both guys staring at me with molten desire in their eyes.

"Did I just black out?"

"Fuck, Bree," Hayden says. "That was the hottest thing I've ever seen. You squirted every-fucking-where."

"What?" I squeak, sitting up and finding the sheets under me soaking wet. "Oh, my God! Did I…Did I pee the bed?"

Brody shakes his head. "No, sweetness, you came hard as hell. Did it feel good?"

"So good," I admit, dropping my head back onto the pillow while I work on catching my breath.

"I can't believe I soaked the sheets," I groan in embarrassment, covering my eyes with my arm.

"Hey," Hayden says, moving my arm away. "Look at me."

Because I'd pretty much do anything for these guys, I do as he says.

"You have nothing to be embarrassed about. Having to change

the sheets was worth watching you come like that. And if we have it our way, you'll be coming like that again soon."

"Hell yes," Brody agrees. "As a matter of fact, I think we should try it again now."

"You're nuts," I tell them both. "That orgasm damn near killed me."

"Maybe," Hayden jokes. "But what a way to go, huh?"

CHAPTER THIRTY
BRODY

I COULD WATCH BREE FOR HOURS—HELL, DAYS. SLEEP, eat, laugh, talk...It doesn't matter what she's doing. I would be content spending the rest of my life simply watching her. And because she's mine, I'm able to do just that. Every goddamn day. Sure, I have to go to work, so I can't watch her all the time, but when I'm not working, I get to be with her. She and Hayden...

I glance at my best friend and girlfriend, who are playing Frisbee on the beach. She cracks up whenever she sends it flying in the wrong direction. Her laughter only getting louder when Hayden attacks her, throwing her gently onto the ground and kissing the hell out of her. If it weren't so glaringly obvious how bad her aim was, I'd almost think she was doing it on purpose just to get a reaction out of him.

She throws it, and he doesn't even bother going after it, just waits until it lands nowhere near him and then grabs it before going after her. She shrieks and runs, but his steps eat up the ground, and he catches her quickly.

His laughter is boisterous, and his smile never falters. He's in love with Bree, just like I am. Some guys are possessive and could never imagine sharing a woman with another man, and honestly, if it were any other man, it wouldn't be happening. But it's Hayden… My best friend, brother from another mother, the man I've loved for years. When I wasn't sure how I felt about guys, he offered himself up on a silver platter for two reasons: one, he would do anything for me, and two, he knew I needed to know how it would feel to be with a man…to be with him.

That night, I learned that regardless of Hayden being straight, he's damn good in bed with either sex, and while it was good, it wasn't enough.

We moved forward, never looking back, and dated a plethora of women, none of them ever being enough…until Bree. I don't know if it's fate or the stars aligning or the best goddamn luck, but when she fell for both of us—and we equally fell for her—it was like everything just came together. I get to be with a woman I'm not only attracted to but thoroughly enjoy being around—a woman I can picture a future with—and have my best friend by my side.

Am I gay or bi or whatever? Eh, not really. I don't look at men and think about them like that. I love women—more specifically, I love Bree. I love the feel of her tight, warm pussy wrapped around my cock, the silkiness of her womanly creamy skin. I love the way her pouty lips curve against mine, and how soft her body is. And fuck, those twin dimples and her smile. I could spend the rest of my life with her and be content.

But when I was with Hayden, I felt something stir deep inside me. Something that I pushed down because I never thought I could have it while also being with a woman. But then Bree mentioned us being together, and those deep feelings clawed their way to the surface, knowing they would be safe with Bree. Because that's what she does. She makes me feel safe in loving her.

"You look like you're lost in your own head," the woman who occupies my thoughts says, dropping in front of me and attempting to give me a quick kiss. Instead, I grab the back of her head, fisting her wet, sandy hair, and crush my mouth back down on hers.

There's an urgency in the kiss, the need to tell her how I feel about her without words.

I love you.

I need you.

You're everything I could ever want.

Thank you for wanting my best friend and me.

When we separate, her eyes are glassy with desire, her lips bee stung from how hard I was kissing her, and her cheeks are tinted pink. "What's going on?" she whispers, sensing my inner turmoil.

I consider saying it's nothing, but instead, I go with the truth since I told myself I'd never hide anything from her again. Not after what happened with Hayden and his dad's company wanting her to sell out of her lease.

"I love you," I admit, praying I don't scare the hell out of her. "I love you, and I need you, and I feel like you're exactly what Hayden and I were looking for all these years without even realizing it. I love him so much, and the thought of being without him hurt my heart, but because of you, I get to have you both," I choke out, throwing it all on the table.

Her eyes widen for a second, then they relax, and the most beautiful smile spreads across her face. "I love you too," she says softly as Hayden drops next to us, oblivious to the depth that the conversation has taken. "I love you both," she says, looking at him. "I never thought I would want to find love after losing Pete, but now I can't imagine not having this feeling inside of me."

She leans in and kisses Hayden and then me. "A large part of me was buried with my husband, and it feels like you guys have resurrected me."

Hayden doesn't say a word. Instead, he lifts her into his arms and starts carrying her back toward the boat. I laugh, following, knowing he sucks at speaking his feelings, and he's about to fuck her seven ways to Sunday to show her just how much he cares.

The moment we're back on the yacht, he deposits her onto the bed and takes his clothes off quickly before undressing her. I stand in the doorway watching, my heart so damn full as he climbs on top of her, attacking her mouth and entering her simultaneously.

I watch as he fucks her with abandon, as she takes every thrust like she was made for him. Because she was. She was made for us both.

He, of course, makes sure she comes first, screaming his name hoarsely, and then he roars out his own release, only stopping once they're both spent.

"Fuck," he hisses, dropping his head so their foreheads are touching. "I love you so much." He glances back at me. "Brody, get the hell over here," he demands.

I chuckle under my breath, walking over and joining them on the bed. He pulls out, and I can't help but get hard at the way his cum mixed with her release slowly seeps out of her pussy.

He notices my face and smirks. "If you want to eat her pussy, just do it."

I glance at her, waiting to see some sort of disgust on her features, but she just looks at me with desire in her eyes. "Or you could work on my ass some more," she says, biting her bottom lip. I love that she wants to be with us both, and it's going to happen as soon as she's ready.

Hayden slides over, making room for me, and I waste no time situating myself between her legs so I can give her another orgasm. With my tongue in her pussy, my fingers deep in her ass, and my cock as hard as a rock, she comes for a second time.

"Your turn," she says, spreading her legs. "I want you in me… now."

She doesn't have to tell me twice. Tugging my shorts down as fast as possible, I guide myself toward her pussy, but she shakes her head. "No, in my ass."

I glance at Hayden lying next to her, trailing kisses along her neck and shoulders. "You heard her," he says, "stick your cock in that ass." He turns her face toward his and captures her mouth.

I grab more lube and coat my shaft, not wanting to hurt her too badly. I know from experience it will hurt no matter what the first time, but I want it to at least be somewhat pleasurable for her. I could go at it from the missionary position, or I could flip her onto her stomach and take her from behind. But as I watch her and Hayden kissing and exploring each other, I pull her legs to the side and slide in behind her. Lifting her leg onto my thigh, I guide myself into her tight ass inch by inch. When I get far enough inside that I know she can feel it, her head falls back against mine, and she lets out a loud moan.

"You okay?" I murmur, kissing her shoulder as I slowly go deeper and deeper inside her.

"It hurts, but it also feels good," she breathes.

Hayden moves closer, creating a human sandwich with Bree in the middle, and bends his head down, taking one of her breasts into his hand and mouth. He sucks hard on her nipple, effectively distracting her and turning her on. When she moans loudly, I push the rest of the way in, filling her ass to the hilt.

"Holy shit." She sighs. At the same time, I curse under my breath. She's too tight, feels too good. This isn't going to last long at all.

I start to move in and out, trying to be gentle, while Hayden inches downward until his head is even with her pussy.

"No way," she moans, trying to push his head away. "I already came twice."

"And you're about to come again," he says matter-of-factly, grabbing her hand so she can't stop him.

And she fucking does, hard and loud, while I fuck her ass until I can't take it any longer. I quickly pull out, not wanting to come in her ass since we haven't discussed it. As she throws her head back in orgasmic bliss, ropes of cum jet out all over her skin, some even hitting her luscious tits. And if I hadn't just come, the sight of her covered in my seed would've done it for me.

"Wow." She sighs, rolling onto her back, looking satiated and spent. "I feel like I'm in one of those pornos I've watched to see how this would all work. Except, it's real life, and the guys I'm with are in love with me."

"Damn right, we are," I say, lifting her into my arms. "Let's get cleaned up. The fireworks are due to start soon."

"I did good, right?" she says as I carry her to the bathroom. When I lift a brow in confusion, she adds, "My ass. It wasn't too bad and felt really good after a few minutes. That means I'm ready for both of you." She waggles her brows, and Hayden and I both bark out a laugh.

"I think we've created a sex fiend," I joke.

"Hey!" She pouts. "I went almost five years without sex. I have a lot to make up for. And I have not one but two sexy guys at my disposal. Can you blame me?"

"Nope, sweetness," I tell her, kissing her pouty lips. "I can't. And you're right. We're both absolutely at your disposal."

CHAPTER THIRTY-ONE

HAYDEN

BREE

What time will you be home? Dinner's almost
ready.

*Home...*I LOVE THE SOUND OF THAT. UNTIL BREE, OUR condo felt like nothing more than the place where Brody and I came to at the end of a long day. But with Bree there, it actually feels like a home. It's been almost two weeks since she forgave me for what happened with my dad and we went away for the Fourth of July.

And every night since we've returned, she's been at our place, cooking us dinner and sleeping in our beds. When she's not at Heart's, she's with us. A few times, she even brought us lunch at the office. And last weekend, we spent the entire two days holed up in the condo, ordering in, binge-watching Netflix, and inside her.

I love it, and if it weren't for her having to go home once the kids get back, I'd never let her leave. But Bree's a good mom, and she's going to want to take shit slow, so they aren't affected by her moving forward from their dad—with two guys.

BRODY

Leaving now.

And so is Hayden.

As the second text comes through, Brody comes sauntering through my office doorway. I've only been working with him for a short time, but the difference in the environment is night and day. Unlike my dad, who acts like he wants your opinion but won't listen, Brody values the words that come out of my mouth.

"I was thinking we should take Bree to dinner tomorrow night. She mentioned the kids will be home Monday or Tuesday, and I'm sure shit will slow down once they're back," he says, obviously on the same page as I am.

"Yeah, sounds good," I say, closing my laptop. "We should make it special. Spend the night somewhere. A little mini staycation."

Brody nods in agreement. "That could be fun. I'll see if my parents recommend anywhere."

"We could go to a winery," I mention. "She loves that shit."

"Good thinking."

Since we work together, we share a car to and from work, which is nice. And since Bree demands—without actually doing so—that we're home at a decent hour for dinner every night, I feel like I've seen more of Brody lately than I did during all the years we've been living together prior to Bree.

The delicious aroma coming from the kitchen has my stomach grumbling in excitement when we walk through the door. We're met with Bree, standing at the stove, stirring something, and thoughts of our future flit through my head: her pregnant with our babies, the kids' laughter filling the silence, her clothes occupying half the closet. Dinners and breakfasts and family trips. I never imagined wanting any of it, but I want it all with her...and Brody.

I glance at my best friend, and I can tell by the dopey expression on his face he's thinking the same thing as me—forever with Bree looks damn good.

"Hey," she says, "how was work?"

"Busy," Brody says, going over and giving her a kiss on the cheek. I follow, giving her one on her neck. We both grab a beer from the fridge and lean against the island.

"How was your day?" I ask, checking out the way her shirt rises when she leans over the stove to turn it off, showing off the swells of her ass since she's only in a pajama shirt and tiny underwear.

"So good." She beams. "Remember how I brought samples by several bakeries last week?"

Brody convinced her to take her baked goods to the next level by distributing them to places that outsource their goods. We compiled a list, and then she created a box filled with samples to take to each business to pitch her products.

"Well, two of them called me today wanting to sign a six-month contract!" She giggles happily. "It's going to mean more work, but with the additional income, I'll be able to afford to hire Jessica full time to do the baking! And if I can get a few more contracts like those two, I should have no problem finding a new place to rent."

I'm bringing my beer to my lips to take a swig, but her words stop me in my place. "Where are you going?"

She takes the pot off the stove and glances at me with a frown. "I have to be moved out of my apartment by the end of the year. I'd rather not be moving in the middle of winter, so I'm hoping to find a place soon. I haven't looked at apartments yet, but with the additional income, I imagine I'll be able to afford something halfway decent now."

Brody and I share a glance. If it were up to us, the only place she and her kids would be moving to is here, but she's not there yet.

"Congratulations," Brody says. "I have no doubt every one of those businesses will be begging you for your baked goods. They're like fucking crack."

Bree rolls her eyes and laughs, handing us each a plate of food. Since it's just the three of us, we eat at the island.

"We should celebrate," I say. "Brody and I were thinking we

could take you away tomorrow night. A quick trip before the kids come home. Think you can have someone go in for you tomorrow and Sunday?"

"Really?" She beams. "That sounds perfect. And I have someone. I've actually decided not to work on the weekends anymore. I've really enjoyed having some time to myself. I think I buried myself under my work after Pete died, and it's been nice finding a balance. I don't want that to stop when the kids get home, so I've promoted two of my part-timers to full time, one of which is in culinary school and has wanted more hours. I've been meaning to do it so Lacey could cut back her hours. She only came on to help me after my grandma passed away."

"That's good," I tell her. "That means we get you every weekend." I waggle my brows, but she doesn't react how I expect her to. Instead, she frowns.

"It won't be able to be like that once the kids are home," she says. "You know that, right?"

"Of course, we do," I say. "But eventually, once the kids know about us, we'll be able to all hang out."

She nods wordlessly but doesn't say anything.

"Hey." I lean over and palm her cheek. "We'll take things slowly. You're a mom first, and we get that." It's one of the things I love about her. How much she loves her kids. I can't wait to meet them and see her with them, but I know it'll take some time. She's worried about how they'll react to her moving forward and the fact that she cares enough to be worried only proves how good of a mom she is.

"Damn right we do," Brody agrees. "And when you're ready for us to meet them, we'll be here."

She smiles softly. "Thanks for understanding."

We finish eating, and then Brody and I work together to do the dishes and clean the kitchen while Bree video chats with her kids. I'm drying a pan when my phone goes off with a text from my sister:

GRETCHEN

I can't believe you seriously left. I didn't take
you for a quitter.

I roll my eyes at her lack of compassion. Not that it shocks me.

ME

Look at the bright side. Now Dad has no
choice but to give you the CEO position.

GRETCHEN

I'd rather beat you fair and square.

ME

Consider it a win-win. You get to be CEO,
and I get to work at a company that actually
gives a shit about their employees.

GRETCHEN

Wait, where are you working? Dad made it
seem like you were just being a brat and
you'd be back.

ME

Fields...I'm done with Shea. Won't be back.

GRETCHEN

All over the stupid business of some woman
you're screwing around with?

ME

There's more to it than that. For one, she's
not just some woman. I love her.

I stare at my phone, waiting for her to text back, but apparently, I've shocked her to the point she's speechless. Probably for the best. My sister might be married, but they're far from being in love. She fits in perfectly with Shea—with my dad—since the only thing she truly loves is her job and power.

"Everything okay?" Brody asks as I pocket my phone.

"Just my sister. Dad made it seem like I'm throwing a tantrum, and I'll be back. I told her I'm done there for good."

Brody dries his hands on the towel and throws it to the side, leaning against the counter. "I looked into buying the building from that asshole who was harassing Bree."

"Benitez?"

"Yeah." He nods. "Figured if I bought it, we could turn it into luxury apartments and keep Bree's coffeehouse."

Fuck, why didn't I think of that? "That's brilliant. How'd it go?"

"I think he would've sold it to me, but Shea has him in with a six-month no-compete contract. Shea pays him a monthly fee during that time in exchange for him agreeing not to sell the building to anyone else. If he can't meet Shea's stipulation of buying Bree's lease out, Shea can walk away, and Benitez can sell it to someone else."

"He must've done that shit after I left. He'll learn soon enough it's not happening." I shrug. "We should put together a proposal and present it to him as a backup option before someone else does."

"I agree. I'm having my legal department draw something up, and I'm offering him more than Shea is." Brody pushes off the counter and walks to the edge of the kitchen to watch Bree talk animatedly with her kids. She's laughing and smiling and looks so damn happy.

"She's not losing that shop," he says. "Not if we have anything to do with it."

"Damn right," I agree.

CHAPTER THIRTY-TWO
AUBREE

"This is the most adorable place I've ever seen." I sigh in awe, taking in the charming bed and breakfast the guys have taken me to. It looks like a cottage straight out of a fairy tale, surrounded by acres and acres of vineyards.

"C'mon," Brody says, taking my hand in his. "Let's get checked in. We have reservations for lunch."

While he speaks to the woman at the front desk, Hayden and I walk around. When we stop in the main room with a gorgeous fireplace with huge comfy-looking reading chairs, I can't help but imagine getting lost in a book here for hours with a coffee in my hand.

"What are you smiling at?" Hayden asks.

"If I were rich, I would build a room just like this. Only I'd have bookshelves lining the walls with all of my favorite books. I'd make myself a cup of coffee every night after the kids are in bed and lounge in one of those chairs, reading for hours."

Hayden smiles softly and wraps his arms around me, his hands going straight to my butt. "And on the floor"—he juts his chin toward the fluffy rug in front of the fireplace—"Brody and I would lay you out and make love to you every single night."

My core tightens at the thought, and I nod in agreement. "I want to be with you both this weekend," I murmur so nobody can hear, "at the same time."

"Ready?" Brody asks.

"More than ready," I tell him.

Hayden chuckles and, threading our fingers together, tugs me away from the pretty room.

I expected our room to be in the cozy little cabin, so I'm surprised when Brody takes us out back and around the side, where I see several cottages just as adorable. The walls are white-washed wood, and cute royal blue shutters frame the windows with gorgeous flower beds perched under each one. There's a wraparound porch with a porch swing, and more potted plants hang from the beams.

The interior is even cozier, with a good-sized country-style kitchen, comfy-looking couches in the living room, and a fireplace that's just as big as the one in the main house. There's even a plush rug in front of the fireplace. I glance at it and then at Hayden, who must know exactly what I'm thinking because his lips curl into the sexiest smirk.

There are three bedrooms and two bathrooms, but Brody insists we share a room—not that he has to because it's a given. Just like I've been sharing a room with them for the past few weeks at their place.

"We have about an hour and a half or so before lunch," Brody says. "If you want to freshen—"

"What I want is to thank you for bringing me here," I say, cutting him off. I wrap my arms around his neck and pull him down for a kiss, wanting him to know how much this all means to me. Ever since we've been together, regardless of the guys' crazy schedule, they make it a point to put me...to put *us* first. It doesn't matter how busy they are. They come home at a decent hour and spend the weekend with me.

When I went to their office to have lunch with them, Brody's assistant made a comment that this is the first time in years she's seen him take so much time off.

And a couple of days ago, when we had dinner with Brody's parents again—this time with his siblings—Savy mentioned the same thing, thanking me for pulling them out of their work-induced fog. But what she doesn't realize is that I didn't have to pull at all—they do it on their own.

One night, when I asked them why they no longer work long hours, Brody simply said, "Why would we want to be in an office when we can be spending time with you?"

"You don't have to thank us," Brody murmurs against my lips. "We'd give you the damn world if you let us." He presses his lips against mine for a soft kiss and is exploring my mouth when Hayden comes up behind me, resting his hands on my hips. He nips at my shoulder, then licks away the bite of pain.

"I want you both...now," I groan as Hayden fists my hair and tugs it to the side, and Brody breaks our kiss, placing kisses along my jawline and then my throat. I let my head fall back against Hayden's shoulder, and he sucks on my earlobe, sending sparks of pleasure straight to my core.

"We need to wait until tonight," Brody says, cupping my face. "If we get you naked right now, we'll never make it to lunch."

"Fuck lunch," I breathe. "The only thing I want for lunch is you."

Brazenly, I drop to my knees between them and stroke the bulges in their pants. They both release a groan in unison, spurring me on. Starting with Brody, I undo his pants and push them along with his boxer briefs to the floor. His cock is rock hard and stands at attention, and I give it a quick, open-mouthed kiss before I turn my attention to Hayden, removing his pants as well. His cock is also hard with a bit of pre-cum beading out of the slit, so I lean in and lick the head, tasting the saltiness before I take him all the way into my mouth.

While I'm sucking Hayden's dick, I reach back and cup Brody's ballsac, gently rolling them in my palms before I work my way up, stroking his cock up and down.

"Fuck, baby," Hayden hisses as he fists the back of my head. With my mouth full of him, he tugs on my hair, and I glance up, our gazes colliding. "You look so beautiful like this," he says reverently. "Can you go deeper?" He trails a finger down my cheek. "Can you take me all the way down that pretty throat?" His dirty words send liquid desire through my body, and I nod adamantly, wanting to please him.

I inhale and exhale a deep breath and then take almost his entire length into my mouth, the head of his cock hitting the back of my throat and making me gag slightly.

"Jesus, you're so goddamned perfect," Hayden coos as I take him in deep over and over again, my eyes watering and tears dripping down my cheeks.

"That's it," he says when I damn near swallow him whole. "Fuck!" He pulls my head back, and my mouth pops off his dick. "Show Brody what you can do before I come down that perfect little throat." Before I can do as he says, he reaches down and pulls my shirt over my head, exposing the new lace set I bought with Lacey the other day. Shopping with her is a lot more fun now that I have two horny men to shop for.

Seeing my new bra has Hayden grinning as his hand delves into my bra and pulls my breast out of the cup, pinching my nipple so hard it borders on pleasure-pain.

"Oh, God," I breathe. "That feels so good."

"Suck Brody's cock, baby," Hayden murmurs, his eyes filled with molten heat.

When I turn to give Brody my attention, I find that he's stroking his cock since I let go of him, and when I take it from him, I give each of his knuckles a soft kiss.

He palms my face and kisses me softly. "I love you, sweetness."

Butterflies erupt in my belly. How did I get so lucky that I have not one but two amazing men who love me? I almost feel greedy.

"I love you too," I tell him. Then I glance at Hayden. "I love you both so much."

Hayden leans in and nips my bottom lip, then my top. "Love everything about you," he murmurs against my mouth before pulling back.

As I take Brody's cock down my throat, he strokes my hair sweetly while Hayden tugs my shorts and panties down my legs.

"Sit on the couch," Hayden tells Brody, who backs up and sits, while I follow, my fingers fisting his shaft. I take him back into my mouth and am deep throating him when Hayden tugs on my hair once again, forcing me to release Brody.

"Bend over this," he demands gently, helping me stand and bend over the ottoman. I have no idea what's going on, but I trust Hayden explicitly, so I don't question him as my stomach hits the soft material and my ass pops up into the air.

"Good girl," Hayden mewls, stroking the globes of my ass. "Go back to sucking Brody's cock."

I do what he says as his hand descends toward my pussy. He pushes a single digit in and curses. "Fuck, you're practically dripping."

Of course, I am. This is what they do to me. Ever since I met them, it's like my libido has been in overdrive in the best way possible.

Another finger enters me, and then his thumb presses my sensitive clit. "Yes, right there," I beg. "Please fuck me."

"Not yet, baby," Hayden says, removing his thumb and fingers and making me pout.

In the next beat, my panties are removed, and then Hayden's large hands grip and spread my cheeks. His tongue swipes up the middle of my ass, stopping at the tight ringed muscle, and I groan, taking Brody deeper into my mouth.

"You want my cock in your ass?" Hayden asks, dripping cold liquid between my cheeks.

"Yes, please," I beg, my voice raspy with want and desire. "Fuck my ass."

I continue to give Brody head, licking up his shaft, sucking on his balls, and kissing the swollen head while he runs his fingers through my hair with one hand and pinches my nipples with the other.

Hayden pushes something cold and hard into my ass—a dildo, if I were to guess—and then starts to fuck me with it. "Damn, I've never been so jealous of a fake dick in my life," he says, pushing it in and pulling it out several times before he pulls it out one last time and throws it to the side. Gripping my hips, he thrusts deep into my pussy from behind, nearly taking my breath away.

"Oh, God!" I yell, squeezing Brody's dick as Hayden fucks me hard and fast. "Yes! Yes!" He feels so good inside me, hitting the most delicious spot that will cause me to explode...and then he pulls out.

"Hayden!" I hiss.

"Shh," he says, widening my cheeks. The thickness of his head pushes past the tight ring of muscle, and I groan in both pleasure and pain.

"Brody, you ready to fuck our woman?" he asks, sinking deep into my ass.

"Fuck yes," Brody replies.

Hayden pulls out, leaving me empty once again, and I sigh in annoyance, turned on and needing them.

"Straddle his cock," Hayden says, giving my ass a playful smack.

Desperately, I scramble over the ottoman and climb onto Brody's lap. Hayden must push the ottoman out of my way because he's suddenly at my back, gripping the curves of my hips as I sink onto Brody's shaft.

"How does that feel?" Brody asks.

"Like I'm stuffed full of a big cock," I moan as he stretches me nice and good.

With a soft chuckle, Brody grips my face and presses his lips to mine tenderly. I'm so lost in the kiss that I don't realize what Hayden's doing until my ass is spread open and his long, thick cock enters me from behind. With Brody in my pussy and Hayden in my ass, I feel beyond full.

"Can you feel that?" Hayden asks as he starts to fuck my ass. I'm not sure who he's talking to until he adds, "Can you feel my cock rubbing against yours?"

Brody groans into my mouth and then releases me. "I feel it," he breathes. "Fuck, this feels so good." He frames my face. "You okay, sweetness?"

"So good," I breathe. "But I'd be even better if you'd make me come."

Brody smirks and nods. "You got it, beautiful."

The guys work in tandem, thrusting in and out of my holes.

Taking me higher and higher.

Brody massages my clit.

Hayden suckles on my heated flesh.

Brody kisses me.

And then Hayden goes deeper, his hands cupping my breasts and tweaking my nipples.

And I explode, my walls clamping down on Brody's cock and sending him soaring as well.

"That's it, sweetness," Brody moans. "Squeeze my cock."

"Fuck, I can feel you both," Hayden hisses. "Tell me I can come in your ass, Bree."

"Yes!" I yell, the thought of my pussy and ass being filled with their cum causes my body to convulse harder.

My head drops onto Brody's shoulder, and he strokes my back tenderly while Hayden leans over me, nipping and kissing my shoulder.

And at this moment, my heart has never felt so full of love. A couple of months ago, I was barely surviving, and now I'm thriving. And it's because of these two. Because of their love.

The thought is both exhilarating and scary...because the last man I loved with my entire heart, I lost. And what I feel for Brody and Hayden in this short amount of time is already so strong that I can't imagine how much deeper my feelings will run a year...or five years from now.

"I never want this to end," I tell them out loud, needing them to know how I feel. "I don't think my heart could handle it if I lost either of you."

Brody lifts my chin and looks into my eyes, understanding the double meaning behind my words. "You'll never have to worry about that," he says. "Neither of us is going anywhere."

"Fuck no, we aren't," Hayden adds.

When I don't say anything, caught up in my own head and wanting so badly for them to be right and for nothing to ever come between us, Hayden grips my chin and tilts my head to the side, forcing me to look at him.

"Hey," he says. "We're. Not. Going. Anywhere. You hear me?"

I nod, but my eyes water, my emotions getting the better of me. When a tear leaks out and drips down my cheek, Hayden leans over and licks it up.

"You couldn't get rid of us if you tried. We're addicted to you, baby, and nothing and no one will take you from us. I promise."

While I appreciate their sureness, unfortunately, sometimes things are out of our control. Peter promised me forever, and look how that ended.

CHAPTER THIRTY-THREE
AUBREE

"Mommy! I missed you so, so much," Evie yells, running through the coffeehouse and straight into my arms. I bend and scoop my little girl up, hugging her tightly.

"I missed you too, sweet girl."

"Hey, Mom," Miles says, walking over and hugging me from the side. "Can I get a brownie?"

I laugh at his nonchalance and nod. "Of course."

I set Evie down and she joins her brother while I give Beatrice a hug. "Thank you for taking them," I tell her. "I didn't realize how much I needed this break."

"We loved spending time with them. They are such a delight and so well-mannered." She pulls back and looks into my eyes. "You're a wonderful mother, Aubree, and you're raising two amazing kids. There's nothing wrong with needing some time for yourself."

"Thank you."

After saying goodbye to my in-laws and Caroline and Lacey assuring me that they have the place under control, I head upstairs with the kids and their luggage to get situated.

"Mom, Evie and I were talking, and we were wondering if we

could have our party at the park," Miles says as I go through his clothes, separating the dirty from the clean so I can do the laundry.

"Yeah," Evie agrees. "Miles wants to play, and I want to paint with my friends."

Since I haven't made any plans and throwing one party instead of two will make everything easier, I have zero issues with that. "Sure, make a list of who you'd like to invite, and we can figure it out."

A little while later, my phone goes off with a text from Brody, asking if the kids have gotten home, and I send him a picture of them scribbling down their list at the kitchen table.

BRODY

Miss you in our bed already, but I'm glad they're home with you again. I know how much you missed them.

I send him a text back, telling him how much I miss them as well, and then put my phone down so I can get a load into the washer and start dinner.

The kids and I spend the evening catching up as they show me all the photos they took with their iPads. After they take showers, we settle in on the couch and watch a movie. Evie falls asleep halfway through, but Miles is still awake at the end. I carry Evie to her bed, kissing her good night, and then join Miles in his room, where I find him sitting in his bed, looking at a piece of paper.

At first, I assume it's his list of friends he's planning to invite to his birthday party, until I get closer and see it's the letter Peter wrote him before he died—well, a copy of the letter. I put the original away so nothing would happen to it. It's been a while since he's pulled it out, so I'm not sure what's going through his head until he looks up at me with tears in his eyes.

"Grammy told Papa you have a new boyfriend. Does that mean I'll have a new dad?"

His words have me freezing, my heart stammering in my chest. I wasn't expecting this, and I have no idea how to answer him. One thing's for sure, Beatrice and I will be having a conversation about being careful of what she says around my kids. They're getting older and can hear and understand what's being said.

"Nobody," I say, sitting on the edge of the bed and framing his face. "And I mean, nobody will ever replace your dad. He was your dad since the day I found out I was pregnant with you, and he'll be your dad forever. He loved you so much, and nobody can ever take his place."

"Okay, good," he says softly, sniffling back his tears. "I don't want a new dad. I want my dad back even though I know I can't have him."

My heart cracks in my chest at his words, knowing exactly how he feels. Then guilt fills those crevices because, unlike Miles, who can never replace his dad, I've replaced my late husband with Brody and Hayden in many ways. Whereas I used to spend hours thinking about Peter, I now think about them. My heart, that once upon a time only beat for my late husband, now beats for two other men.

"I miss him," Miles murmurs, glancing down at the letter that's never going to be enough to quell the need he has in him to feel like his father is here with him. He's gone, and nothing will ever bring him back.

"Me too," I tell him honestly. "Every single day."

"Can you read me his letter?" he asks like he used to when he was little and couldn't read. Now, he's old enough to read it on his own, but I know he's not asking because he can't read it. He's asking because he doesn't want to be alone in his thoughts and feelings. Nobody wants to mourn alone.

"Of course," I tell him, settling next to him against his headboard. I clear my throat and then begin reading Peter's final words to his son.

Dear Miles,

I'm writing you this letter so you have something

from me once I'm gone. Words will never be enough, but it's all I have to give you. I love you, my boy. You, your mom, and your sister are my entire world, and I want you to always remember that. If you're reading this, it's because I've gone to heaven. It's okay to be sad. I'm sad. But once you're done being sad, I want you to be happy again and know that I'm watching you from heaven.

When you give your mom a kiss and a hug, make sure you give her two—one from you and one from me. Right now, you're four years old, but one day, you're going to grow up, and I always imagined being there as you did. Since I can't be there, here are some things I want you to know:

It's okay to fail. Everyone fails until they succeed. Just make sure you keep getting up.

Follow your dreams and passions.

One day, you're going to like girls. Treat them the way you would want someone to treat your mom and sister.

It's okay to cry.

Always try to use your words instead of your fists.

Always hold the door open for a woman.

Learn how to tie a tie.

Money can't buy happiness, but money pays the bills, so get a job you love but can also pay the bills.

When picking a wife, remember you can't do better than your mom.

It's okay to be the man and support your wife, but it's also okay to support her dreams.

Cooking, cleaning, doing the laundry, and caring for your babies is not only the woman's job.

A happy wife is a happy life.

One day, your mom will find someone new to love. That doesn't mean she doesn't love me anymore. It means she's ready to move forward, and I'm okay with that. Make sure he's good to her and if he is, be supportive. One day, when your sister and you leave home, I don't want her to be alone.

When your sister gets married, walk her down the aisle, and when you give her away, give her two kisses: one from you and one from me. The same goes for your mom.

And last but not least, always remember that I love you and I wish I were there with you. If you ever need me, know that I'm listening and am here with you.

Love always,
Dad

By the time I finish reading the letter, I'm a mess, and my heart aches. Miles sniffles and takes the letter from me, folding it back up. "I don't know a lot of what he said," he admits, "but I'm never getting a wife or moving out. I'm going to live here forever, and so is Evie."

I stifle a laugh at his innocence and kiss the top of his head. "You both can live here for however long you like, but when you're ready to move out one day, that will be okay too. And when you're older, you'll understand more of what your dad wrote. Just know that he loves you and is watching over you."

I turn off his light and partly close his door, then head to my room. I can feel my phone buzzing in my pocket, and I'd bet it's Brody or Hayden, but I don't have it in me to respond. I know Peter said he wanted me to move forward, but I can't help feeling guilty.

While the kids were away, it was easy to live in a fairy tale, feeling like a princess who had found her prince—or, in my case, princes—but the moment they returned, it was as if the clock struck midnight, and I turned back into a pumpkin.

"NIGHT, MOMMY!"

I give Evie an exhausted kiss good night, then go to Miles's room to kiss him as well.

"Night, Mom," he says, rolling over and closing his eyes.

It's late, and I'm exhausted. Between Jessica quitting unexpectedly—she apparently applied for an internship without mentioning it and got it—and one of my ovens going out and needing to be replaced—which will take weeks because the part is on back order—which means it's taking twice as long to get the baking done, I'm ready for this week to be over. The kids' birthday is coming up, and I've done nothing to prepare for them.

As I brush my teeth and wash my face, I make a mental note to buy invitations and call to make sure the park pavilion is available tomorrow. Then I climb into bed, missing Brody and Hayden like crazy. I haven't seen either of them since the kids returned almost a week ago, and like the amazing guys they are, knowing I need to take things slow because of my kids, aside from them texting to tell me they miss me and see how things are going, they haven't asked or complained once. And somehow, that only makes me feel that much more guilty.

Since my eyes aren't tired yet, I turn on my e-reader to read a chapter since reading always helps me fall asleep. The book I'm reading is about a poly relationship—I know, I know, how cliché—but even though it's romance and obviously not reality, it's nice to read about people in the same situation as me.

Of course, the part I'm on is where they're all about to be together sexually, and as I read, I can't help thinking about the last time I was with Hayden and Brody. When we spent the night at the cottage Upstate. We missed lunch…and dinner, but it was worth it. The way they devoured me, working together to pleasure me…

I continue to read, but unlike with my guys and me, in my book, while the men are pleasuring the heroine, they're also pleasuring each other.

My thoughts go to Brody and Hayden…and what it would be like to watch them kiss or go down on each other.

The images run through my head like the best movie reel, and before I know it, I'm sticking my hand down the front of my shorts and circling my clit with my fingers. I'm near my orgasm when my phone vibrates with an incoming call. Hayden. I ignore it, desperate for release. But when it stops and then starts again, I stop mid-stroke and answer it because he hasn't called me since the kids got home. *What if something is wrong?*

"Hey, is everything okay?" I breathe, cringing when my voice comes out breathy, and hoping he doesn't notice.

"Where the hell are you?" Hayden barks.

"What?" I ask in confusion. "I'm at home."

"Alone?"

"Yes."

"Then why the hell does it sound like you're being fucked?"

Even though he can't see me, my face heats up at having been caught. "I'm…"

"Don't lie to me, Bree."

Dammit! "I'm doing it to myself," I whisper.

There's a long beat of silence, and then he says, "Please hold."

A few seconds later, Brody says, "Hello?"

"I'm on the phone with Bree…and she's fingering herself."

"Hayden!" I hiss in embarrassment.

"What? Why?" Brody asks, sounding hurt.

"Because I miss you guys," I admit. "And a woman has needs."

"Needs that we would gladly meet if you let us see you," Hayden says.

"The kids aren't ready for that…I'm sorry."

"Don't be sorry," Brody murmurs. "Were you at least thinking about us?"

My body heat increases. "Of course, I was…but the fantasy isn't as good as the real thing."

Hayden chuckles. "You're fantasizing about us, baby? Tell us about it."

"Wait," Brody adds. Two seconds later, my phone is beeping to switch to a video chat.

Holy shit, they want to have phone sex.

I hit accept, and their gorgeous faces appear on the screen. It's dark in my room, but with the light from the city shining in, it's enough for them to see me.

"There you are," Brody says, smiling softly. "We've missed that face."

"I've missed you too. Hence me resorting to…" I shrug. "You know."

"Tell us about your fantasy," Hayden says, his eyes alight over the screen. "And don't leave anything out."

When I remember that I was fantasizing about them being together, I clear my throat and dart my eyes away sheepishly.

"Don't be shy," Brody says. "We've been in every one of your holes. Nothing you could fantasize about would be embarrassing."

"Actually, I wasn't imagining us together," I admit. "Well, I was there, but you two were together."

Brody's brows hit his forehead, and Hayden smirks.

"Tell us what you were imagining," Hayden says.

"We were in the room together, and I watched as you guys kissed and then…" I swallow thickly, my thighs clenching in desire. "Brody got on his knees and took you in his mouth."

"Fuck," Brody curses while Hayden's smirk widens.

"What happened next?" Hayden asks.

My hand instinctively slides back down my shorts, my finger going to my clit. I'm soaked and sensitive. "Brody gave you head."

"And what were you doing while I was sucking his dick?" Brody asks, his voice hoarse.

"I was watching."

"Fuck," Hayden hisses. "What are you doing right now?" His heated gaze sears into mine. "Are you touching yourself, baby?"

"Yes," I croak.

"Does it turn you on to think of Brody sucking my cock?"

Oh, God! "Yes."

"What else turns you on?" Brody asks.

I open my mouth to answer, but I'm so close to coming, it's hard to speak.

"What about you riding Brody, taking his cock deep in your pussy, while I plow into his tight ass from behind?" Hayden murmurs. "Does that turn you on?"

The explicit visual sends me soaring over the edge, and I climax harder than I ever have by myself. My eyes squeeze shut, and white spots dance behind my lids.

When I open them, Brody and Hayden are staring at me with lust-filled eyes.

I should be embarrassed that I just came while on the phone with them, but I don't even have it in me to care because it felt too damn good.

"We need to see you soon," Brody says softly.

"Like now," Hayden growls.

"I can't," I say. "The kids are here."

Both guys nod in understanding, but I still feel like shit because all they want is to be with me, and while I might've gotten off, they didn't. How long until they give up on me? Until they're so sexually frustrated, they turn to someone else?

The thought causes tears to prick my eyes, and before I can hide them, Hayden notices. "What's wrong?" he asks, concern replacing the lust.

"I'm sorry I can't be with you guys right now. If you can just give me a little bit more time…" I don't know what's come over me or why I'm suddenly so emotional. My period is due soon, so maybe it's that.

"Hey," Brody says gently. "You don't have to apologize for being a mom. Yeah, we miss you, but we're patient, and we'll wait as long as you need."

"We love you, Bree," Hayden adds.

I take a deep breath and nod, feeling silly. I know these men. They love me and wouldn't go elsewhere because we can't be together for a couple of weeks. I mean more to them than that.

"I love you too."

"Get some sleep, sweetness," Brody says with a soft smile. "We'll talk soon."

"Be good for Grammy, and don't go overboard."

"We know," Miles and Evie say in unison.

"Please let me give you some money," I offer Beatrice. Just her taking the kids to pick out decorations and two cakes while I bake is enough—yes, I've ordered their cakes because I don't have time to bake two specialty cakes. With Caroline and Lacey both home with colds, and still being down an oven, the last thing I need is the kids complaining while I bake. When Beatrice offered to take them to pick out the stuff for their party this weekend, I could've kissed her.

"It's not happening," she insists. "It's my treat. We'll be back soon."

Once they're gone, I get to work. I'm several trays of muffins and scones in when I remember I never let the guys know today isn't happening after all. Lacey had originally offered to watch the kids, but she came down with a cold. Then Caroline called in, saying she was feeling under the weather, which put me behind on my baking. I meant to let them know that I can't meet up with them, but I got busy.

ME

> Rain check? I'm stuck in the shop baking.
> I'm sorry.

HAYDEN

> Are the kids with Lacey?

ME

> She's sick. They're with my MIL, but Caroline
> called out. Since I had to work the front
> instead of baking, I need to get it all done for
> tomorrow.

BRODY

> It's okay.

It's not, though. They may say it is, but it's not. Dating someone means actually seeing them. It's been two weeks since I've seen the guys, and I've passed the point of desperation. And based on their texts, I'm almost positive they feel the same way.

We talk every night after the kids go to bed and text throughout the day, but I miss being with them. I'm stressed and exhausted, and I just want them to hold me. I want to feel their mouths on mine and their hands on my body. I want to lay my head on their chests and fall asleep to the thumping of their heartbeats.

I'm lost in thought when there's a knock on the door. When I walk out to see who it is, my heart picks up speed. Because standing on the other side are Brody and Hayden.

I quickly undo the lock and pull them inside, hugging each of them as tightly as I can. "This is the best surprise ever, but I told you I can't go anywhere."

"We know," Hayden says. "That's why we came to you."

"I have to bake." Just as the words leave my mouth, the timer goes off.

"Smells good in here," Brody says, walking to the back ahead of me.

"They're blueberry muffins." Slipping on my oven mitt, I pull the trays out and set them on the cooling racks. "I still have at least another hour to go. I'm sorry. I wish I could leave, but my oven is broken and—"

"Stop," Hayden says, pulling me into his arms. "We aren't asking you to leave. We miss you, and if that means hanging out here while you bake, that's fine by us."

Emotion clogs my throat as tears fill my lids, and when Brody leans in and kisses the crown of my head with Hayden still holding me, a choked sob escapes. I drop my head against Hayden's chest and lose it.

Neither man says a word while I cry into Hayden's shirt. A hand rubs my back, while another rubs my arm, attempting to comfort me. When I finally get myself together, I exhale a deep breath and glance up at Hayden, who's looking down at me with concern etched in his features.

"What's wrong?" he asks, tucking several strands of hair behind my ear. "Talk to us, please."

"I just feel a bit overwhelmed at the moment," I admit through a sniffle. "The broken oven doubles my baking time. My baker quit, two employees are sick, the kids' birthday party is this weekend, and I haven't gotten it all together. And then there's you guys. I haven't seen you in almost two weeks, and instead of failing at one relationship, I'm failing at two." By the time I've gotten it all out, my cheeks are covered in tears, and snot drips out of my nose.

Hayden lifts me and places me on the counter, then grabs a paper towel and dabs the tears from my cheeks. I take it from him and clean my nose.

"Have Brody or I complained once about not seeing you?" Hayden asks once I'm halfway decent.

"No, but—"

He presses his fingers gently over my lips and shakes his head. "Do we miss you? Yes. Do we tell you that? Of course. But we know you'd spend time with us if you could. Right now, seeing you like this, my only concern is how stressed you are, and I don't like that you're adding our relationship to that pile. We love you, and being with us should never feel like a burden or like you're failing."

"I just…" I choke up again and wipe my eyes. "I just feel like I can't do it all. Like everything is falling apart, and I want to go back to when we were in that cottage. When everything felt simple."

Brody steps closer and smiles. "We can go back any time you want, but right now, tell us what you need from us to make it better."

"Aside from a second working oven," I joke. "I just need you both to kiss me and make me forget about all the stress for a few minutes."

"Done," Hayden says, just before his mouth descends on mine. He tastes like what fairy tales and happiness and love are made of, and I sigh into the kiss, wanting to get lost in everything that is him.

When he breaks the kiss, I pout, wanting more, until I realize why he broke the kiss. He backs up so Brody can take his place, his hands gripping the curves of my hips and pulling me toward him. He leans down and licks the seam of my lips and then gently pushes his tongue into my mouth.

My thighs clench around his waist, my ankles locking behind him, never wanting this to end. But just like Hayden, he ends the kiss all too soon.

It's not enough, though. I need more, so I lift my shirt over my head, silently telling them what I want…*what I need.*

And thankfully, they don't have to be told twice. Within seconds, I'm laid out on the counter while Hayden licks and sucks on my breasts, and Brody pulls my shorts down.

They work together to bring me to an orgasm. And like a tidal wave, it crashes into me quick and hard, taking me under.

"Holy shit," Brody murmurs as waves of pleasure roll through me. "That's it. Come all over my fingers."

"I need you," I tell them. "In me, now." I pull myself into a sitting position and then spread my legs, glancing from Brody to Hayden. "Both of you."

Brody goes first, sliding my legs over his forearms and slipping into me slowly. His mouth connects with mine, and he fucks me with slow and deep thrusts while kissing me the same way.

"You feel so good," he mutters against my mouth. "I missed being in you, kissing you…"

A second orgasm starts to build, but before it can surface, he's draining his release into me and then pulling back so Hayden can take over.

The second Hayden slams into me, his mouth crashes against mine. He fucks me with abandon as if he's starving for me. And that orgasm that was close to surfacing erupts through me like a volcano.

"Fuck, fuck, *fuck*," Hayden roars, stilling his movements as he comes deep inside me.

We both take a moment to catch our breath, and when he pulls out, I can feel their cum dripping out of me.

"I better get cleaned up," I say with a small laugh, already feeling like some of my stress has been alleviated.

I jump off the counter and kiss Hayden and then Brody. "Thank you," I say to both of them.

"What the hell are you thanking us for?" Brody asks, one brow quirked up in confusion.

"For being patient with me, for showing up here. For giving me two mind-blowing orgasms…" The guys chuckle and shake their heads. "I'll be right back!" I grab my clothes and run to the bathroom in the back.

Once I'm cleaned up, I get dressed and head back to the kitchen. Only, when I get there, it's empty.

And then I hear voices coming from the front. *They probably went looking for treats…*

"Guys?" I yell out.

When I get out there, I don't find them looking for food. Instead, they're dressed and talking to Beatrice and my kids.

"The door was unlocked," Beatrice says with a smirk.

Shit! In my excitement to see the guys, I forgot to lock the damn door.

Oh my God, if the kids would've shown up a few minutes earlier, they would've walked in on us having sex. They would've been scarred for life!

"Who are you?" Evie asks, her head tilting to the side curiously.

"I'm Brody." Brody points at himself and then at Hayden. "And this is Hayden. We're friends of your mom's."

"I've never heard of you," Evie says, her face scrunching up like she's trying to figure out a puzzle.

"Are you her boyfriends?" Miles asks. "Grammy told Papa that she has two boyfriends."

Beatrice's eyes go wide. "Oh, I—"

I want to protect my kids, but I won't lie to them, and I won't belittle my relationship with Brody and Hayden either. I'm proud to be with them, to be loved by them, and I won't hide that from my children.

"They are my boyfriends," I admit before Beatrice can finish her sentence.

"You said you didn't have one," Miles says, his eyes narrowing.

"No, I said no man will ever replace your dad." I walk over and kneel in front of my children so I'm at their level. "And I meant that. Your dad will always be your dad. But do you remember the part of his letter when he said he wants me to find love again?"

The kids nod. I've read their letters from him enough that they probably have them memorized, even if they don't understand all that they say.

"I found love with Brody and Hayden."

"You still love Daddy, though, right?" Evie asks.

"Of course. I will *always* love your dad."

"And you love us too, right?" she adds.

"I love you more than brownies, cupcakes, and blueberry muffins combined."

A happy smile spreads across her face. "I love you more than brownies, cupcakes, blueberry muffins, *and* chocolate chip cookies!" She throws her arms around me, and I hug her tightly.

When we break apart, Miles still stands there with a blank expression.

"Miles, is there anything you want to say or ask me?"

He glances over at Brody and Hayden who stand nearby, watching our interaction, and then looks at me.

"I think it would be best if you guys go," I tell Brody and Hayden. Miles never has trouble speaking his thoughts, so if he's not saying anything, it's because he's uncomfortable. Regardless of how I feel about them, my children will always come first.

Brody and Hayden both smile in understanding.

"It was nice meeting all of you," Brody says as they walk toward the front door.

"Wait," Miles says, shocking everyone. "Dad said I have to make sure they treat you good." Oh, my heart…It seems he understands more of what his dad wrote than I thought he did.

"He did write that," I agree, my words laced with raw emotion.

"How will I know if they're treating you good if they leave?"

I glance at Beatrice, who has tears in her eyes. She's read Peter's letters as well.

"I think in order to know, we'll have to spend time together," I tell Miles. "Are you okay with that?"

He thinks for a moment before he says, "Yeah," then steps closer to me. "How do I know if they treat you good, though?" he asks, back to sounding like the almost nine-year-old he is.

"Well," I say, kneeling in front of him. "If I smile and laugh a lot, that means I'm happy. And if I'm happy, that means they're treating me good."

Miles nods in understanding. "You laugh and smile a lot with Evie and me. That means we treat you good, right?"

"You definitely treat me good," I choke out, trying to fight the tears about to fall whether I like it or not.

"Okay," Miles says after a moment. "I'm hungry. Can we go eat dinner?"

I stifle my chuckle at the change of subject. "Sure, sweetie."

I stand and am about to tell Brody and Hayden that I'll see them soon when Miles speaks first. "We're going to dinner. I'm going to watch and make sure my mom laughs and smiles. If she does, then you can be her boyfriends."

"Where would you like to go to dinner?" Brody asks Miles, his voice rough.

"Evie and I like pizza. You want pizza, Evie?"

"Yes!" She jumps up and down. "And I'll make sure Mom laughs and smiles too," she tells Miles as she walks to the front door. Then she turns around and glances at the guys. "Do you have a puppy?"

They shake their heads.

"Where you live, can you have one?" she asks.

Oh, geez.

Before I can stop them from answering, Hayden says, "Sure," with a shrug.

Shit!

Evie perks up, then quickly schools her features. "You should probably get a puppy. When we saw the puppies at the park who need homes, they jumped all over Mommy and made her smile and laugh."

I snort at my conniving daughter, who should be too young to manipulate grown-ass men. She begged for a puppy that day, and when I told her we couldn't have one where we lived, she asked if we could move to where we could have one. Of course, I told her that wasn't going to happen.

Hayden grins wide. "We'll take that under consideration."

"Consideration?" she asks, her nose scrunching up. "Is that closer to a yes or a no or a maybe?"

"Umm, a maybe?" Hayden says, though it comes out like a question.

Evie's face falls. "Everyone knows maybe means no."

Brody chuckles. "Then it's closer to a yes," he says, glancing at me and winking.

Evie's smile returns. "Cool. Let's go get pizza."

CHAPTER THIRTY-FIVE

HAYDEN

Bree's kids are adorable mini versions of her—smart, witty, and as sweet as those damn brownies I'm addicted to. When they walked into the coffeehouse and nearly caught us fucking their mom on the kitchen counter, I thought for sure Bree was going to freak out. Instead, she shocked the hell out of me—and based on Brody's facial expression, him as well—when she admitted to her kids that she's found love, and Brody and I are her boyfriends. And then again when she agreed to all of us going out to dinner.

"Can we get pineapple?" Evie asks her mom when we walk into a pizzeria down the street from where they live. We're planning to get a couple of pies and take them over to the park across the street so we can hang out and get to know the kids a little.

"Ugh, not you too," Brody groans.

"What?" Evie asks, her hand going to her hip like she's eight going on eighteen. "You talking about my pineapple?"

Brody barks out a laugh. "Yes, my stepmom loves pineapple. Pineapple does not belong on pizza, ever." He draws out the last word in exaggeration.

"Thank you!" Miles says, throwing his hands up in the air.

"Finally, someone on my side. Mom and Evie always want pineapple. It's so gross." He fake gags. "Pizza should have sausage and pepperoni, not fruit!"

"Hey," Bree says. "Don't mess with our pineapple."

"You ladies can get that girly sh—stuff," Brody says, quickly catching himself. "Us, men, will get the manly pizza."

Bree snorts out a laugh. "Okay, *men*, enjoy your manly pizza."

"Yeah, and there's three of you, so you get less." Evie sticks her tongue out at her brother and twirls around with an attitude I didn't know an adorable little girl could possess.

Brody glances at me and silently laughs.

I pull out my phone and send him a text:

ME

I have a feeling that things will be a whole lot less boring with these kids around.

Brody checks his phone and grins, then texts me back:

BRODY

I love it. Now, we just have to make Bree smile and laugh so they actually like us.

ME

Truth

BRODY

Worst-case scenario, we buy them a puppy.

I crack up laughing and pocket my phone, not bothering to respond. I honestly wouldn't put it past Brody to buy them a damn puppy.

After we get the food and drinks, we take them over to the park and find a bench to eat on.

"Mom, this is the park for our birthday, right?" Miles asks.

"It is," she tells him. "I booked the pavilion over there." She points in the direction of a small pavilion.

"Did you get the bounce house?" Miles asks.

"And the balloon person?" Evie adds. "Oh! And the face-painting person?"

"That's for girls," Miles says, his nose scrunching up in disgust. "Mom, can we get an obstacle course bounce house and get it with water? And also, Shane said for his birthday his dad is getting him a big blow-up movie screen to watch a movie on when it's dark. Can we get one for our birthday?"

"Yeah!" Evie squeals. "That would be so cool. And can we get stuff to paint pictures with?"

As Bree's eyes bounce from one kid to the other with a look of horror etched in her features, something tells me she didn't book any of that nor was she planning to.

"Umm," she says after several moments. "I booked that pavilion," she says slowly, pointing at it again. "And I thought we would grill some burgers and hot dogs, and you guys can play with your friends. We could, um, maybe..." She swallows thickly. "Why don't we talk about this later, once we're home? Right now, let's eat, and afterward, if you want, you can go play on the playground."

"But don't we have to book it now?" Miles asks. "The party is in a few days."

Bree glances at Brody and me and winces. I'm not sure what's going on, but it's obvious she doesn't want to discuss this with Brody and me around. Could it be because she didn't invite us? Is she worried we're going to ask to go? I make a mental note to remind her later that the ball is in her court. Brody and I would never do anything she isn't comfortable with.

"Miles," she says softly yet firmly. "We'll talk about this at home."

Both kids' shoulders slump, and I expect them to argue, but instead, they both nod and take their pizza.

The mood is now a bit somber, the kids quietly eating while Bree appears to be lost in her own head. Not wanting the evening to be ruined, I try to make small talk with the kids, but neither one is really interested in conversing. Don't get me wrong—they're both polite and answer, but their earlier excitement has dissipated.

When Bree asks the kids if they want to go play, they both run to the playground and straight over to the swings.

Bree, Brody, and I follow, sitting on the bench in front of them. Since she seems down, I take her hand in mine and kiss her knuckles. "You know we're taking this at your pace, right?"

She glances at me in confusion.

"You seemed uncomfortable discussing the party in front of us. I just don't want you to think we expect to be invited. Would we love to go? For sure. But we know you need to take things slow, and you telling them about us and that we're your boyfriends means a lot."

"Yeah, it does," Brody agrees, taking her other hand in his. "You're calling the shots."

Bree smiles at me, but it's strained. "You're welcome to come to the party, but honestly, you'll probably be bored. We're just grilling and doing cake. I had no idea the kids wanted to do all that stuff." She looks at them, a frown marring her face. "They're going to be disappointed, but that's part of parenting. Some days, I'm the best mom ever, and others...not so much."

"You might not be able to book all that at the last minute, but you could probably book some of it," I point out. "I can help you make some calls and see who has availability."

Before Bree can respond, Evie yells, "Mom, come watch me on the monkey bars!" as she flies off the swing and runs toward the jungle gym equipment.

Brody and I both pull out our phones at the same time.

"What are you doing?" I ask.

"Probably the same thing as you." He laughs. "Finding places available for the party."

I GLANCE AT OUR GROUP CHAT, SERIOUSLY PROUD OF Brody and me. Between the two of us, we managed to find a bounce house with water that has an obstacle course, a clown who does balloon animals, a princess who does face painting, and a company who rents blow-up screens—all of which are available for Sunday.

"Why hasn't she replied yet?" Brody asks from next to me. It's been almost an hour since we shared with her all the links, thinking she would call us her heroes since she seemed to think she wouldn't be able to pull it all off.

"Maybe she's busy."

"Yeah, maybe, but she always responds somewhat quickly."

That's true. She does.

We both get back to work since we have a shit ton of stuff to do for a meeting next week with a potential new business venture.

Hours go by, and when my phone goes off, I see Bree's responded, but her response is definitely not what I was expecting:

> **BREE**
> Thanks.

"What the hell is going on with her?" Brody asks, barging into my office. "Bree doesn't do one-word answers. Did we do something wrong?" He plops down on my couch and glares at his phone.

"She said thanks. It's hardly a fighting word."

He types out something on his phone, then my phone goes off with a message.

> **BRODY**
> Which ones are you going to book? I like the obstacle course, especially if it means I'll get to see you in a bathing suit again. ;)

A few seconds later, Bree texts back:

"What the fuck?" I drop my phone on the desk, confused as hell. "What's going on with her?"

"I don't know. Maybe she doesn't want us getting involved."

We both stare at our phones, waiting for her to respond, but it becomes clear after several minutes that she's not going to.

"I'm going to see her," Brody says, standing. "Something is going on, and I'm not going to let her hide behind her damn phone. You coming?"

"Of course."

I shut down my computer, and then we head out. Heart's is closed when we get there, but we can see the kids running around and laughing.

I knock, and when they see us, they smile and wave, and Miles yells for their mom, who steps out from the kitchen and doesn't look nearly as happy to see us as her kids.

"Something's wrong," Brody says under his breath as Bree unlocks and opens the door.

"Hey, I wasn't expecting you," she says, letting us in.

"We thought we'd surprise you," I say. "Thought we could do something this afternoon."

"Oh! Can we go to the arcade?" Miles asks. "Shane went with his mom and said it's so cool."

"Not today," Bree says, and her tone brooks no argument. "I need to finish baking for tomorrow."

Miles groans. "It's so boring here."

"Why don't you go play on your iPad?" Bree suggests, sounding like she's ten seconds away from losing her shit.

Miles perks up. "Really?"

"I thought Miles already used all his time?" Evie asks.

"Mind your own business!" Miles snaps, grabbing his iPad and handing it to his mom.

She types something and hands it back to him. "I gave you one hour."

"Thanks!" He runs to a table and sets up his iPad.

"Hey!" Brody laughs. "That table is device free!"

"That's only for the customers, silly," Evie says with a laugh. "Mommy lets us use our iPads, so Miles doesn't whine like a baby."

"I'm not a baby," Miles grumbles.

"Yes, you are," Evie taunts.

"Am not!"

"Okay, okay," Bree says, breaking up the argument. "Evie, please leave Miles alone."

"But I'm so bored." She pouts. "I wanna play Monopoly, and he won't play with me."

"Because it's boring with only you," Miles says. "I always win anyway."

"Nuh-uh," Evie argues.

"Yes-huh!" Miles yells back.

"Enough!" Bree snaps. "As soon as I'm done, I'll play with you. But if you keep fighting, I won't ever get done."

"I'll play with you," Brody offers.

"Me too," I add.

"Really?" Evie exclaims.

"You don't have to do that," Bree says, sounding utterly exhausted.

"We want to," Brody tells her. "You go bake, and we'll play Monopoly with Evie. Just don't get mad when I buy Park Place and you go broke paying me rent." Brody winks, and Evie looks at him like he's grown two heads.

"That's the adult version," Bree explains. "This is the SpongeBob version. You want to buy The Crusty Crab and SpongeBob's Pineapple house." She glances back and forth between us. "Are you sure you're okay hanging out with the kids?"

"We're all good," I tell her. "Go bake. We'll be here when you're done. And if you want to thank us, feel free to pay us with brownies and cupcakes." I shoot her a playful wink, but she doesn't take the bait, the frown on her face still going strong.

"Okay, well, if you need to go or if they're acting up, just let me know." And with that, she disappears into the kitchen.

"You sure you don't want to play?" I ask Miles when I catch him eyeing us.

"I guess I could play one game." He shrugs, walking over and joining us at the table.

We pick out our pieces, and Evie hands out the money, and then we start playing with her going first since she's the youngest—by four minutes.

"You guys excited about your party?" Brody asks, making conversation—and being nosy since Bree won't talk to us—as Evie rolls the dice and then moves five spaces.

"I'll buy it," she says, depositing the right amount of money into the makeshift bank. "I'm excited to see my friends." She glances at Miles as Brody hands her the card.

"Me too," Miles agrees, rolling the die. "And the cake. Grammy got me a *Minecraft* cake."

"I got an American Girl cake," Evie says with a smile. "And she got me pink glitter for the table."

Miles scrunches up his nose. "Just make sure you keep it on your side of the table."

Evie rolls her eyes, and Miles moves several spaces.

"I'll buy it," he says, handing Evie the money.

"So, uh, did your mom ever decide if she was doing the balloon guy or anything?" I ask, trying to dig a little deeper. Are Brody and I playing dirty? Yeah, but you have to use what you got, and we're not above getting some info out of the kids. I'm not sure what we're looking for at this point, but I think we're both hoping the kids will say something that will clue us into why we were invited to the party one minute and not the next.

Evie frowns. "No. Mommy said no one can do it."

Brody and I share a glance. We checked, and there are definitely people available.

"There's no movie screen either," Miles adds as Brody rolls the die. "Or bounce houses."

"I'll buy it," Brody tells Evie, handing her the money for the place he landed on. "You owe me two dollars back."

"Mommy got us two piñatas and let us pick out the candy yesterday," Evie says, giving him change. "And after we move to our new house, she said we can have a sleepover with our friends."

This doesn't make any sense. We sent her all the info. Everything the kids are saying isn't available is. So why the hell would she lie?

I roll the die, trying to figure out what's going on. Brody pulls out his phone, and a second later, a text comes in.

BRODY

You thinking what I'm thinking?

I move four places, buy it, then text Brody back:

HAYDEN

I don't know what the hell I'm thinking. What are you thinking?

BRODY

She told the kids none of it's available, she told us not to go to the party, and they're moving into a new house soon. She doesn't have the money and is embarrassed to tell us. She's probably trying to save up to rent somewhere else because that asshole is evicting everyone, and wherever she moves will be more than where she lives now.

Fuck, I feel so stupid. I didn't put that together because my mom would throw us the biggest parties every year to show off. We lived in an expensive home. When we wanted something, we got it. My parents sucked at the emotions, but in its place was materialistic possessions because my family has never lacked for money. Even if I quit working tomorrow, the trust fund I was given when I graduated from college from my grandparents meant I was set for life.

Bree never discusses money. I knew she had to find a new place to live by the end of the year, but I didn't know she was struggling. Then again, how would I know? I've never asked about her money situation, and she's never brought it up. I guess I assumed she was doing okay since she turned down Benitez when he tried to buy her out of her contract.

The thought has me cringing because once again, I'm an idiot. I've never owned anything sentimental before. Everything I buy is strictly business. I buy properties and sell them. But this coffee-house isn't just a business to her—it's her *heart*. That's why she took Brody's advice to try to distribute her products, so she can make more profit. She's been busting her ass, baking every damn day for several hours a day so she can simply survive.

ME

We're going to handle the party, right?

BRODY

I don't know…She might get upset that we overstepped.

"Yes!" Evie squeals. "You landed on my Crusty Crab," she says to her brother. "You owe me fifty dollars." Her smile spreads across her face and twin dimples pop out—identical to her mom's.

"Hey, Miles," she says when he grudgingly hands her the money. "Wouldn't it be cool if this money was real? We could buy Mommy a new house, and she'd be so happy."

That does it…I type out a text to Brody:

Some might assume my wanting her to move in with us is because of her money situation, but the truth is, I miss the hell out of her since the kids got home and she stopped spending the night. If we can solve her financial problems *and* have her and the kids under our roof, why wouldn't I be all for it? Bree is ours forever—and that means spending our lives together under one roof. The sooner that happens, the better.

CHAPTER THIRTY-SIX
AUBREE

My kids are nine years old today. My once teeny tiny babies are nine freaking years old. It's also the day of their party. I've tried to make the party as special as possible but feel like I've failed because it isn't what they wanted…what they hoped for.

My kids aren't spoiled brats—contrary to what they sounded like the other day when listing off all the stuff they wanted for their parties. But since they go to a private school—that my in-laws insisted on paying for because I can't afford it, and it was Peter's wish for them to attend the same private school he went to—they come across children who are well off and some are downright wealthy. And because kids don't actually understand the value of a dollar, and I refuse to burden them with my financial woes, they don't understand that what they were asking for costs a lot of money.

So I lied and told them that a lot of people are on vacation because it's the summer, and I wasn't able to find any of the stuff they want. And then I pushed Brody and Hayden away when they were only trying to help by finding me vendors that I could book at the last minute. A part of it was because I was embarrassed for them to show up at the party and see it's lacking everything they can afford—it's the reason I don't invite them up to my place unless necessary. And the other part—which has me feeling like shit—is that I resented the fact that they could afford everything I can't. They sent me bounce houses and clowns and a princess that would probably make my daughter cry in happiness and didn't even consider the cost…because they don't have to.

Now, it's the day of the party, and I wish I hadn't pushed them away. All they want is to be a part of my life, and I keep shoving them out the door at every turn, which is unfair to them on many levels.

I consider texting and telling them I'd love for them to be there today, but my pride prevents me from actually typing out the message.

Evie steps out of her room, twirling in the American Girl leopard dress Beatrice bought her that matches her doll, and my heart sinks as I wonder if I made a mistake by not selling out of my lease. It would've meant having money in the bank since the little bit of savings I have is dwindling quickly, thanks to the distributors raising their prices, and Heart's turning a smaller profit because of it. And on top of that, I've been looking at apartments, and holy shit, the kids and I will be living in a damn shoebox—if we're lucky. But when I imagine my grandparents' pride and joy being demolished, I know I did the right thing. Besides, if I sold out of the lease, I'd either have to find a new job or open Heart's somewhere else. And since everything has gone up in price, wherever I find to lease will put me back in the position I'm in now.

"You look so pretty," I tell Evie, pulling my phone out of my pocket and snapping her picture.

"Why thank you," she says, doing a curtsy like she's royalty. "Is it time to go yet?"

"Soon. Grammy and Papa are coming to pick us up, so we don't have to carry all the food and decorations to the park."

"Okay! I'm going to brush Molly's hair while I wait," she says, then skips down the hall with her doll tucked under her arm.

"Miles, you almost ready?" I ask, peeking into his room.

When he doesn't answer, I step farther in and find him sitting on the edge of his bed, staring at the photo of the four of us. It was their last birthday before Peter passed away.

"Hey." I sit next to him and pull him against my side, kissing the top of his head. "You okay?"

"I miss him," he says softly. "I wish he were here."

"Me too, buddy," I choke out, suddenly missing Brody and Hayden. One shouldn't coincide with the other, and really thinking about my late husband should probably make me not want to be around them, but every time I think about him, it reminds me how short life is and how our loved ones can be taken from us at any moment. And those stupid details like me being embarrassed or having too much pride to text them are ridiculous and only hurt us all.

"Can we go visit him soon?" Miles asks, referring to his dad's gravesite.

"Of course." I kiss his cheek. "Go brush your teeth and get your shoes on. Grammy and Papa will be here soon."

He nods and walks out the door, leaving me staring at the picture of the smiling family who had no idea that a few months later, their happiness would be taken from them in a blink of an eye.

With that thought, I pull my phone out of my pocket and dial Hayden's number. He answers on the first ring.

"Hey, baby, you getting ready to party?"

Of course, he holds no grudge toward my decision to uninvite them. "Is Brody with you?" I croak out.

"Yeah, is everything okay?"

"Yeah, can you put me on speakerphone?" I ask, glancing at the picture one last time before I walk out of Miles's room and into mine, closing the door so the kids don't hear me.

"Hey, sweetness," Brody says. "Are the kids excited for their birthday?"

"Yeah," I choke out, unable to hold back my emotions. "But I'm calling because…I'm so sorry."

"Bree, are you crying?" Brody asks.

A second later, the phone rings in my ear, and I click accept to turn the call into a video call. The guys appear over the screen, and their worried faces send me over the edge.

"I'm so sorry I pushed you away," I sob, wiping my tears so I can see them. "The truth is, I can't afford the party the kids want, and when you guys sent me all that info, it made me feel worse. I know you were only trying to help, but I let my pride get in the way of just telling you the truth, and instead, I uninvited you. And I'm sorry."

I sniffle through my sobs. "We haven't really talked about it, but I'm kind of in a weird place right now financially. I had no idea how expensive apartments are nowadays until I started apartment hunting because I went from living with my husband to living where I live now, and it scared the crap out of me. And on top of that, several of the distributors for the coffeehouse have had price increases. My profit has decreased by over fifteen percent because I haven't raised my prices."

I take a deep breath in and then release it. "Anyway, I'm sorry for the way I've been acting, but I'd really like it if you'd come to the kids' party, if you don't have plans. You'll probably be bored, but I want you there. I want you in our lives. If it's not too late."

Brody speaks first. "Of course, we'll be there. We get that you've been doing this alone since Peter died, but you have us now. Even if we're just someone to talk to, we're here."

"I'm going to work on that." When Hayden hasn't said anything, I say, "Hayden, do you…want to come?"

"Of course, I do," he says with a sigh that makes me nervous.

"Are you mad at me?" I whisper, sounding like a kid instead of a grown-ass woman.

"No," he says. "I just…I want to give you and your kids the

world and I hate that you're struggling when Brody and I could do that. I love you, and all I want is for you and your kids to be happy. I know you're independent, and I respect the hell out of that, but if it were up to me, you'd let us take care of you."

"And I love that you love me enough to want to do that but respect me enough not to."

"Mommy! Is it time to go yet?" Evie yells through the door.

"Yep, one minute," I tell her. Then to the guys, I say, "Thank you for being patient with me."

"Always," Brody says back. "We'll see you soon."

"Mom! Look at the bounce house!" Miles gasps.

"And there's a princess!" Evie squeals.

"That has to be an obstacle course," Miles adds in awe. "And there's water coming out of it!"

I stare at the setup in front of us in confusion. Ponies, bounce houses, face painting, a clown walking around with balloon animals. The pavilion looks like *Minecraft* and American Girl threw up all over it. This doesn't make any sense because I didn't order any of this.

"Did you do this?" I ask my in-laws, who shake their heads.

"Did they double book the pavilion?"

Which would make sense, except what are the odds both parties have the same double themes?

And then I see them sauntering toward us wearing nervous smiles, and I know who did this. And while I should probably be pissed that they did it behind my back, the excitement on my kids' faces prevents me from saying anything other than, "Thank you," when I hug Hayden and then Brody.

"Is it our party?" Miles asks with hope-filled eyes.

"Who else's party would it be?" Brody asks with a laugh, ruffling his hair. "Are those your friends playing?"

Miles nods.

"Then it must be your party."

Miles goes to run toward his friends but stops and turns around and flies at me, nearly knocking me over. "You're the best mom in the whole world," he says, then runs off.

Evie gives me a hug after him, telling me she loves me more than double chocolate chunk brownies, and then takes off after her friends, and I'm left completely choked up with emotions.

"I can't believe you did all of this. How did you manage to pull it all off that fast?"

"I'd like for you to meet my aunt Amalia," Brody says, pulling an older woman into his side. "She specializes in this stuff."

"Thank you," I tell her, giving her a hug. "It's so nice to meet you. This is all amazing."

"You're very welcome," she says warmly. "This was easy compared to some of the events I've put together over the years. I need to get going, but everything is handled." She gives Brody a hug. "Let's do brunch soon."

"Thank you," I tell the guys again. "This means so much to the kids and me." Tears fill my lids as I watch Miles and Evie running around and laughing with their friends. This is a party they'll remember and talk about for a long time.

"We got you," Brody says, kissing my cheek. "Always."

"Damn right, we do," Hayden says. "Now, how about we go check out that obstacle course?" He leans in and whispers, "I'm dying to get you wet."

Before I can retort, he picks me up and throws me over his shoulder like I'm a sack of potatoes and stalks toward the bounce house.

"Hayden!" I screech. "Put me down! I can't get wet. I need to grill the food."

"The only thing you're doing is having a good time," Hayden says. "And we brought you a change of clothes."

"Can I go in the water?" Miles asks, running up next to us.

"Yep," Hayden says. "We brought you and your sister a change of clothes too."

Miles yells in excitement and runs straight for the obstacle course.

"Miles, help me!" I shout.

Hayden gets to the big inflatable thing, and that's when I see it… a huge pool of water. "Hayd—"

Before I can finish yelling his name, Hayden drops into the water, taking me with him. "I can't believe you!" I hiss. "You are so dead!"

Reaching into the water, I cup my hands and then push a shit ton of water at Hayden, soaking his entire face. He tries to bat away the waves of water as I continue to do it over and over again.

"That's what you get!" I say through a laugh.

"Oh, yeah?" he splutters. "It's on!"

He grabs me by my hips and drops me into the water, and then proceeds to tickle me. I scream and shout, flailing my arms and legs, laughing so hard, I'm almost positive I'm going to pee myself. I'm drenched, my hair is a mess, and I'm sure the little bit of makeup I put on is running, but I don't give a shit.

"C'mon, Miles," Hayden yells over at my son, who I see is standing near us, observing. "Come tickle your mom."

"Miles, don't you dare!" I shout playfully through my laughter.

"Miles, I'm holding her down," Hayden says, grabbing my hands and forcing them over my head. "Now's your chance."

Miles glances back and forth between us, and I hold my breath, waiting to see what he'll do. He was emotional this morning about missing his dad, and my dating is new for him. I know he's watching to see if these guys are worthy of being with me.

His eyes meet mine, a sly smile spreading across his face, and then he jumps into the mini pool of water and starts tickling me. And as I howl with laughter, for the first time since Pete passed away, I feel like we're really going to be okay.

"I DON'T THINK I CAN WALK," MILES MUTTERS, HIS HEAD landing against the side of my arm in exhaustion.

"Me neither," Evie adds with a tired sigh as her head falls into my lap, and she cuddles against me on the bench.

It's almost nine o'clock, and the kids have played, laughed, and eaten their hearts out. Even though Amalia said it was all taken care of, I didn't feel comfortable leaving until everything was cleaned up and picked up by the rental companies, which means my kids got to play extra long. Unfortunately, that also means my in-laws left a long time ago, taking their vehicle with them.

"All right, everything is back to the way it was," Brody says, walking over and smiling down at the three of us.

"Thank you for everything."

"I think you've thanked us a dozen times," Hayden says. "Stop it." He leans down and presses his lips against my forehead. "We love you, and it's our pleasure to make sure you and your kids are happy." Butterflies erupt in my belly, and I close my eyes, letting his words resonate deep within me.

They love me...Despite losing my first love and best friend, I've found two guys who love and care about me, who care about my kids enough to make their entire day. I have no idea how I got this lucky, but I vow never to take them for granted.

"C'mon," Brody says. "Let's get you three home. I drove here." He bends so he's at Evie's level. "Would you like me to carry you, princess?"

She nods and tiredly sits up, lifting her arms so he can pick her up. He gently takes her into his arms, and she wraps her legs around him, her head dropping onto his shoulder and her eyes closing. My heart expands at the sight. At my daughter trusting the man I love enough to let him carry her.

Miles sits up and stands.

"You good?" Hayden asks him.

"Yeah, I'm nine now. I'm practically a man. I can walk."

Hayden stifles his laughter and nods, extending his arm to fist bump Miles, who reciprocates.

Gathering all the gifts they got, we head to Brody's vehicle. The drive is quick, and he parks in the front so they can help me carry everything—as well as Evie—up.

Brody lays her in bed and then leaves the room so I can change her into her pajamas. After kissing her good night, I head over to Miles's room to say good night. Only before I enter, I hear him talking to someone. I peer inside and find Hayden and Brody standing with Miles, who's holding the picture frame in his hands that contains the photo of the four of us from their last birthday with him.

"That's my dad," he says. "He wrote me a letter that said to make sure he's good to her, and Mom said that means she has to laugh and smile."

Miles goes to his drawer and pulls out the letter. "It says I have to be supportive, but I don't know what that means." He shows the letter to the guys, who take it and read it.

"I think it means to be okay with it," Brody says, his voice hoarse. "Like, if she's happy, it's okay to let her date him, but if she's not happy, then you shouldn't be okay with it."

Miles nods in understanding. "She laughed and smiled a lot today." I suck in a sharp breath, his words causing me to choke up.

"We like when she laughs and smiles," Hayden says.

"Me too," Miles agrees. "And I don't want her to be alone."

Oh, my heart. He's referring to the part of the letter where Pete told him that eventually, the kids would leave and wanted me to find love so I wouldn't be alone.

"She'll never be alone, buddy," Hayden says. "She's got you and Evie."

"Yeah, but it says right here we're gonna leave." He points at the letter.

My hand goes to my chest, clutching it over my heart.

"I don't know when we're leaving, but I don't want her to be alone," Miles says solemnly. "If you want to love her, I'm okay with it."

As I watch my nine-year-old do what no kid should ever have to do at his age—be the man of the house—a piece of my broken heart that I never thought could be pieced back together after losing Peter slides into place.

"Thank you," Brody chokes out. "We do love her very much. And I promise, no matter what, she'll never be alone."

Another jagged piece fits into place.

"I know you have a mom and a dad," Hayden adds. "But if it's okay with you, we'd like to be your friend. And if you ever need anything, we're here…always."

And just like that, my heart feels as if it's almost whole again.

CHAPTER THIRTY-SEVEN
BRODY

"There they are," Bree's friend Lacey says as Hayden and I walk through the door of Heart's, thanks to her letting us in. It's after hours, so the shop is closed, but they're still here closing up. "Heard you were the reason the kids had the best birthday ever." Her brows rise for dramatic effect. "Their words, not mine."

When Hayden and I shrug, a grin spreads across her face. "I wish I could've been there, but my son had his end of football camp award ceremony, so I was out of town. But I heard what you guys did. Thank you. I haven't seen her this happy since..." She clears her throat, not needing to finish her statement. "She works hard, *moms* even harder, and doesn't give enough to herself. She needs someone to put her and her kids first."

I'm about to respond when I hear Bree speak. "Miles, I understand you're bored, but I have to work, so I need you to chill out for a little while, please."

I glance over and see Bree walking out of the kitchen with Miles on her heels. Her face is etched in frustration, but as always, she speaks with the patience of a saint. She's been so busy this week we haven't seen her at all. She's still looking for a new baker, and until then, she's doing it all on her own. But it's Friday, and we insisted on spending some time with her and the kids.

"But Mom," Miles moans.

Bree looks up, and when she sees us standing there, a small smile graces her lips. "Hey," she says, walking over and kissing me and then Hayden. "Did we have plans?"

I chuckle softly. The woman has so much going on that she can't even remember whether we made plans.

"Shoot, we did, didn't we?" She groans, then glances at Lacey. "Don't you need to get going? Your husband will not be thrilled that his wife is late for their anniversary dinner."

"He married me for better or worse," Lacey jokes. "You sure you're okay? If you need me to—"

"I'm good. I promise," Bree assures her. "Go. Enjoy your anniversary weekend. I'll see you Monday."

Once Lacey is gone, Miles starts whining again that he's bored, and Bree takes a deep breath, her eyes going to the ceiling like she's praying to God not to let her lose it on her child.

"Hey," I say, pulling her away from everyone. "Why don't Hayden and I take the kids to the park while you finish up here, and then once you're done, we can go back to our place for dinner and a movie?" We've wanted to bring the kids to our place. We're hoping to eventually convince Bree to move in with us, and the first step is to make sure the kids are comfortable there.

"I couldn't—"

"Yes! Please, Mom," Miles begs, obviously hearing what I said despite me trying to speak low enough so he couldn't.

"Kids have bionic hearing," I mutter. "I'll remember that."

This makes Bree bark out a laugh. Fuck, I love that sound.

"Guess I can't say no now." She rolls her eyes playfully. "But you're sure you're okay with that? I have an interview with a potential baker in"—she glances at her watch—"thirty minutes. She seems promising, and if it works out, it will mean I won't be working as much."

"You don't have to explain shit to us," I say, needing her to know we're not about to add to the weight on her shoulders, "but that makes me happy because you seem a bit stressed."

"I am," she admits. "I got two more contracts, which is amazing, but that also means more work. Hopefully, this interview goes well."

"You focus on that, and we'll take the kids to the park and then meet you back here," Hayden says.

"Yes!" Miles fist pumps in the air. "Evie! We're going to the park."

"Yay!" She comes running out of the kitchen with a box in her hands. "I made you cupcakes," she says, thrusting the box at me. "Both of you."

Opening the lid, I find two sprinkle-covered cupcakes. "Thanks, princess. They look delicious," I say, closing the box.

"You're welcome." She beams.

After saying goodbye to Bree, we take off to the park. Miles loves all sports, so on the way, we stop at the store and pick up a basketball, and while we're there, Evie gets chalk.

We spend the afternoon playing with the kids, who, when they're not cooped up in the bakery, are damn good kids. I can't really blame them, though. At their age, my mom had me in camp all summer. It was probably to pawn me off so she wouldn't have to deal with me, but I loved everything we did. Which gives me an idea…

"You did what?" Bree gasps, glancing around to make sure the kids can't overhear. "Brody, that's too much. I…"

"It's only four weeks of camp," I say, shrugging it off. "The kids have a month of summer left, so why torture them and yourself when they can be having fun for the next four weeks? The sports complex had a couple of spots available. Evie will be doing dance, gymnastics, and swimming, and Miles will get to play a bunch of different sports." She opens her mouth to argue, but I speak over her. "And before you ask how you're going to get them there and pick them up every day, you're not. Hayden and I will. The great thing about running my own company is that I can come and go as I please. Hayden and I will pick them up before we go into work and get them at the end of the day."

Tears fill her eyes, and she throws her arms around me and pulls me down. "Thank you," she murmurs, placing a soft kiss on my neck. "You and Hayden are the best boyfriends. I don't know what I would do without you."

"Well, you're never going to have to find out." I kiss her lips, and she sighs into me.

"Carina, the woman I interviewed, is amazing, and I gave her the job," she says, stepping back slightly. "She's going to be baking full time. It will be a bit costly, but the new contracts will help even it out. I'm hoping to get a few more contracts. I have several places that sounded interested. At least now, I won't have to stay late or go in extra early."

"That's awesome, sweetness." Knowing she'll have help makes me feel better. She's stretching herself too thin, and it's only a matter of time until she snaps.

"How about we order in some Chinese and let the kids pick out a movie?"

"That sounds like a perfect Friday night," she says with a smile. "And maybe if they fall asleep, we can get some adult time in later." She waggles her brows, and I chuckle at how adorable she is.

Leaning down, I kiss each of her dimples. "Now *that* sounds like a perfect Friday night."

"THEY'RE BOTH ASLEEP," BREE WHISPERS, GLANCING AT the two kids passed out on their blanket bed in the middle of the living room.

"We wore them out at the park," Hayden says. "You know, if you want to just spend the night…"

"I want to do more than spend the night," Bree says, standing. "I need to use the restroom. Meet me in Hayden's room." With a flirtatious wink, she saunters out of the living room and down the hall. We generally sleep in my room, but I imagine she mentioned Hayden's since it's farther down the hall, which means farther away from the sleeping kids.

After making sure the alarm is on in case they wake up confused, we head back to Hayden's room and close the door. I've never had kids before, so I'm not sure how this all works. Is it okay to leave them out there while we do what we're about to do in here? What if they wake up?

"Hey, Bree, are you sure they're good out there?" Hayden asks as if reading my mind.

She doesn't answer, but a second later, the bathroom door opens, and she walks out in only her bra and underwear. They're nothing special: plain black cotton that covers all the important parts, but holy shit, does she look gorgeous. The swells of her breasts are spilling slightly out of her cups, and her hard nipples are poking through the material. Her underwear is those boy shorts women love, and when she walks past us, we get an eye full of her plump ass cheeks peeking out.

"I turned on the alarm," I say, my gaze trained on Bree.

"They sleep all night," she says, climbing onto the bed and crawling to the center, "but even if they do wake up, they'll just call out my name."

She turns around and sits up against the headboard. "But if

you're worried, we should probably hurry, just in case." She sucks her bottom lip into her mouth, biting down seductively, and Hayden and I both take that as our cue to attack.

"Wait," she says before we make it over to her, halting us in place. "I've been thinking about my fantasy. The one I told you about when we video chatted."

"I don't remember it," Hayden says, playing dumb because there's no way either of us could ever forget that night. "You're going to have to tell us again."

Bree's cheeks stain pink. "Well," she says slowly, her gaze flitting from Hayden to me since we're standing next to each other, "it was about you guys."

"Hmm," Hayden says. "I think I might recall something about that. You'll have to be more specific."

Bree sucks her lip into her mouth shyly. "It started with you two kissing."

"Is that what you want?" Hayden asks. "You want to see Brody and me kiss?"

Bree nods slowly, and my cock thickens behind my pants at the thought. "Yes," she says, voicing her thoughts. "I want to see you kiss."

Hayden turns toward me. "You okay with this?"

I've barely nodded my okay before his mouth is on mine with such force, our teeth clash. The kiss is hard and unyielding. We haven't done this in over ten years, yet it's as easy as it was the only other time it happened. He palms the side of my face and then deepens the kiss, his strong lips curling against mine as his tongue slides in and devours me.

When he pulls back, my lids slowly open, remembering where we are, and who we're here with. I take a deep breath, slowly moving my eyes toward Bree, afraid to see the look of disgust on her face, terrified that she'll realize fantasy isn't always the same as reality.

But when our eyes meet, the only thing I see is want and desire.

Her chest heaves, her lids are slightly hooded, and her fingers are plucking at her hard nipples.

"What else did this fantasy include?" Hayden asks, his voice sounding as turned on as I feel.

Bree's tongue darts out across the seam of her lips. "Brody," she breathes, "on his knees, sucking you off."

Hayden nods, then pops the top button and unzips his pants, lowering them slightly. When he pulls his cock out of its confines, it's thick and hard with a single vein running from root to tip, just the way I remember.

"Well, you heard her," he says gruffly. "Get on your knees and suck me."

When I glance back at Bree, she's watching intently with her thighs parted and one of her hands between them, stroking her clit.

That's all I need to see to do as she wants—as Hayden demanded. I drop to my knees and take his length in my hand, stroking it a couple of times. It's smooth like velvet and hard as a steel beam. And when I put him in my mouth, he tastes like the perfect mix of cleanliness and masculinity.

I suck his cock deep and rough, the sounds of Bree moaning spurring me on. Hayden's shaft thickens, and I assume he's about to come until he steps back, and his dick pops out of my mouth.

"Does that turn you on?" he asks Bree, who's fingering the hell out of her pussy.

"So much," she breathes.

"What happens next?" he asks her, knowing her fantasy ended there—at least from what she told us over the phone.

"I...I don't know," she croaks, clearly close to an orgasm.

"What do you want to happen next?" he asks.

"I want you to fuck me." She spreads her legs farther, and she's so wet that she's glistening in the bit of light coming in through the slats of the blinds. "While Brody fucks my ass."

And because she doesn't have to tell either of us twice, we do just that—twice. And when she's sated and sleepy and can barely keep her eyes open, we carry her and her kids up to the guest bedroom, so they can sleep in a comfortable bed.

"I like this," Hayden says, eyeing Bree and her kids in the king-sized bed. "All of us under one roof."

"You and me both," I agree.

"PLEASE, MOM," MILES BEGS. "CAN WE PLEEEEAAAASSSSE stay here?" Miles clasps his fingers together and lifts them in a praying gesture. "They have a PlayStation with the most awesome games, and Brody said I can play if you say yes." I stifle my chuckle at his puppy dog eyes.

"Fine," Bree says, giving in. "Evie, do you want to come with me?"

We glance over at Evie, who's sitting on the couch with Hayden in front of her. She's brushing his hair and sticking bows in it.

"I'll stay here," Evie says. "I still have to do Hayden's makeup and paint his nails. And he said he'll paint mine too."

"All right," Bree says. "But you two better behave."

"We will," the kids say in unison.

"And if they don't," she says, her eyes meeting mine, "bring them to the coffeehouse and I'll put them to work." She gives me a chaste kiss. "Thank you."

She gives Miles a kiss next, then Evie, then kneels in front of Hayden to give him a kiss. When he leans in, Evie chides, "Don't move, or you'll ruin your hair," making Bree laugh.

The morning is spent playing video games and hairdresser—Evie gets a hold of me after she's done with Hayden, and although she can't do my hair, my face and nails are game. When afternoon comes, and the kids are hungry, I get an idea.

"Who wants to make homemade pizza?"

Both kids shout in excitement.

"All right, go get dressed, and then we'll go to the store so we can pick up the ingredients."

While we wait for them to get ready, I text Bree to let her know our plans since I don't want to leave without her knowing where her kids are, and she says she'll be back around four o'clock. She's training the new baker and a part-timer who'd like more hours, which means they need to learn how to close the shop.

ME

Want to do dinner and a movie again?

Now that she's crossed the line and lets us hang out with the kids, if it were up to me, we'd hang out every night—especially since they're already comfortable at our place and seem to like Hayden and me.

BREE

You really want to spend another night at home after babysitting two kids all day?

HAYDEN

We can go out if you want.

BREE

I can't go out…I meant YOU GUYS. Why would you want to be trapped at home all night after being stuck at home all day?

Hayden glances over at me and shakes his head.

"She'll get it eventually," I tell him. "She just needs time."

ME

I don't think you seem to understand. Hayden and I aren't babysitting your kids. We're caring for and spending time with our girlfriend's children while she busts her ass at work. And tonight, after you get home, we want nothing more than to order in dinner and watch a movie with you and your kids. We hope that one day when you're ready, we'll all live under one roof as a family. We're not trapped or stuck. We're in love with a woman who has two kids. Two kids who are pretty damn amazing, just like their mom.

BREE

And now I'm crying in the middle of the coffeehouse. I love you.

HAYDEN

We love you more. See you later.

"Ready!" Evie yells, flying down the stairs. "Can we get pineapple for the pizza? Please?"

"Pineapple is not meant for pizza!" Miles shouts, coming down after her. "We need sausage and pepperoni and lots of cheese."

"I want pineapple," Evie argues.

"No way," Miles says back.

"How about we all make our own pizzas, and you guys can put whatever you want on yours?" I say.

Evie glances at me. "Whatever we want?" she asks slowly.

"Sure." I shrug, proud of myself for ending that argument before it started.

Two hours later, the kids insist on sending their mom pictures of their pizzas. Miles's is pepperoni, Cheetos, sausage, and Doritos, and Evie's is M&M, Twix, mini marshmallows, and pineapple.

And as I hit send on the text, I think to myself that before I agree next time, I'll make sure to ask questions...seek clarification. It's like being in a business meeting. I wasn't prepared.

But next time, I will be.

CHAPTER THIRTY-EIGHT
AUBREE

"Is there a reason I keep ending up in a bed sandwiched between my kids instead of with you and Hayden?" I ask sleepily, crawling into Brody's bed since he's already awake. It's early. Three thirty in the morning. But I have to get going to meet my new baker. I probably should've spent the night at my place, but the kids are starting camp today and begged to sleep here, which doesn't surprise me since they've asked to spend the night the past two nights as well.

Hayden said by sleeping here, they can sleep in instead of getting up early with me, and I couldn't argue with that.

What I can argue with, however, is why all three nights we've slept here, I've started off sleeping in one of the guy's beds and ended up in a different bed.

"There is," Brody says, setting his phone down and giving me his full attention. I love that no matter how busy he and Hayden are with work, when I talk, they stop what they're doing and listen. I noticed over the weekend that they do the same thing for my kids. Several times they would be texting or emailing, and when my kids wanted or needed them for something, they stopped and gave them their attention.

"When I was growing up, my mom went through boyfriends and husbands like one goes through underwear. Sometimes, I would wake up and find her in bed with a guy I didn't know, and it made me uncomfortable." He takes my hand, threads his fingers through mine, then looks at me and smiles softly. "When your kids see us sleeping in the same bed, I want them to know it's because we're a family. I want them to understand what is happening and to feel comfortable with it.

"I love that you're comfortable with staying here with them, and that you want to go to sleep and wake up with Hayden and me. I just feel that when we do that, it should be because we've agreed to spend our lives together."

"Isn't that what we're doing?" I ask, a bit confused. "I thought what we're doing is serious, that we're in a committed relationship. That's the only reason I allowed you to meet my kids."

"We are," he says. "But dating isn't the same thing as getting married and creating a life together."

His words have my head spinning. "We can't get married," I blurt out. It's against the law to marry two people, and there's no way I'm choosing one of them over the other.

"Not in the eye of the law, but we can still put a ring on your finger and have a ceremony. One where we exchange vows in front of our family and friends."

I imagine walking down an aisle somewhere, dressed in a gorgeous white dress, and waiting for me is Hayden and Brody, both wearing sharp tuxes and prepared to say their vows to me. Before, I couldn't even fathom marrying another man, let alone two, but now, the thought has my heart swelling in my chest, butterflies attacking my belly.

"I want that," I admit out loud.

"You want what?" Hayden asks, strolling into the room and

dropping down on the other side of Brody, since Brody is in the middle, and I'm sprawled out next to him.

"Brody was saying that even though we can't get married legally, he wants to have a ceremony, and I was saying that I want that too. I want to commit myself to you both in every way possible, even if that means we do it our own way."

Brody and Hayden both grin.

"Good," Brody says, palming the side of my face. "When we get married and move in together, we'll spend every night together in one bed." He leans in and brushes his lips against mine. "I can't wait for you to be our wife."

"Mommy! Look what I can do!" Evie screeches as I step out of the elevator. It's been a long day, but the second I see her excited face, just before she raises her arms and flies into a cartwheel, I can't help but smile.

"Wow, that was really good," I tell her as she does two more.

"I know, right? Camp was so much fun. I got to do lots of gymnastics and dance, and we went swimming, and I jumped off the tallest diving board. Miles was too scared, so he didn't jump, but I told him it wasn't scary, so if we go swimming again tomorrow, he's gonna try it."

"I'm not scared," Miles says from the couch, where he and Hayden are playing video games. "It was just really tall, and I didn't feel like walking up all the steps."

"And that's completely fine," I tell him, sitting next to Hayden.

"How was camp?" I ask Miles.

"Good. I met a friend. His name is Matthew, and he likes hockey like me."

"How was your day?" Hayden asks, pausing the game so I know I have his attention.

"Long. The espresso machine is giving me problems. I'm going to have to have someone come out and look at it. And the guy who fixed the oven said it was good to go, but when I was baking this morning, dozens of muffins burnt, and the fire alarm went off." I sigh, remembering the fire department coming out, despite me trying to tell them it was fine. "Now, I'm going to be charged, and I'm still down an oven and now an espresso machine."

"Is there anything I can do?" he asks.

I shake my head and then lean down and press my lips to his. "You're already doing it," I whisper. "Thank you for helping with the kids."

"Oh, Mom!" Miles says, dropping his controller and turning toward me. "Coach Henry said if you say it's okay, I can play on the hockey team. Matthew is asking his mom too. Can I play? I have the papers for you to sign in my backpack."

"That's awesome. I'll read over the papers once we get home, but I don't see why not." Speaking of which…"Why don't you guys start cleaning up, so we can get going?"

"Now?" Miles asks. "But I'm playing with Hayden."

"And I have to show Brody my cartwheels," Evie adds. "He told me to show him when he gets home."

"You're leaving?" Hayden asks.

The three of them stare at me with various amounts of confusion and disappointment, and I feel like it's three against one.

"I'm going to get a drink in the kitchen," I say slowly, my gaze meeting Hayden's.

He looks at me confused but then catches on and says, "I'll join you."

Once we're alone, I lean against the counter, and he cages me in, kissing me softly. "Missed you today."

"I missed you too. Mondays are rough after the weekend."

He trails kisses along my jawline. "Stay here tonight."

"The kids need to take showers, and I need to make dinner," I say through a groan as he places a kiss above my pulse point, making it a point to nip playfully at my flesh. "I'm sure I have laundry to do from their day at camp," I add.

"They can shower here," he says, lifting his head and looking at me. "Brody can pick up dinner on his way home. And we have a washer and dryer here. Besides, with us taking the kids to camp, it's easier to stay here so they don't have to get up so early with you. Brody and I got them ready and out the door just fine this morning."

"Hayden," I say with a light laugh. "The kids have four weeks of camp. We can't stay here the entire time."

"Why not?" he asks, kissing me again. This time, his tongue slips past the seam of my lips, and I really wish we were alone so I could get lost in him.

But we're not, so I gently push him back.

"Because this isn't our home."

"Huh?" he asks in confusion, clearly distracted.

"You asked why we can't stay here," I remind him with a soft laugh. "This isn't our home," I repeat.

Hayden simply shrugs. "It could be."

A knot forms in my belly at the thought of living here with them as a family, but I push it away because it's too soon.

"Stay," he says, resting his hands on my hips and nuzzling his face into my neck. "Just for tonight," he murmurs, running his nose along my jawline. "Please."

"Bree!" Savy, Brody's stepmom, pulls me into a hug. "It's so good to see you." She pulls back and glances to the left of me. "And you must be Miles and Evie," she says warmly. "I've heard so much about you. I'm Savannah, Brody's stepmom, but you can call me Savy." She points at her husband. "And this is his dad, Benjamin, but you can call him Benji." She winks playfully and her husband groans, shaking his head.

"You can call me Ben," he says. "Did you bring your suits? The kids are already in the pool."

"Yes!" Evie exclaims. "It's under my clothes."

"And can you swim on your own?" Ben asks both kids.

"Yep," they both answer.

"Well, then, head on back and have fun."

They both waste no time flying through the house as if they've been here before, and I glance at Brody, who laughs. "I'm going to make sure they get in okay," he offers, walking by and giving his dad a handshake, his stepmom a kiss on her cheek, and then stopping and kissing my forehead.

"Where do you want these?" Hayden asks, holding up the box of treats I brought for the end of the summer Labor Day barbecue Savy and Ben are throwing before the kids start school next week.

"I'll take those," Savy says with a glimmer in her eye. Lifting the top, she takes a whiff and sighs. "Mmm, they smell so good."

We head out back and find Brody's aunt and her husband, Gerald, lounging by the pool while the kids take turns going down the pool slide. Brody introduces me to Gerald since I already met his aunt at the kids' birthday party and then pulls me onto his lap on a lounge chair, so we can watch the kids swim and play.

The kids were good swimmers before, but since they spent the past month at camp, swimming almost every day, they've turned into the most adorable little fish, confident in the water. I honestly don't even know what I would've done without Brody and Hayden signing them up and taking them and picking them up from camp the past four weeks. Bringing them to work isn't as easy as it was when they were little and loved to help me.

"Brody mentioned your kids go to King's Cross," Amalia says. "Brittany goes there as well." Brittany is her and Gerald's teenage daughter, who's not here today because she's at a cheer event with her friends.

"Really? What a small world," I tell her. "Peter went there as a kid." I realize my mistake the second Amalia's brow furrows. One thing that sucks about being a widow is having to explain why since it's not normal for a woman my age to have lost her husband.

But before she can ask and I have to answer, Brody wraps his arms around me from behind and squeezes comfortingly, then says, "Peter is the kids' father. He passed away a few years ago."

"Oh, I'm so sorry. I didn't know," Amalia says.

I smile gently at her. "It's okay."

"Are you attending the open house tomorrow?" she asks, changing the subject.

"Theirs is Tuesday since the kids are in elementary school," Brody says, shocking the hell out of me.

"How did you know that?" I ask.

"They told us," Hayden says, "when they asked if we would go."

"And we told them we had to check with you first," Brody adds. "They told us about it on their way home from camp. Apparently, this is the first year they'll have different teachers. Miles isn't thrilled, but Evie seems okay with it."

Miles isn't thrilled because he takes his role as big brother seriously, which drives Evie crazy since he's only four minutes older.

"We told them that if we don't go, we can meet you for dinner afterward," Hayden says. He doesn't mention spending the night because I told them we have to go back to sleeping at our place now that school is starting since all the kids' stuff is there.

Both the kids and Hayden and Brody weren't thrilled. And truth be told, I'm not either, but it's too much work going back and forth between the two places, especially when the bus goes to my place to pick the kids up and drop them off every day. It was justifiable when the guys were taking them to camp, but now that camp's over, we have no reason to continue staying there.

And it's too soon to consider moving in together. I mean, it's only been a few months. That's not enough time to make such a serious decision...right?

Yet the past month we've been staying with them has gone smoother than I ever could've imagined. The kids adore Brody and

Hayden, and the guys clearly feel the same way. In the past month, we've created this routine that feels comfortable and right. Every day I think it can't be this easy to bring all these pieces together, yet it is that easy. The kids have taken over the two guest rooms, each wanting their own bed, and I sleep with Evie in her room. *Jesus, her room, like it's actually hers.* A huge ball of emotion fills my throat at the thought of going home tonight and not sleeping under the same roof as the guys.

"Hey," Brody says, pulling me from my thoughts. "If you don't want—"

"Of course, you guys can come to the open house," I choke out, trying and failing to get my emotions in check.

Brody eyes me. "Then what's wrong?"

"Nothing," I whisper, not wanting to do this with everyone here.

Brody opens his mouth to argue, but before he can get the words out, Evie calls his name.

"Brody, come and play Marco Polo with us!"

"Yeah!" Penelope agrees. "You can be Marco!"

"Hayden, they have a basketball hoop. Come play!" Miles adds.

Since the guys can't say no to my kids, they both get up, throw their shirts onto the chair, and jump into the water.

The kids squeal in delight as Brody chases after Evie and Penelope, and Hayden lifts Miles onto his shoulders to dunk the ball into the hoop. And as I watch them laugh and play, I can't help but wish that tonight we would be under the same roof. It might have only been a short time since we've been together, but Brody and Hayden have had no trouble burrowing themselves into my kids' and my heart in that amount of time.

CHAPTER THIRTY-NINE
AUBREE

Knock. Knock. Knock.

"Mommy, someone's here," Evie yells from somewhere in our apartment. It's the kids' first day of school, and we're running behind because...well, it's the first day of school, and that's how it sometimes goes when you have two kids.

Thanks to Viviana, my new baker, I no longer have to get up early or stay late baking. With the schedule we've put together, she'll be handling it all since her entire job is to bake. It's going to cost me a pretty penny, but with the kids getting older and not wanting to wake up at the crack of dawn or hang out in the bakery all afternoon, it's worth it.

As I step out of the bathroom, Evie says, "Who is it?" I'm too far away to hear who answers, but she says, "It's Hayden and Brody," letting me know. "Can I open the door?"

"Go ahead."

She unlocks the door, then swings it open, and my gorgeous boyfriends are standing on the other side, dressed to the nines in their corporate suits.

"What are you doing here?" Evie asks, giving each of them a hug.

"Hey, guys!" Miles says, coming out and giving both of them a fist bump. "What are you doing here? We have school."

I can't help but smile at how they've won over both of my kids—not unlike how they won over my heart in the same way and just as quickly.

"We know," Hayden says as they step inside. "We brought breakfast." He pulls a bag out from behind his back.

"And good luck gifts," Brody adds, showing his own bag.

"You brought me a gift?" Evie gasps.

"Yep," Brody says, opening the bag and pulling out the backpack Evie wanted but they were out of at the store when we went school shopping. She decided to keep the backpack she had because she couldn't find one that she loved, and I told her we would check back again later.

The second she sees it, she squeals and hugs both of the guys again. "Thank you! Thank you! I love it. I need to switch all my stuff out."

"And this is for you," Hayden says to Miles, handing him a box.

He snaps it open, and his eyes widen. "It's like yours," Miles says in awe. A lump fills my throat, choking me with raw emotion. The other day, Miles mentioned how much he loved Hayden's watch. Hayden told him that his grandfather bought it for him for his high school graduation, telling him that he got him a watch to remind him how precious time is and to never waste it. To live life and make the most of it. A couple of months later, he passed away. Miles told him that he loved it and said he never had a watch before. Then he asked me if his dad had a watch—and was bummed to learn he didn't.

"It's the same brand," Hayden says, "but in your size." He takes it out and puts it on Miles's wrist. "It's to wish you a good year at school."

"Thank you," Miles says, "I love it." After admiring it for a moment, he says, "Are you coming to my hockey practice after school?"

"Of course," Hayden says.

"Wouldn't miss it," Brody adds, grabbing the bag of food and pulling a box out. We eat the muffins and pastries they brought while the kids talk about the friends they're excited to see. Evie reminds me she has gymnastics—thankfully, both their new sports are at the same place—and then we head down to wait for the bus. After wishing them an amazing day at school, they jump on the bus, waving before the door closes and they're off.

"You didn't have to come by this morning," I tell Hayden and Brody once the kids are gone, "but thank you." As I give them each a kiss, thinking about how happy my kids were this morning, how happy they've been the past several weeks, it feels like our family is finally healing, and I can't help but feel like the two guys in front of me have a lot to do with that.

HAYDEN

Dinner tonight to celebrate the kids' first day
of school?

BRODY

We can go out or bring the food to you.

ME

My place sounds good.

"I LOVE THIS."

"Love what?" I glance at my best friend in confusion. We've just finished with the morning rush and are cleaning the tables during the downtime before our next rush hits.

"You, happy," she says with a soft smile. "I forgot what it looked like after Peter passed away, and I was worried I'd never see it again. But those guys have done the impossible. They've made you genuinely smile again."

"Sometimes I think I'm crazy for allowing myself to love two men. For exposing my children to a situation that is not the norm. But then I think about how short life is and how blessed I am to have found not one but two men who love me and my kids after thinking I'd never find anyone after Pete."

I glance at the time. It's still early, which gives me an idea.

"Go ahead," Lacey says with a smirk.

"What?"

"Oh, like you weren't thinking about going to see the guys for a little office romp." She laughs. "I have things under control here. Go get laid."

"Have I ever told you that you're the best friend a woman could ever have?"

"Yeah, yeah. Have fun."

Less than twenty minutes later, Hillary, Brody's assistant, lets me know that the guys are in a meeting, but if I want to wait in Brody's office, I can, and they should be done shortly.

On my way back, I notice Hayden's name on a plaque on the outside of a door. It must be his office. Since the door is open, I step inside and find it's empty, nothing proving this is his office...until I see the drawings on the wall. Drawings Evie made. I step around his desk to get a closer look, and my eyes land on several pictures—of us, of my kids and me. If I didn't know better, I'd assume Hayden had a wife and children—a family.

My heart expands at the thought that he cares about us so much he proudly displays my daughter's drawings and our photos in his office.

I leave his office and head back to Brody's since that's where she told me I could wait, and when I get inside, I'm shocked to find the same things in Brody's office—shocked because I didn't expect either of them to have their offices filled with drawings and pictures as if they're displaying the evidence of having a family.

A family.

They love my children and me and want to be a part of our family.

"Hillary mentioned you were here," Brody says. "Everything okay?"

I glance up at him, my eyes blurry with unshed emotion, and find both him and Hayden standing there, looking concerned.

"What's wrong?" Hayden asks, stepping toward me. "Did something happen with the kids?"

"You guys have drawings...and pictures..."

Their features both contort into confusion.

"From Evie," I explain, though I'm so choked up with emotion, it's hard to speak. "The drawings she made you guys. And pictures," I add. "I saw them in Hayden's office, and they're in yours." I point at the picture frame on Brody's desk.

"Of course, we do," Hayden says, bridging the gap between us and pulling me into his arms. "It's bad enough we have to go hours, sometimes days, without seeing you guys. The office is where we spend the majority of our time."

"I love you," I breathe, wishing there was a better phrase to describe how I feel, how full my heart feels. "I love you both so much."

I press my lips against Hayden's, tasting his warmth, his love. "I want you...now."

I hear the door close, but I pay it no mind as Hayden lifts me onto Brody's desk and tears my clothes off my body.

Brody joins us a few seconds later, and the guys work together to undress me while kissing me, touching me, and making me feel good.

I kiss Hayden and stroke Brody.

I can't get enough. It's never enough. I always want more of them. Of their bodies, their heart. I want it all. Maybe that makes me selfish, but when you've experienced the bad, you tend to cling to the good. When you've felt the loss, the heartbreak, you grab ahold tightly to the people who are alive and able to love you.

Hayden enters me first, pounding into me with such vigor that if he weren't holding my legs, I'd probably fly off the desk.

"God, you feel so good," he groans. "You're ours, baby. You know that, right?"

His eyes meet mine, filled with promises of love and lust and… tomorrow.

"Tell us you're ours," he growls, slamming into me over and over again.

"I'm yours," I breathe as Brody pinches my nipples, kisses my neck, and massages my clit. "I'm both of yours."

Hayden slows down and leans in, his lips brushing against mine. "And we're yours," he murmurs against my mouth. "All fucking yours."

With his words, I come hard around his cock and all over Brody's fingers.

Hayden finds his release, and then with a soft kiss, he pulls out, and Brody takes his place, entering me slowly. I'm drenched from my orgasm and Hayden's cum, but Brody doesn't care. He groans as he slides in and out of me, filling me with his length. He kisses me sweetly, murmuring how much he loves me and how important I am to him.

Hayden stays close by, touching me the way Brody just was, working me up toward another orgasm. He nips at my heated flesh and strokes my clit. And then I'm coming again, taking Brody over the edge with me.

"I want this," I tell them once I've come down from my orgasm, needing them to hear the words. "I want both of you, forever."

Brody cradles my face. "That's the plan," he murmurs, kissing me softly.

"As long as you'll have us," Hayden adds, squeezing my hip.

CHAPTER FORTY

AUBREE

BRODY

There's a box on your bed for you. Be ready
to go at 6:00.

I STARE AT THE TEXT FOR SEVERAL SECONDS IN
confusion before I respond.

ME

Be ready to go where?

HAYDEN

Just be ready. No questions.

ME

What about the kids?

Just as I'm hitting send, Beatrice comes strolling into the shop
with a conspiratorial smile on her face.

"Grammy!" Evie squeals, running over to give her a hug.

"Hello, sweetheart. How are you?"

"Good. I'm doing my homework." Evie shows her the world map

she's coloring. "This is where we live." She points at the state of New York. "Mommy said tomorrow we're going to look at new places to live." She glances at me. "Will we still live here?" she asks, her finger on the map.

"We will. It just won't be in this building anymore."

It's been almost a month since school started and the kids are doing well in separate classes. They've both made friends and have several from previous years. Miles loves hockey, and Evie adores gymnastics.

The coffeehouse is busy, and I've picked up several more accounts from shops and stores that wish to carry my product. I've started seriously looking at apartments since I'd like to be in our new place before winter, and because of my supplemental income, it feels like we'll be okay to move. It will suck having to travel to work, but I don't have a choice, thanks to the building owner refusing to renew anyone's leases. We can live month to month until the building sells, but then we'll only be given two weeks' notice to move out, and I'm not playing that game.

"Will we live with Hayden and Brody?" Evie asks.

"We totally should," Miles cuts in. "They have an elevator that goes right to their house, and they have the best game room."

"You'd be okay with us living with the guys?" I ask curiously. The kids have never lived with anyone but their father and me, and unfortunately, their dad passing when they were young means they don't remember a lot of it.

"Yeah," Miles says. "You smile and laugh a lot, so I told them it's okay to be with you." My heart squeezes in my chest, remembering the conversation I overheard him having with the guys the night of his birthday.

"Me too!" Evie adds.

"Hey, kids," Beatrice says. "We should get going."

"I'm ready," Miles says, grabbing his backpack and hitching it over his shoulder.

"Where are you going?" I ask.

"We're spending the night with Grammy," Evie says matter-of-factly.

"You're…" And then it hits me. The guys must've planned this and told the kids about it.

"Have a good night," Beatrice says, giving me a kiss on my cheek. "We'll see you tomorrow."

Once they've left, I finish closing the shop and head upstairs to see what the guys have left for me. On the center of my bed is a big black box with a red bow. Inside, I find a blue maxi dress. With a V-neck and slits running up the sides, it's the perfect combination of sexy and classy. It's paired with gorgeous black heels, and underneath I find a sexy bra and panty set.

I take my time getting ready, straightening my hair and applying my makeup. Since I haven't had time to get my nails done lately, I paint them myself, reading for a little bit while they dry. Once I'm dressed, I stand in front of the full-length mirror and smile. I look like a princess. A beautiful princess who is happy.

My gaze goes to the picture on my bedside table. I pick it up, looking at Pete and me. It was taken at our wedding. We were both smiling hard, excited for what the future would hold. Neither of us having any idea that our happily ever after would be so short-lived. All I wanted was to love and be loved. To create a family that I never really had. Sure, I had my nana, but it wasn't the same—I wanted a husband to hold me and kiss me, to be my partner in all things. I wanted a father for my children, someone to wake up and go to bed with. To cry and laugh with.

And for a short time, I had that…until I didn't.

I stare at the picture in my hand and think back to the day at Fields—seeing the photos and drawings Brody and Hayden had hanging up, showing how much the kids and I mean to them.

Taking the photo with me, I walk through the apartment, realizing that not a single photo has been taken after Pete passed. I've been so wrapped up in mourning that it's like I forgot to celebrate the people who are still here.

I make the decision right here and now that when we move, I'm going to put up newer pictures of the kids and add in pictures of Hayden and Brody. They're in our life, and if I have it my way, they'll stay in our life for however long the fates will allow.

There's a knock on my door, and I set the frame down so I can answer it. On the other side, I find Brody and Hayden standing in sharp tuxes, their faces clean shaven. Both men are holding a bouquet.

"You look stunning," Brody says, kissing my cheek and stepping inside.

"Perfect," Hayden adds, following.

Since the flowers both have vases, I thank them and set them on the center of the table, then grab my clutch that holds my ID, phone, and money.

"I don't know what the occasion is," I tell them, "but I must admit as much as I love you in a suit, these tuxes make me want to rip them off and have my way with you." I wink playfully, and they both smile wide, making my heart melt.

"It's been four months since you agreed to go out on a date with each of us," Brody says, taking my hand in his and kissing the top. "We're taking you out to dinner to celebrate."

When we get downstairs, I find a sleek black limo waiting at the curb for us. Hayden opens the door for me, and I tell Brody to slide in first, wanting to sit between the two of them.

The ride to dinner is spent with the guys feeling me up and kissing me, telling me how beautiful I look and how much I mean to them. If I were dating one of them, I would feel cherished and loved, but dating them both is almost too much. Sometimes, when they're doting on me, I wonder if I'm enough for them. If they're missing out because there's only one of me to two of them, but then I shut down my insecurities because if I wasn't enough, they wouldn't be here, showering me with love and attention. They're wealthy, good looking, sweet, and selfless. They could have their pick of women—but they want me:

the curvy, single mom, widow. And they love me just the way I am.

We arrive at the Pierce Hotel—a luxury hotel that I've only ever seen in passing—and the guys escort me to the restaurant that's on the rooftop. The hostess takes us back to a private room with a candlelit square table. After pulling out and pushing my chair in for me, the guys sit on either side of me.

I'm assuming they handled the details ahead of time because the server doesn't take our order. Instead, he brings out a bottle of the wine I love and pours us each a glass.

"How did Miles do on his math test?" Brody asks after taking a sip of his drink. "It was today, right?"

"He thinks he did good," Hayden replies before I can. "He texted me this afternoon and thinks he got them all right."

"What? When?" Brody pulls out his phone, his brows pinched together.

"Not in the group chat," Hayden explains. "I texted him earlier about his hockey game on Monday and asked."

"He's so damn nervous," Brody says with a chuckle. "We should take him to practice on Sunday to get him hyped up."

"Hell yeah," Hayden says. "He's going to kill it as goalie."

As the guys talk about my son, my gaze volleys between them, listening, watching, and taking it all in. Two years ago, Lacey set me up on a blind date with some corporate bigwig who worked with her husband. I tried to refrain from bringing up my kids, wanting to keep the date about me, but when it came up, and I mentioned my kids, I could immediately see the shutters dropping. The date might as well have ended at that moment because once he knew I was a single mom, there was nothing left to say. This is why I told them I had kids when I first went out with Brody and Hayden. I figured it would push them away, and I could say I tried, then go back to being a lonely, mourning widow.

Only instead of pushing them away, they embraced me being a single mom and they didn't stop there. Without expectation, they've developed their own relationships with my children. Relationships that aren't just for show to win me over—no, they care about them and connect with them. We're at dinner, celebrating our four-month anniversary, and instead of discussing getting laid—which hasn't happened in over a week thanks to life—they're talking about hockey games and math tests.

"Hey, what's wrong?" Brody asks. It isn't until he knocks me out of my thoughts that I realize I've teared up, my emotions getting the better of me.

"Nothing," I say honestly. "Everything is perfect."

Hayden's brow furrows. "Then why the hell are you crying?" He swipes at a tear that's leaked out and is sliding down my cheek.

"I just...I'm..." Jesus, how do I explain how I feel? I take a deep breath and just go with whatever comes to me. "I love you both so much. I love that you love my children and that you think about them. That you think about me. I didn't even know we have an anniversary date," I say through a watery laugh. "And..." I sigh, my gaze flitting between the two of them. "I'm happy."

Those two words shouldn't send me over the edge, but they do because after living through the childhood I did, then finding love and shortly after losing it, then losing my nana, happiness has been really hard to grasp. But between my children, who were the only things keeping me afloat since losing Pete and my grandma, and Hayden and Brody, I've finally found happiness again, and it feels so damn good.

"Every time I imagined what happiness looked like, it seemed so far off. It was wrapped around my marriage, the life we were creating. After he died, that happiness looked different. It wasn't as vibrant, full of color. Don't get me wrong—my kids are my entire world, but I craved the happiness that comes from adult conversations, lazy mornings in bed...orgasms." I feel myself flush, but I'm not embarrassed. Hayden and Brody make me feel safe to say whatever's on my mind.

"I didn't think I'd ever find that kind of happiness again. But then you two came along. You gave me back the happiness I longed for. Filled my heart with a kind of love that I didn't think I'd ever feel again." I lift my hands and thread my fingers through both of theirs. "Thank you for not giving up on me when I pushed you away. Thank you for loving me, for loving my kids."

Hayden shakes his head, and Brody chuckles under his breath.

"What?" I ask, worried I said something wrong.

"We had this huge speech planned, and then you swooped in and stole our thunder," Hayden says, his tone half playful and half serious. "Fuck it." He shrugs, then pushes his chair back. "We were going to wait until after dinner to do this, but after everything you said, now seems like the perfect time."

Hayden gets down on one knee, and then Brody joins him. I know what this means, but I can't quite wrap my head around it until Brody pulls a ring box out and opens it, exposing a gorgeous princess-cut diamond ring with two matching outer bands.

"The middle one is the engagement ring," Brody explains.

"But instead of one wedding band, we had it designed so you'll have two," Hayden adds. "They fit around the center band, symbolizing the three of us as one unit."

"Aubree Heart," Brody says, his eyes locking with mine. "We know that in the eyes of the law, you can't legally marry us both, but we would love it if you would wear our ring. And one day…"

"Soon," Hayden cuts in. "Really fucking soon."

Brody rolls his eyes, and I laugh at how adorable they are.

"One day *soon*," Brody says, "we would love to marry you and put our rings on your finger that symbolize our commitment and love to you, as well as your kids, the law be damned."

Brody plucks the middle ring out of the cushion as Hayden says, "And for the record, the kids are aware, and Miles has given us his approval."

"Evie too," Brody adds. "And Beatrice…"

"And Lacey." Hayden chuckles.

"Pretty much, we've gotten everyone's approval but yours,"

Brody says with a light laugh. "So, Bree, will you make us the luck-
iest guys in the world and marry us?"

"Yes," I choke out. "I would love nothing more than to marry
both of you."

Brody slides the ring onto my finger and then pulls my face down
to his, kissing me softly, passionately. "Thank you," he murmurs
against my lips.

He ends the kiss, and Hayden pulls me into his arms, his mouth
crashing against mine. Claiming, taking, demanding.

When the kiss ends, I glance down at my ring, my heart filled
with so much love. Then I look at my two men, who want me
forever, and the only thing I want is to begin forever with them,
right now.

"I know we haven't eaten dinner yet," I say, "but is there any way
we can skip it and go back to your place to celebrate?"

Hayden barks out a laugh. "Oh, baby, we're not going back to our
place tonight. We booked a suite here, where we plan to spend the
entire night showing you just how happy we are that you're wearing
our ring."

Oh, hell yes.

Well, in that case…"Check, please."

CHAPTER FORTY-ONE
HAYDEN

"NOVEMBER FOURTH."

"What?" Bree's head pops up in shock. "That's only in like two weeks."

"What about November eighteenth?" Brody offers. "My aunt Amalia said she can have it planned without issue. Do you want a big or small wedding? I'm assuming not in a church. We can do a destination wedding. Hawaii, Italy...Puerto Rico is beautiful this time of year."

Bree's eyes widen. "I-I don't know. What do you guys want?"

"Whatever ends with you attached to the two of us for the rest of our lives," I tell her truthfully. The fact is, guys don't give a shit about the details. As long as Bree is happy, I'm happy. And since my parents will no doubt have a conniption when they find out I'm entering a polyamorous relationship, they won't be attending. I haven't spoken to my father since the day I walked away from Shea Realty. It was the best decision I could've made. I never understood how toxic working with my dad was until I walked away.

Without him being able to pit my sister and me against each other, Gretchen and I have finally established a relationship, which has been nice. She hasn't met Bree yet, but she knows about her, and Brody's and my relationship with her, and she supports it, wanting me to be happy.

But she—as well as my parents—will meet her tonight at the charity gala we're attending that Brody's parents host every year for Speak Up—a nonprofit organization they started after Brody admitted to being sexually harassed by his mom's ex-fiancé when he was a teenager, which came close to being assault. They hated that Brody was scared to speak up and wanted to find a way to support kids in the same position he was in, so they started Speak Up—and every October is the annual charity gala they host to raise money for it. Tonight, Brody and I will be attending with Bree and her kids.

"I don't really have many people to invite," Bree admits sheepishly. "Other than Beatrice and Steven and Lacey and her family. That's pretty much it. But I wouldn't want to make everyone travel and on such short notice. So maybe a small wedding at a hotel or something, and then we can go away somewhere?"

"Whatever you want is fine with us," Brody says.

"I want to be a flower girl!" Evie exclaims, twirling around in her dress that she's wearing tonight. As soon as she saw it, there was no stopping her from putting it on. Especially since we made sure to have one made for her creepy doll that looks like her. "Molly wants to be one too," she adds, referring to said creepy doll.

"When we move in, can I keep the room I sleep in now?" Miles asks.

"Oh! Can I have an American Girl room since Mommy won't be in my room anymore?" Evie bounces up and down excitedly. "And can we get a bed for Molly? She's so squished sleeping with Mommy and me here."

"Umm…" Bree glances at us with wide eyes. "We haven't…We haven't discussed where we'll live."

"Well, your lease is up soon, right?" Brody points out. "And since we'll be married, it only makes sense that we'll all live together. And this place can fit everyone."

"Yeah," Bree breathes, glancing at Miles and Evie, who are watching and listening. "Can we go talk in the kitchen?"

"What's going on?" I ask once we're out of hearing distance.

"You guys didn't…" Bree swallows thickly. "You're not rushing this because I have to move out of my place, right? Like, you don't feel bad and are trying to fix things…"

"What? No," Brody says, grabbing her hips and pulling her toward him. "We love you and want to marry you. But if you want to wait, then we can wait. Move wherever you want, sign whatever lease you want. And once you're ready, we'll marry you. And then wherever you're living, whatever lease you've signed, we'll cancel it and move you guys in here. Or we can get a new place. A house or a brownstone somewhere…"

"We can do whatever you want," I add, stepping toward them and cupping her cheek. "All we want is to be with you. If you want to wait…"

"No," she breathes. "I want to marry you, and I know you want to marry me. I just wanted to make sure you're not putting a rush on it because of my living situation."

She pulls her phone out and glances at it. "What about December ninth?"

Brody and I look at each other and nod.

"That's perfect," Brody says. "It's two weeks before Christmas, which will give Amalia and you time to plan the wedding and enough time for you guys to move in afterward and spend our first Christmas together as a family."

The mention of Christmas has her lips turning down slightly, and I know it's because she's thinking of her late husband and how he passed away on Christmas.

"How do you feel about living here?" I ask.

"I'm okay with it. It's bigger than any place the kids and I have ever lived, and it's not too far from Heart's. And maybe we can go on a little trip over winter break with the kids," she adds softly.

"December ninth it is," I say, kissing the corner of her mouth. "And we can definitely go away. Whatever you want, baby."

"Okay," she breathes, smiling sweetly. "I guess I better cancel the real estate agent then." She glances from Brody to me. "We're really doing this, huh?"

"Damn right, we are," Brody says. "In less than two months, we'll officially be a family."

"OH, BREE," SAVY COOS. "YOU LOOK STUNNING. AND LOOK at you," she says to Evie. "You and your doll look so beautiful in your matching dresses."

"Her name's Molly," Evie says. "And guess what? Mommy said we can be the flower girls at her wedding when she marries Brody and Hayden. And we get more pretty dresses!"

Everyone's eyes swing over to Bree and straight to her hand, which houses the engagement ring we gave her.

Since Brody tells his parents everything, they already know, but that doesn't stop them from giving their congratulations since this is the first time they've seen Bree since the engagement took place. Amalia croons over how perfect the ring is, and Savy asks if we've picked a date yet.

I'm so absorbed in everything that is Bree that I don't realize my parents have arrived, and based on the way they're glaring, they overheard everything.

"Hayden," Mom hisses, confusion and shock marring her otherwise perfectly Botoxed features. "What's going on here? I don't understand."

"We'll talk later," I tell her, not wanting Bree to overhear anything negative that will come out of my parents' mouths.

"No," Dad says, refusing to let it go. "We'll talk now. You can't be serious. Sharing a woman with Brody Fields? What the hell are you thinking? Do you have any idea how bad this looks?"

"Oh, Joseph, Kassandra," Savy says without missing a beat and saving my ass. "I didn't realize you'd arrived." She politely gives each of them a kiss on their cheeks. "Thank you for being here. How are you?"

"We were good...until now," my dad says. "You can't really approve of this...*arrangement*."

"Actually, we do," Ben says, stepping into my father's face. "Brody and Hayden are happy, and that's all that matters. Love comes in all different forms, and we support their decision to be together."

"This is insanity," Dad barks. "How could—?"

"Enough," I demand. "Now is not the time or the place to discuss this."

"You're absolutely right," Dad says, "and had you told us, then we wouldn't be finding out about it now."

"It only happened a week ago," I explain. "And we haven't exactly been on speaking terms since I left Shea. I wasn't even sure you'd be here tonight."

"First, you embarrass our family by walking away from Shea over a woman," Dad spits. "And now I learn you're passing her back and forth with your friend. What the hell is wrong with you?"

"Joseph, if you can't drop this, I'm going to have to ask you to leave," Ben says softly yet firmly, his tone brooking no argument.

"Fine," Dad says. "Kassandra, let's go." He grabs Mom's hand and pulls her through the throng of people toward the door.

As I watch them leave, wishing not for the first time I was born into a different family, I pray Bree didn't hear any of that. That somehow, she got pulled away to talk to someone, and when I turn around, I'll see she's none the wiser. But when my eyes land on hers, I know she witnessed the entire exchange. Thankfully, when I look for her kids, they're at the dessert table with Amalia—out of hearing distance.

"Ignore them," I say, lifting her chin to look at me. "There will always be people who don't understand, who don't get it. And unfortunately, my parents will always be those people. All they care about is their pristine image. And unless my sister and I fall into line, allowing them to make us their personal puppets they can pull the strings on, they'll never support anything we do."

"I don't want to come between you and your family," she murmurs, her eyes showing a sadness I don't like.

"They did this, not you. It doesn't matter what I do, I'll never please them, and I'm done trying. Forget them. I already have. You, Brody, and your kids are my future. You got me?"

"Okay," she whispers, but she looks anything but okay.

Wanting to somehow salvage the evening, I glance around for a way to distract Bree when I notice several couples dancing on the dance floor. Extending my hand, I bow dramatically and say, "Dance with me, my lady?"

I know it works when a small smile tugs on the corners of Bree's cheeks, and she nods, placing her hand in mine.

I guide her to the dance floor and wrap my arms around her waist. She's wearing a gorgeous dress that shows off every one of her perfect curves as well as her entire back. I can't help but run my fingers along her smooth flesh as she encircles her arms around my neck, and we sway to the music.

"Your skin is soft," I murmur, dipping my head and kissing the corner of her mouth as my hands descend to the swells of her ass. "And you smell so damn sweet." I run my nose along her jawline and place a soft kiss to the sensitive spot just below it, leaving my lips on her long enough to feel the thrumming of her pulse. "It's taking everything in me not to take a bite out of you right here." I sink my teeth into her flesh, and a shiver runs through her body.

"Hayden," she half groans, half chides, tilting her head to the side to give me better access. "You can't say stuff like that here."

"Why not?" I ask, licking the slight pain away.

"Because..." She leans up on her tiptoes, and her mouth grazes the shell of my ear. "When you talk like that, you turn me on. And I can't be turned on *here*."

She pulls back slightly, and our eyes meet. The desire I see in hers has me pulling out my phone and sending a text to Brody.

ME

Keep an eye on the kids for a few minutes. I'm about to fuck our girl seven ways to Sunday.

BRODY

Lucky bastard. On it.

I've been to this venue enough times to know the family bathroom is cleaner than most people's houses and has a comfortable couch.

When I see Brody sitting at the table with his family and Bree's kids, I take Bree's hand in mine and pull her off the dance floor. After looking to make sure no one is watching, we slip inside.

"What are we—?" she begins to ask, but before she can finish her question, I slam my mouth down on hers and lift her into my arms, carrying her over to the counter.

"We need to be quick," I murmur against her mouth.

She parts her lips to argue, but when I tug her panties down her legs and then thrust my fingers inside her, finding her drenched, her argument is lost in her throat.

"Fuck, you're so wet," I mutter, trailing kisses along her neck.

As I'm finger-fucking her to make sure she's ready for me, she clamps down on my hand with hers, so my fingers are inside her, but I can't move them.

"Wait," she breathes. "What about Brody?"

"He knows," I tell her, nipping at her flesh. "Who do you think is watching the kids?"

"I-I can't," she says. "I'm sorry, but I can't do this without him."

My head snaps up at her admission.

"I know we haven't discussed it," she says, "but…I don't like choosing. I want you both…always."

I think for a moment, trying to wrap my head around what she's saying, and then it hits me—every single time we've been with her has been together. She's never been with just Brody or just me. It's always the three of us.

"Okay," I tell her, taking out my phone and sending a text to Brody to have his stepmom watch the kids so he can get his ass in here.

"What are you doing?" Bree asks.

"Making sure you don't have to choose." There's a soft knock on the door, and I give her a quick kiss before I open it slightly to make sure it's Brody. Once I know it is, I let him in and relock the door.

"Jesus, look at you," he says, walking straight toward her.

"She's soaked," I tell him. "Feel her."

I spread her legs, and Brody sticks a couple of fingers inside. "Fuck," he groans. "You're dripping wet." He leans in and gives her a kiss. "I heard you need to be fucked."

She nods. "By both of you."

"How do you want it, sweetness?" he asks. "One at a time, or in both holes?"

We've fucked her ass enough by now that she barely needs lube to take us both, but to be on the safe side, we always carry travel packets with us.

"Both," she says, her cheeks staining pink.

"Then that's what you'll have," he tells her, lifting her off the counter and carrying her over to the couch. "Hayden, sit down and get ready for our girl."

I do as he says, unbuttoning my pants and pulling my hard as hell dick out. Once I'm seated, Brody hands Bree over to me. She's holding her dress up, so it's easy to slide right inside her. She's wet and warm and fucking perfect. Using my shoulders to steady herself, she begins to ride my cock. I'm so lost in her hot as fuck heat that I don't realize Brody's joined in until I feel his cock rubbing against mine through Bree's walls.

"Is that what you wanted, baby?" I ask, nipping her bottom lip with my teeth. "You wanted to be fucked by both of us?"

"Yes," she moans. "It feels so good. I feel so…full."

She continues to fuck me while being fucked by Brody, and I watch as she swivels her hips, working my dick over like a pro. She's gotten so good at this—taking us both. At first, she was shy, but over time, she's come in to her own.

"Oh, God, Brody," she groans. "Fuck my ass harder, please."

He does as she demands, and she throws her head back, her eyes rolling upward in pure bliss. You'd never know how dirty she is by looking at her. She's like those cupcakes she loves to bake. From the outside, they're sweet and pretty, but with one bite, you realize they're not just simply cupcakes—they're filled with the most delicious cream. Messy as fuck but worth it.

"I'm close," Bree gasps. "Oh—" Not wanting to chance anyone hearing her, I cover her mouth with mine as her walls tighten around my cock like a vise, sending me straight over the edge after her.

"Holy fuck," Brody grunts, just before he pulls out of her ass and finishes in his hand. "Thanks for the invite," he says with a smirk.

"Don't thank me. Thank our woman. She said she wants us both…always."

Brody's brows rise at that information, and I shrug.

"Is that okay?" Bree asks, her head resting on my shoulder while my dick softens inside her. "I don't know how it's supposed to work, but I like being with you both."

"Whatever you want is what you'll get," Brody says, walking around and kissing the top of her head. "You want us both, you'll have us both…always."

"That's what I want," she says, sighing in contentment.

After we clean up, we head back out, and if anyone notices our absence, they don't mention it.

With my parents and their negativity gone, we're all able to relax.

A few people give Brody, Bree, and me a curious look, but everyone thankfully keeps their questions and opinions to themselves.

"Have you thought about where you want to have the wedding?" Savy asks Bree over dinner.

"I'm not sure. Maybe at a hotel or somewhere cozy, like the bed and breakfast we went to," she says, glancing at Brody and then me.

"Oh, that would be sweet," Amalia says. "I'll add it to the list of venues to look at."

"We'd like to pay for your honeymoon as your wedding gift," Ben says. "Brody said you guys are going to go away over winter break once the kids are out of school, but we'd like to pay for a trip for just you three."

"And if Beatrice can't watch the kids, we'd love to," Savy adds.

"Oh, we couldn't ask you to do that," Bree says, shaking her head. "That's way too much."

"We want to," Savy says, placing her hand over Bree's. "We tried to pay for the wedding, but Brody refused." She glares playfully at Brody. "Any ideas where you might want to go?"

"I don't know," Bree says. "I've never been anywhere."

"Really?" I ask.

"Nope, I don't even have a passport."

"Well, we need to change that," Brody says. "What about Italy or Paris? They're both known for having amazing food. Right? Maybe you can meet some of those crazy chefs on that food show."

At his words, Bree's face falls. "Excuse me," she breathes. "I need to use the bathroom."

She takes off, and Brody and I exchange a look before we get up and follow her.

"What's wrong?" I ask when we catch up to her in the bathroom.

She's standing in front of the mirror, tears sliding down her cheeks as she tries to stop them with a tissue.

"I'm sorry," she says. "I didn't mean to—"

"Hey," I say, turning her to face us. "Don't apologize for getting upset. Tell us why so we can fix it."

"It's not something you can fix," she says. "I was supposed to go to France. Pete paid for me to study with some of my favorite chefs. It was his Christmas present to me. He had just given it to me right before he…" She chokes out a sob. "Right before his heart stopped."

Oh, fuck.

"I never went. Beatrice offered to watch the kids so I could go, but I couldn't find it in me to leave them. With Pete gone, I was all they had. It was just too hard."

"I'm sorry," Brody says, wiping under her eyes. "I didn't know. Fuck Paris," he jokes. "Nobody wants to meet those over-the-top chefs anyway."

Bree snorts out a laugh. "Actually, I totally would," she says with a watery smile. "Your words just caught me off guard and brought back memories of that day."

Brody and I pull her into a hug and hold her until she's calm and ready to go back out and join everyone.

The rest of the evening goes smoothly. We talk and eat and dance. At the end of the night, Ben and Savy give a speech, thanking everyone for coming out and supporting a cause that's close to their heart, and then we take off. Since it's the weekend, Bree and the kids spend the night. Bree cuddles with us until she's ready to fall asleep, and then she moves to the bed she shares with Evie.

"We should order a bigger bed," I say to Brody once she's fast asleep. "I don't see her wanting anything other than to sleep with both of us once they're living here."

"You okay with that?" Brody asks. Despite us being best friends, and me making it clear I'm okay with everything we've done together, he sometimes worries that his attraction to me will push me away.

"I'm more than okay with it," I assure him. "I'll start checking out beds, so we can have one here before they move in."

As I'm pulling my phone out to do a search, a text comes through from my dad:

DAD

I need to see you in my office Monday morning at eight

I must make a noise of disgust because Brody asks if everything's okay. "Yeah, just my dad and his bullshit." I send a quick text back letting him know that's not happening, then set his contact to mute, not wanting to deal with his crap tonight.

"Let's look at some beds," I say, clicking on the internet. "It needs to be big and comfortable."

"Make sure it's waterproof too," Brody adds. When I give him a brow up in question, he smirks. "You see how wet our woman gets? Just wait until we have her in our bed every goddamn night."

And because he isn't lying, I add waterproof to the search.

CHAPTER FORTY-TWO

AUBREE

ME

Lunch today?

BRODY

Only if I can have you ;)

HAYDEN

Can't. Sorry.

"Where's Hayden?" I ask Brody thirty minutes later when I walk into his office with a bag of food from the deli we love.

"I'm not sure," he says, pulling me into his arms and kissing my lips. "You smell like cupcakes." He runs his nose along my jawline and then playfully nips at my bottom lip before brushing his lips against mine.

"I was baking this morning," I tell him. "Viviana had an appointment."

"Mmm, any chance you brought me one?" He tugs me closer, and his leg parts my thighs, rubbing against my center.

"No, sorry."

"That's okay," he murmurs, sucking my lip into his mouth. "I'll just eat you instead."

After the gala, we discussed the mechanics of our relationship. The guys mentioned that while in a perfect world, the three of us could always be together, there will be times when one of them has to go out of town, and they're okay with me being with only one of them. They don't consider it cheating in any way.

I get it...I do. And I can see where they're coming from, but my head and heart aren't exactly on the same page. I like being with them together. I fell in love with both of them, and I love being with both of them.

They insisted they were okay with doing it my way. But I also know they're men who have needs and wants—I love that they both need and want me—and it isn't fair to make one go without if the other isn't available. So I promised them I would try.

But it's easier said than done because as I kiss Brody, I can't help feeling like Hayden should be here.

As if Brody can sense my hesitation, he pulls back and looks at me. "You okay?"

"Yeah, I just wish Hayden were here with us." I shrug. "I know I said I'd try, but..."

"Hey," Brody says, framing my face. "It's okay. We love that you care about us enough that you want to be with both of us. And we won't push it, but we just need you to understand that if you're with one of us without the other, that doesn't mean you love the other one any less. We're not going to get jealous or keep track. There's no point system here. Promise."

"I know. I just think I need a little bit of time. Maybe when one of you goes away, and I'm so horny I can't handle it, I'll break the ice and give in."

Brody chuckles and gives me a chaste kiss. "Let's eat lunch, sweetness. If I can't eat you, then I guess I'll have to settle for this sandwich."

ME

Lunch today?

BRODY

Can't do lunch, but how about dinner after
the kids' sports?

HAYDEN

Sorry, can't.

ME

Everything okay?

HAYDEN

Have a lot going on with work.

"I FEEL LIKE I HAVEN'T SEEN HAYDEN IN FOREVER," I TELL Brody later that night as I take a bite of my pizza. After the kids finished hockey and gymnastics, we met Brody at the arcade they love to play at so we could eat while they played. "Is everything okay with him?"

It's been a week since the gala and his parents finding out about our relationship, and ever since, he's been...different. I can't quite pinpoint how, but he's been quiet, distant, and I'm starting to worry.

"I'm sure he's just busy with work. We have a huge project he's the point of contact on. I'll check in with him tonight when I get home."

"I miss him," I admit. "I miss both of you."

Brody pulls me into his arms and kisses my cheek. "Are you trying to imply that you're so horny you're ready to give in? Because if that's the case, I can take care of you. Just say the word."

"Very funny," I say with a giggle. "I'm not horny. Well, not desperately so...yet." I give him a peck on his lips. "Make sure Hayden's okay, please?"

"Of course."

"WHAT DO YOU THINK?" AMALIA ASKS. "THE CEREMONY can be held here, and the restaurant is the perfect place for the reception afterward."

"It's beautiful," Lacey says.

"It's perfect." I twirl around, taking in the indoor wedding venue. It's part of Brookstone Vineyard and Winery, the vineyard that Hayden took me to on our first date months ago. Built out of gorgeous rock, it's big enough to hold a small wedding yet also intimate. Since we'll be getting married next month, it'll be cold outside, so an indoor venue is a must. "But it's an hour and a half drive from the city," I add, remembering the long drive here.

"No matter where we book, it will be a bit of a drive," Brody points out, sliding his arm around my waist. "The question is, can you see yourself being married here?"

"And we can make a weekend out of it," Amalia adds. "I spoke to the owners, and they said we can book rooms for Friday and Saturday night. We can do a brunch Sunday morning before everyone heads home."

"What do you think?" I ask Hayden, who's been quiet today. I keep asking if everything is okay, but according to Brody and him, he's just been busy with work—so busy, this is the first time I've seen him in two weeks. I'm missing the hell out of him, horny as hell—just as Brody predicted—and if he doesn't tell me what's going on soon—or fuck me—I'm going to explode—and not in the orgasm sort of way.

"I think..." He glances down at me, and my stomach clenches at the way his eyes are glistening with...*is that sadness?* Dammit, Hayden! What's going on with you? "I think it's perfect," he finally says.

"Yeah?" I ask, feeling deep down that something is wrong. Something more than a man overwhelmed with work. "You're okay with us getting married here?"

Hayden nods, plastering a fake smile on his face, and lead fills my stomach. I want to demand that he tells me what's wrong, but since we're in front of Lacey and Amalia, I keep it to myself. The kids are with Beatrice since I knew they'd be bored driving up here and back. I told them we'd go pick out their Halloween costumes when we got home since Halloween is this week.

"Okay, we'll do it here," I say, unable to muster the enthusiasm I should have about deciding on the place where the guys and I will be saying our vows.

Amalia claps excitedly. "Perfect! I'll handle everything and keep you informed of anything you need to know. Next week, we have an appointment with the boutique for you to try on dresses and with the bakery to pick out your wedding cake."

"Thank you," I tell her, forcing a smile past my nerves. "I couldn't do this without you."

The ride home is filled with Amalia going over various details and asking questions about color schemes and foods and such. Brody's driving his SUV, and he drops her off first, then Lacey next.

"We're getting the kids at Beatrice's?" Brody confirms once it's just the three of us.

"Yeah, we—" I begin, but Hayden cuts me off.

"We need to talk," he says. I'm sitting in the back seat next to him, so I look over at him, but he doesn't make eye contact with me. "Can you ask her to watch the kids a little longer?"

"We're supposed to take them to pick out their costumes," I say dumbly, knowing whatever he needs to talk about won't be good.

"All right," he says.

"So…are we going to get them now?" Brody asks, confused.

"Yeah," Hayden says.

The afternoon is awkward, and I almost wish I would've picked the kids up later, but thankfully, they're too busy at the costume store to notice the tension. Evie picks out a cute cheerleader costume, and Miles goes with Creeper from *Minecraft*. Once we've purchased them, we head back to Brody and Hayden's place since it's the weekend. The kids pick out a movie to watch, and both pass out not even halfway through it.

Brody carries Evie to bed while Hayden carries Miles. After kissing them both good night, I find Brody standing in the hall with a frown marring his features.

"Something's wrong with Hayden," I whisper, emotion clogging my voice.

"Yeah." He nods. "But he won't tell me what. He said he needs to talk to us. He's in the living room."

"Okay." I follow Brody down the stairs, where we find Hayden sitting on the couch with his face in his hands.

When he hears us, he lifts his head, and his eyes are glassy again, like he's holding his emotions in and refusing to let them out.

"We need to talk," he says, his tone devoid of all the emotion his face is showing.

I go to sit next to him, but as I sit, he stands, like he can't bear being near me. Brody sits in his place, and Hayden walks around the coffee table, out of touching distance.

"I've made a decision," he says, his eyes not really looking at us but instead past us. "I won't be getting married to Bree."

A piece of my heart cracks, like he's stepping on it, and my organ can't withstand the pressure.

"I don't want to be in this relationship anymore."

His foot is now pushing down harder, causing several pieces to fragment. It hurts, and it's hard to breathe.

"And I'm moving out."

And just like that, like a bomb has been placed inside my chest and has exploded, my heart shatters into a million tiny pieces.

"You don't want me anymore?" I croak out, unable to stop myself from asking. I heard what he said, and I understand the words, but I don't want to believe them.

"No," he says simply, still refusing to look at me.

"Why? Is it because I said I only wanted you both together? I told you that I can try to be with you separately," I stammer, tears filling my eyes.

"It's not that," Hayden says, swallowing thickly.

"Then why?" I ask, sniffling back my emotions. "What did I do wrong?"

His eyes roll toward the ceiling, and he releases a harsh breath. "It's not you. I thought I could do this, but I can't." His gaze slowly shifts to Brody, who has yet to say a word. "And I won't be working at Fields anymore. If you need me to give my two weeks, I can, but I'd prefer to cut ties immediately."

My eyes flit between Brody and Hayden, unsure what to do or say. It's one thing for Hayden to break up with me, but for him to move out and quit his job? This doesn't make any sense. They've been best friends for years, more like brothers. And then it hits me...

"You're walking away so Brody and I can be together," I say, tears streaming down my cheeks. "But you know I won't choose, so you're making the decision for me by cutting yourself out of the equation."

"Is that what you're doing?" Brody asks, his voice hoarse.

"If that's the case, then I'll walk away," I sob. "I'm not going to come between your friendship." I stand, blinking fast so my vision will clear. "I told you I didn't want to come between your friendship, and you said this is what you wanted!" I cry. "I was afraid of this happening, of one of you not wanting me anymore, and you said you wanted me forever."

I cry harder, unable to help myself.

"It's not just you. I don't want to be with Brody either," Hayden says, emotionless, like he didn't just end an engagement, relationship, and friendship all in one go. "I'm not gay or bi, and I don't want to share, and I don't want to be in this relationship anymore. I'm done." He takes a step back, and I swear it feels like he's taking my battered heart with him. "I'll be by Monday while you're at work to move my stuff out."

He turns on his heel and starts walking toward the door, and I gasp for air, trying to catch my breath. This can't be happening. It doesn't make any sense. Hayden said he loved me. So why is he leaving?

"Hayden," I cry out, jumping off the couch and running after him. "Please don't do this." I pull on his hand, trying to stop him, but he won't even look at me.

"Hayden, please!" I speed up and swivel around in front of the elevator so he can't leave. "Tell me how to fix this, and I will." I'm aware of how pathetic I sound, but I can't stop myself. My parents walked away, and my husband and grandma left me. I gave Hayden my heart because he promised to be careful with it. This is exactly what I was terrified of—giving what was left of my heart away and being left with a hole in my chest.

Only now he's not just leaving me, he's leaving Brody and…"The kids," I blurt out. "They love you so much. You can't leave them. You can't leave *us*. Please, tell me how to fix this."

When he still won't look at me, I step toward him and jerk his chin, forcing him to make eye contact. His eyes are bloodshot, like he's trying with everything in him not to cry.

"There's nothing you can say or do to make me change my mind. Now, please move." His words are spoken like a robot, and I'm momentarily stunned speechless.

I glance back at Brody, who's still sitting on the couch, frozen in his spot. "Brody!" I yell, and his eyes connect with mine. "Do something! Make him stay, please."

His face falls, finally showing emotion, and he stands and walks toward us. I release a harsh breath, thinking he'll talk some sense into Hayden, but instead, he wraps his arms around me and moves me to the side so Hayden can leave.

As he presses the button and then steps inside, I scream and cry, begging Brody to stop him, to fix this, but he keeps holding me while Hayden walks out of our life.

When the door is closed, I push away from him, stumbling backward. "Why didn't you stop him?" I yell. "You should've made him stay!" He tries to approach me, but I shake my head, wrapping my arms around myself in a protective manner. "You guys promised," I sob. "You promised to love me forever, and now he's gone, and you just let him walk away."

Brody's staring at me with tear-filled eyes when I hear the soft voice of my son. "Mom," Miles whispers. "What's wrong?"

This seems to wake Brody up because his eyes snap toward Miles, who's standing at the bottom of the stairs.

"It's okay, buddy," Brody says, his voice trying to be soothing but failing.

"No, it's not," Miles argues. "You and Hayden said you'd make my mom happy, but she's crying. That's not happy."

Oh, God. Another sob wracks my body before I can get control of myself. "Miles, it's okay," I tell him, forcing myself to get control of my emotions. Before anything else, I'm a mom.

"Why are you crying?" Miles asks. "Is it because Hayden left?"

Dammit, he must've been standing there when Hayden and I were at the door. Who knows how much he heard.

"Sometimes people have bad days," I say, trying to explain. "Hayden is having a bad day, so he left, and that made me sad, but I'm okay."

"Is he coming back?" Miles asks.

"Of course, he is," I say.

"Bree," Brody says softly, obviously disagreeing with my answer.

"He is," I tell Brody, glaring at him. "He'll be back."

I refuse to believe this is the end. I don't know what's going on with Hayden, but I'm going to find out and then fix it. Because despite the way he was acting tonight, I know damn well he loves me and Brody and my kids. Feelings don't just flip on and off like a damn light switch. Something happened, and I'm going to figure out what.

CHAPTER FORTY-THREE
BRODY

IT'S CRAZY HOW QUICKLY THINGS CAN CHANGE. ONE minute, I was on top of the world with the entire future ahead of me. I was engaged to the woman of my dreams, planning my life with her and my best friend, and the next, Hayden is walking out the door, taking our hearts and plans for the future with him.

Bree begged me to say something, to do something, but I couldn't speak, couldn't move. A million thoughts were running through my head with just as many words I wanted to say, but not a single one came out of my mouth.

So instead, I let my best friend walk out the door. Then, after calling Beatrice so she could take the kids, I spent the next thirty-six hours trying to comfort Bree. At the same time, she cried in my arms, asking me heartbreaking questions like if Hayden left because of the kids, or if she did something wrong. She questioned everything about herself, allowing her insecurities to get the better of her. Had Hayden been anywhere near me, I would've punched him in his face for doing what he did, making her feel that way.

I don't know why he walked away, but I'm sure as hell going to get some damn answers…which is why, instead of going in to work, I'm sitting on my couch, waiting for him to show up.

At nine o'clock on the dot, he walks through the door, his steps faltering the second he sees me sitting, waiting.

"You were supposed to be at work," he says, his tone devoid of all emotion.

"That's all you have to say to me?" I stalk toward him. "A lifetime of friendship and that's all you have to say?" I get in his face, and he backs up against the wall, showing zero emotion. "Fuck work. I'd say my best friend walking away is a bit more important than going to work." I cage him in, and we both stand like this for several seconds—me, trying to get ahold of myself so I can get some answers, and him, waiting for me to speak.

When I'm finally calm enough to speak, I say, "She spent the last day and a half crying." Hayden at least has the decency to flinch before schooling his features.

"She thinks she did something wrong. She questioned her weight, if she's good enough in bed, if she's pretty enough. Then she moved on to her kids, asking if they were behaved enough, or if maybe it's because you want your own. She said she'd give us however many kids we wanted. After that, she wondered if maybe she's not lovable. Her mom and dad didn't love her enough to stay. From there, she questioned if she was destined to always be left behind. Because you know, everyone she's loved has either left or died."

I look Hayden in the eyes, and despite him refusing to show any emotions, I can see it in his features, my words are killing him inside, yet he did this. He caused this. And he won't tell me why.

"Say something!" I slam my fist against the wall because I have so much anger built up, but I'd never touch Hayden, not violently.

When he doesn't say a damn word, I continue. "She was so distraught I had to have Beatrice take the kids for the rest of the weekend. She barely slept, wouldn't eat, just fucking cried. Oh," I say with a bitter laugh, remembering something else. "Then she apologized. Our sweet, too damn good for us fiancée apologized for being the reason I lost you as well."

When he finally speaks, the words that come out of his mouth have me wanting to kill him. "I need to pack my shit, so if you wouldn't mind backing up so I can do that, I'd appreciate it."

"You'd appreciate it?" I mock, close to losing my shit. "What the fuck is going on, Hayden?" With shaky hands, I cup the sides of his face. "Talk to me, please."

Liquid emotion shines in his glassy eyes, but he doesn't say anything, and just when I think he's never going to, he speaks. "Love her enough for us both, please," he chokes out, his gaze finally meeting mine. "Remind her every day how perfect she is, that she deserves to be loved, and…" He closes his eyes for a moment, and when a single tear escapes from under his lashes, trailing down his cheek, I know this isn't what he wants. He's doing this for a reason —one he won't disclose. "Please take care of her and the kids," he says, his eyes meeting mine once again. "Give them the entire world. She'll get past this. She'll get over me because she has you."

"Hayden," I say. "Whatever's going on…"

"Please don't," he begs, shaking his head. "Please let me walk away. It's hard enough as it is. Just know that it's nothing either of you or those amazing kids did. This is on me."

He slides out and around me, and I stand where I am, watching him go to his room. I want to yell and scream and make demands, but I don't because deep down, I know he's not walking away because he doesn't love us…He's walking away because he does.

"IT'S ALL GONE." BREE STANDS IN THE MIDDLE OF Hayden's room, surveying the empty space. I'd stayed for a few minutes to see what he was going to do, hoping he would come to his senses, but when the movers showed up, I left, unable to watch.

"You let him leave," she says matter-of-factly. "You promised you would handle it. This is handling it? Letting him move out? Good job." She glares at me, and I remind myself that she's lashing out at the person who's still here. She isn't mad at me. She's heartbroken over Hayden leaving.

"I have to go," she says, a small sniffle giving away her hard exterior. "Beatrice is bringing the kids home after practice."

"Or you guys could stay the night," I offer, not wanting to be away from her—and also dreading being alone in this big place.

"I don't think that's a good idea. Miles is upset about Hayden making me cry, and I haven't told him he left for good."

"Okay," I say, feeling like even though I'm not the one who left, I'm losing her just the same.

After she's gone and the place is too quiet, I grab my jacket, wallet, and phone and go out for a drink. I end up at Lush, one of the bars Fields owns, and order a drink. Then another, and another. I'm three, maybe four deep when my dad sits beside me.

"What are you doing here?" Ever since he retired, it's rare to find him in the city.

"Hayden called," he says, making me drop my drink and give him my full attention. "Said you might need someone tonight and that I could find you here."

Fucking location app. When Bree told us she uses it to keep track of where her kids are, Hayden suggested we sign up as well. God forbid something happen to Bree or the kids, we could pull up the app and see where they are. I honestly forgot about it, but he clearly didn't.

I pull out my phone to see where he is and laugh bitterly when it shows his location is unknown. Then I turn my location off as well —because fuck him—and down my drink, motioning for the bartender to bring me another once my glass is empty.

"Did he also tell you that without any reasoning, he quit his job at Fields, broke up with Bree, and moved out?" I ask, looking over at my dad.

When his eyes widen, I know Hayden conveniently left all that out. I throw back the drink the bartender sets down and then slam my glass on the bar top. "What I need is for my *friend* to come back."

Another drink is placed in front of me, and I shoot it back. But before I can motion for another, my dad shakes his head, cutting me off.

"Getting drunk isn't going to fix things."

"Nothing will fix this, but at least getting drunk will numb the pain."

I raise a finger to get the bartender's attention, then gesture for another drink, but my dad shakes his head again, throws down a few bills, and wraps his arm around my shoulders. "C'mon, son," he says. "How about you come home with me tonight? Savy is making dinner, and I know your brother and sister would love to see you."

"I appreciate it, but I'm not good company tonight," I mutter once we're out of Lush and standing by the valet. Knowing I had every intention of getting shit-faced, I didn't drive, but Dad showing up put a damper on that.

"We don't need you to be good company," he says. "We just want to be there for you. I don't know all that's going on, but I don't think you should be alone tonight. Come home with me, have a home-cooked meal, and then if you want to close yourself off in a room, we won't stop you. But at least we know you're not alone."

Because I can tell he's worried, and I really don't want to be alone in that condo, I agree and go home with him. Just as he said, Olivier and Penelope are happy to see me, and Savy made delicious pot roast, one of my favorites. Nobody questions why I'm home on a random Monday night, and after dinner's cleaned up, they don't say a word when I excuse myself to the guest room that used to be my room before I officially moved out after college.

I open a drawer and find some shirts and pajama pants in my

size. Since the room has an en suite bathroom, I take a quick shower to rinse off, get dressed, and then drop onto the bed, staring at my phone.

It's been hours since I spoke to Bree, and I hate that she left upset. I hate even more that I don't think there's any way I can fix this. Not unless Hayden tells me why he left, and from the way he was talking, I don't think he's going to do that any time soon.

Refusing to let Bree push me away, I check the time and see the kids would be in bed by now since it's a school night, then video call her, hoping she'll answer.

I'm shocked when she actually does. And my heart breaks when her blotchy, tearstained face comes over the screen. She's lying in her bed, the covers surrounding her, and even sad, she looks so damn beautiful.

"Hey," I say softly, afraid to say anything else.

"Hey," she says back, fresh tears filling her eyes. We stare at each other for a few moments before she speaks.

"I'm so sorry," she murmurs, crying softly. "I shouldn't have been so mean to you earlier." She sniffles back a sob, and I know she's trying to keep it together so the kids don't hear her.

"Sweetness," I say, mustering up a smile so she knows I'm not mad. "I love you, and I hate that you're hurting. And it's killing me not to be able to make it better."

"You're hurting too."

"I am."

"Do you think…?" She swallows thickly. "Do you think if we broke up, he'd go back to being friends with you?"

I think back to Hayden's earlier words and shake my head. "I think he wants us to stay together. He asked me to love you enough for us both."

Her eyes widen, then fill with fresh tears. "Why can't he just love me himself?"

"He does. I think he loves you so much that he felt the only way to love you was to walk away."

"That's not how you love someone," she mutters, her mouth forming the most adorable pout. "Did he say anything else?"

"He said to take care of you and the kids and to make sure you guys know it's nothing you did."

"I really miss him."

"I do too." It's not about the distance—it's feeling like he's broken our connection. The only time we were apart was during high school when his parents forced him to go to boarding school—a family tradition—but we never stopped talking, and whenever he was home, we hung out. It's a bad feeling, wondering if or when I'll speak to or see him again.

"Brody," Bree says, snapping me from my thoughts. "I was thinking about the wedding…"

I nod, mentally preparing myself for the blow—for her to tell me that she's calling it off. I already put it in my head this was coming. Bree made it clear she never wanted to choose. Hell, she didn't even want to have sex with one of us without the other. But as I hold my breath, waiting for her to confirm, I know no amount of mental preparation can prepare me for losing my best friend and my soul mate in the same week.

"I think we should push the wedding back a little bit." Push it back—not call it off. Or is that her way of calling it off without saying it? "Brody…"

"You still want to marry me?"

"Of course, I do," she says. "I want to marry you both. And I'm going to. I just think we should push it back a little to give us some time to get Hayden back."

Oh, fuck, this woman. "Bree…I don't think—"

"You said it yourself. He loves us, and the reason he walked away is *because* he loves us, not because he doesn't want us. The stuff he said Saturday night was to hurt us, push us away. I'm going to find out why he's pushing us away, and then I'm going to bring him back."

And because I can hear the determination in her voice, I don't argue. I just nod and start mentally preparing myself for the day when she realizes Hayden isn't coming back, and I have to comfort her again. Then I pray that when that day comes, she'll still want me. Because I'm not sure I can handle losing both of them.

CHAPTER FORTY-FOUR

AUBREE

AS THE ELEVATOR ASCENDS TO THE TOP FLOOR, I READ over the texts I've sent the past week to Hayden that have gone unanswered. They show as delivered, so I know he's seeing them, but he's not responding, and since his location is turned off, I have no way of knowing where he is, so I can go to him and drag his ass back to where he belongs.

I considered finding out where his family lives and going there, but since his parents are not Team Bree, I scratched that. I checked all his social media, but he hasn't posted on any of them, so they're useless. Then I remembered he has a sister, who, despite him not being close to, he's mentioned he cares about. Since I've hit dead end after dead end, I figured it can't hurt to reach out and see if she knows where I can find her brother.

"Good morning, welcome to Shea," a woman, who looks to be in her mid-forties, says with a sweet smile. "How may I help you?"

"I'm here to see…" I'm about to say Gretchen when a masculine figure steps out of the doorway, speaking to another gentleman. Even with his back to me, I'd recognize that hair, those shoulders, that ass anywhere. Which doesn't make any sense because why the hell would Hayden be working here again?

"Ma'am," the woman says, "how can I help you?"

"Does Hayden Shea work here?"

Her brow furrows in confusion. "He does, but he's in a meeting right now. Do you have an appointment with him?" She starts typing on her keyboard. "I don't see—"

"I don't have an appointment," I say, feeling like I'm missing something here. Hayden left this place because he hated working for his dad, so why would he return? He's mentioned on several occasions he has plenty of money, so why wouldn't he hold out for another job he'd enjoy? Why come back here where he was miserable? It doesn't make any sense.

Or maybe this is why he left us? He wanted to go back to work for his dad but was scared Brody would get upset? No, that can't be right. He chose to leave Shea and go to work with Brody.

"Ma'am, if you don't have an appointment…"

Hayden begins to turn around, and since I don't want him to see me here, I take off toward the elevator. Once I'm out of the building, I call Brody, who answers on the first ring.

"Did you know Hayden is working at Shea again?"

"How do you know that?"

"Did you know?"

"No, I didn't know that, but how do you know he is?"

"I saw him," I admit.

"At Shea?"

"He won't answer my texts, so I was going to speak to Gretchen to find out where he is. Instead, I saw him coming out of a meeting, and the receptionist confirmed he's working there."

Brody curses under his breath. "I have to go into a meeting myself, but when I get out, I'll ask around and see why he's back there."

"Brody, something is up. It can't be a coincidence that he left us and then went back to work for his dad."

"I know, sweetness. I promise I'll look into it after my meeting."

"Hey," I say before we hang up. "I love you."

"I love you too."

We hang up, and I snag a cab back to the bakery so I can check on things before the kids get home from school. As I'm walking across the sidewalk, I notice a few gentlemen standing in front of my window talking while pointing at the building.

"Can I help you?"

"Are you the owner?" one of the gentlemen says.

"Yes, and contrary to what that sleazy building owner, Benitez, says, I will not be bought out, so you might as well look for another building to buy."

"Actually," the second gentleman says, "it's already been sold."

Goose bumps prick my skin as a shiver runs straight up my spine. "By whom?"

"Shea Real Estate Investments."

No...No. No. No. "But I didn't sign off," I say dumbly. "He can't tear down my coffeehouse."

The gentleman flips through a bunch of papers attached to a clipboard, then looks up at me. "He's not tearing it down. But we have been advised to get measurements for the remodel."

He's not tearing it down...

"He's not trying to kick me out?"

The man looks at me with confusion. "From the notes I have here, Heart's Coffeehouse and Bakery is remaining."

"And what will this building become?"

"A luxury condominium complex."

This doesn't make any sense. Hayden's dad was determined to buy me out, set on turning it into a wellness spa. I pull out my phone to call Hayden when it clicks…

He left.

He's back working for his dad.

They're not kicking me out of the building.

"Oh, Hayden, what did you do?"

"You're back." The woman from earlier plasters on a smile, clearly not thrilled with seeing me again. Oh, fucking, well.

"I am. And I would like to meet with Mr. Shea."

"Hayden's currently—"

"Not Hayden. I would like to meet with Joseph Shea, the CEO."

"Unfortunately—"

Knowing she won't let me back, I step around her desk and stalk down the hallway in search of his office. The woman calls out for me, but I ignore her, on a mission to find him. When I see the plaque on the door indicating his office, I knock once and then open the door, not giving him a chance to refuse me.

"Ms. Heart." Joseph stands, looking a mixture of confused and annoyed. "I'm in the middle of—"

"What did you do?"

"Excuse me?"

"What did you do to get Hayden to leave us? To get him to come back to work for you? I know you did something! And I'm not leaving until you tell me what you did."

CHAPTER FORTY-FIVE

HAYDEN

BREE

I need you to meet me at Brody's place
ASAP.

It's an emergency.

I STARE AT THE TEXTS, WONDERING IF I SHOULD GO OR not. More than likely, it's not an emergency, just a way for Bree to get me to talk to her. But at the same time, what if it *is* an emergency?

My office phone beeps with an in-house call from my dad, summoning me like his stupid little puppet, and I make the decision to go. If nothing else, I'll get to see Bree and maybe Brody for a few minutes. It'll hurt like a bitch when I have to walk out the door again, but fuck, I miss them.

My phone vibrates with a call from my dad, and I send him to voicemail, then send a text to him that I'm dealing with an emergency and I'll call him later.

He responds with a message demanding me to go see him immediately, but I ignore him and take off to the condo.

When I arrive, my heart pounds in my chest at the thought of seeing them. It's been a little over a week since I've seen either of them in person or heard their voices, and I'm craving them like a damn addict.

Without thinking, I type in my code and use the card I still have to take me up to the top floor, and when the doors open, I find Bree standing there with Brody.

"You came," she says.

"You said it was an emergency," I murmur, masking my expression, knowing it will only make things worse if I show any emotion.

"It is," she says, walking toward me. "I want the truth. Why did you walk away?"

I open my mouth to spew my go-to lie, but before the words come out, she adds, "And don't you dare lie to me *again*. You promised me the truth...always. You at least owe me that."

I close my mouth and consider how to go about this. Telling the truth will defeat the entire purpose of what I've done. And then it hits me...She said *again*. Is it possible she knows I was lying when I left?

"Hayden, please," she says softly, palming my face gently. "Tell me why you left."

"It's not going to change anything," I murmur, my eyes locking with hers before they go to her plump lips, wishing I could kiss her.

"That's okay," she says. "I just...I need the truth."

THE DAY AFTER THE CHARITY GALA

DAD

We need to talk.

I ignore his text, just like I did last night, not giving a shit that he needs to talk to me. There's nothing I *need* or want to hear from him.

I'm about to put my phone away when a second text comes through that gets my attention.

DAD

It's regarding your girlfriend's little bakery.

ME

What about it?

DAD

Call Carly and schedule a meeting.

Such an asshole. Since there's no way I'm not finding out what's going on regarding Bree's bakery, I call Carly and schedule an appointment for this afternoon.

When lunch rolls around, I let Hillary know I have an appointment and won't be in for the rest of the day and then take off.

My dad runs behind in his previous meeting I'm sure to spite me, and finally, nearly forty minutes after our scheduled time, Carly lets me know he's ready to see me.

"Son, how nice to see you," Dad says. "Drink?"

"Get to the point, please. I have shit to do. What is it you need to talk to me about?"

He picks up a stack of papers and drops them in front of me. "Turns out Violet and Roy Heart were all too trusting. Although back then, times were different." He shrugs. "People would shake hands and consider it an agreement. But things have changed over the years, and now, it's very difficult for a verbal agreement to stand in court, especially when both parties are deceased."

I stare at the papers in front of me, but I can't make heads or tails of what I'm looking at based on the bullshit my dad is spewing.

"Let me," he says, flipping the pages to the last one. "I have another meeting in fifteen minutes, so we'll have to speed this up."

He points at the lines at the bottom of the page. "This is the contract between Violet and Roy Heart and Sal Benitez, where they agreed to a ninety-nine-year lease on the property where Heart's Coffeehouse and Bakery resides. What's missing?" He taps his finger right over the blank lines...Fuck, they're blank. How can that be?

I flip through all the pages, looking for somewhere they might've signed, an initial, anything that can hold up in court. But there's nothing. Neither party ever signed the damn paperwork. Which means Bree has no rights as far as her coffeehouse goes.

Fuck, if my dad buys the property, she's screwed. He'll kick her out in a heartbeat and without paying her a dime since she has no leg to stand on without a signed contract.

"What do you want?" I ask, knowing that's why he called me here. He knows what that business means to Bree and what she means to me, and there's only one reason he would point it out.

"I want to make a deal," he confirms with a smirk I'd love to punch right off his damn face.

"What do you want?" I repeat.

"For you to stop embarrassing the Shea name. I want you out of that ridiculous relationship and back here working where you belong."

"And you'll what—cancel the sale?" I volley as my mind runs with possible ways to save Bree's coffeehouse. If I can convince him that we're over and that I'm back at Shea just long enough for Brody to—

"The sale's already done," he says, stabbing my ideas with a fucking knife. "You think I'd risk you walking away as soon as I cancel it, so Fields can swoop in and scoop it up?" He barks out a humorless laugh. "Hell no. I bought it. The deal is done. And as long as you work for me and stay away from them, she can keep her little bakery."

His words wrap around my heart, squeezing, piercing, bleeding me out. Without thought, I bring my hand up and rub my chest, seeking reprieve but knowing I won't get it. Dad doesn't say anything, letting me stew in my thoughts. He's covered all his bases, leaving no room for any loopholes. Except…

"How are you going to put a spa there?"

"I already found another property for the spa. This purchase was strictly done to ensure you'd come back to where you belong. It will make a great luxury condominium complex. Surprisingly, that bakery has a decent clientele. With a few necessary upgrades, it'll fit in just fine…as long as you hold up your end of the bargain, that is."

"I need time to think," I tell him, standing. It's hard to breathe, and if I don't leave soon, he's going to witness me losing my shit.

"You have one week to return to where you belong. If you're not here on Monday morning, she's gone."

"Even if I do return, you have to know I'll never want to be here. I'll resent you for forcing me into this, for destroying the little bit of happiness I found."

"You'll get over it. You're meant to be the CEO of Shea, not working as a lackey at Fields. You'll thank me one day." He presses the button for the intercom. "Carly, let my next appointment know I'm ready." And just like that, I've been dismissed.

Taking the contract with me, I spend the next several hours combing through it, hoping to find a loophole. When I don't find one, I take it to an attorney friend and ask him to look over it. When he tells me that without any signatures, the contract isn't worth the paper it was typed on, I know what I have to do.

PRESENT DAY

"You should've told me," Bree says. "You should've given me the choice."

"I know what you would've chosen," I argue, "and I wasn't going to put you in that position. My family did this to you, and it was up to me to fix it. I know how much Heart's means to you. It's all you have left from your grandparents. It's more than just coffee and cupcakes. It's your past, your present, your future. It's your livelihood. I wasn't going to let you have it ripped out from under you."

Bree steps toward me and cradles my face in her gentle hands. "I've lost enough people in my life to know that Heart's is just a dwelling. The heart of it is inside me, where nobody, not even your dad, can reach. My grandma took me in when my parents weren't capable of loving me the right way. She showed me what love looks like, and it's not four walls at the bottom of a building. It's you, me, Brody, and my children."

She smiles softly up at me. "I know without a doubt my grandparents would not only understand but would want me to choose you…choose love over a location."

"Bree…" I swallow thickly, hearing her words but not wanting to accept them. She shouldn't have to choose. "I can't let you—"

"I already did."

Her admission has me stumbling back. "What? What did you do?"

"I had a letter of termination of my lease drawn up, and I gave it to your dad. It wasn't really necessary since the contract wasn't even signed, but I did it, so legally, it's been handled. I have ninety days to move my stuff out of there before he locks me out."

She presses her lips to mine. "I love you, Hayden, and I appreciate what you did. I don't like that you didn't speak to me, but I know what you did was out of love, so I'm going to forgive you, but in the future, we handle things together." She takes Brody's hand in hers and tugs him toward us. "The three of us."

I don't know how the hell I got this lucky to have someone like Bree love me, but I vow to spend the rest of our lives making it up to her.

"HEY, MAN, CAN WE TALK?"

Brody closes the fridge and slowly turns around, glaring my way.

"Oh, now you want to talk?" he says, popping the top off his beer. "I think that ship sailed the moment you chose to walk away instead of talking to me."

It's late, and even though it's a weekday, Bree and the kids spent the night. We had a conversation with the kids about what happened, and I apologized to Miles and Evie for making their mom cry.

She explained to them about the coffeehouse, how she has to find a new one, and that I was upsetting her because I was trying to fix it. I'm not sure if they completely understand what happened, but Miles seemed to forgive me by the end of the night.

Brody, on the other hand, hasn't said a single word to me all night.

"I know I fucked up…"

"You know you fucked up?" he mocks. "Fuck that! You don't know shit." He stalks toward me and gets in my face. "You're lucky Bree is a fucking angel and willing to forgive you, but I'm not." He slams his beer on the counter next to me. "An entire lifetime of friendship and instead of talking to me, you shut me out."

"I didn't have a choice."

"You always have a choice!" he barks. "You chose to walk away. You chose to say the shit you said. You broke her heart, and I had to try to pick up the shattered fucking pieces. You weren't there, watching her cry for days. Helpless!" He pounds his chest with his fist. "I thought I was gonna lose her too. Do you know what it feels like to think you're going to lose the two people who mean the most to you?" I open my mouth to say something—what, I'm not sure— but he speaks first. "And don't you dare say you know because you made that decision. You did that! And Bree might be forgiving, but I'll be damned if you ever do that shit to her again."

He grabs me by the shirt and slams me against the wall. I brace myself, ready for him to hit me, and I wouldn't blame him, but before he does, Bree runs into the kitchen and pushes him away from me.

"Enough," she hisses. "Enough."

"No, fuck that!" Brody barks. "He should be hurting, just like we were." Tears prick his eyes, and he looks away from me and at her as she takes his face in her hands. "He fucking hurt you, and just like that, you let him back in. I can't go through that again." He shakes his head. "I can't see you crying like that again. He's either got to be all in or out. You almost canceled the wedding. You were crying for days."

He glances at me. "While you were accepting your decision, did you know that she refused to? She was running around like a detective, refusing to give up hope. Swearing she was going to get you back. You gave up before even trying, and she never fucking gave up."

"Brody, please," Bree says, forcing him to look at her. "None of us are perfect. All we can do is love each other and live for today and hope for tomorrow. I love that you're protecting me, but all I want is for us to learn from this and put it behind us."

She reaches over and takes my hand, pulling me toward Brody so we're standing next to each other. "I just want to love you both and be loved by you. Everything else be damned."

She reaches up on her tiptoes and kisses Brody, then turns and kisses me. "Now," she says, a sexy smirk quirking up in the corner of her lips. "It's been way too long since I've felt either of you inside me. So I say we take advantage of the kids sleeping and get reacquainted with each other...on a personal level."

And because neither of us can—or want to—say no to that offer, we follow her to Brody's room, where we spend damn near the entire night making up for the lost time.

BONUS SCENE - BRODY

"You're still awake?"

Hayden's standing in the doorway, dressed in a pair of sweats, sans shirt. We've just spent hours making love to Bree. After everything that went down, she was needier than usual, and we were both willing and happy to give her that extra attention.

But once she fell asleep, I couldn't stay in that room, in the bed with Hayden, so when I knew she wouldn't be waking up until morning, I left and came out onto the balcony to get some fresh air.

"It would seem so," I clip, still pissed at Hayden.

"Can I join you?" he asks, already walking over to have a seat next to me.

We sit in silence for several minutes, and I think it's going to stay that way until he turns to face me.

"I'm sorry." His eyes are glassy with emotion. "I know I already said it earlier and Bree forgave me, but I owe you an apology."

He reaches over and threads our fingers together, and my stomach knots. Hayden has been my best friend for years, and what he did hurt. I love how big Bree's heart is and that it's so open to forgiveness, but what Hayden did fucking hurt.

"You've had my back every day for the past decade, and I can't imagine a life without you in it," he says, his words laced with raw emotion. "I know I hurt you, and for that, I'm sorry. But you have to understand that I didn't make my decision lightly. I've watched you for years struggle with finding yourself in this world and when my dad threatened to take it all away…"

"That's what you don't understand," I tell him, our eyes meeting. "My happiness isn't only contingent on Bree. It's on you as well.

We're in this together, the three of us. And you're just as important to me as she is."

Hayden nods in understanding. "I love you, and I'm sorry I didn't come to you. In the future, I will."

"Good, because we can't run Fields and Shea Enterprises together if we aren't on the same page."

"What?" His eyes go wide. "It's…It's not…"

"It will be," I tell him. "I spoke to my dad, and he's agreed. I don't want you to work for me at Fields. I want you to be my partner."

"Fuck," Hayden chokes out.

"I love you," I tell him. "And I wouldn't want to be in this life with anyone but you." I stand. "Now, let's go back to bed. We have a woman who needs us to make up for lost time."

Hayden grins. "I call her ass."

CHAPTER FORTY-SIX
AUBREE

WEDDING DAY

"You look beautiful," Lacey says, fluffing my dress. "Are you nervous?"

I glance at myself in the mirror, dressed in a strapless, satin, sparkly floor-length wedding gown that shows off all of my curves. My hair is down in waves, with a beautiful rhinestone tiara on the crown of my head that Lacey loaned me as something borrowed and something blue. Laying across my neck is a beautiful necklace the guys gave me yesterday as my something new. It has an elegant white gold cupcake in the center to symbolize my love of baking and how I met them. And on my wrist is a delicate bracelet that was my grandma's as my something old.

I look like a princess straight out of a fairy tale ready to marry my prince—or in my case, princes. But what has my attention isn't the dress or my hair or the jewelry I'm wearing. It's my genuine smile.

"No," I tell Lacey. "I'm not nervous. I'm happy." Something I never thought I would truly be after Pete died.

She smiles at me through the mirror. "You deserve to be happy," she says, squeezing my hand. "And I'm honored to be a part of your big day."

Since we're not having a traditional wedding service, Lacey will be standing at the altar, walking us through our vows. It was only fitting since the only reason I gave either of them a chance in the first place was because of her.

There's a knock on the door, and then Miles walks in, dressed adorably in a black tux with a powder-blue tie that matches the rhinestones on my tiara and the flowers on Evie's dress. "I have a gift for you," he announces, holding up a small rectangular-shaped box. "It's from Hayden and Brody. They said you're not allowed to cry."

"Thank you," I choke out, wondering when the heck my little boy grew up.

I take the box from him and carefully sit on the couch, not wanting to wrinkle my dress before the wedding. I untie the ribbon, vaguely aware of the photographer hired to take pictures during the wedding.

When I remove the tissue paper, I find a note, and I know I won't be able to contain my tears.

Bree,

One of the most important things as your husbands is to stand by your side and help make sure all your dreams come true, so today, as we begin our lives together, we'd like to give you the gift Peter wanted you to have: to study in France with some of the best pastry chefs in the world. We can't bring him back, but we hope by making one of your dreams come true, we're able to honor his last wish. We love you, and we can't wait to spend the rest of our lives by your side.

Xo Hayden and Brody

Nestled underneath, I find five round-trip tickets to Europe dated for this summer, along with a voucher to study with some of my favorite chefs.

"Mom," Miles says. "You're not supposed to cry."

"Come here, sweetie." He walks over, and I pull him into my arms. "Sometimes, when people are so happy, they cry." He looks at me, confused, and I laugh, hugging him tightly. "I promise, I'm very happy."

"Okay, it's time," Savy says, walking into the room. "Are you ready to walk your mom down the aisle?" she asks Miles, handing him the pillow holding the rings. Instead of walking myself down the aisle, the kids will be walking with me. Miles is in charge of the rings, and Evie will be dropping flower petals as we go.

"I'm ready," Miles says, taking it from her.

"Me too!" Evie sing-songs, swinging her basket of petals in the air.

The music starts, and everyone gives me a quick kiss before heading out to have a seat. I double-check my makeup to make sure it's not splotchy from the emotional note and gift, and then with a deep breath, the kids and I walk to where Brody and Hayden are waiting.

When we arrive at the altar, Evie and Miles step to the side as we practiced, and Brody and Hayden each take one of my hands in theirs.

With a soft smile, Lacey begins to speak. "We are gathered here today to celebrate the love and commitment between Brody Fields, Aubree Heart, and Hayden Shea…"

ONE WEEK LATER

"Just sign here and here and initial right here," the attorney says. "This is for the lease agreement."

I scan the verbiage even though I've already read through the entire contract several times—at Brody's demand—and laugh when I see the length of the agreement. Ninety-nine years. The same length of the contract my grandparents had.

When Brody and Hayden brought me to the building they purchased, I wasn't all that surprised. One thing about my husbands is that they'll do everything in their power to make sure I'm happy—and owning my own coffeehouse and bakery makes me happy.

I sign and initial where I was told, and then the notary does the same before adding her stamp to it.

"You're going to sign here." He flips to the next page. "And here."

Because I can't legally marry both of them, I felt it was best if I didn't legally marry either one. Instead, we had a beautiful cere-mony where we exchanged vows in front of our family and friends and then spent the night celebrating our commitment to one another.

I'm keeping my last name—Heart—and the guys insisted on drawing up paperwork that would ensure that if anything happened to them, the building would become mine, so nobody could ever do what Benitez did to me. They also added the kids and me to their life insurance policies and wills, wanting to ensure we're taken care of. I hate the thought of anything happening to them, but I love that they want to make sure we'll be financially okay if, God forbid, something does happen.

I finish signing, and the attorney shakes my hand, letting us know he'll file everything and get certified copies sent to all of us, and then he and the notary leave.

"We have about an hour before Samuel gets here," Brody says, glancing at his watch while Hayden closes the door behind them. "I think that's enough time to celebrate."

Because our lives and businesses are in the city, the guys suggested we take the top two floors of the building and create our family home. Samuel has been hired as the architect to design it, and I'm apparently in charge since they want me to create my dream home.

"And how do you want to celebrate?" I ask coyly, knowing exactly how they want to celebrate. The day we said I do, I stopped taking birth control. They had asked if I was okay having more children, and since I'd love nothing more than to have mini Haydens and Brodys running around, I said yes.

We agreed that whoever's baby I have first will use protection the next time so we can assure I have a baby with both of them, and the children will have their last names with mine hyphenated.

"You know exactly how we want to celebrate," Hayden says, fisting the back of my hair with one hand and lifting me onto the desk with the other. His mouth comes down on mine as Brody spreads my legs, pulls my panties down, and goes to town, eating me out.

With my mouth and pussy being tongue-fucked, I come fast and hard. Hayden kisses me harder to muffle my moans until I've come down from my climax.

The guys work together to remove my clothes, and then Brody flips me over so my chest is pressed against the top of the desk and my ass is in the air. Hayden walks around to the front, stroking his hard length while Brody parts my legs and teases me with his cock.

I open my mouth wide and take Hayden's entire length into my mouth at the same time Brody enters me from behind.

"Fuck, baby," Hayden groans, stroking my cheek as he fucks my mouth. "It feels so damn good with your warm, wet mouth around my cock."

"You should feel her pussy," Brody breathes. "Fuck, I'm gonna come." His fingers tighten on my hips, and his thrusts turn erratic. A few seconds later, he stills, and his warm seed coats my walls.

Hayden pulls his cock out of my mouth and walks back around the desk.

"My turn," he says, spreading my cheeks apart and slamming into me. Because he was already close, he fucks me fast and hard while Brody reaches under and strokes my already sensitive clit.

My orgasm hits me hard as waves of pleasure shoot through my entire body. My feet wobble slightly in my heels, my legs feeling like Jell-O, and when I try to get a grip, Hayden pulls out and lifts me back onto the desk.

He runs his large hand down the center of my chest, pushing me onto my back, and then lifts my legs over his shoulders, slamming back into me. I pant unabashedly as he fucks me with abandon until he finds his release, draining every last drop into me.

I'm still lying with my back on the desk, trying to catch my breath, when I feel fingers prodding at my entrance.

"What are you doing?" I ask, too tired to sit up.

"Making sure it all stays in there," Hayden says, pushing his fingers inside me.

"What?" I try to sit up, but a strong hand gently pushes me back down.

"Stay like that for a few minutes," Brody says. "I read it increases the chances of pregnancy."

"It wha—" And then it hits me. I open my eyes and see both guys kneeling between my legs, watching their cum drip out of me —and pushing it back inside.

"Fuck, that's the best sight in the world," Hayden says.

"Yeah, it is," Brody agrees.

I should probably be embarrassed or grossed out, but the truth is, I love how much they love me. How much they want me. What we have is unconventional, and many wouldn't approve. We're making it up as we go, and we have no idea what we're doing half the time.

But the one thing we've learned along the way is that you can't help what the heart wants. And my heart wants Brody and Hayden…forever.

CHAPTER FORTY-SEVEN
BRODY

"Shit," I curse under my breath. "I left the Hedenburg contracts at the office."

Hayden glances up at me from playing video games with Miles. "I don't have anything here with me."

"I'm going to have to run to the office." I slam my laptop closed.

"Oh! Can I go?" Evie asks, running over from the table where she was coloring pictures with Molly. With Christmas right around the corner, Bree is swamped at the bakery with holiday orders. Since it's the kids' winter break and they have no school, Hayden and I are chilling with them while she works.

"You want to go with me to the office?" I ask, knowing there has to be an ulterior motive. Evie is absolutely adorable…and always up to something.

"Well, I was thinking we could go ice-skating since the rink is near your office." She bats her lashes, and I chuckle.

"Sure," I say, making her squeal in excitement. "You wanna go, Miles?"

"Yeah, I'll grab my skates." He drops the controller and runs up to his room. It's only been a couple of weeks since Bree and her kids moved in, but the transition has been pretty easy because they've spent so much time here.

Since it's going to take a good year for the new place to be done, we told the kids we'd take them to pick out stuff to decorate their new rooms once the holidays are over. Bree's now sharing my room with Hayden and me, and Hayden's room has become a guest room.

After the kids are ready to go, we pile into my SUV and drive over to my office so I can grab my files. Since the rink is within walking distance, I leave my vehicle in the parking garage.

"Look at that pretty tree!" Evie exclaims, pointing at the decorated Christmas tree. "Oh! That one is so beautiful." She runs over to it and reaches up, palming an ornament.

"Can we get a tree?" she asks, hitting me with her best puppy dog eyes. "Please."

"Evie," Miles says.

"What?" she argues. "Our house is so big. It can fit the prettiest, biggest Christmas tree ever." Her eyes meet mine. "Please, Brody." Then she looks at Hayden. "Please, Hayden."

Hayden glances at me and shakes his head, knowing neither of us can ever say no to her. We've already gotten shit from Bree a few times because of it…speaking of which.

"Maybe your mom wants to get the tree," I point out. Bree hasn't mentioned it, but isn't that something women love to do?

"She's too busy," Evie says. "She's at the coffee place all the time. We should surprise her."

"Well, it is Christmas," Hayden points out. "And she has been busy…"

Between the holiday baking and having to pack up to move from there to the new location that's under construction, she has been a bit preoccupied.

"Yes!" Evie says. "We should get her a tree and ornaments. It will make her so happy."

Miles is quiet the entire time, so I ask him, "What do you think?"

He glances at Evie, then says, "Okay." He doesn't sound too thrilled, but then again, most boys probably aren't too thrilled about decorating a Christmas tree.

We spend a little time at the rink since Miles insisted that he still get to skate—despite Evie wanting to skip the skating and go straight for the tree—and then we head over to the store to get the tree.

Like a true woman in the making, Evie shops till she drops. After we get a huge fake tree, she picks out a ton of ornaments. Then she insists we get stockings with the first initial of our names on each one.

When she grabs an extra one with a paw print on the front instead of a letter, she says, "Just in case Santa decides to get me a puppy since I live where one is allowed."

Hayden and I laugh, both noting to check out puppies for sale once we have time. After the stockings are in the cart, she grabs a bunch of other decorations until the cart is overflowing. We haul it all into my vehicle and then head home.

"So do we decorate or wait for your mom?" I ask the kids once we have it all inside the house.

"We decorate," Evie says. "And we'll save a few for Mommy. That way when she gets home, she'll see it all and be so happy."

"All right." I shrug. "Let's get this party started."

CHAPTER FORTY-EIGHT
AUBREE

A WEEK BEFORE CHRISTMAS

I'M EXHAUSTED. BAKED OUT. *If I never see or smell another sweet, I'll be completely okay with that,* I think as I step out of the elevator and into the foyer.

Before I can call out that I'm home, I notice something that wasn't there when I left this morning—Santa Claus. I walk over to it, and it starts swinging its hips, singing "Jingle Bells." I screech in shock and jump back. *What in the actual hell?*

I step toward it again, and it starts up again. It must have a motion detector. Where the hell did that thing even come from?

"Bree? You home?" Hayden calls out from somewhere.

"Yeah," I shout back, stepping away from the creepy Santa and heading into the living room. "Do you know why—?" My words are cut off when my eyes land on the beautifully decorated Christmas tree that's taking up a large section of the living room.

From there, I notice stockings hanging from the fireplace, each with an initial on the front. And next to the tree, hanging on the wall, are several Christmas coloring pages.

My thoughts go back to the last time we celebrated Christmas when Pete was alive. After the kids woke up, before we started opening presents, Pete insisted on taking a family picture using the self-timer on his phone. It's the picture the kids keep by their bed. The four of us and in the background is the Christmas tree, the stockings, and the kids' Christmas pictures they colored and hung on the wall. This room looks like our family Christmas picture on steroids.

"Why would you do this?" I choke out, fully aware that I'm crying, but it doesn't make any sense. Why would the guys take that picture and do this? They've never once tried to recreate what Pete and I had.

"Oh, shit," Brody curses under his breath. "Bree…"

"Why?" I cry out. "Why would you take that photo and recreate it? I don't understand."

Hayden and Brody look at me with confused expressions, and then my eyes go to Evie, who has silent tears sliding down her face.

"Oh, sweetie." I run over to her and pull her into my arms. "Are you okay?" I glance up at Brody and Hayden and glare. "What is wrong with you?"

"They didn't do it," Evie says softly.

"What?" I ask, confused.

"They didn't do it," she repeats, her cries getting louder. "I did." She pulls out of my arms. "I'm so sorry, Mommy," she says through her tears. "I just wanted to make Christmas happy again like in the picture. Because you're always sad on Christmas since Daddy died."

Oh, my heart. I wrap my arms around her and hold her tightly, hating that my children have suffered because I've been so busy mourning my late husband. I had assumed because their father died on Christmas, they would hate the holiday too, but they're little and innocent. This entire time, they've been going along with my lack of Christmas for me because I was sad.

I look over and find Miles standing to the side, watching. "I tried to tell her no, but she wouldn't listen," he says solemnly.

"Are you mad at me?" Evie asks.

"No, sweetie. I'm not mad," I say, needing to make this right. "I love the tree and the stockings and your beautiful pictures." I look at Evie and smile. "You're right. This all makes me very happy, just like in the picture."

"You promise?" Evie asks.

"Yes." I walk over to the tree and run my fingers along the various ornaments I can tell the kids picked out, which reminds me…"I'll be right back."

I run into Hayden's bedroom, which is now the guest room and houses several of my unpacked boxes. I rifle through them until I find what I'm looking for, and then head back to the living room, where I find everyone sitting quietly, worried because I freaked out and scared that I was upset.

"These are from when your dad was alive," I say, handing the box to Evie. She opens it up and inside there are ornaments. "This was our first family ornament," I tell her.

"It has all our names," she says, smiling at me. "Even Daddy's."

"Yep. And this one"—I pull it out and hand it to Miles—"is your first Christmas ornament."

He takes it from me and looks at it. "I don't remember these," he says softly.

"No, you were too little. But every year, we would buy a new ornament for Christmas to hang on the tree. I saved these for you guys."

"This is mine?" Evie asks, taking the princess crown ornament out of the box.

"Yep, that was your first ornament."

"Can I hang it on the tree?" she asks.

"Of course, you can."

She eyes the family one. "What about this one?"

"That should definitely go on the tree," I tell her. "That way, it will be like your dad is with us for Christmas."

The kids take the ornaments over to the tree, and while I watch them hang them up, Brody and Hayden come over, wrapping their arms around me.

"I'm sorry," I whisper. "I shouldn't have accused—"

"Shh, sweetness," Brody says. "I should've asked you first. It's just, Evie looked at me and…"

"She totally gave you the puppy dog eyes," I say with a laugh.

"Yeah," Brody groans.

"Well, it's a good thing she didn't say she wants a damn car," I mutter.

When neither guy says anything, I glance at them and notice their guilty expressions. "She didn't ask for a car, right?"

"No," both guys say in unison.

"Mommy, can we finish decorating the tree?" Evie asks, hopefulness filled in her eyes.

"Absolutely." I stand and walk over to join them. We spend the next hour decorating the rest of the tree while we listen to Christmas music. Once it's done, Evie turns the lights on and squeals over how beautiful it is.

"Can we watch a Christmas movie?" she asks, clearly in the holiday spirit.

"Sure," I tell her.

We pile onto the couches, and Brody clicks on Netflix. As he's scrolling through the different Christmas movies, I notice six stockings hanging on the fireplace instead of five. One of which has a paw print on it.

"Why does that stocking have a paw print?" I lean in and whisper to Hayden.

When he doesn't say anything after several seconds, Miles answers for him. "That would be for the puppy Evie asked Santa for."

BONUS SCENE - AUBREE

"Do you think there's something wrong with me?"

Hayden and Brody glance up from their phones and put them away to give me their full attention.

"What are you talking about?" Brody asks.

"It's been six months since I got off birth control and I'm still not pregnant." The doctor said it can take time for my cycles to adjust since I'd been on birth control for so many years, but I thought I'd be pregnant by now.

"Hey, come here." Hayden leans over and grabs my hand. He pulls me down onto the bed between them and they both roll over so they're facing me.

Since we're in Paris for a month, instead of booking a hotel room, the guys rented a house so we'd be more comfortable. The kids each have their own rooms and the three of us share one room with a California King bed.

"I guess I thought I'd be pregnant by now," I murmur. "What if something's wrong with me? Or I take so long getting pregnant the first time, I can't do it again?"

"Stop it," Brody says, turning my face toward him. "Sure, we'd love to watch you swollen with our baby, see a little mini version of us running around..."

"Can you imagine a mini version of Brody?" Hayden chuckles. "God help us all."

Brody glares, making me laugh.

"We're already a family," Brody continues. "You, me, Hayden, Miles, and Evie. And if that's all we ever have, that's enough for me."

"And me," Hayden adds. "And if you do get pregnant, regardless of whose DNA it has, it will be all of ours."

"We love you," Brody says. "And as long as you're by our side, we'll take you however we can get you."

"And look at the bright side," Hayden adds. "The longer it takes, the longer we get to work on making a baby with you."

"Hell yeah," Brody agrees, getting up and moving so he's between my legs.

He hooks his thumbs into my panties and pulls them down my legs, then spreads my thighs so I'm completely exposed to him.

"Hey, Hayden." Brody smirks. "I noticed you didn't have any dessert earlier at dinner. I was thinking we could split this delicious piece of pussy."

"Fuck yeah," Hayden says. "And after we eat it, we can fill it with some cream…make it even sweeter."

I can't help but snort out a laugh. I was in such a somber mood tonight, but like always, my husbands know just what to say to make me feel better.

Brody drops down and, without wasting any time, starts to lick up my slit while Hayden works on pulling my nightgown over my head.

He pulls on my nipples, knowing how much it turns me on while Brody eats me out. Within minutes, I'm screaming out my orgasm, and before I've even had time to come down, Brody is entering me in one fluid motion while Hayden leans down and kisses me.

Brody fucks with slow and deep movements, hitting the spot that will no doubt send me over the edge again, but before I can find my release, he finishes and pulls out, so Hayden can have his turn.

Thankfully, he picks up right where Brody left off, and with his hard and quick thrusts, he sends me flying high, following along with me.

When he pulls out, I'm about to close my legs so I can go to the bathroom to get cleaned up, but Hayden pushes my legs back open.

"You feel this?" he says, pushing their cum inside of me with his eyes locked on mine. "That's us inside you. Right where we belong." Hayden smirks. "And it's where we'll be every damn day for the rest of our lives. You're all we want…"

"And you're all we need," Brody adds, leaning over and kissing me. "Everything else is just a bonus."

CHAPTER FORTY-NINE

AUBREE

THE FOLLOWING CHRISTMAS

"Do you hear that?" Brody asks.

"No," I mutter.

"You sure?" Hayden asks.

"The kids are asleep," I assure them. "And if you wake them up at three in the damn morning, I'm going to kill you," I say.

"Fine." Brody groans and reaches toward me, palming my breast.

"No way," I hiss. "I'm trying to sleep. Just because you guys are excited for Christmas doesn't mean we have to get up in the middle of the night."

"Look, Miles! Santa came!" Evie whisper-yells.

"I knew I heard them!" Brody says as the guys dart out of bed and out the door.

"Guess we're doing presents at three in the morning," I say to myself as I drag my ass out of bed, exhaustion weighing down on me.

"Mom! Check out all the presents," Evie says when she sees me. "And look, Piper, Santa brought you some presents too," she says to her one-and-a-half-year-old black Labrador Santa brought her for Christmas last year. Brody rescued him from the animal shelter—a puppy someone got and couldn't handle—and put him under the tree. Evie was so excited she cried; the two of them have been inseparable ever since.

I plop onto the couch and cuddle up with Brody and Hayden, watching as the kids open present after present. When only a few are left, Evie says, "Brody, Hayden, this one's for you!" She hands them the present, and they look at me.

Hayden undoes the wrapping and then opens the box, pulling an ornament out.

"Oh, it's a family ornament," Evie says. "But we already got one," she points out.

"This one's different," I say. "Hayden, read the names out loud."

"Hayden, Brody, Evie, Miles, Bree, and..." His eyes dart up to me. "Baby?" he chokes out. "Are you—?"

"Pregnant?" Brody finishes.

"Yep," I tell them both. "I'm eight weeks along."

Brody pulls me onto his lap, and Hayden lifts my shirt.

"You're going to be dads," I murmur as Hayden kisses my soft belly. "Merry Christmas."

CHAPTER FIFTY

AUBREE

SIX MONTHS AFTER THE BABY IS BORN

"Bree!" Hayden shouts from downstairs. "You here?"

I glance at myself in the mirror one last time, then yell back, "In our room."

A few seconds later, my husbands step through the door of our bedroom and then stop in their tracks as they take me in—dressed in a lacy red bra and panty set that shows more than it covers.

"Holy shit," Brody says. "Where are the kids?"

"With Beatrice," I say with a knowing smirk. With us having two eleven-year-olds and a six-month-old, our alone time is limited.

"Fuck yes," Hayden says, stepping toward me.

"Nuh-uh." I playfully waggle my finger back and forth. "I'm in the mood for a fantasy."

Brody's eyes light up, knowing exactly what that means. Ninety-nine percent of the time, our relationship revolves around the guys and me, but every once in a while, when I'm in the mood, the guys will act out one of my fantasies that involves the two of them.

"Strip," I tell them both. Then in my way too tall heels, I saunter past them and make a show of climbing onto the bed, sticking my butt in the air as I slowly crawl to the center.

By the time I turn around and spread my legs, showing off my crotchless panties, they're both naked. As I take a moment to enjoy the sight of my husbands' fit bodies, Hayden asks, "What's your fantasy?"

"It starts with Brody and you stroking each other...Getting one another hard." The guys do as I say, and move closer, their hands reaching out and gripping the other's shaft and pulling their cocks in a jerking motion, up and down.

While I watch them grow harder and harder, I reach down and pluck at my sensitive nipples, loving the way Brody's movements are slow and gentle and Hayden's are rougher.

"I want you to kiss," I add, my voice raspy with desire.

Hayden's hand comes up to palm the side of Brody's face, and as they continue to stroke each other, their mouths connect in the most erotic way. From where I'm lying, I can see Hayden's tongue enter Brody's mouth. Brody moans, his chest rising and falling in quick succession.

I move back down the bed until my legs hang off the edge, and then I spread my legs.

"That's enough," I murmur, my fingers gliding across my wet slit. Watching them kiss and touch is such a turn-on. By the time they get anywhere near me, I'm already drenched.

The guys stop kissing and step apart, their hands still on each other's cocks.

"What happens next?" Brody asks, his eyes trained on my center.

"You kneel between my legs and eat me," I say to Brody. Then to Hayden, I add, "And while he eats me, you fuck his ass."

Brody groans, then releases Hayden's cock so he can drop to his knees in front of me. His hands palm the inside of my thighs, and he delves straight in, parting my lips and licking up my center. When he gets to my clit, he focuses his attention on it, massaging the most delicious circles over it.

As he licks and sucks me, my eyes go to Hayden, who's dripped lube down Brody's crack and is prepping him with his finger.

"Fuck." Brody gasps.

"That feel good, baby?" I ask, reaching down and stroking the side of his face.

"So good," he groans as Hayden enters him from behind. I can't see him fucking him, but every time he thrusts forward, Brody sucks hard on my clit, taking me closer to the edge.

"Yes! Yes! " I chant when he pushes a couple of fingers inside me and curls them in the perfect way that has me coming so hard, it feels as though I'm going to black out.

As soon as I come down from my high, I push his head back and slide down the end of the bed, so I can kiss Brody while Hayden continues to fuck him.

Reaching underneath, I find his hard cock and stroke it up and down, fucking him with my hand while he makes love to me with his mouth.

"Fuck, I'm gonna come," Hayden growls. At the same time, Brody's cock swells, and spurts of cum fill my fist. Hayden pulls out and rips the condom off just in time for it to jet out all over Brody's back.

"That was quite a fantasy," Brody says after we've showered and are in bed with both of them lying on either side of me. Brody peppers kisses across my neck and shoulder, and Hayden is gently massaging circles along my outer thigh that's hooked over his leg.

"Yeah, it was," I agree. "But reality is better than the fantasy. Especially when my reality ends with me telling you guys a little secret."

Both guys stop what they're doing and look at me. "What secret?" Brody asks, his tone filled with hope.

"Check your nightstand drawer," I tell him, trying to keep my excitement in check so I don't ruin the surprise.

Brody rolls over and opens the drawer. He reaches in, and when he finds what he's looking for, he jumps up, his gaze going straight to my belly. "Are you serious?" he says, his eyes filled with raw emotion.

"Yep," I choke out. "I'm pregnant...again."

Want to know how the night in college went down between Brody and Hayden?

Check out their steamy bonus scene on my website.
www.authornikkiash.com

ABOUT THE AUTHOR

Nikki Ash is a USA Today Bestselling author of contemporary romance, focusing on single parent, secret baby, and surprise pregnancy romances. She spends her days and nights getting lost in words. When she's not writing, she's reading. From the Boxcar Children, to Wuthering Heights, to the latest single parent romance, she has lived and breathed every type of book.

Nikki resides in South Florida with her husband, two children, and dog that she considers to be one of her kids. When she's not reading or writing, she's traveling the world with her family—in search of inspiration.

Would you like free books?
Join my newsletter today